KT-498-715

'Loved this book, read it in less than a day as I just **COULDN'T PUT IT DOWN**' *Celie*

'**I LOVE ALL ALICE PETERSON BOOKS** and this is no exception. She really makes the characters come to life and I recommend this book' *mommyj*

'I raced through this book. Although the subject matter is different, it **TUGGED AT THE HEARTSTRINGS IN THE SAME WAY THAT JOJO MOYES' ME BEFORE YOU DID**' *SoozBuch*

'Another great read from Alice Peterson…Loved the characters and the story line. As others have said, **YOU WILL LAUGH AND CRY**. Couldn't put it down and sad when I had finished it' *Anne*

'I loved this book. In fact I love Alice Peterson's books because you relate to the people in them. They are **REAL PEOPLE, WHO HAVE NORMAL LIVES, FEEL NORMAL EMOTIONS AND MAKE NORMAL DECISIONS** . . . I did not want the book to end' *Anon*

'This was a **WONDERFUL AND EMOTIONAL READ OF LOVE, LOSS AND PICKING YOURSELF UP** and carrying on with the hand you've been given. I found Peterson's writing was fantastic, and had me turning the pages until I reached the end. It deals with a sensitive topic with grace and empathy, and you'll certainly be moved by Rebecca's story. **A HEART-WARMING AND TOUCHING READ**' *Chloe S*

'I TOTALLY FELL IN LOVE with the characters and felt myself wishing they were my friends too' *Clara*

'I couldn't put it down. It was funny, the WRITING WAS SUPERB and it was in parts rather sad! Alice Petersen has a real talent of describing the characters in such a detailed way that you feel you know them. I really recommend this book' *EmmaH*

'I wish I could give this book more than 5 stars!' *Miss McMahon*

'THIS MADE ME LAUGH OUT LOUD. Was very well written and felt real, like you could be friends with the characters' *Emma Mitchell*

'Really loved this book, the story was interesting and the characters were FUNNY AND ADDICTIVE. Looked forward to reading every night. A lovely story of family, friends and romance' *Louise*

'One of the MOST SPECIAL STORIES I've ever had the pleasure of reading . . . A MUST READ' *Megan Reading in the sunshine*

'The BEST BOOK I have read in a long time' *Jen*

'This book has it all. It tugs at the heart strings and is an EMOTIONAL ROLLERCOASTER RIDE' *Sarah-Jane*

Reader reviews for Alice Peterson

'**ABSOLUTELY BRILLIANT**. There's not enough stars for this book really, it's worth so much more than the lousy 5/5 I can offer it' *Pajama Book Girl*

'I am not totally sure if my review can describe how much **I LOVED THIS BOOK**' *Agi*

'I have never cried over one book so much. The story is **INSPIRING, HEART-FELT, REALISTIC AND BEAUTIFULLY PORTRAYED**. It was unpredictable and had me staying up to finish it . . . I can't tell you how uplifting and emotional this story is but you can see for yourself' *Rachael*

'I found this book totally **SPELL-BINDING** and **AN ABSOLUTE JOY** to read. I read this book in 2 sittings, the last one ending at 3am this morning ... when you are engrossed in a brilliant book, who cares what the time is! I laughed, I cried (no, sobbed) . . . Loved it!' *Gail*

'The book is magical – a true gift of emotions. **READING IT HAS ENRICHED MY LIFE** and I'll certainly be reading more from this author' *Amanda*

KT 2151219 1

'Peterson's writing is simply brilliant, honest and frank, emotional and very touching . . . **IT WILL STAY WITH YOU LONG AFTER YOU TURN THAT FINAL PAGE**. An utterly amazing book' *Chloe*

'I would defy anyone not to **FALL IN LOVE** with this novel' *Fabulous Book Fiend*

'This was one of those books that was **HEARTBREAKING BUT TRULY INSPIRATIONAL** at the same time, I literally could not put it down and read it in a day. The story flowed effortlessly and I found myself **GRIPPED ALMOST FROM THE FIRST PAGE**' *Sharon*

'Made me **LAUGH OUT LOUD AT PARTS AND I HAD A TEAR IN MY EYE AT OTHERS** - not many authors find the right balance between serious and humor but Alice does' *Lindsay*

'Each book is totally different from the others, with diverse stories and all the books are written with **DEEP COMPASSION AND UNDERSTANDING** . . . I just loved all her books and cannot wait for the next one to be published!' *O Kleinova*

'It's rare that you find a book that delivers **HUMOUR, DRAMA, TENSION AND EMOTION IN EQUAL MEASURE** – I simply could not put this book down and read it from cover to cover in a single go . . . In a sea of clichéd, run-of-the-mill books about modern relationships, this really cuts through with a completely different perspective' *Anon*

One Step
Closer
To You

Also by Alice Peterson

Another Alice
M'Coben, Place of Ghosts
You, Me and Him
Letters From my Sister
Monday to Friday Man
Ten Years On
By My Side

One Step Closer To You

ALICE PETERSON

The moral right of Alice Peterson to be
identified as the author of this work has been
asserted in accordance with the Copyright,

All rights reserved. No part of this publication
may be reproduced or transmitted in any form
or by any means, electronic or mechanical,
without permission in writing from the publisher

A CIP catalogue record for this book is available
from the British Library

Quercus

First published in Great Britain in 2014 by

Quercus Editions Ltd
55 Baker Street
7th Floor, South Block
London W1U 8EW

Copyright © 2014 Alice Peterson

Kingston upon Thames Libraries	
KT 2151219 1	
Askews & Holts	01-Oct-2014
AF	£7.99
ST	KT00000116

PBO ISBN 978 1 78206 183 0
EBOOK 978 1 78206 184 7

This book is a work of fiction. Names, characters,
businesses, organisations, places and events are
either the product of the author's imagination
or are used fictitiously. Any resemblance to
actual persons, living or dead, events or
locales is entirely coincidental.

10 9 8 7 6 5 4 3 2

Printed and bound in Great Britain by Clays Ltd, St Ives plc

Typeset by Ellipsis Digital Limited, Glasgow

1

2010

'Polly, can you tell me when you've felt most happy?' my counsellor, Stephanie, asks towards the end of our session. I've been seeing her for over six months now. She's sitting opposite me, dead straight hair framing her pale freckled face, pen poised in her slender hand.

'Happy?' I say, as if it's an alien emotion.

'It could be anything. Being happy doesn't have to be the result of a momentous occasion.'

I take a sip of water. 'I loved Dad taking Hugo and me out on the lake when we were little.' Hugo is my younger brother. 'We'd go out every Sunday. I liked the routine,' I reflect. 'School was OK too, when I wasn't getting into trouble.'

Stephanie waits for more, her neutral expression giving nothing away. She's always digging around in the vain hope that something will emerge from somewhere deep inside me.

'That's a hard question,' I mutter. Happiness, a sense of calm, it's always been over there, never with me. In the past I've always searched for excitement; thrived on thrill-seeking.

'Take your time,' Stephanie says, the clock behind her desk ticking.

Many people might say that their happiest moment was when they gave birth to a healthy son or daughter, or when they fell in love. I have a one-year-old son, Louis, but I'm not with Louis's father, Matthew, anymore. I think about the first time I met Matt. Did he make me happy? Looking back, no. But he made my pulse race, especially in the early months of our relationship. I can still feel his penetrating gaze from the other side of the bar that very first night we laid eyes on one another. He had the gift of making me feel like I was the only person in the room. I see us dancing, our hot bodies pressed against one another. Then I picture us sitting side by side in the taxi later on that evening, heading back to my flat, Matt's hand creeping up my skirt, that flirtatious look in his eye. I shiver when I see that smile, that smile that wanted to own me. I was flattered at first, intoxicated by his attention: how could any woman not be? I shift in my seat, wanting to blot him out of my mind. I wish I could stop looking over my shoulder; that his face would stop haunting me.

Go back to the question, Polly. When have I felt most happy? 'Having Louis,' I pretend, when I can't think of anything else. Truthfully the birth of my son and the first year were far from how I'd imagined. I wonder if that's the same for other mothers. I don't regret him for a single second, but what would Stephanie think of me if I told her I'd almost walked away from him? Left him defenceless in the park? I close my eyes, not wanting to cry.

'Polly?' Stephanie says, 'Don't worry, we . . .'

I raise a hand to stop her, seeing myself as an eight-year-old back at my childhood home in Norfolk, in the kitchen, wearing a rosebud apron and matching chef's hat. I see myself mixing sultanas into a creamy cookie dough with a wooden spoon. When Mum's not looking I dip my finger into the bowl. It tastes of sweet buttery heaven. I can't resist plunging my finger in again. 'Polly, there won't be any left,' Mum ticks me off, before creeping up behind me and dipping her finger into the mixture too, laughing with me. Mum rarely laughed so when she did it felt like a prize. I loved cooking with her because it was just the two of us, no Hugo stealing the limelight, no Dad, only Mum and me. Next I see us dropping small spoonfuls of batter onto baking sheets. Mum sets the oven timer, but I can't stop peeping through the glass door to see the biscuits rising, the edges turning a delicious golden brown.

'Cooking,' I mutter, still dressed in my rosebud apron, my mother by my side.

'Cooking? You mean your job?'

Since breaking up with Matt, I now work in a café baking cakes and serving soup to the locals in Belsize Park.

I shake my head. 'With my mother, when I was little.' I particularly remember the weeks leading up to Christmas, making mince pies while listening to carols on the radio. I hear Mum singing along to 'Once in Royal David's City' as she greased the baking tray. I inhale the comforting smell of cloves, grated nutmeg and cinnamon. I see myself carefully cutting the pastry with my silver star-shaped cutter to give the mince pies little hats. Little hats. That's what Mum and I called them.

'I wish my entire childhood had been spent in the kitchen cooking,' I say to Stephanie. 'Mum didn't worry or frown; I stopped being naughty for a while. I think it's why I enjoy my job so much now, it reminds me of those times.' I take another sip of water. 'I loved the build-up to Christmas, wrapping presents and decorating the tree with Hugo. It was all so perfect until the family actually arrived.'

Stephanie looks at me as if she can almost relate to that: the build-up to the party is often better than the party itself.

'I remember one year . . . it was the year when I began to realise things at home weren't quite as they seemed. In fact, things were a mess, our family was one big lie.' I stop, glance at the time. My hour is up.

'Tell me more, Polly. We've still got a little time left,' she says, ignoring the sound of the ticking clock.

2

1989

My name is Polly and I'm nine years old. It's Christmas Eve and Mum is frantically searching my wardrobe. 'I don't know what you do with your things, Polly!' She's looking for my red velvet dress. I know exactly where it is. It's hidden under my bed, torn and caked in dry mud.

In the end we agree that I wear my silver star-patterned skirt for the family party tonight, and I breathe a sigh of relief when finally she leaves my bedroom. Quietly I shut my door and crouch down beside my bed to pull out my dress. I'd forgotten all about it being there until now. On the last day of term it was non-school-uniform day and I'd had a fight in the sports field, close to the girls' loos, with one of the girls in my class. Imogen loves to mimic my younger brother Hugo, calling him 'Cyclops', because he's blind. She had two friends with her, laughing as she pulled cross-eyed faces, imitating Hugo squinting. I charged towards her, like

5

a bull, before both of us went into the mud. We wrestled and fought to lots of cheering until I heard my dress rip and felt a hand trying to pull me up. It was Janey, my best friend, begging me not to get into trouble again.

'Anyway, Cyclops is a superhero,' she said to Imogen, 'and Hugo has two eyes, not one, stupid.'

I put on my skirt and blouse, wondering how I can get the dress clean and fix it without Mum noticing.

I hear footsteps approaching my bedroom. I shove the dress back underneath the bed. I'm relieved when Hugo pokes his head round the door. He's two years younger than me, but already taller.

'Are you coming?' he asks. He's dressed in a dark purple waistcoat, smart trousers and Dad has polished his shoes.

I take Hugo's chubby hand and together we walk downstairs. Mum and Dad explained why my brother is partially sighted. When he was born, he couldn't breathe so was put onto an oxygen machine. The doctor said the rods and cones in his eyes were killed at birth.

'Cones?' I'd said to Dad. All I could see was Mr Whippy ice cream with chocolate flakes.

Dad tried to explain. 'Hugo has . . . how can I put it? Faulty wiring. Sometimes there can be problems at birth, but it doesn't mean we don't love him just the way he is.'

'So my birth wasn't difficult?'

There was a long pause. I don't think he answered. He was probably still thinking about Hugo's rods and cones.

As Hugo and I almost reach the bottom of the stairs, 'No more steps,' I say, with one to go. He steps forward and I grab him before he can fall. 'Not funny, Polly!' But we both giggle because Christmas Day and opening presents is only one day away now.

Granny Sue and Granddad Arthur, Mum's parents, always come round on Christmas Eve. They live in Devon, in a cottage by the sea. Dad's sister, Lyn, is also coming. Auntie Lyn is widowed and lives on her own in London. Tonight, for the first time ever, Mum is allowing me to stay up until at least nine. Normally Hugo and I are packed off to bed before they even sit down to dinner.

The doorbell rings, three times. That'll be Granddad.

'Now the party has begun!' he says as I open the door and throw my arms around him. He's wearing a navy spotted tie and smells of bonfires and aftershave. Granny Sue pushes past us in a long stylish coat, scarlet lipstick and high heels, carrying a plate of food. Granny Sue used to be blonde and glamorous, I've seen pictures of her when she was young. Dad says she still is goodlooking. She used to be a professional cook. Granny Sue's hands are famous because she's been on adverts carving turkey. Dad says they were a handsome couple in their day, Granddad Arthur and Granny Sue. People wanted to be like them.

Hugo and I follow Granddad into the sitting room, eyeing the bulging bag that clinks by his side. Granddad remarks on the twinkling lights in our Christmas tree and all those presents stacked in piles underneath it. 'All for me!' he beams at us, before slipping off his coat and telling us nothing beats a real log fire. I watch as he sits down and takes a couple of bottles out of his bag. Aware of my gaze he winks at me. 'No presents for you, Polly! I hear you've been a very naughty girl this year.'

He roars with laughter, before presenting me with a small box wrapped in silver paper that immediately I shake before adding to my pile.

Mum's right. Granddad can't talk; he shouts. He can't laugh; he roars. He can't ring the doorbell once; he has to ring it three times. He's like a giant ray of sunshine appearing on our doorstep.

Auntie Lyn arrives next, and Granddad almost crushes her in his embrace. She's wearing a spotty red dress with her famous beige tights. Since she lost her husband she doesn't smile that much, not even at Christmas.

Soon we're all in the sitting room chatting about school and stuff. I'm telling Auntie Lyn about my nativity play, but Mum interrupts me, 'Hugo sang a wonderful solo too. He played the Mad Hatter.'

'How about a little music now to get the party going?' suggests Granddad. Dejected, I follow him into the hallway, towards our music machine on a shelf stacked with CDs. I help Granddad find some music and soon my good mood returns as he twirls me round the room to Johnny Cash's 'Ring of Fire'. Hugo dances with Mum, in between pretending to play the guitar. My father takes a couple of photographs. 'Come on, Lynny, it's Christmas! Let your hair down!'

'Best not,' she says, shrinking further away from him. Sometimes I think she's scared of Granddad. I don't know why when he's so much fun.

I sit at the table, next to Granny Sue and opposite Granddad Arthur. Dad lights the candles and Granny Sue compliments the table that Mum and I decorated earlier this afternoon, after we'd made the mince pies listening to the carols on the radio. Hugo and Dad were busy watching *It's a Wonderful Life* while Mum and I were opening boxes filled with beautiful glass candlesticks, gold candles, ivy, berry and ribbon decorations and our special red star-patterned tablecloth with matching napkins. I made some place names using my gold marker pen. Mum also bought some crackers, but we're saving those for tomorrow.

As Mum dishes out piping-hot fish pie, she talks about going to church tomorrow. 'It's hard timing it with the turkey,' she says, her brow furrowed. 'Maybe we should eat in the evening, but the children are exhausted by then.' Mum is *always* worrying about something. Granddad Arthur says she'll be flapping and worrying in her grave.

I notice her watching as Granddad pours the last of the wine into his glass. 'Why do we eat turkey every year? Makes you windy.' He winks at me and I giggle as he helps himself to another drink from a new bottle and offers some to Auntie Lyn. 'Same goes for stinky sprouts!'

Auntie Lyn places a hand over her glass, pursing her lips.

Granddad frowns. 'Oh come on, Lynny, it's Christmas! Get legless!'

'Dad!' Mum says, but I find it very funny.

'I'm driving,' she replies, refusing to look at him.

There's a strange silence. Mum's face reddens.

'Anyway, this fish pie is delicious.' Dad raises his glass. 'Three cheers for the chef.'

'Be careful of the bones,' Mum warns in her worried little voice.

'Behave,' I hear Granny Sue muttering to Granddad.

I feel sorry for Granddad. He's always being told off.

'I am very *very* proud of our family,' Granddad repeats over pudding, his eyes watering. 'We've had some tough times but Hugo is an inspiration. That little boy . . .' Granddad takes a deep breath, 'he'll have one heck of a life ahead of him and it won't be easy.' He wags a finger. 'But he's a strong little lad and . . . well . . . I can see great things . . .' He stumbles on his words, takes another gulp of wine. 'He's got balls.' Granddad hiccups. 'You know, it's a big bad world out there, but he's a brave boy. And then there's beautiful you, Polly. You'll have the boys eating out of your hand, I bet, bees round a honey pot.'

Shy, I play with my spoon, not sure exactly what he means.

'Polly, you have such a happy future ahead of you . . . oh boy, if I could have my life again . . .'

'What would you do differently, Arthur?' asks my dad.

'Oh . . . everything, right, Sue? Wifey here thinks I'm a failure.' He nudges Auntie Lyn, who smiles at him awkwardly.

'I do not,' Granny Sue tuts. 'When have I said that?'

'You don't have to.' He wipes his mouth with the sleeve of his shirt.

Dad has told me Granddad Arthur hasn't worked much in his life. He lost jobs as quickly as he found them.

'Why?' I'd asked.

'It's complicated,' Dad replied.

'I *am* a failure,' Granddad says, pushing his food to one side, 'and it's all my fault.'

I sit up. 'What's your fault?'

'Can we change the subject?' suggests Granny Sue. 'It's Christmas.'

Why does everyone keep on saying, 'It's Christmas'?

'We've always been very good at changing the subject, Lynny,' Granddad says. She squiggles in her chair. He leans closer. 'They never want to talk about *the truth*.'

'You're drunk,' she says, edging away again. 'Very drunk, Arthur.'

He edges towards her once more. 'Well, as Churchill

11

said, "You're ugly, you're *very* ugly. But I shall be sober in the morning!"' He leans back in his chair and roars with laughter, but no one else does. I'm not sure what's so funny. Mum and Dad look angry and Granny Sue furious, as if she might explode.

'Dad, *please*,' Mum says, gesturing to me. 'You promised.'

'All right, all right, loosen up everyone.' He finishes off his wine and reaches for another bottle.

'Arthur, you've had enough.' Dad swipes the bottle from him.

'Says who?' he snaps, before knocking over the pot of salt. He takes a large pinch in his fingers and throws it over his shoulder. 'Bad luck spilling salt, Polly.'

'You need some black coffee,' Mum says, manically tidying up the salt.

'She should be here,' Granddad Arthur says as he fishes out a packet of cigarettes from his pocket. 'We go to church, get preached to about forgiveness . . .'

Mum stops dead. 'Dad!'

Granddad shakes his head. 'But we can't even do it in our own family. We pretend like everything is normal, here we are on Christmas Eve, blah blah blah.' He's waving his arm in the air.

'Dad! Now is not the right time . . .'

'It's never the right time. She should be here.'

I frown. 'Who should be here, Granddad?'

'No one.' Mum stares at him.

12

'Secrets,' Granddad says. 'The thing about life, Polly, is . . .'

'I think it's time you left.' Dad walks over to Granddad.

Granddad shakes his head with regret. 'You can bury your head in the sand, but the thing about life is it will always bite you back, it'll come back to haunt you when you least expect it.'

'Polly, come,' Mum demands, taking me firmly by the arm. 'Say goodbye and up to bed. We need to put some sherry and biscuits out for Father Christmas.'

'I'll take her up,' says Auntie Lyn, relieved to get up from the table.

I kiss him goodnight. His cheek is sweaty; his lips and hair sticky. Granddad barely looks up at me. Reluctantly I follow Auntie Lyn out of the room, before glancing at him, shoulders slumped, his eyes fixed to the floor. He looks sad, as if Christmas is over.

With brushed teeth and an empty stocking at the end of the bed, I can't sleep. I hear muffled voices outside and footsteps on our gravel drive. Something makes me walk over to my window. Carefully I lift the curtain and see figures walking towards Granny Sue's car. Granny Sue doesn't like staying here. She always books a hotel close by.

Dad is holding Granddad by the arm. Granddad stumbles, crashes into the side of the car and falls. Dad tries to help him up but Granddad pushes him away. Mum opens the passenger door and they shove him inside. As the car drives away Dad puts an arm around Mum.

I get back into bed. What did Granddad mean by secrets? *She should be here.* I pull the blankets around me, feeling something uncertain, something I don't understand, and I don't like it. Surely I'm not supposed to feel like this, not when it's Christmas.

3

2013

My name is Polly. I'm thirty-three years old, a single mother
to my five-year-old son, Louis, and I live in north London.
Each morning I pray for a sober day and before bedtime
Louis and I tell each other all the things in life we are
grateful for: my brother, Hugo, comes top of the list, custard tarts a close second. I work in a café in Belsize Village,
run by a Frenchman called Jean. Half the café sells cookery
books from across the world; the other half is the kitchen
and eating area, where I cook soup and bake cakes for the
locals. I attempt to go jogging as much as I can to run off
licking the wooden spoon. I've been seeing an addiction
counsellor called Stephanie for the past four years, and
finally, every Friday lunchtime I go to my AA meeting.
Sometimes I go to a couple of meetings a week, I squeeze
them in when I need to, but Friday is always my regular
slot. AA is my oxygen. It doesn't matter how busy I am or

what else is going on around me, my recovery comes first.

As I make my way towards the church, close to Louis's school in Primrose Hill, I think about the friends I have made in AA. Firstly, Harry. Harry is in his late seventies, grey-haired and slight in build. He's always dressed in a tweed jacket one size too big for him and occasionally a matching cap that he models at a jaunty angle. Harry loves to be in charge of the kitchen, serving hot drinks and bis-cuits. The first time I came to a meeting, all snotty-nosed and red-eyed, Harry plied me with sweet tea and gave me his cotton handkerchief with an embroidered 'H' in the corner. He hasn't had it easy. He suffered abuse in his childhood and became addicted to alcohol in his twenties, drinking heavily into his fifties, until his doctor told him he had the choice either to carry on drinking or die in six months. He has been clean now for over twenty years and to celebrate each anniversary he takes his wife Betsy out for a slap-up meal.

Next is Ryan, a music producer in his late twenties, sleepy brown eyes, who always looks as if he's just rolled out of bed and shoved on a pair of jeans and sneakers. Over the past four years he's sported orange, pink, black and blond hair, but currently it's his natural brown, which suits him. He plays the guitar and has a rescue bulldog called Kip. Louis and I once met Ryan and Kip in the park and Louis had an instant crush; Ryan is impossibly cool. If I were a little younger, or the old Polly . . .

There's also Neve, two children, just turned forty,

divorced, but now in a happy relationship with a former addict. She left the corporate world and has since become a yoga teacher. Neve has an open, angelic face, which makes it hard to imagine that by the age of fifteen she was addicted to cocaine, drink and sex. Basically, she wanted the largest piece of whatever was put in front of her. She chaired the first meeting I went to. Everything she said echoed my life. She was also funny, describing how she'd been pulled over and breathalysed on her way to the meeting. 'When the policeman asked me the last time I'd had a drink I replied, smugly, let me tell you,' she'd added with a wink, '"Twenty-ninth September 2005, 5 p.m., Phoenix Airport, Arizona, sir!"' I was in awe of how she'd turned her life around, so much so that I plucked up the courage to ask her to be my sponsor – a person who helps you to stay sober through the AA programme. 'I'd love to, Polly,' she'd said at the end of the meeting, before adding, 'but you've got to promise me one thing. You swear you'll never *ever* lie to me.'

And finally there's Denise, in her late fifties, dark roots and dyed blonde hair. She's had many jobs, mainly in retail and now works part-time for Sainsbury's, behind the cheese counter. Denise's mother was an alcoholic who didn't make it to fifty. Her father chucked her out on the streets when she turned sixteen. She has a mustard tinge to her skin and the crumpled lines on her face give away her forty-a-day habit. She lives in a council flat with a ginger cat called

Felix, and since giving up smoking, has taken up knitting instead.

I enter the church hall, waving to Harry behind the tea and biscuits table, before taking a seat on the back row, next to Denise, who's knitting something in pale blue today. She tells me it's a cardigan for her grandson Larry. 'He was called Larry, 'cos my daughter always used to say when she was preggers, "He's as happy as Larry."' She chuckles as she carries on, giving me a flash of her nicotine-stained teeth. 'Didn't see you last week, sweetheart?'

I tell her Louis and I spent Christmas and New Year with my parents in Norfolk.

Neve enters shortly after me, dressed in yoga pants that show off annoyingly toned legs and a sheepskin coat. Her short brown hair is pulled back at both sides in a couple of clips, accentuating her high cheekbones and deep-blue eyes. Out of breath, she sits down next to me and says, 'So blooming glad Christmas is over.'

Ryan strolls in next, wearing headphones. Just behind him is a tall man with thick dark hair and a beard, his shoulders hunched awkwardly as he looks for a space to sit down. 'What is it?' Neve asks when she sees me shrinking into my seat.

'I know him.'

Her eyes light up as she says, 'He's handsome in a beardy kind of way. Who is he?'

He turns round, as if sensing someone is talking about him.

'An ex?' Neve whispers.

I shake my head.

'Your gynaecologist?' There's that flash of mischief in her eyes.

'Shh! I don't have one, luckily.'

'Your Botox man?'

'Bog off.'

'Your doc who tells you not to drink and smoke,' chips in Denise with a husky chuckle, her knitting needles clickety-clicking.

Neve turns to me, the colour in her cheeks fading. 'It's not Louis's dad, is it? Matthew?'

'Whoa, Matthew's here?' says Ryan, catching half the conversation as he approaches us with a mug of tea, laces undone and headphones now round his neck. I still get a knot in my stomach whenever someone mentions Matthew's name.

'Everyone calm down,' I say, feeling far from calm myself. 'He's a dad from school, that's all.'

'Oh, right.' Neve seems disappointed.

Ryan scratches his head in confusion. 'Who's a dad from school?'

Neve gestures to the back of a man wearing a navy jumper. 'Do you think he saw you, Polly?'

'Don't think so.'

I explain to Denise, Ryan and Neve that his name is Ben and his niece, Emily, is in Louis's class. Emily started school during the second half of the Christmas term last year. When I'd asked Louis about Emily's father, he'd said, 'Emily doesn't have a mum. Her heart was attacked. Her uncle Ben looks after her instead.' Part of me is pleased to see him here. I have an ally, someone I can be sober with at school fundraising events, a kindred spirit at the school gates. I've wanted to talk to him and now I have an excuse. The other side of me likes to hold on to my privacy. I like being new Polly at the school gates, unscarred, the mother who has left her past behind.

'Hi. My name's Colin, and I'm an alcoholic.'

'Hi Colin,' everyone replies. Colin is chairing the meeting, sitting at a table in the front of the room, next to the secretary, dressed in a grey cable knit jumper. 'It took me a long time to admit I was an addict. I pictured old men in mouldy clothes with rotting teeth, clutching a whisky bottle in a brown paper bag and sleeping in skips.'

There are smiles and mutters of agreement in the room. Harry, sitting a few chairs away from me, wipes his forehead with a handkerchief, before finishing off his slab of Battenberg cake.

'We're good at fooling ourselves, but in reality my sofa was my park bench.'

As Colin continues, my mind drifts to Ben. How is he managing with Emily? What happened to Emily's father? Is this his first AA meeting?

'I started drinking heavily when my divorce papers came through.' Colin shakes his head. 'I used to dream about lie-ins and freedom, no child jumping on the bed at six in the morning. Truth is when the kids were with my ex suddenly I had all this time on my own. I was also still in love with my wife, which didn't help, and in complete denial that it was over. I didn't drink to be social. I'd drink to get plastered. One time I vandalised public property, another time I went round to my ex-wife's house and thought it was a great idea to hit the new boyfriend. "Don't blame me! I was drunk!" That was the excuse. Addicts need an excuse to drink, never want to accept responsibility. "It's Friday," or "I've had a bad day at work."' Colin smiles wryly. '"It's Christmas!" That's a great excuse to drink even more because *everyone* gets wasted at Christmas. Looking back now, I reckon all my cherry-faced cousins were pissed on whisky and mulled wine.'

I think of Granddad, that very first time when I was allowed to stay up for supper on Christmas Eve. On Christmas Day, he had fallen backwards into our tree and blamed it on Hugo getting in his way, when in fact Hugo was nowhere near him. In my teenage years I saw a darker side to Granddad. His jokes weren't so funny anymore. He became a sad and lonely figure. I understood why Mum talked to him as if he were a child and why he and Granny Sue had slept in separate bedrooms for years. It had nothing to do with Granddad 'snoring'. Granny Sue didn't want to be woken up by Granddad staggering home from the pub.

'Then something made me sit up,' Colin continues. 'My six-year-old daughter became ill. I had a choice now. It was a case of "Do I run?" or "Do I face life and be there for her?" Basically, I had to sober up and be a proper man, be a dad.'

I watch as Ben heads abruptly out of the room. Neve glances at me. Should I follow him?

When Colin finishes his talk, the secretary opens the meeting to anyone who wants to share. A woman raises her arm. Colin nods.

'Hi. I'm Pam and I'm an alcoholic.'

'Hi, Pam,' everyone says.

Will Ben come back?

'Thanks, Colin,' she begins. 'I haven't touched a drink for nearly five years now.'

There's clapping. Maybe he's outside having a cigarette? Neve encourages me to go.

I tiptoe out of the room and head outside to a small group of people smoking. I see Ben in the distance. Unsure if I should go after him, I see him glancing over his shoulder. Caught off balance, I take a step back before waving tentatively. But it's too late. He's turned round, hands back in pockets as he walks away.

4

After the meeting, I jog back home. I live in a tiny rented two-bedroom flat in Primrose Gardens, off England's Lane, in Belsize Park. I had no idea how beautiful and green this part of north London was until I moved here. Hampstead Heath is only a ten-minute walk away from my flat. Primrose Hill and Regent's Park are equally close.

Inside the block of flats, before heading upstairs I glance in my cubbyhole to see if I have any interesting mail. It's all junk except for a credit card bill, which I decide can stay there.

The moment I walk through the front door, Louis charges towards me in his pilot's costume. 'Have you been a good monkey for Uncle H?' I ruffle his bushy brown hair.

He nods. 'We played pirates.'

'Thanks, Hugo.' I touch his shoulder. 'I really needed to go today.'

'How were your breakdown friends, Mum?' asks Louis.

Recently, Louis overheard Hugo and me talking about

AA and my breakdown friends, as Hugo calls them. He'd walked into the kitchen in his pyjamas and said, 'What's an alcoholic?'

Hugo and I exchanged glances. 'It's someone who drinks a little bit too much,' I replied.

'So if I drink too much Ribena, am I an alcoholic?'

'No, sweetheart.'

He waited, clearly not understanding.

'It's if you have too much wine or beer, grown-up drinks.'

'Uncle Hugo drinks beer *and* wine. Are you an alcoholic too?'

I can't remember how we poured water over this heated conversation. I think it had something to do with having a biscuit before going back to bed.

Hugo, Louis and I head into the sitting room that now resembles a bombsite.

Louis grabs his play sword and swishes it in my direction, exclaiming, 'You're dead!'

I stagger to the floor, clutching my chest in defeat. 'Right.' I spring back to life and look at my watch. It's early afternoon. 'Let's tidy this mess up, go for a walk and then do you fancy something to eat?' I ask Hugo. 'My treat.'

'Pizza Express!' shouts Louis, jumping up and down.

Hugo sticks close to me in the dark. Every now and then I take his arm to steer him along the road and make sure he doesn't headbutt a lamppost or trip over a toddler. Hugo is six foot four with thick dark hair like mine, and a soft plump tummy held in by a wide leather belt. He makes me, an average five foot six, look like a midget beside him. We often wonder how we came out of the same person, me joking that I need a stepladder to kiss him hello. Though on the podgy side, he's fit and always challenging himself to climb mountains and ski down black runs. His latest feat was climbing Mount Kilimanjaro. He promises Louis that when's he older he will take him trekking up a mountain. It'll be a strictly boys' holiday, a time to bond.

Uncle Hugo and Louis are close. When I left Matthew, Hugo became a father figure to his nephew. He doesn't spoil or indulge Louis to make up for the fact his dad is out of the picture. If Louis believes he can get away with eating a second chocolate marshmallow biscuit, he can think again. 'I can see more than you realise,' Uncle Hugo says, wagging a finger.

'Careful. Step here,' I say.

'Up or down would be helpful.'

'Sorry. Down.'

Pizza Express is in Belsize Park, close to the cinema with the comfy leather seats. When inside the restaurant, I slow down to allow Hugo to adjust to the darkness. A waiter leads us to a table by the window. It's packed since it's still the Christmas holidays. I notice Louis glancing at the next table, watching a dad going through the menu with his son.

One of the waitresses comes over with a small pot of pens and crayons and a paper place mat for Louis to colour in.

'Well, I'm guessing they're not for me,' Hugo says, already charming her.

I order apple juice and dough balls for Louis before reading the menu out for Hugo. Hugo can't read in a dark restaurant. At work he reads from a computer screen, the typeface blown up. It's clear he's partially sighted since his eyes are inverted and he has a strong squint. His sight is in the corner of his eyes, so it's hard for him to look directly at someone sitting opposite him. He tells me that when he is lost in a strange place with no one to guide him he finds it easier to walk in sidesteps. He calls it his sexy crab walk.

'Lasagne,' Hugo says, stopping me mid-sentence. 'That'll do.'

When we order our food the waitress asks if we would like to see the wine list.

'No,' says Louis, looking up from his place mat, pen in hand. 'My mummy is an alcoholic.'

Oh, Louis!

'Oh right,' she says, blushing, before she flees from our table as fast as she can.

As we wait for our food, Louis is zooming his toy police cars around the floor, playing good cop, bad cop. 'Don't go too far,' I call out to him.

'So how was the meeting?' Hugo asks.

Without mentioning names I tell Hugo that I saw someone from school there, adding that they didn't stay for long.

'Maybe he or she didn't feel comfortable?' Hugo suggests. 'Hugs not drugs isn't for everyone.'

'Excuse me, we're not all raving hippies.'

'Did this person see you?'

'Think so. Apparently his sister had a heart attack. She died, Hugo. She would have been around our age.' I chew my nail. 'He must be going through hell.'

'When you next see him, talk to him.'

I nod. 'By the way, how did your date go last night?'

'I don't think we'll be heading down the aisle any time soon.'

'No snap, crackle and pop?'

'None.'

'Oh bollocks. This one sounded so promising, too.'

Hugo has joined an online dating agency. He tried to persuade me to join a single-parent dating website too, but right now I'm happy being on my own. The idea of meeting strangers in pubs doesn't appeal anymore. Besides, there's a lot to be said for being on your own. I feel in control when it's just me; I can do what I like, see who I like, wear my yoga pants most of the time and eat ice cream out of a tub in front of the new series of *Strictly Come Dancing*. My last relationship, with a lawyer called David, ended nine months ago. He was six years older than me and on paper every woman's dream: good-looking in that male model catalogue way, old-fashioned in that he liked to pick up the tab in restaurants, he didn't like football (hurray), was a good listener (rare) and was refreshingly honest about how much he wanted to marry and settle down, when most blokes can't even commit to a second date. I met David in an art gallery. I was gazing at a sculpture of a man's head by Picasso when I became aware of a tall dark stranger watching me. 'I'm glad I don't have such a large nose,' he said, guessing why I was smiling, before introducing himself. We went out for dinner that night and to my surprise Louis and a recovering alcoholic didn't put him off. As our relationship progressed he was positively supportive, suggesting he gave up booze too. David could not have been more different from Matthew. I told myself that it didn't matter that my pulse didn't race when we were together or that my head wasn't intoxicated by thoughts of him when we were apart. Those kind of relationships spelt trouble. And for a time I did enjoy feeling safe and part of a couple. Our relationship lasted a year. Mum only met him twice but was bitterly disappointed when we broke up. Janey was infuriated when I kept on saying he was too perfect, especially when her last date had quibbled over the bill, saying he hadn't eaten any garlic bread. Hugo liked him, but knew there wasn't enough spark. Another factor against us was that David wasn't a natural with kids. He and Louis didn't hit it off as I'd hoped. I could tell David was irritated if Louis cut into his weekend paper time or spilt juice over his paperwork. When David began to talk about holidays and us moving in together I knew, from my reaction, that I had to break up with him. The pressure of more commitment was keeping me awake at night. I knew I was lying to myself and to David, pretending my caution was Louis. I wasn't ready because I wasn't in love with him.

'She kept on saying "poor you",' Hugo says, bringing me back to his date. 'She didn't get the fact that when you're born blind it's all I have ever known so there is no need to feel sorry for me. I only wish I'd been able to see the price of the wine she was merrily ordering. It was literally poor me by the end of the night.'

Hugo tells all his stories on air. He's a journalist and radio presenter. When he left university he did work experience for the BBC, longing to break into broadcasting or journalism and began working for them on the production side soon afterwards. He moved to the other side of the microphone five years ago, when he began writing a blog about being partially sighted and it received so many hits that he was given his own midweek show on Radio 2 called *How I See It*. Hugo is honest about everything, from the barbecue fluid left in the fridge that he almost mistook for fruit juice to how he gets around on the tube and buses, to films and books, political views and most popular of all, the single scene in London.

My mind drifts to Ben again. I wonder if he takes Emily

out for meals. I've never seen him out and about, or bumped into him at the supermarket. I'd say he's about forty, but then again beards can age people.

'Polly?'

'Sorry.'

'You're still thinking about that guy from school, aren't you?'

I'm wondering why he left so abruptly.

'Maybe he'll go to another meeting,' Hugo says. 'It can be pretty daunting first time.'

Back at home, later that evening, I say goodnight to Louis. He's been unusually quiet since we left Pizza Express. His pilot costume now hangs on one side of his wardrobe, next to his clown suit. Fido the toy dog is under the duvet covers with him. It was one of Uncle Hugo's toys, so ancient now that Fido's fur is threadbare and he's missing an eye. 'He's half blind,' Hugo had said. 'Rather apt, don't you think?'

'We thank our lucky stars for Uncle Hugo, don't we?' I say. 'What was the best thing you did today?'

'Mum?'

'Yes?'

'Why doesn't Dad visit me?'

I take a deep breath. Understandably, Louis is beginning to ask more questions, especially when we go out and see families together in parks and restaurants. 'Daddy has to work out his problems,' I say. 'He has many problems, it has nothing . . .'

He pushes my hand away from his cheek and for a second the angry look in his eyes reminds me of his father.

'What problems? Where is he?'

'He had to go away . . .'

'Where?'

I have no idea. 'Louis, he . . .'

'Doesn't he want to see me in my pilot costume?'

'No, I mean yes . . .' I wish I knew the right thing to say. How much should you tell a five-year-old? 'He can't come home, Louis.'

'Where is his house? We can go and see him.'

I shake my head.

'Louis, your dad has problems,' I repeat, adding before he can interrupt, 'things I can't explain to you, but that doesn't mean he doesn't love you.'

Later that night, I sit down on my rocking chair in the corner of my bedroom. It's my favourite spot in the house, my thinking spot. From the window I can see the communal gardens and the larger neighbouring houses with their bay windows. Often I try to imagine what each family is like behind closed doors.

As I rock back and forth, I vow that one day, when Louis is old enough, I will tell him the truth about his father. I feel guilty that I'm raising him as a single mum, but at the same time, if Matthew never showed up again I'd be relieved. Finally I've reached the stage where I don't look over my shoulder all the time; I feel safe at night. I'm lonely, but then everyone gets lonely, right? But at last I sleep without worrying about creaks and night-time noises. I don't have nightmares that he might be outside, watching us.

I don't blame anyone for the choices I made. I had to fix myself. I've made a start, and want nothing and no one to threaten the life Louis and I now have.

But I can't stop Louis from asking questions.

My parents kept too many secrets. I can see my mother now, buttoning up her lips whenever I asked anything personal. She kept my Aunt Vivienne a secret for years.

When the right time comes, I will tell Louis about my past and what has led us here.

5

1991

It's Sunday, the day before Hugo goes to a special boarding school for the blind. Hugo is seven. I'm nearly eleven years old.

Hugo and I walk down to the boathouse with Dad, dressed in our bright yellow life jackets. Dad is going to take us out in the boat before lunch. Mum is cooking a special good-luck meal: roast chicken with oven chips, Hugo's favourite.

We live in Norfolk, in a house by a river and lake. We moved here six months ago, to be close to his school. I was sad to leave London, but Mum and Dad reassured me that London isn't going anywhere and that I can always visit my old friends. 'Dad has a new job in Norwich,' Mum explained. He works in an insurance company. 'It's a fresh start for all of us.'

When Mum and Dad drove Hugo and me to our new home for the first time I felt carsick as we bumped along a narrow winding road. 'Are we nearly there?' I kept on asking. Our house was in the middle of nowhere! Granny Sue wondered why we'd wanted to live so far out in the sticks, but Mum and Dad fell in love with the house and were keen for us to have a garden to play in and room to explore.

Except Mum is always worried when we go outside to play. 'Don't play in the woods, there might be adders,' she says. Or it's, 'Don't go too near the water, you might fall in and drown.'

As we approach the old boathouse I breathe in the smell of bracken and seaweedy water. Dad helps Hugo onto the boat. It's old, wooden and rocks gently from side to side when Hugo clambers in. I follow and Dad asks me to be a good girl and fix one of the oars into the rowlock. When we're ready, Dad uses one oar to push us out of the boat-house and into the open space.

Hugo always looks so happy when he's out on the water. He stretches his podgy arms, the sun beating down on his round dimpled face. I lean over the boat, trail my fingers in the water. Hugo copies me.

'You know what Mum says, Hugo,' I tease. 'There might be huge pike and we all know pike have very sharp teeth.' Hugo sits up straight, puts his hands on his lap.

'We're nearly at the sunken boat now,' I tell him.

'How did it sink, Papa?' he asks.

It doesn't matter how many times we've heard this story, Hugo and I still love it.

34

'Well, it all happened about a hundred years ago. Two lovers . . .'

'Kissy kissy,' says Hugo, nudging me.

'Behave, or I won't finish the story,' says Dad. 'Two lovers weren't allowed to be together. Their families hated one another.'

'Why?' we ask.

'They just did, OK! Otherwise we'll never finish the story. They couldn't see one another in daylight so they decided to meet every night in the boat, when the clock struck twelve and their parents were in bed, fast asleep. So they'd meet down at the boathouse. It was very romantic, the lake was beautiful in the moonlight, but one evening there was a terrible storm. The girl was anxious, said maybe they should go back inside. "Where is your sense of adventure?" the boy asked, encouraging her into the boat. There was thunder and lightning, it was a wild night, the small wooden boat rocking from side to side. She begged him to stop, but he was determined to prove he was brave, that nothing could stand in the way of their being together. Well of course they lost an oar and hit a submerged tree trunk, just here,' Dad says, as we row up to the sunken boat and look down into the murky water. It's spooky. Even the seats are still there. I imagine the girl with long red hair, splayed out in the water, weeds coming out of her mouth.

'And they drowned,' Dad says. 'And that was the end of them.'

I shiver each time I hear the story.

'They haunt the lake, but in a good way,' Dad continues, 'reminding us never to take foolish risks.'

I stare at the murky water, wondering what other secrets lies beneath it.

The following morning, Dad, Mum, Hugo and I eat breakfast. Dad has taken the day off to drive Hugo to his new school. He knows Mum will be too upset to travel home alone. Besides, he wants to say goodbye too. 'Please can I come,' I try again, pushing my porridge away, lumps sticking in my throat.

Mum butters her toast. 'You have school.'

I hold back the tears and look beseechingly at Dad.

'No, Polly,' she snaps. 'We've talked about this.'

'Dad?'

I try one last time.

'Best do as your mum says.'

Why doesn't he ever stand up to her?

'Please can she come,' says a small voice from across the table.

Later that morning we're on our way to Hugo's school in Dad's old bottle-green BMW. We play car games and Dad sings his favourite song, 'Meet me in St Louis'. It always makes Hugo and me laugh, especially when he sings the words, 'hoochee koochee' and 'tootsie-wootsie'.

When we reach the gates of Hugo's school, Mum orders Dad to stop the car. I hold Hugo's hand until Mum unbuckles his seatbelt and sits him on her knee in the front, stroking and hugging him.

Slowly we approach a tall grey stone building with wide, open green space on either side of the driveway. The school looks like a castle with turrets and lots of narrow windows. We approach a courtyard with a fountain, cupids spraying water. Dad turns off the engine. I notice a tall wiry man with a moustache and dressed in a suit walking down some steep stone steps and approaching our car. 'Wait,' Mum says. Hugo's hands are clasped around her neck.

Nervously I step outside and look up at the imposing building, already feeling scared for my brother. I can't imagine living here. I bet this place is haunted. Dad opens the boot and lifts out Hugo's trunk, packed with all his new clothes to start his new life. He shakes the tall man's hand. Dad tells me this is Mr Barry, the headmaster.

Mr Barry shakes my hand too, welcoming me to the school. He smells of cigar smoke. 'Hello, Hugo,' he says. Hugo rushes back to Mum. 'I don't want to go,' he says, suddenly tiny and fragile, lost in her arms.

When Mr Barry tries to prise them apart, Hugo lashes out at him, hitting his arm.

'Hugo,' my father says tearfully, taking him to one side, 'you're going to be fine. You'll be so happy here, and it's only a few days until we'll see you at the weekend.'

Tears are streaming down Hugo's face; his eyes are red and crumpled. I rush to the backseat of the car and pick up Fido, Hugo's favourite toy dog. I thrust it into his hands, 'Whenever you feel sad, think of us in the boat,' I say, before Dad tells me to give my brother one last hug and then we must go.

'Matron will help him settle in,' assures Mr Barry. 'We'll take great care of him.'

As we pull away, back down the long school drive, we hear Hugo wailing. Dad says, 'Don't turn round.' But it's too late. Mum and I see Mr Barry restraining Hugo from running after us. Fido is tossed on to the ground.

'What have we done?' Mum says.

That night, I can't sleep. On my way to the bathroom I hear Mum and Dad talking in the kitchen. I creep downstairs and sit on the bottom step. My heart lifts. Maybe they're saying they might collect Hugo tomorrow?

'You know it's the right thing, Gina,' Dad's saying. 'The sooner Hugo can be with other children like himself, the better. We've got to be brave, let him go.'

'I know, but I feel guilty. He's only seven, he's so young.'

'The specialist said now is the right time. I know he's only little, but Polly's school could *never* give him the same opportunities.'

Mum has explained to me why he is going too. All the pupils have eyesight problems, the classes are small, and the teachers will be able to help children like Hugo overcome barriers. The specialist had told Mum and Dad how important it was to integrate Hugo with others like him as soon as possible. The longer they waited the harder it would be, not only for them, but for Hugo too.

'This was your idea. I took the promotion for Hugo! For you!' Dad continues.

'I know!'

I hear a bottle being opened.

'Here,' Dad says.

'No.'

'Come on, you can have a small one, Gina.'

'No.'

'For God's sake, one won't hurt!' I'm not used to Dad raising his voice. 'It's brandy.'

'No.'

'Think of it as medicine. It'll help you sleep.'

'I don't want it! It's poison!' I grip on to the banister when I hear glass shattering against the floor.

'Gina, you're not Vivienne!'

Who's Vivienne?

'Don't you dare mention her name in this house,' Mum shouts now.

'Fine, but if I want a drink, I'll have one. He's my son too.' He pauses. 'It's going to be strange without him but we have Polly to think about. She needs us to be strong.'

'I know, but . . .'

'You're tough on her.'

'It's hard not to love Hugo more.'

Fighting back the tears, I jump up.

'Polly?' they call.

I rush back upstairs and into my bedroom, hiding under the duvet, tears rolling down my cheeks as I pretend to be asleep when Mum opens the door.

6

2013

It's Louis's first day back at school after the Christmas holidays and we need to leave in fifteen minutes. 'London's burning, London's burning,' I sing, gathering his packed lunch. 'Get the engine.'

'*Fetch* the engine!' Louis corrects me.

'Pour on water, pour on water!'

Louis leaps off the sofa and clambers into his toy fire engine that somehow Uncle Hugo and I had assembled over the Christmas holidays. Our flat is open-plan. One room merges into another so I can see Louis from the kitchen putting out the fire with his party balloon pump that acts as an imaginary hose.

We need to leave in five minutes.

'Sing it again, Mummy.'

I shake my head. 'We'll be late.'

'What did the big tomato say to the little tomato?'

'Don't know. Now, come on, put your socks on!'

'Ketch up. Why don't we have a car?'

We can't afford one, that's why. 'We have legs, Louis.'

'Maisy's dad has legs and a car.'

'Good for him. Now come on!' I say, urging him to put his other sock on.

Finally I help him into his coat. Zip it up. On go the gloves and the woolly lion hat. We gather his PE kit and rucksack. I try not to think about the chaos left in the sitting room. As we're about to head out of the door, 'Mum, I need the loo,' he says.

Louis and I race across Primrose Hill, there's no time to admire the BT tower or point at the pretty apricot house today. When Louis slows down to admire a small dog, asking the owner if he can pat it, I grab his hand and yank him away, terrified that the headmistress will tell me off for being so late.

Ben and Emily arrive in a heap at the school gates at the exact same time as us. I notice Emily's coat is buttoned skew-whiff and her hair is in an odd sort of plait. 'I used to get to the office at 6.30,' Ben mutters out of breath as we make our way towards the classroom. A voice in my head tells me to ask him out for a coffee.

I help Louis hang up his duffel coat and put his school bag into one of the pull-out trays before he darts over to his friends, who are sitting at a table covered in fake grass and toy farm animals. 'Oh silly me!' he says when he realises he hasn't signed himself in. There's a seaside chart on one of the walls; each child is a sea creature. Louis grabs a Velcro-backed crab with his name on it and thrusts it in the sandy section of the picture, next to all the other crabs. 'Well done,' I say, kissing him goodbye. 'Be good.'

Outside the gates, mums congregate in small groups, while I talk to Jim, our stay-at-home dad, keeping an eye out for Ben at the same time. Jim has two children; Maisy, who is one of Louis's best friends, and Theo, two years old and clutching Jim's hand, dressed in red cords that clash with his carrot-coloured hair. Jim is slim and fit from spending hours in the gym. When his two children are older he wants to train to become a sports teacher. When he first pitched up at the school gates there was a wave of curiosity around him. When one of the mums saw him in the swimming pool dressed in his snug-fitting pair of trunks that left little to the imagination, ripples of excitement were shared at the school gates the following morning.

Just as Ben heads towards us, hands deep in pockets, head down, it seems I'm not the only one keeping an eye out for him. Gabriella, Italian and voluptuous, totters towards him in her heels and fake fur coat carrying a bright orange dish. She's married, but that doesn't stop her from flirting. 'I don't believe it,' Jim says, humour in his voice. 'Why don't I get a lasagne anymore?'

Ben has attracted lots of attention for different reasons. Losing his sister and adopting his niece has made him both a subject of pity and something of a local hero. I sense this makes Ben deeply uncomfortable, and I'm guessing this is why he never hangs around, giving nobody the chance to get to know him, not even busty Gabriella.

I watch as she touches Ben's arm and flicks her dark wavy hair as she tells him to how to heat the lasagne. Her hand rests on his shoulder as she asks him how he is feeling with a sympathetic nod. Before I know it, I'm over there. 'Sorry to interrupt,' I say to Gabriella, before turning to Ben, 'but I was wondering if you'd like to join Jim and me for a coffee.'

'I don't drink coffee,' Ben replies, Gabriella standing close to him, reeking of Italian perfume.

He glances at his watch. 'But I've got time for a ginger tea.'

Jim, Ben and I sit at our usual corner table in Chamomile, a small lively café on England's Lane, close to my flat and always packed with locals.

Jim and I discover Ben lives in Chalcot Square, a cluster of imposing houses, each painted in different shades of pastel. Ben apologetically tells us he used to be a broker in the City, back in his twenties. He's thirty-six now. 'It's fine, you can hate me.' He shrugs. 'I know we're world-wreckers. To be honest, I went into the City because I didn't know what else to do. No imagination.' His mouth curls into a slight smile and I decide there's something attractive in his manner but looks-wise he's definitely not my type. I've always preferred blonds.

'Well someone has to run our economy,' admits Jim.

Ben shrugs. 'You know, it wasn't all that bad but I had to give it up in the end. The lifestyle wasn't for me.'

Is that why he was at AA?

'What do you do now?' I ask.

'Accountant. Deeply unglamorous,' he says with that dry smile, 'but I like being freelance, being my own boss, and I work for some really interesting clients, a lot of them in the creative industries. To be honest it's useful now, working from home. I need to be around for Emily.'

'How's Emily doing?' Jim asks.

'The headmistress told me she's quiet, subdued, which isn't surprising. As I'm sure you know my sister, Grace, Emily's mother, died last summer.'

We nod. 'I'm so sorry,' I say, trying hard not to do that sympathetic nod. 'I've wanted to talk to you for a while, but wasn't sure you . . .'

He stops me. 'It was sudden.' Ben gives nothing away in his eyes as he tells us she died from hypertrophic cardio-myopathy, a heart condition that causes enlargement of the heart muscle. She had no symptoms; they didn't even know she was unwell. She died in the early hours of the morning. 'Emily had gone to wake her up. Poor child.'

Jim and I remain silent.

Ben explains that he is Emily's only living blood relative. 'Grace and I were close. When she had Emily, she made me promise I'd be her guardian if anything happened to her. Of course I agreed at the time, believing that if anything bad was going to happen, it was going to happen to me. You see, Grace was fit and happy. She was an acupuncturist, worked from home. Unlike me, she'd barely touched a drink or smoked in her life. She lived in the country, didn't believe in polluting the environment so cycled everywhere and meditated each morning. She was only three years older than me. Ironic thing is she'd kept on joking about not wanting to turn forty. She died only a few days before. Why does the world behave in this absurd way? I should be the one in the grave.' He shrugs. 'I'm not married, have no commitments, I'm all she has, so I owe it to Grace to be there for her, but to be honest I'm not sure I'm cut out to be a dad. I'm not even a dad, am I? I'm Emily's uncle, but now that Grace is gone, it's like she doesn't even know me anymore.'

I wait for Jim to say something. He doesn't. I'm about to, but Ben beats me to it. 'Sorry, bet you wished you'd never asked me out for a coffee now.' He grabs his pack of Marlboro Reds, saying he'll be back in a second.

Five minutes later Ben is still smoking outside. Jim opens the lid of the lasagne dish to take a peep. 'Gabriella once made me a tiramisu. Her husband must be the size of a

46

house.' He pauses. 'What do you think happened to Emily's dad?' He doesn't wait for an answer. 'Poor Ben, he must be . . .'

'Shut up.'

Jim looks up. 'You shut up.'

'He's coming,' I mouth.

'Oh.' The lid slams back on as Ben returns to an awkward silence. 'Please don't stop talking about me.' He sits down, tosses his cigarette pack on the table.

'I'm sorry. I was just saying to Jim,' I improvise, 'that I can't imagine what you're going through, but being a single mum I do sort of understand the pressure and I'm happy to look after Emily any time.'

Jim backs me up. 'Me too, mate. If there's anything I can do.'

'Well, there is something.'

'Yes?' both Jim and I say.

'Those muffins look pretty good.' Ben gestures to the glass cabinet filled with cakes and pastries.

Over muffins, Jim tells Ben about Violet Reid, head of the PTA. 'She thinks I'm a weirdo not working. I love to wind her up, tell her I'm busy all day with a feather duster.' Jim pretends to dust our table. 'This one time, right, before a meeting I overheard her saying to one of the other mums . . .' Jim prepares himself to mimic Violet with her la-di-da voice, '"I'm all for men being more hands-on and changing the odd nappy, but if my hubby suddenly started walking round the house in a pinny I swear I'd lose all respect for him!"'

'What do you call men like us?' Ben looks at Jim, a tiny glint of humour now in his eyes.

'Stay-at-home-dads or lazy sods, according to Granny-in-law,' Jim says. He goes on to tell Ben what his wife, Camilla's family, think about their swapping the traditional roles and how Christmas with them en masse is always a challenge. 'Truth is Milla wasn't cut out to be a stay-at-home mum and missed being a lawyer, and she earns more too. I was hating my job with the local council so it made complete sense to us, but Granny doesn't see it like that. Christmas Day went from bad to worse,' Jim continues, enjoying the captive audience. 'Not content with calling me a lazy sod, she says, "I mean, what do you *do* all day? It's not right my daughter has meetings up to her eyeballs while you fanny around eating muffins!"' He picks up his blueberry muffin and takes a large deliberate bite, making Ben and me laugh.

'Jim, I wish I could clone you,' I say. 'Seriously, most men are too proud to do what you do.'

If only they knew about Matthew. Jim knows my relationship went badly wrong and he's aware I go to AA, but that's only half the story. I shudder hearing his voice. *'If I hear that baby crying one more time before I've had a coffee I swear I'll throw it out the window.'*

'He does everything, Ben,' I carry on, wishing I could

wipe away those memories. Rub them out like a teacher rubs things out on a blackboard.

'It's not a hardship,' Jim declares. 'It's a choice and a privilege. I think it's fine having someone look after your child when they are so tiny, like puppies in your arms that you feed and rock to sleep, but I wanted to be around when Theo said his first few words. I think it's important that one of us looks after our children. Sorry, that was crass,' he says to both Ben and me. 'I wasn't thinking.'

Ben nods. 'What I'm struggling with is how do you know the right thing to do, the right way to bring them up? At night I'm lying awake thinking this girl, this little person, her happiness now rests in my hands. It terrifies me.'

'Me too,' I confess.

'This morning she asked me to plait her hair,' Ben continues.

'Ah, the hair thing,' says Jim. 'It gets easier with practice.'

'I'll give you a lesson,' I suggest.

'You and me, Ben, we're in the minority, so we need to stick together.' He raises his mug to Ben's.

'To stay-at-home-dads-slash-uncles then,' Ben says.

'And single mums,' Jim adds.

I join in. 'So stick that up your pipe and smoke it, Granny.'

When Jim heads off to pick Theo up from nursery, Ben and I leave the café.

We walk along the pavement, quiet in our thoughts until I pluck up the courage to say, 'Ben, do you mind me asking . . . ?' *Tell him you saw him at the meeting.* I wimp out. 'Where's Emily's father?'

'Oh, right. Him. When Grace told him she was pregnant he did a runner. She wrestled with the decision, but she'd always wanted children.'

'Your parents, are they around to help?'

'Mum is no longer with us and my father died when I was four. My stepdad's still around, sadly.'

'Anything "step" is never the easiest of relationships.'

'Forget the title,' he says sharply. 'It's about the person, the man, and in this case he's a horrible jumped-up little man.'

We turn into Chalcot Square.

'Right, well I'd better get to work,' I say, feeling that conversation was killed. 'It was great to . . .'

'Are you around tonight?'

'Tonight?'

'I wouldn't mind taking you up on that plaiting lesson. Emily keeps asking for a fish plait?'

'French plait?'

'Yeah, maybe that was it. Who knows, but you sound very clued up in this area, so if a French plait is something you can teach me, I might earn brownie points and Emily might be a bit happier.'

He mentions her name with little emotion, which unsettles me. 'It's a date. Well, not a date *date*.' Oh put a sock in it, Polly.

'Shall we meet after school? We can eat Gabriella's lasagne,' he says, gesturing to the orange dish. 'You'd be doing me a favour. She's cooked enough to feed the south of England.'

'I'd like that.' I'm not so sure Gabriella would, mind you.

'Good. Well, I'll see you later.' And for the first time that morning his smile reaches his eyes and I catch a glimmer of the man he could be, underneath that mask of loneliness.

7

Ben leads me into his sitting room. I stare at the modern fireplace, the brown leather sofa with matching armchairs that look as if they've never been sat upon, and the stark white walls. 'I'm bored,' Louis says, clearly realising that this isn't a child-friendly place. No toy diggers, trucks or toolboxes scattered on the carpet, only pristine wooden floors.

'Why don't you play a game with Emily?' I suggest, distracted by a painting with a giant orange splodge in the middle of it.

Emily edges away from us as if we're poisonous. She hasn't said a word since we collected her from school. I can't imagine what's going on inside her head. She probably doesn't know either. She must be confused and scared, yet unable to express it, and from the little I know about Ben, I doubt he can help her either, especially when he's grieving too.

'Do you want to read your book, Emily?' Ben asks, as if

reading from a script. 'Or have a snack before dinner? Juice? Watch television?'

Unsurprisingly they opt for television and a juice.

I follow Ben into the white kitchen, with nothing on the counters except a music system and coffee machine. In the middle of the room is an island with two modern silver stools. He opens the fridge, reaches for the milk and two cartons of apple juice. He switches on the kettle. 'Cup of tea?'

'Thanks,' I say, feeling faintly uncomfortable in this show home. I look at Louis and Emily watching television, their mouths wide open like goldfish. 'The moment that thing is on, they turn into zombies.'

Ben hands me a mug. 'Emily probably watches too much, but I don't know what else to do with her. She won't play with her toys.'

Toys? What toys?

I saw you at the meeting.

'Maybe she needs counselling,' Ben continues.

'Um. Maybe.'

Throwing money at the problem probably isn't the answer. But then again, if he can't talk to her . . .

I look around the kitchen. She needs a home filled with fun and love. She needs to understand what's going on. I have no idea how a child sees death. It's frightening enough for an adult to lose a parent, so what does it mean for Emily? She needs Ben to talk to her about Grace to keep her memory alive. Does she ask questions, like Louis is beginning to with his father? It's hard for Louis to understand why he has no dad when the man is still alive.

Louis jolts me from my thoughts, saying he needs the loo.

'Sure. Just round the corner, last room on right,' Ben says. Louis wants me to come with him, clingy when we're not at home.

As we walk down the hallway, hand-in-hand, I can't help taking a quick peep into Ben's room. There's an exercise bike and double bed, a bedside table with nothing on it. No photographs or things that tell me anything about him. This flat isn't a home; it's more like a stage where the actors don't know their lines. We all have four walls around us that can be filled with laughter, hope, security, love and all other kinds of feelings. These walls house sadness. When Matthew and I lived together they housed fear.

We all eat lasagne (delicious, thanks, Gabriella) round the dining room table. 'Then Polly's going to teach me how to plait your hair, Emily,' says Ben stiltedly. 'Come on, you must be starving.' He takes the fork, scoops some food on to it.

Emily turns her head away from him. Ben puts the fork down. 'You need to eat,' he says, fighting not to lose his patience.

'Mummy says if I don't eat I'll shrivel up!' Louis waves his fork in the air.

'I don't have a Mummy anymore,' Emily says. 'She's dead.'

It's the first thing she has said this afternoon and it makes me want to cry. I glance at Ben, who looks lost.

'I'm so sorry, Emily,' I say. 'You must miss her very much.'

She nods. 'Her heart went wrong. Mummy said you go to heaven,' Emily continues, shoving food from one side of the plate to the other.

'What is heaven?' Louis asks.

'It's a place where all the most wonderful things are,' I say. 'All the things that make you happy.'

Louis thinks about this. 'Custard tarts?'

'Oh yeah, loads of custard tarts.'

'Is there a garden?' Louis continues, 'So I can play stomp rocket?'

'Yes,' Emily says to my surprise, 'there is one big garden with flowers and lots of dogs.'

Emily is a beautiful girl with her long shiny auburn hair, heart-shaped mouth and oval green eyes. She just needs to eat. She's nothing but skin and bones. A puff of wind could surely blow her over.

'And cars? We don't have a car. Do you have a car, Emily?'

She nods. 'Uncle Ben has a car with no roof.'

'Not for long,' he mutters.

'I want to see heaven,' Louis announces. 'When can we go, Mum?'

'We can't. People don't come *back* from heaven.' Please stop asking awkward questions, Louis.

'Oh. Why not?'

I cough. 'Well . . .'

'Maisy's name was written in the red book today,' he interrupts me, thankfully. I remind Ben that Maisy is Jim's daughter, noticing how relieved he looks that we've changed subjects too.

'Why was she in the red book?' I ask.

'She flushed lots of paper down the toilet.'

'How do you know?'

'She came into the classroom with toilet paper stuck on her skirt!' Again Louis howls with laughter, thinking this has to be the funniest thing ever.

'What's the red book?' asks Ben.

'If your name is in the little red book it's because you've been very naughty,' says Louis, rather self-righteously.

'Do you think your name is in it?' I ask him.

He blushes, even his ears turning pink. 'I don't think so, Mum. No.'

'Do you think your name might *possibly* be in there?'

He pauses. 'Possibly.'

'Do you think you probably *are* in the red book?'

Louis puts down his knife and fork, taking his time to answer. 'I probably am, Mummy, yes.'

There's a pause before we all laugh, even Emily. I catch Ben looking at her, as if she has never laughed before. She eats a mouthful of lasagne, and then another. Mentally I am urging her to eat just one more. As we clear up the plates,

Ben tells me that Emily's eaten more tonight than she has in weeks. 'You'll have to come over more often,' he whispers.

'OK, so you take a strand in the middle, here,' I say, 'and then you go to the sides . . .'

'He's not scratching the floor, is he?' asks Ben, looking over his shoulder at Louis racing his car around the flat.

'Concentrate on this, please,' I tell him before muttering, 'control freak.' It takes one to know one.

He raises an eyebrow. 'Bossy-boots.'

'Ow.' Emily pulls away, touching her hair.

'Sorry, sweetheart. You take this strand over the other and then you take another from here . . .'

'I'll never be able to do this,' murmurs Ben, watching avidly. 'It's harder than astrophysics.'

'Don't be silly.'

'Don't be silly,' Emily repeats.

'And then you plait some more . . . like this . . . and look . . .' I tie the hairband at the end of the plait and swivel Emily round to face me. 'So pretty.' She touches the back of her head tentatively, before saying, 'I like you.'

My heart melts. 'Well that's good news, because I like you too,' I say. Ben and I swap positions on the sofa, Ben asking Emily to sit down on the floor again, in front of him. He rolls up his sleeves as if he means business. We undo the plait; Ben brushes her hair.

'Ouch!' she shrieks. 'Uncle Ben!'

'Wimp,' he says, and for the first time tonight I think he's enjoying himself. 'Like this?' Ben grabs a section of Emily's hair.

I lean towards him. 'Gently. That's right, bring it over this strand . . .'

'It's coming loose, oh shit, I mean sugar.'

'Oh shit,' repeats Louis, charging around the house, now with his emergency helicopter.

'Oh shit,' Emily joins in.

'My fault, sorry,' murmurs Ben when I tell Louis off for saying the 's' word. 'There.' Ben ties the plait together with a bright pink band.

'Not bad,' I judge. It's wonky and won't stay in for long, but, 'you have potential. Go and have a look in the mirror, Emily.' She slopes off towards her bedroom. I urge Ben to follow her.

Emily's room is smaller than Ben's, with a single bed, pink-spotted duvet, and a toy sheep on her pillow. There's another modern painting on the wall, this one with a red splodge in the middle. It looks like a nosebleed.

'It's nice,' she says, heading out again, avoiding eye contact. Ben perches on the edge of her bed, sighs as if he has the world on his shoulders.

I sit down next to him, wishing I knew all the right things to say. I glance around the bare room before Ben tells me, 'I was close to Grace, we used to talk on the phone most days, she was always nagging me to come and stay.'

He smiles sadly. 'I knew Emily well enough, but I've never been that great with kids, as you can probably tell. The idea of having one myself . . .' He inhales deeply, as if it were never on the agenda. 'And now she's here, it's like we're almost strangers.'

'It's bound to take time,' I reassure him. 'Where are her toys?'

He gestures to the window box at the foot of her bed. I open it, and inside are dolls, a basket filled with wooden fruit and vegetables, a toy till and a pair of wooden stilts, everything heaped up. 'She doesn't want to play with them anymore,' he says.

I think about this, completely unqualified in this area, but something tells me that Ben needs to try a different tactic, because it can't get much worse. 'She probably does, but maybe you need to play with her. Does she have a picture of her mum?'

'I've got albums.' He looks out of the window. 'I thought it might upset her, you know, seeing photos of Grace. At night I find her looking out into the sky.' He stares ahead. 'Asking for her Mummy.' He turns back to me, panic in his eyes. 'I'm not sure I'm cut out for this.'

'Yes you are.' I sit down next to him. 'You're all she's got, Ben. She's lost the most important person in her world, she can't lose you too.'

'I know, but . . .'

'You're her uncle, her *father* now.'

We sit silently. I want to ask him about AA. 'Ben, do you mind me asking but . . .'

'You saw me.'

We glance at one another awkwardly again until I say, 'You didn't stay long. I wanted to come after you . . . Was it your first time?'

'No, been to a few. I'm not sure it's for me, all that sharing stuff, talking about *feelings*.' He pulls a face. 'Listening to how old Bob found himself in the dustbin but crawled his way out of it.'

I find myself smiling. 'It's not all like that. I've met some incredible people.' I think of music producer Ryan, lovely old Harry, my sponsor, Neve.

'Why were you there?' He stares ahead.

'Drink. You?'

'Drink and drugs. Drink *went* with the drugs. A couple of glasses of wine, a line of coke. My dealer was on speed dial.' He shrugs. 'This was years ago, Polly, when I worked in the City. I went into rehab when I was thirty, haven't looked back. I don't know . . . I wasn't wavering the other day, or maybe I was, but what with losing Grace and Emily living with me, life has been a little crazy.'

I look at Ben. He's got money, the designer suit, looks (if only he'd get rid of that beard) the cushy pad, but all I can see is emptiness inside. 'If ever you need to talk, if you need a friend . . .'

He turns to me, warmth in his dark-brown eyes. 'You've already helped with the plait situation.' He pauses, pressing his head into his hands. 'I am worried about losing clients. I can't seem to focus, I need to . . .'

'Listen,' I interrupt, 'anyone would be struggling right now in your shoes. Don't be too hard on yourself.'

He nods. 'When did you start drinking?'

'Twelve.'

'Twelve!'

'Oh believe me, people start younger than that.'

'Why did you?'

'I don't know. I felt nothing inside,' is all I can say. 'Escape, I guess. The only time I felt at peace was when I drank. You?'

He thinks about this. 'The normal route to life, you know, marriage and children, it seemed pretty dull. I was determined not to go down the same path as my mum and stepdad. They had a marriage I wouldn't inflict on my worst enemy,' he confides. 'I thought I was better off living the high life, drinking and partying to excess, I didn't want to invest in any relationship that got in the way of my freedom. I see now that that way of living is no route to happiness.' He stops, runs a hand through his thick wavy hair. 'Boy, this is getting a bit heavy. I hardly know you.'

'Sometimes it's easier to talk to complete strangers.'

'Not *quite* so complete now.'

We smile, and in that moment I see something flicker between us, something that tells me we are going to become good friends.

8

1994

I'm in the kitchen being told off, my father telling Mum to calm down. She's spitting with rage as she reads a letter from my headmistress. 'Why did you do it, Polly?'

To earn money to buy cigarettes, I set up a hairdressing camp in one corner of the playing field with my best friend, Janey.

'She said she liked it, Mum.' The girls brought along a picture from a glossy magazine of a hairstyle they liked and Janey and I copied it. It was all going so well until Lucinda wanted a short spiky hairdo like Helena Christensen's. I thought I'd copied it faithfully, but clearly from the letter Mum is reading, Lucinda's parents are furious.

'Lucinda was pleased!' I stress again.

Mum steps forward, hits me so hard across the cheek that even Dad is shocked.

I stagger back, tears stinging my eyes.

She tells me how disappointed and ashamed she is of me, and soon her words become a blur. I can't listen. All I hear is, 'Go! You're grounded for a month.'

Slowly I head upstairs, feeling guilty and wretched. I stop when I overhear Mum talking to Dad. 'I'm not being hard! My mother hit us all the time, never did us any harm. If we're not careful she'll turn out like Vivienne.'

I catch my breath. Vivienne? Why is that name familiar? I recall sitting on the stairs the night after Hugo was dropped off at school. *'Think of it as medicine,'* Dad had said. *'It'll help you sleep.'*

'I don't want it! It's poison!'

'Gina, you're not Vivienne!'

Vivienne. Who is she?

Later that night, I lie awake, missing Hugo. I wish I could go into his bedroom, talk to him like we used to.

When Hugo left home three years ago a light switched off in the house. When we sat down to supper, none of us could look at the empty seat opposite mine. We'd gone from a comfortable square to an awkward triangle. Mum can't disguise anymore that he is undoubtedly her favourite child. Hugo is ten now, but when he was eight his school was approached by the British Ski Club for the Disabled. I can still recall Mum's excitement when she had told Dad and me that they had selected only three of the pupils to train and compete for the Paralympics. 'And guess who they've picked!'

I want Mum to look at me with that same pride, but at my school we're lucky to get forty-five minutes of sport a week. By the time we've changed into our kit and trekked to the lacrosse field it's time to turn round and get changed again. I'm not jealous of Hugo, not at all. I really look forward to seeing him each weekend and particularly love our cooking sessions. I am in charge and we make apple crumble and chicken pie for our Sunday lunch. Often we'll pretend to be on a television show demonstrating our skills. Hugo says he wants to be a newsreader or chat show host when he grows up. I smile, remembering how one time when we were making sultana scones, Hugo mistook the jug of gravy sitting in the fridge for milk. We howled with laughter, bits of chicken fat bobbing about in the mixing bowl, Hugo saying, 'Now, folks, that's *not* how to do it.'

We go for long walks by the lake and Hugo promises he won't tell Mum and Dad that I smoke, though admits he wishes I didn't, saying my teeth will turn yellow. He laughed at me when I told him I wanted to be a pothead and play in a band with Janey when I'm older.

When he's gone I feel lonely and the house plunges into darkness. Unable to sleep, I get up, walk over to my wardrobe, open the door and nestled on one of the shelves, underneath a couple of jumpers, is a half bottle of wine. Curious, I'd nicked it from Janey's kitchen one evening after school, shoved it in my rucksack without even Janey knowing. I wonder if she's been grounded for a month?

I tiptoe downstairs into the kitchen and open one of the cutlery drawers. In the darkness I feel for the corkscrew. Got it. Quietly, I head back to my room.

I plunge the corkscrew into the top of the bottle, twist it round. Finally I pour some of the golden liquid into my glass. Tentatively I take a sip. It slides down my throat easily; I feel warmth coursing through my body. I take another sip and squeeze my eyes shut, feeling another hit of syrupy warmth and sunshine. That's better. I feel good. I take another. And another. Soon all the worries about no more pocket money and being grounded fade away. The burn of Mum's palm striking my cheek disappears. I can't explain why, but I feel like an outsider, as if I don't belong in the family. Sometimes I think Mum hates me. I shut my eyes and try to blot out those words I overheard sitting on the stairs outside the kitchen, *'It's hard not to love Hugo more.'*

I empty my glass and pour myself another. I smile, not feeling so alone anymore. The wine takes me to a happy place, far away from home.

9

@GateauAuChocolat Lunch today! Chorizo & cannellini bean soup along with our famous gateau au chocolat. What a feast!

I work in a café in Belsize Village called Gateau Au Chocolat. Belsize Village is a small enclave tucked away on the junction of Belsize Lane, a hidden part of London that thankfully few tourists have found. What I love about the village is that most of the shops and cafés are independent. There's the local launderette, the family pet shop, the delicatessen selling a mouth-watering array of cheeses, salads and pâté. It's off the beaten track, and I like being off the beaten track.

When I enter the café, I'm welcomed by the familiar smell of freshly made garlic and rosemary bread and winter soup cooking on the stove. I walk past the front table covered in hardback cookery books, delectable covers illustrating curries from India, homemade pasta and fish marinated in herbs from Italy, barbecued meat from Australia and pies with golden crust tops from the Brits.

On the shelves that line both sides of the shop are further cookbooks. One side is divided into sections, including vegetables, cheese, meat, baking, bread, coffee, parties, health, books for kids and spices and herbs. The opposite side is divided into countries.

Our test kitchen is at the end of the shop. It's small with white tiles, a modern cooker and stove; copper pans hang from hooks, and we have an old-fashioned mixer and white porcelain cake stands, along with a blackboard where we write up the lunch menu for the day. There are five small tables that can seat two to three people, and then a larger communal table that can sit six, just in front of our mural-painted walls of lobsters, chilli, cans of soup and olive oil bottles. There's a squishy sofa that customers enjoy with a cappuccino and a book. There are also shelves stacked with chef magazines and olive oils for sale, along with my boss's red wine, produced in his own vineyard in France.

I share the kitchen with Mary-Jane. Mary-Jane is in her late fifties and has worked here ever since the café opened ten years ago. She comes from St Helena, a tiny tropical island in the South Atlantic Ocean, famous for being where Napoleon was exiled and died. She's short and plump with a mop of thick dark hair and a determined stride. When I came in for my interview with Jean almost four years ago, she was standing at the sink in her marigolds, steely-faced and certainly not about to make me feel less nervous. 'Mary-Jane is special,' Jean assured me, giving her a wink that she ignored, 'but she's not too good at . . .' he clicked his fingers, 'small talk.' Mary-Jane shooed him away with her hand, as if he were an annoying fly, but I could see the affection between them.

She grunts when I say hello, before approaching me with the soupspoon. 'Taste,' she orders. I taste and give it the thumbs-up because, as usual, it tastes delicious.

Like me, Mary-Jane had had no professional experience before she began working here. Her passion for food came from her grandmother, who loved to bake. She was famous for her fruitcakes and coconut fingers – slabs of fresh sponge cut into slices and rolled in icing sugar and coconut. Granny lived with the family. Mary-Jane's father was a farmer; he grew fruit and vegetables. When Mary-Jane talks about her childhood, it's the one time that her eyes light up and she often giggles as if she were a young girl again. 'Dad used to grow bananas, Polly. On a Saturday morning we'd help him pick them off the trees and bunch them together with string, and then we'd hang the bunches on the side of the donkeys' saddles. We had beautiful donkeys, I can even remember their names.' She smiled, as if she were standing by the banana tree that moment with them. 'Prince, Violet and Ned. We had guava trees too: they grew wild and Granny used to make the best guava jelly. We'd eat it on toast after school.'

'Find a boss who will make you a coffee every day,' Jean says as I'm writing the menu on the blackboard. He's standing by the cappuccino machine, dressed in his blue apron. Jean is in his early fifties, tall and fit from swimming every day, with brown hair and probing eyes.

When he hands me a cup I can tell he's in a good mood. Jean's behaviour is as unpredictable as the weather. Often he loses his cool in the kitchen, spatulas and crockery flying across the kitchen. But today he blows Mary-Jane and me a kiss before disappearing upstairs to prepare his workshop on cooking with wild mushrooms.

As I stick my apron on and begin to assemble all the ingredients I need for my cakes and pavlova, I think about how working here was only meant to be a stopgap. It was something to do to help me through the early months after my break-up with Matt, and to earn some money, but more importantly to distract me from drinking. During the early days of rehab, I needed a sense of purpose until I felt ready to think about a new career or going back to teaching. In my early twenties, when friends, including Janey, were still at university I was lost as to what I wanted to do with my life. In the end, I enrolled on a one-year Montessori teacher-training course just off Oxford Street. It was hard work, practical and written exams at the end of the year, but I still managed to keep up my drinking and smoking habits full-time, rolling out of bed when my alarm clock shrilled at me, head pounding, only to be cured by another coffee and cigarette at breakfast. I passed my exams and found work, teaching children at

Barn Owls Nursery in Earls Court. I enjoyed playing games and singing alphabet songs with the children – it seems like another world now. I gave up work after giving birth to Louis, though always intended to return to teaching. After my break-up I couldn't go back. It reminded me too much of my past. I needed something new.

During my unorthodox interview at the café I felt intimidated by Jean. He sat me down and began to describe how he had cooked all over the world. 'America was like walking into my television set, Polly, it was as if I were on *Miami Vice*. Have you been there?'

I shook my head, staring at my CV placed in front of him that surely showed an underachiever. As to my travelling experiences, well, I'd been stoned in France and drunk in Thailand, so drunk that I'd had a blackout for three days, waking up to find an old Thai lady trying to force me to drink some awful herb tea. Jean went on to tell me that he'd left school when he was thirteen to make his own way in the world. 'My father, he said I could leave school if I work, not sit around doing, what is it you say . . .' He clicked his fingers until it came to him, 'sweet Fanny Adams. All I wanted to do was be a chef. And you Polly, did you enjoy school?' he asked, finally flicking through my CV, looking fairly uninterested.

'I wasn't an A-grade student,' I confided, realising there was little point pretending, my nerves finally subsiding. 'I wrote, "Happy Christmas" on my maths mock exam paper.

Got 3 per cent for that. Apparently that was for writing my name and the correct date.'

That was when Jean and I clicked. 'You're funny, Polly. You make even Mary-Jane laugh, no mean feat,' he said, gesturing to her chuckling at the sink in her Marigolds, 'but is your cooking as bad as your mathematics?'

I smiled at that, before shaking my head vigorously. 'I can bake cakes, biscuits, pancakes, meringues, you name it, I can do it. I've loved cooking since I was a child, I've just never had this opportunity, so if you'll let me . . .'

I watched as Jean scrunched my CV into a tiny ball and threw it over his shoulder. 'I'll give you a trial run. When can you start?'

Almost four years on and I'm still working here, partly because I love the job and partly because Jean allows me to be flexible, working my hours around Louis. My role is to bake the cakes (we have a selection of three, daily) and I serve the lunches and chat to the locals, all part of the job since it's a goldfish bowl here; there are no doors to hide behind since it's open-plan. I have to pinch myself, knowing I'm so lucky to be here, although I worked so hard in my one-month trial to prove to Jean I deserved a chance. I sweated at the oven and put so much passion into my food, telling myself I had to make this work. I'll never forget when Jean tasted my chocolate chestnut torte and said, 'Pure, undiluted chocolate heaven. Trial over, Polly.

The job is officially yours!' I threw my arms around him and Mary-Jane clapped.

Being here has made me fall in love with baking all over again. When I'm rubbing butter into flour to make a bread-crumb mixture I find it therapeutic; it takes me back to my happy childhood memories, cooking mince pies with Mum or apple crumble with Hugo.

I take a file out from the shelf. The first cake is a choco-late layer cake with icing. As I sift the flour, soda and salt into a mixing bowl my mind wanders to Ben. Since I went to his flat two weeks ago we've met again, twice. Slowly I'm discovering more about his past. His stepfather runs a men's fashion shop in central London. When I'd asked what he was like Ben said, 'Well, at my mum's funeral he called me a bastard, so that should give you an idea.' Ben's eyes didn't give anything away. Perhaps it's buried too deep, just like Emily's grief. I discovered Grace had lived in Hampshire, in a village called Crawley. 'I called her the village witch,' Ben had said with a small smile when describing how she'd tried to cure his smoking habits with acupuncture. It was Grace who had urged him to seek help, get out of the City and stop drinking. 'She was the only one brave enough to tell me that I was ruining my life.' Ben told me that he'd stayed with her for almost six months after his stint in rehab and during that time he'd helped her to get going with her acu-puncture business, managing her finances and accounts. At that time Grace was alone and pregnant, so in many ways they both needed support. Ben certainly needed the distraction and Grace's failed relationship – her boyfriend disappearing the moment she'd told him she was pregnant – had left her heartbroken. Yet she was determined to make a success of working from home, plus it would give her flexibility when her baby was born. 'She encouraged me to think about managing other people's finances professionally. After Emily was born I moved back to London and went on a three-year training course. I qualified as a chartered accountant. Not very rock 'n' roll but to my surprise I enjoyed it.'

I make a well in the centre of my bowl and add the sunflower oil, sugar, vanilla extract, eggs, yoghurt and cooled chocolate, inhaling the sweet smell. When Mary-Jane isn't looking I dip my finger into the gooey mixture. 'Saw that,' she says.

While Ben and I were making pancakes with the children, laughing as Ben had tossed one into the air and onto the floor, he'd asked me how I came to work here, saying he must pop by sometime and sample one of my cakes.

I told him I'd found the job through my Aunt Vivienne, who goes out with my boss, Jean. 'Nothing like a bit of nepotism.'

He detected there was more to this. I'm learning Ben is sharp and naturally curious. 'And?' he pressed.

'You know I said our family was plagued by secrets?' I inhaled deeply. 'I didn't get to know about my Aunt Vivienne until I was fourteen.'

'How come?'

'Long story.'

Ben had looked at Louis and Emily, now engrossed in eating their pancakes. He turned to me and shrugged. 'We've got time.'

10

1994

'I feel ill, Mum,' I say when she asks me why I'm not dressed for school.

'What kind of ill?' She stands at the bottom of the stairs, dressed in her navy jacket, matching skirt and heels, dark hair pinned back from her face.

'Sick.'

Mum comes upstairs and touches my forehead. 'Do you think you're coming down with something?'

I nod.

She feels my glands before glancing at her watch. Normally Mum drives me to school and then goes to work. She is a part-time fundraiser for a charity for the blind and partially sighted in Norwich.

'You don't look great,' she admits reluctantly. 'I'll call the office.'

'No! I mean, no Mum, you go to work, I'll be fine on my own.'

The thermometer reads normal. Mum leaves a plastic bowl and for a second I panic, thinking she might find the empty wine bottles under my bed. She says she'll be home at lunchtime. She looks at me, almost with affection. 'But promise to call if there's any problem, darling,' she says.

Later that morning, I'm enjoying a toasted cheese sandwich in front of *Friends*. I wonder if Janey made it to school? I'll call her later. Last night we pretended to be upstairs doing our French homework, but instead we were smoking out of her bedroom window and drinking Baileys. I ran home giggling, my steps light, before I raced up to my bedroom, saying 'Yes!' when Dad called out, 'Polly, is that you?'

The telephone rings from the kitchen. Bugger. That'll be Mum again. I hear the answer machine beep but it's a voice I don't recognise.

When I enter the kitchen to make myself another sandwich I'm strangely drawn to the red light flashing on the answer machine. I press the button before opening the fridge.

'Georgina, it's me, Vivienne.' No one calls mum Georgina. Yet her voice sounds familiar somehow. *Vivienne.* I shut the fridge, forgetting what I was looking for. 'I'm back. Dad gave me your number. I hope we can meet. I know it's been many years, but . . .' She trails off. 'How is Polly? I often think of you all,' she continues. 'You didn't respond to my letters.

77

Oh listen to me, I promised I wouldn't rant on the answer-machine, that I'd only say hello. Please call me.'

Mum arrives home at lunchtime, laden with shopping bags. She stands at the sitting room door, asks me how I am.

'Someone called earlier.' I follow her into the kitchen. 'She left a message.'

'Who was it? Did you get some sleep, darling?' Mum begins to unpack the groceries, asking me to give her a hand.

'Vivienne?'

She stops unpacking. Sits down.

'Mum? Who is she?'

'My sister,' she replies in a small voice, staring ahead.

'I didn't know you had a sister?'

Silence.

'Mum?' I sit down next to her.

'She . . .' Mum presses her head into her hands. 'She killed someone.'

'What! Who?'

'Stop! Polly, please, stop!'

I hand Mum a piece of kitchen roll. She blows her nose, wipes her tears.

'Mum, I'm scared.' I don't like seeing her so upset. 'Why didn't you tell Hugo and me you have a sister? What happened?'

To my surprise Mum takes my hand firmly in hers.

'She was drunk behind the wheel and killed her baby, my nephew,' she says, as if it were only yesterday. I wait, sensing there is even more. 'And she killed my brother, he was sitting in the front . . . *She* was the one that survived.'

It's been ten days since Mum told me about her sister, and Vivienne is visiting us today. She's coming for tea. It's a Saturday and Hugo is back at home. Mum wanted us all to be together. 'What do we call her?' Hugo says to me quietly in the kitchen as he helps me lay the table for lunch. Dad is outside mowing the lawn. Mum is frantically tidying the house. All morning she's been nagging us to tidy our bedrooms and put away our things.

'It feels odd calling her Aunt Vivienne when we don't know her,' Hugo adds, placing a knife the wrong way round.

'Don't call her anything,' I suggest. 'Say hello, that's all.'

'Is she a bad person, Polly?' he asks, as if she could be a murdering monster.

'I don't know.'

'Why is she visiting us now?'

'I don't know, Hugo.'

'I wonder what prison was like? Do you think she'll talk about it? I still can't believe Mum didn't tell us.'

I nod. 'Makes you wonder if she's hiding any more secrets from us.'

Mum's explanation for keeping Vivienne a secret was that Hugo and I were too young to understand the damage

79

she had caused to the family, and then the older we became the harder it was to stir up painful memories. 'Sometimes it's too painful to dredge up the past,' Mum reasoned, Dad backing her up. 'You need to let things be.'

Part of me wanted to argue and say that Hugo and I had at least deserved to know we had an aunt; the other part of me could see how much Vivienne's forthcoming visit was upsetting Mum. I tried to imagine if someone had killed Hugo recklessly in a car crash, drunk behind the wheel. I wouldn't be able to forgive them. But things are beginning to make sense now. Granddad Arthur at Christmas saying 'She should be here.' Mum not touching alcohol. 'Gina, you're not Vivienne,' my father had said.

Dad has been able to explain a little more to Hugo and me about Vivienne. He told us that after she was released from prison she couldn't settle in one place, she needed to leave the country and her memories behind. She fled to America.

'How? Why?' It all sounded so mysterious and tragic.

'I'm not sure, Polly. Don't ask too many questions,' Dad had begged. 'We just need the afternoon to go smoothly, no dramas.'

Over lunch Mum can't eat. An hour before Vivienne arrives she's twitching at the curtains. Dad tries to relax, says he's going to watch the tennis on television. He enjoys Wimbledon. Hugo and I don't know what to do; we kill time going for a walk by the lake. I smoke a couple of cigarettes.

Hugo asks if he can have a puff. He coughs and splutters. 'It tastes like the kitchen bin, Polly!'

Five minutes before she is due to arrive, Hugo and I sit side by side on the sofa, now on our best behaviour. After my walk Mum made me take my jeans off and put a sundress on instead, 'And please brush your hair, Polly,' she'd ordered, before even snapping at Hugo to pull his trousers up.

Dad is helping Mum make the tea. I can hear cups and saucers being laid out on a tray, Mum determined to use the best china. What will Vivienne look like? What will we talk about? Will this visit upset Mum? I begin to chew my thumbnail, unsure I want to meet her now. Will I like her? *Should* I like her, after what she has done?

We hear a car approaching. I turn to look out of the window, see a taxi parking outside the front door. My heart is beating fast. Hugo grips my hand and I squeeze it back, glad we are in this together. We are a small family, only Auntie Lyn on our father's side, whom we rarely see. We aren't used to relations visiting, let alone an estranged aunt who killed Mum's brother and her own son before being locked up behind bars.

Vivienne enters the room behind my mother, wearing a cream sundress and wide leather belt with gold clasps, showing off her slim waist. Hugo and I stand up as Mum introduces us.

Her arms are tanned and adorned with bracelets. Long

dark hair sweeps down her back. She is nothing like Mum, who keeps her hair short and practical. Tentatively Vivienne comes over to me first. No one says a word, until Mum finally mutters, 'This is Polly.'

Vivienne runs a hand through her hair, her face free of make-up except for deep-red lipstick. I also notice she has two earrings in both ears. I feel paralysed. I just stand there, gazing at this beautiful gypsy-like woman. She clutches my hand and looks deep into my eyes. To my surprise she begins to cry and I don't know where to look. 'Silly me,' she says, wiping away her tears. 'Always been a soppy old cow.' She laughs, her light-brown eyes still fixed on mine. 'It's just . . .' She turns to Mum, 'so lovely to be here.' Mum nods curtly, as if this is a business meeting. They couldn't be more different, but despite myself I find I am drawn to her warmth. She isn't what I expected at all; she doesn't seem like the terrible person Mum has talked about.

Vivienne moves on to Hugo. 'I've heard so much about you,' she says. 'Your mother tells me you're a fine skier.'

Hugo nods. 'My school have chosen me to train for the Paralympics and the World Championships,' he claims with pride. 'I train at the dry ski slopes all the time.'

'When I lived in Los Angeles, I used to take myself off skiing at Mount Baldy.'

Hugo giggles and Vivienne tells us she thinks the name is funny too.

Hugo points to a scar above his eyebrow. 'I had stitches. I love going fast, too fast sometimes.'

I glance at Mum, so buttoned up. She can't sit still, fidgeting like Hugo and me during a sermon at church. Dad pours the tea and tells Vivienne I made the coffee and walnut cake. 'Do you like cooking, Polly?' she asks.

I nod, vigorously. 'She's very good,' Mum adds. It's the first time my mother has complimented me and my head swims with pride.

'Perhaps you'll be a chef one day,' Vivienne says, before telling me my cake tastes like heaven. 'Maybe you'll live in Paris and run a patisserie.'

Over tea Vivienne talks to Hugo and me, asking us questions about school and what we enjoy. I notice how graceful her hands are, placed gently around her teacup. She smiles and laughs generously, but there is also a sadness that haunts her face. Part of me wants to shout at Mum, tell her to make Vivienne feel more welcome, forgive her; but I have to keep on reminding myself why Mum is reserved. I answer questions politely. It is as if Vivienne has cast a spell on me to behave. Never before have I been so careful about my grammar. Mum keeps on hopping up and down, refilling mugs and cutting more cake, even though none of us are really all that hungry.

I am disappointed when Vivienne's taxi arrives. She

says goodbye, hugging Hugo and me as if we are long-lost friends. Mum and Dad walk her to the car.

'She was awesome,' says Hugo with surprise. 'I really liked her.'

'Shush!' I watch them from the window. It looks as if Vivienne is upset. Mum is shaking her head. Dad opens the passenger door, but Vivienne stays put. She is saying something to Mum. Oh I wish I could hear! I think they are arguing. Maybe Mum is saying she can't visit us again. Vivienne glances towards the window, as if she senses I am watching. She waves goodbye. Tentatively I wave back.

When she's gone I'm left confused. I feel sorry for Mum: her visit was clearly painful, but Vivienne also brought a ray of sunshine into the house, just as Granddad Arthur used to.

That night Hugo sits at the end of my bed. 'What did she look like, Polly?'

I wish with all my heart I could wave a magic wand and let him see. I'd do anything for my brother, but I can't help with this. 'Oh Hugo, she had this amazing wild hair.' I picture it; chocolate-brown, just like mine, tumbling down her back like a waterfall. 'And brown eyes, like Mum's. She wore these sparkly sandals and lovely jewellery.'

'Do you think Mum will let us see her again?'

'Hope so.'

'Me too.'

When Hugo goes to bed, I shut my eyes. I see her tears, hear the warmth in her voice, taking such an interest in my life that I almost believed I could have an exciting future. A patisserie in Paris! Tired, I fall straight to sleep, only to stir when I hear footsteps across the landing. My bedroom door creaks open and I see the shadow of my mother standing at the end of my room, until quietly she slips away.

@GateauAuChocolat It's chickpea soup & Indonesian marinated chicken with roasted sweet potatoes & as if that isn't enough, apple caramel cake.

The first regular to arrive at the café is our local famous author, in her eighties, who hobbled here two years ago, after breaking her wrist and cracking both ribs falling down her stairs. 'It's a curse getting old,' she'd said, before explaining she couldn't cook for herself. Her elderly friend often accompanies her; they call us 'Care in the Community'. Without asking I serve them both some soup and a glass of red wine, 'Medicinal,' as they call it.

Next comes our local serial flirt, an illustrator who works from home. I haven't seen him since Christmas. He scans the menu board and orders the chicken, 'And maybe, pretty Polly, if I have room, a slice of your apple caramel cake.'

'You always have room.'

He smiles. 'How are you, Mary-Jane? Been on any hot dates?'

Mary-Jane bristles. 'You're lucky I don't pour this over you,' she tuts as she places the jug on the table.

Soon there's a real buzz, everyone talking across the tables and Mary-Jane and I are rushing around serving soup, camomile and mint teas or Jean's red wine to go with their chicken. I slow down when I see Ben opening the front door, and notice at once that he's shaved his beard. It makes him look younger. Jean turns to see who I'm waving at. 'You dark horse, Polly.'

I smile. 'He's a friend.'

'Single?'

I'm sure Aunt Vivienne bribes him to squeeze gossip out of me.

'Think so.'

Jean shrugs. 'Cute. Gay?'

'Straight.'

'In that case why aren't you two at it *like rabbits*?'

'So delicately put, Jean.'

He laughs. 'I try my best.'

Before I have to time to explain that he's not my type, Ben kisses me on the cheek.

'Like the new look,' I say, touching his chin.

When Jean is thankfully upstairs giving a cooking demo on bread-making, and all the regulars have left, Mary-Jane and

I finally have our lunch. I serve myself some chicken and sit down next to Ben, asking what he's bought, gesturing to the bags under the table.

'Clothes. Emily was moaning that—'

'That's great!'

'Sorry?'

'She's talking.'

He nods. 'The headmistress spoke to me, says she keeps on asking her teacher if her mum is coming back.' Guilt is etched on his face. 'You were right, Polly. I need to stop pretending this hasn't happened. It's not helping her, or me for that matter, so at bedtime we've begun to tell each other stories about Grace.'

'What was she like?'

'Amazing. Independent. Wore her heart on her sleeve. Annoying too, because she always had to be right. I've told Emily about the holidays we used to go on as children, how Grace and I could swim for hours in the sea . . .' his voice falters, 'pretending we were fish. Sorry,' he says, hiding his emotion with a cough.

'Carry on,' I encourage, believing it's good for him to talk about her.

'She was passionate about Chinese medicine and helping people. I envied that in a way. I told Emily about her school days, at boarding school like me. Our stepfather couldn't wait to get us out of the way. She once dunked a towel in the bath and wrung it over the headmistress's head.' He smiles. 'Emily liked that one, but I told her not to be getting any ideas, that I didn't want to see her name in that red book.'

I laugh at that. 'Did she tell you any stories?'

'She told me how her mummy had once left a needle sticking out of her patient's forehead, between her eyebrows. There have been lots of stories about Patch too.'

'Patch?'

'Grace felt guilty that Emily didn't have a brother or sister so they got a rescue dog, a half this and a half that, who knows what Patch was, but . . .'

'When did Patch die?' An idea is forming in my head.

'About a year ago. He had a tumour, died very young, poor Patch. I remember Grace asking me how she could explain death to Emily,' he says with more than a trace of irony. 'Why?'

'No reason.' Just that one of the customers was saying earlier today that her neighbour's dog, a Scottie, had had four puppies and she was struggling to find a home for the last girl.

'Let's see what you bought,' I ask, still wondering if I'm crazy thinking Ben could handle a puppy on top of everything else? I can't imagine one in his immaculate flat, but then again, maybe it's exactly what their home needs?

Ben fishes out a selection of items.

'What?' he says, catching me looking at an uninspiring mushroom-coloured skirt with matching polo-neck.

'Was this the only colour it came in?'

Ben stares at me as if I'm talking astrophysics.

'Grace must have bought her things, you know, in pretty colours?'

'Yeah, but they're too small for her now . . . I just grabbed . . .'

'I can tell,' I say, a little too harshly, as I come across a pair of sludgy khaki dungarees. 'Has Emily got a party dress for Maisy's birthday?' Jim's Maisy is five this weekend. She's having a bouncy castle party on Sunday.

'A dress? No! We should get her something.'

Ben must sense I'm taken aback at the 'we' since he says, 'You will help me, won't you?'

The look in his eyes is so beseeching that I feel a flood of affection towards him. 'Of course.' I fold the clothes back into the bag. 'Let's take this stuff back and . . .'

'Take what stuff back?' Aunt Viv says, joining us in the kitchen. I hadn't noticed her come in. Aunt Viv has worked for Jean for five years, managing the shop area part-time. She heard about Jean's café by pure chance. After Louis was born Aunt Viv had returned from America for good, but needed to find work. She happened to be sitting on the bus scanning the job section of the newspaper, when she overheard a Frenchman complaining that all his staff were hopeless and leaving the country. They ended up talking, Jean offered her a job, and they fell in love almost overnight. Jean's perfect for her in that he's unconventional, well-travelled and fiery – which keeps Aunt Viv on her toes – but deep down he's kind at heart.

I introduce Ben to Aunt Vivienne, and when he hears her name I can see his ears prick up. I'd told Ben all about her that night in his flat. He'd listened intently to the story of her first visit, asking what happened after that. Well, Vivienne did visit us regularly, but I always felt it was carefully stage-managed by my parents. Each time Aunt Viv arrived, we were ushered into the sitting room and rarely left alone. I always had this feeling Mum was eavesdropping. I told Ben about one time when Aunt Viv had asked if Hugo and I could show her the sunken boat. Mum sent out a search party, i.e. my father, when we weren't back after an hour. When we were on the boat, alone, just the three of us, Hugo and I felt much more at ease. Aunt Viv talked little about the past, she never mentioned Mum's brother, or prison, or losing her child, but what she did say was that after seven years of hell, Granddad Arthur had saved her by buying a ticket to America. He had an old school friend in LA, who was willing to have her to stay. He paid for her flight and enough to pay for a short stint in rehab; the rest was her responsibility. 'There is something about the ocean. It helped me heal,' she told us.

'I can see the family likeness,' says Ben, jolting me from my thoughts. Aunt Viv's dark hair, now peppered with grey, is coiled loosely in a clip, and she's wearing a red woollen dress with suede boots.

'We are alike,' Aunt Viv says, 'except I've got a lot more wrinkles, damn it!'

I explain that this is Ben, the one I met at school; his niece is in Louis's class. 'And we're going shopping on Saturday to buy her a dress,' I tell Aunt Viv, reassuring Ben that I haven't forgotten.

When Ben leaves, Aunt Viv looks at me quizzically. 'He's charming.'

I realise my friendship with Ben is going to be a source of gossip. Already school mum Gabriella is pouting, unable to hide her jealousy when I told her how much I'd enjoyed her lasagne. I couldn't help myself. Every now and then my naughty side comes out. Gabriella will be at Maisy's party this weekend. I will try to behave.

12

I'm at Ben's flat, helping Emily get ready for Maisy's birthday party. In return, Ben is playing pirate games with Louis. I notice small changes each time I come round. Ben has bought a couple of rugs to warm up the wooden floors and there are more photographs scattered around the flat, including one of Ben as a young boy dressed in his cricket whites, on the bookshelf. There is also a picture of Grace holding Patch on Emily's bedside table. She's fairer-skinned than Ben, with striking auburn hair and hazel eyes, just like Emily's.

Radio 2 is on; it's Hugo's weekend show and he's talking about funny shopping experiences. It makes me think of yesterday. We found Emily a green sequinned dress in Monsoon, but not without a lot of 'I'm bored!' comments from Louis and I could tell Ben was well out of his comfort zone as we shopped for matching accessories.

As I plait Emily's hair in the sitting room I ask her to tell me about Patch. She says he was a cross between a Dalmatian and a Scottie. I let go of the plait. 'How did *that* happen?'

She twists round and stares at me. 'How did what happen?'

'Nothing. Sorry, carry on.'

'Last Friday, after a particularly heavy night,' Hugo says live on air, 'I stumbled into the office and sat down at my desk with my usual bacon and egg McMuffin and cup of coffee, ready to eat my way through my hangover. Being partially sighted, there are various pieces of equipment that make my office existence easier. Actually they are *essential* – none more so than the anglepoise lamp on my desk.'

'It's Uncle Hugo!' says Louis, when he and Ben charge into the room. 'My Uncle Hugo is famous, Emily!'

'So on this particular morning,' Hugo continues, 'I switched on my computer, turned on my lamp only to hear this ominous phutting sound followed by a little bang. My extra light source was stuffed, so before tucking into my hangover breakfast I had to go to the closest supermarket and buy a light bulb.'

'Shh,' I say to Louis when he asks when we're leaving.

'Locating the relevant light bulb successfully, I headed for the till,' Hugo continues, 'where the following dialogue took place: "How much is this, please?" I ask in my politest tone. Silence. "How much is this, please?" I ask in a slightly louder tone, but still nothing. Mildly angry and impatient by now, thinking about my McMuffin getting cold, I demand, "Come on, mate, do me a favour, I can't see very well. I'm blind." To which the cashier sitting behind the one serving me says, "Yes, and she's deaf."'

I burst out laughing.

'Oops,' Hugo says. 'That put me in my place. You're listening to Hugo Stephens on Radio 2. If any of you have had funny shopping experiences, I'd love to hear from you. Now, let's take a break with a bit of something to relax us all on a Sunday morning . . .'

Marvin Gaye's 'Let's Get It On' begins to play.

Ben laughs. 'He's quite funny, your brother, for a blind guy.'

'And you're quite funny, for an arsehole.'

'Arsehole,' Emily repeats, followed by a small laugh.

Ben raises an eyebrow at me.

'Sorry,' I mouth, but when Emily jumps up and gives us a twirl in her new dress and French plait it's clear that we're making progress.

Ben looks as if he has stepped onto foreign soil when he walks inside the local community centre and stares at the bouncy castle at the far end of the room, already filled with five-year-olds jumping up and down to One Direction. I know from hiring out a castle myself that the rules are only eight children allowed on at one time, but it looks as if Louis's entire class is giving it a go, the castle rocking from side to side like a ship on choppy waters. Heads will bang or teeth will be knocked out at any minute.

We take off our coats and hand presents over to Jim, who is dressed in jeans and a thick woolly jumper, house keys sticking out of his back pocket.

ALICE PETERSON

Some of the parents have already left, making the most of
the free babysitting, but Emily clings to both of us, making
it clear that leaving isn't an option. Louis charges towards
the bouncy castle and leaps on to it. I haul him back, whip
off his trainers and make him promise to be careful.

'Promise,' he says, diving towards Maisy again and just
missing the fist of one of the children who has decided it's
much more fun punching the walls.

Jim asks if I'll do the music for pass the parcel and
musical statues. Camilla, his wife, is in bed with flu. 'She
works too hard,' he mutters. 'Not her fault, but she picked
a lousy day to be ill.'

Distracted, I watch Ben take Emily's hand, encouraging
her to have a go on the castle with the other children. She
won't budge. I decide to wait, fighting all my instincts to
butt in. Gabriella approaches him, wearing a low-cut navy
dress and high-heeled boots. I watch as she bends down to
Emily, giving Ben a good view of her ample cleavage.

'She used to flirt with me,' says Jim nostalgically.

'But now there's a new kid on the block,' I say, still
annoyed with myself that it bugs me. She bugs me. She's
married. I watch as Ben and Gabriella help Emily on to the
castle. Gabriella whispers something into his ear.

'Do you think she's attractive?' I ask Jim, attempting to
sound casual.

'Yeah, she's gorgeous in that curvy Italian way.' When
he sees my face he adds, 'But not as hot as you, of course.'

96

I kiss him on the cheek, making him blush. 'I've trained you well. That's the right answer.'

The children sit in a circle for Eugene the magician. There have only been two bouncy castle injuries. Luke, who wears Ben Ten glasses and shorts all year round, even in the snow, is nursing a nosebleed; Maisy has a sore foot. Gabriella's daughter, whose weight is substantial, stood on it.

Eugene enters the circle with his collection of tired props. 'It's the same guy every time,' I tell Ben quietly.

'Why call your child Eugene? Just call them "Kick me",' he mutters.

Eugene is in his early sixties. He has thinning grey hair and a rather unfortunate gap between his front teeth. After a series of half-hearted tricks with his coloured tissues and then a rabbit appearing in a hat (it doesn't worry them that they saw it last time), Eugene steps towards the birthday girl, asking if she will pick a card.

'Is this your card?' he asks, eyes wide with enthusiasm.

Maisy shakes her head, wipes her red snotty nose with the sleeve of her jumper.

'Oh dear. Is *this* your card?' He waves the card, showing it to all the children. 'It is, isn't it?'

'No.' Maisy giggles.

'This *must* be your card!'

'No!'

ALICE PETERSON

And then, like magic, Eugene produces a card from behind his neck.

Everyone claps, even Emily.

Later that afternoon Ben, Emily, Louis and I head back to my flat, armed with slabs of chocolate pirate ship cake and party bags. Without much prompting Louis and Emily play sweet shops in his bedroom, giving Ben and me a moment to flop on to the sofa and shut our eyes.

'Gabriella fancies the pants off you,' I can't help saying, breaking the silence.

'Lovely tits.'

I roll my eyes. 'So predictable.' Long pause. 'She's such a flirt. I think her husband's always away. She must get lonely,' I reflect.

'Jim has a crush on you.'

'No he doesn't.' But then I do confide to Ben that Jim *did* have a small crush, about a year ago. It was during a bad patch in his marriage, when his wife was always working, even at weekends, and it was driving him mad. There was this one moment, over coffee, when he began to say I was the only one he could talk to. I remember him reaching for my hand, loneliness killing the usual shine in his eyes. I don't fancy Jim, and besides, I knew he loved his wife and I was dating David the lawyer. I told him to talk to her. So many times people kill their relationships through lack of communication or misunderstanding. 'I don't know why I was giving Jim relationship advice,' I add. 'I mean, look at my track record.'

'I'm not ready for a relationship.'

'I think Gabriella's after a hot steamy affair, Ben.'

'I've had my fill of that too, Polly. Can't do it anymore. I want something real. You know, I've rarely had sober sex.'

I turn to him, curious. 'Is anyone else in your family an addict?'

'My stepdad.' He pauses, as if knowing what he's about to say is going to unsettle me. 'I don't believe addiction is genetic.'

I shift in my seat. 'I do.'

'Polly, we're not puppets.' Ben wobbles his arms and hands in front of me. 'See that glass.' He's gesturing to the tumbler of water on the coffee table. 'Imagine that's wine. No one is forcing me to pick it up. No one was forcing me to do an all-night session, from eleven to noon the next day . . .'

'Yes, but . . .'

'Are you saying you didn't have a choice? That someone was holding a gun to your head and making you drink?'

There is nothing judgemental in his tone but still I feel my blood coursing through my veins. It doesn't work like that. I tasted wine and that was it. It was like a virus. I would love to have a civilised glass of wine with dinner or be that person in the pub who jangles her car keys at the bar saying, 'just the one.'

'My grandfather was a heavy drinker. Aunt Viv was an alcoholic. I picked up the bad gene,' I insist. 'I'm praying Louis doesn't have it.'

Ben remains unconvinced. 'I believe we mirror our childhoods. If we're fed fizzy drinks and burgers as kids, we'll probably feed our children that crap too. If . . .'

'Hang on . . .'

'Let me speak,' he says, his tone firm. 'My dad died when I was four, in comes my controlling stepfather who hits my mother, and who drinks like a fish and, in return for his charming behaviour, we get shipped to exotic islands for our holidays. Mum loves the glamour, boasts about how most families go to Cornwall but here we are on a private yacht, drinking champagne. She didn't want to hear me crying about how my stepdad stamped on my favourite record or hit me with his belt. I loved my mum dearly, and I know she loved me, but she protected my stepdad, made endless excuses for him. "He's stressed, he's busy, don't worry, Benjamin." My stepdad's addiction was catching. Mum was beginning to lie too because she didn't want to admit our family was shattering into tiny little pieces. I don't think she knew half the time if he'd come home after work. If he didn't, she'd pretend to herself it was work pressures, but the truth was he was drinking. He had the *choice*, Polly. He chose to be a wanker. Mum also chose to stay with him. Perhaps being brought up by an alcoholic stepfather makes me more predisposed to drink, but I still have that choice.

That's why I have a problem with relationships now! I can't commit because I don't want to turn out like him, but it's my problem, up here.' He taps his head. 'We have to take responsibility for ourselves.'

'I do take responsibility,' I stress, raising my voice. 'I never have blamed anyone but myself. That's why I go to meetings and make sure I see my counsellor every week. I can't mess up again. I have to work hard at it. Me, Ben, no one else messed up but me, but I still think I had something in my genetic make-up, something that made me unable to stop. Hugo was lucky he didn't have the rogue gene.'

Ben turns to me. 'Shall we not talk about this?'

I lean back into the sofa. 'Perhaps. Before we kill one another.'

At that moment my mobile rings. Relieved for the interruption I pick it up off the coffee table, glance at the screen, not recognising the number. 'Hello?' I wait. Hear nothing. 'Hello?' I repeat before ending the call. Oh well. I turn back to Ben.

'Who was it?' he asks.

'No idea. Probably a wrong number. What made you stop?' I go on, wondering if I'd have ever pulled myself together without Louis or Hugo and Aunt Viv, or my friends in AA.

'This is going to sound mad. Don't laugh, but I had this dream about my real dad. He was a pilot. I remember him being a big kind man; he'd sit me on his lap and read me stories,' he says nostalgically. 'He told Grace and me always to have dreams, that we could be anything we wanted to be. Anyway,' says Ben, trying to blot out the pain of losing him so young, 'he told me to stop the drink, the partying, the drugs, the women. He wanted me to leave the City before it killed my soul. I woke up drenched in sweat, thinking I was going mad, but as the day went on I was convinced it was real, that it was a message. I'm not in any way religious,' he mentions.

'So what happened next?'

'I knew he was right. I'd often thought I needed help but each time I talked to Mum she'd tell me there was nothing wrong in enjoying a good old drink. Mum never wanted to talk about anything deep. She wanted everyone to be happy, brush all the bad stuff under the carpet. But I knew I couldn't sustain my lifestyle. Grace did too. I couldn't hide what was going on inside of me anymore.'

'What was going on?'

'Nothing. That was the whole problem. I felt nothing.'

'What did you do?'

'Went to see a doctor. Grace came with me. I quit my job and booked myself into rehab in South Africa. Best time of my life. I watched some amazing cricket.' He smiles, surely underplaying how hard it must have been. Ben turns to me. 'There's something I've been wanting to ask you for a long time, Polly.'

'Go on.'

'What happened to Louis's father?'

'It's complicated.'

'How come?'

'I met the wrong man.'

'In what way?'

'Every way.'

'He didn't stick around?'

'I left him.'

'Were you married?'

'No. We were only together for two years.'

'Where is he now?'

'I don't know, hopefully miles away.'

'Let's put him on the North Pole.'

'That's not far enough.'

'Does Louis ask where he is?'

'Sometimes. Since school he's begun to ask more questions.'

'Does he miss him?'

I think about this. 'Yes. He doesn't miss Matthew, he was too little to know him, but he misses having a dad. He's beginning to compare, see his friends with both parents.' In a way it's good for him to spend time with Emily; to understand that families aren't always like the pictures of a house with four windows and a pretty front door, daisies in the garden, sunshine and figures of a mummy and daddy holding their child's hand.

'Emily hasn't asked me at all about her father, maybe it's because he's never been around.'

We sit quietly for a moment. 'I enjoyed today,' Ben says. 'Who would have thought going to a bouncy castle party could be quite fun?'

'I saw you dancing with Emily. She's really coming out of herself, you know.'

For a brief moment his eyes glow with pride. I picture Ben when I first met him at the school gates, his head down and hands deep in pockets.

Later that evening, when I've kissed Louis goodnight, I think about Matthew. I didn't tell Ben even half of the truth about him.

13

'How are you feeling today?' Stephanie asks. Stephanie Green is my counsellor. She's in her mid-forties, with chestnut-brown hair styled into a neat bob and blue eyes that narrow when she's listening to me.

'I couldn't sleep last night,' I tell her. 'I was thinking about something Ben said. We didn't have an argument, exactly, more a discussion. He disagrees with me that addiction's genetic. His stepfather was an alcoholic, but no one else in his family drinks. What do you think?'

'I think it can be. There's also learned behaviour. Your friend Ben grew up as a child watching a grown-up drink. As a child you only know what you see. Many people are born with the potential for addiction. Sometimes it gets realised, sometimes it doesn't. Often there's a catalyst. I don't think it happens by accident, there is always something underlying going on and, from my experience over the years, I see a certain personality type. The main thing is, whatever the reason, we learn from our past and take responsibility.'

She stops, as if she's talked too much. Sometimes I wonder if she's talking from her own experience.

I've seen Stephanie for the past four years and our relationship is professional, but there is no doubt we are getting closer; yet I know nothing about her. Her room is cosy, shelves filled with books and there are always flowers on her desk, but no photographs. There's nothing personal that hints at the life she has outside this room.

'Tell me more about Ben,' she says, making sure the conversation leads back to me. 'Is he a new friend?' Stephanie likes to build a picture of my life.

I end up telling her all about him, not realising how much I am talking until our time runs out.

On my way home, I realise that's the first time Stephanie has offered any encouragement over a friendship with a man. She was always quiet when I told her about my last boyfriend, David the lawyer, the one I met in front of the Picasso sculpture. She did smile once when I marvelled at how controlled he was in all aspects of life. He lived by the motto, 'Everything in moderation'. I told Stephanie that if I opened a bar of chocolate it would be wolfed down in virtually five seconds. I teased David, calling him Mr Two Cubes as he'd only allow himself two cubes of dark chocolate after supper, before carefully wrapping it back in its silver foil and putting it back in the fridge. I see now, that it was never going to work between Mr Two Cubes and me.

*

It's bedtime. Louis has been quiet since I picked him up from school and took him to the café.

'What's the best thing you've done today?' I ask, tucking him up in bed.

'Nothing,' he mumbles, his little jaw clenched.

'Louis, is something wrong?' I stroke his hair.

A thundercloud descends over his face. 'Everyone at school has a daddy, where is mine?'

'Oh, Louis, we've talked about this.'

'Luke's dad helps him take his shoes off at school, and his coat.'

'Emily doesn't have a daddy,' I say. 'She has Uncle Ben. Sometimes in life things aren't as simple as they should be, but you have Uncle Hugo and . . .'

'But he's not my daddy! Where is he?' He kicks his feet under the duvet.

'He has problems.'

'What problems?' More kicks. 'Why can't I see him?' He hurls Fido the dog on to the floor, tears rolling down his face. 'I want my dad,' he sobs.

I sit on my rocking chair, unable to sleep.

I stayed with Louis until finally he drifted off.

Not a day goes by when I don't feel guilty that Louis doesn't have a father. Stephanie tells me I must move on, that the only thing I can do is learn from a bad relationship. She's right, but it still doesn't stop me wishing I could rewind time and do things differently.

If I could do one thing differently, I'd go back to that night when I first met Matthew. I was teaching nursery children back then, but I would come home, strip out of my uniform and party all night.

We met in a bar.

I knew he was trouble.

I should have listened to Hugo.

Should have walked away.

14

2006

I run down the corridor and into the kitchen, leaning against the counter to catch my breath. The school mums can't see me like this! I've just been promoted to head teacher! I can't lose this job. I *love* my job. Thank heavens it's Friday. I press my head into my hands. What was I thinking last night? I shouldn't have gone out again. I told Hugo it wasn't a great idea to have his birthday party on a Thursday. No one can get trashed if they have to go to work the next day. His argument was that a few of his friends were going away at the weekend; it was the only night when everyone was around. I dig into my handbag to find my breath freshener. I almost choke. It smells nothing like mint but it certainly beats breathing toxic fumes all over the parents.

As I mix the paints, ready to make Christmas cards with the children, I have a hazy memory that Hugo was in a grump with me last night. I tell myself I'll stay in this evening. I'll clean the flat. I'll cook, maybe bake us something. Hugo and I share a poky two-bedroom flat in Shepherds Bush, off the Uxbridge Road. On the whole it works well, except sometimes I sense he disapproves of my lifestyle. Come the weekend I'm ready to party and often crawl home in the early hours of the morning, not surfacing from my duvet until late afternoon. But come on, Hugo, I'm twenty-six. That's what weekends are all about. We're young! Everyone drinks in their twenties. I left school when I was eighteen. Hugo read English at Durham. He loves socialising and has many friends, but unlike me he has never enjoyed the party scene because he feels vulnerable in crowds or dark nightclubs. 'If I go to the loo and people move to the dance floor, I can't find them again,' he says. 'If it's a place I've never been before it's even worse, Polly, especially if they've had a few drinks and forget about me.'

After mixing the paints and setting the tables up in the classroom, I apply some make-up to try and look half decent.

Believe it or not, I love my job. I teach a class of eighteen two- to three-year-olds. The one thing I have always enjoyed is playing with children. Mum says I have a real gift with them. 'Probably because you haven't grown up yourself,' she adds. Typical Mum. Can't give a compliment without a put-down too. Anyway, I don't want my own children just yet. I don't want any responsibility beyond helping them learn their alphabet, add and subtract and blow their noses.

As I brush my long dark hair and pin it back at both sides,

I think back to my own schooldays. I left with three under-whelming A levels: two Ds and an E. Mum insisted I retake them, Dad paid for a tutor over the next year and I did sur-prisingly well (three Bs) when they suggested that if I did better the second time round, I could go to Paris for a year to learn French. Paris seemed so glamorous. It reminded me of Aunt Viv's comment about going to Paris to run a patisserie. Well, I didn't cook so much these days but I could stroll along the Champs-Elysées and have a Parisian affair.

I was twenty when I returned, broken-hearted. The French had been fine; I'd passed both the oral and written exams but my love life had taken a battering. I'd met someone called Adrien who worked at the Rodin Museum and mod-elled part time. I can see us now, running down the streets in the pouring rain, laughing, kissing and holding hands. One time we were so stoned that we'd gone into a church, I can't even remember where now, and had grabbed the priest saying, 'We're in love. Marry us!' When he'd asked if my parents knew what I was up to, I had replied, as if acting on a climatic scene of *Romeo and Juliet*, 'My parents won't understand! They'll think I'm too young!'

Adrien left me a few months later. 'I have met someone else,' he'd said nonchalantly. Looking back now, I have no regrets. It was innocent love and inevitably it had to come to an end. When I returned home, I wanted to be in London. I found work ushering at *Les Misérables*. I moved flats con-stantly, kipped on floors to save cash, until finally I'd saved up enough to move in with Hugo. We'd always wanted to live together, since we were young.

I wipe away a glob of mascara before glancing at my watch and making a run for the classroom.

I stand at the front of the class. 'And what noise does a dog make?'

'Woof woof!' they all reply, a few of them laughing.

'And can we say PIG?'

'P . . .' they pronounce, 'I-G.'

'And what noise does a pig make?'

'Oink oink!'

I glance out of the window; it's a glorious winter's day, the sky a clear blue. 'Right. Tell you what. It's too nice to be stuck in here,' I say, thinking the fresh air will be good for all of us. I help them pop on their coats and scarves. Some of them have brought woolly hats. There's lots of buzz and laughter as I lead them out into the playground, the sun beaming on our faces. 'Life is about being outside four walls,' I tell them.

I could do this for hours, I think to myself as we sit down in a circle and sing the curly caterpillar song. At the end of our song Lottie, one of my favourites, throws her arms around me, saying, 'I love you, Miss Polly. Can we sing song again?'

During playtime, I head to my usual quiet spot where no one can find me, at the back entrance to the school. I reach for my crumpled pack of cigarettes, am about to light up when my mobile rings. It's Hugo. I didn't see him this morning before he left for work. 'Polly, you have got to say sorry to Alex's girlfriend.'

'Why? What did I do?'

'You practically jumped on him.'

'Jumped on who?'

'You were flirting with Alex all night! It's not funny, Polly!'

I compose myself. 'I'm sorry, really sorry.'

'It's not me you should be saying sorry to.' When he hangs up, finally I light up, trying to pick my scrambled brain, but still I can't recall much of last night. I won't go out this evening. I hold my stomach in; to my delight I can feel my ribs. I'll cook a special meal for Hugo. Have an early night. I'm going to start a detox programme. No booze for a month and protein shakes in the morning. Playtime is almost over so I call Hugo back, picturing him stewing at his desk. Hugo is now a radio broadcast assistant for the BBC.

'Hello?' he says. When friends call, Hugo can't see the name that comes onto the screen to indicate who's contacting him.

'It's me.'

'Oh you,' he sighs. 'What?'

'Are you in tonight?'

'Yep.'

I always know he's cross when he speaks in clipped tones. 'I'll cook for us.'

'You don't eat.'

'Please, Hugo, I'm trying to say sorry here. I'll call Alex's girlfriend too.' To my surprise a tear runs down my cheek. I'm tired and hate arguing with him. 'I'll cook us something really nice.'

There's a long pause. 'Mum's spaghetti carbonara?'

'Deal.' I smile with relief before asking, 'Did I really make a massive fool of myself last night?'

'You need to say sorry.'

I cringe, knowing that means yes. What's the matter with me? 'Your friends must think I'm crazy.'

'A little. Polly, I'm . . .'

'I'm not drinking for a month,' I pledge before he can say he's worried about me again.

After work I return home with all the ingredients for Mum's carbonara. I also bought Hugo a special gooey chocolate pudding, one of his favourites. I pop it in the fridge, glancing at the bottle of wine in the door. I close the fridge, then open it again, and almost jump out of my skin when my mobile rings.

'What's happened?' I ask Janey, immediately sensing something is wrong.

'Will and I, we're over,' she says tearfully. 'He's seeing someone else.'

'Oh Janey, I'm so sorry.'

Janey met Will during her first year at university. They

were inseparable throughout college; they then moved into a flat together in Balham, but in the last six months she'd begun to suspect he was having an affair after one too many late nights 'working'. The final straw was their recent weekend away, in some country hotel, when all he'd wanted to do was sleep and make secretive calls on his mobile. 'I really need to see you, Polly.'

I hesitate. 'The thing is, I promised Hugo I'd stay in. Why don't you come round here? We can talk about it? I'm cooking. There's plenty of food.'

'I couldn't eat a thing. Oh please, Polly,' she begs now. 'I need to see you. Hugo won't mind, will he?'

When I return to the table with our bottle of wine, Janey tells me about confronting Will after yet another late night in the office. 'I told him I deserved better,' she says, the tears resurfacing.

'You do. You deserve so much more,' I say, reaching for her hand.

'And the least he could do is tell me the truth.'

'What did he say?'

'That he was seeing someone, she's called Clare, she's been working with him on his latest film, that he didn't set out to hurt me, all that crap. Oh, Polly.'

I rub her shoulder and stroke her hair. 'It's better to know,' I assure her. 'I understand it's painful, and you're feeling hurt and betrayed, but . . .'

'Polly,' she cuts in, looking up at me with red eyes. 'If I'm honest, it's been over for months. I lost Will a long time ago, I just didn't want to admit it. In a funny way I'm relieved. Now I can get on with my life, stop worrying about why he hasn't come home at two in the morning. He was with her, Polly. Go fuck yourself, Will.' She raises her glass to mine. 'I can sleep,' she goes on. 'I don't have to share my bed with a lying dirty rotten cheating snoring scumbag. Oh, that feels better,' she says with a brave smile.

'I bet. Carry on.'

She shakes her head. 'Can we make a pact?'

'Depends.'

'It's Christmas and practically our last night before we head home, right?'

I nod. Janey and I will be going back to Norfolk together. Her parents still live locally to mine.

'So let's get plastered and no more mention of Will.'

'Will? Who's Will?'

As the night goes on, Janey and I order another bottle. I realise there's no point trying to cut down before Christmas. I'll adopt a strict regime in the New Year. The main thing is that Janey has cheered up.

'I can have sex with someone else,' she announces, polishing off her glass and refilling mine. 'I can have a first kiss again. Polly?'

'Go on,' I say, distracted by a guy leaning against the

bar, pulling funny faces at me. He has scruffy dark-blond hair, pale skin that accentuates piercing blue eyes and he's wearing a casual white shirt with jeans. Love that look. Always preferred blonds. Polly turns round to the bar. 'The one in the white shirt's cute,' she says.

My mobile rings. It's Hugo. I turn it off, numbing my guilt with more drink. I need to be here, to support Janey.

When Janey staggers to the loo, I catch the guy in the white shirt staring at me again. He makes his move, as I knew he would. 'I bet she goes, mate,' I overhear his friend in the leather jacket jeering.

'I'm so sorry,' he says. 'I'm not with him.'

I shrug, trying to keep cool.

'I couldn't help noticing you're on your own,' he says.

'Not for long.' I circle the rim of my glass. 'There's no need to worry about me.' I lean towards him. He leans towards me.

'I'm Matthew. Matthew Cook.'

'Polly Stephens.'

Janey returns to the table.

'My friend Graham and I wondered if we could buy you both a drink?' Matthew says to us.

'Champagne would be lovely, thanks,' I suggest.

He raises an eyebrow. 'You have expensive taste. The girl wants champagne,' Matthew calls over to his friend, before heading back to the bar saying my wish is his command.

Janey giggles. 'Get in there, Polly. He is *so* into you.'

'Do you want to stay?' I ask her. 'If you're not up to it, we can go.'

'Shut up, will you, and remember our pact. This is *just* what I need.'

Minutes later they join us at our table with a bottle and four glasses. Matthew places himself by my side. Graham, plump and modelling the half-shaved head look, sits next to Janey. She's fared rather worse than me, I think to myself.

'So, what do you do?' Graham asks Janey and me, pouring the champagne.

'I'm a location manager. I organise studios and sites for adverts and television dramas, things like that,' Janey replies.

'Teacher.'

'Miss, I've been naughty,' Matthew says. 'I think I need a *spanking*.'

We all laugh, Matthew's thigh pressing against mine.

'You?' I ask Matthew.

'Bit of this, bit of that.'

'Which basically means he does nothing,' claims Graham.

'My mum tells me never to trust a bit-of-this-bit-of-that man,' says Janey, clearly attracted to him too.

'Does she now? Well, if you really want to know, I'm a property developer. I'm my own boss.'

'Which basically means he does nothing,' Graham says, making us laugh again.

'Don't listen to him. Graham's jealous of my success.' Matthew refills my glass. 'I've just sold my pad in Islington for a small fortune. Lived in it for six months, did a loft conversion, tarted it up, made a *killing*.'

'In that case, mate, I'll put your rent up,' says Graham, explaining to Janey and me that Matthew's squatting with him while he hunts for the next project.

'At the rate I'm going I'll be retired and living in St Tropez by the time I'm forty.'

'Dream on,' I say.

'*You* deserve a spanking for that, Miss Stephens,' he replies, his eyes playing with mine.

Soon we've drunk two bottles and are on our way to some nightclub in Soho, where Matthew knows the bouncer. He assures us we won't have to queue.

We lurch down some steep steps and into a dark space, music making the walls vibrate. Next, we're knocking back tequila shots at the bar, the room beginning to spin. 'Seriously arrogant,' Janey slurs, 'but he's hot and he can't take his eyes off you.'

'What about Graham?' We both turn to look at him.

'He's nice, but I like a guy with a bit more hair.'

We laugh hysterically. 'I love you, Janey, and you're going to be fine. You're better off without Will. You deserve so much more.'

'I love you too, Polly.' We hug. 'Be careful, honey,' she adds. 'I like this guy, but . . .'

'Careful of what?' I exclaim, as Matthew pulls me on to the dance floor.

I love this feeling. I'm dancing. I'm free. I wave at Janey, beckoning her to dance with us. She and Graham remain at the bar. Soon Matthew's hands are travelling down my back and around my hips. My top is coming loose; I feel his hands against my bare skin. As he twists me round in his arms I feel sweet anticipation for the night ahead. I nearly fall. Matthew steadies me in his arms, before saying quietly, 'Let's get out of here.'

I can see a wild streak in his blue eyes that makes me feel alive.

'And do what?'

'Play scrabble.'

I push him away, he reels me back in, hands clasped around my back, our bodies pressed together.

'I have plans with a beautiful woman.' His eyes don't leave mine.

'Where is she?'

'You're funny.'

'You're sure of yourself. So what are these plans?'

He whispers them into my ear, his face brushing against mine, his breath warm.

I'm giggling as I try to unlock the front door. 'Hurry up,' Matthew is saying, kissing my neck, 'or I'll fuck you right here.'

Hugo's bedroom door is shut. We head into the kitchen. I open the fridge. 'Later,' he says, putting the bottle down and taking my hand. 'Come on.'

I lead him into my bedroom, shut the door and he pushes me against it. We kiss, urgently, passionately. He unbuckles his belt and the zip of his jeans. He presses his mouth against mine again. Then he reaches his hand up my skirt and pulls one of my legs so I'm half straddling him. He grabs my arse, hoists me up, everything happening so quickly. His hand is back up my skirt, peeling my knickers off. I want him now. Now. In seconds he's inside me. 'You like that,' he murmurs when I groan with pleasure.

The following morning I find Hugo in the kitchen, already showered and dressed for the gym. I glance at my watch. It's only nine o'clock.

I flick on the kettle. How had last night happened? I can't remember getting home, or saying goodbye to Janey. Did we even say goodbye? I must call her to see if she's OK.

Back to last night . . . I think Matt and I hailed a cab. I remember his hand creeping up my skirt.

I grin. The sex was amazing. Rough but incredible, and I want more. After our door sex we'd finished off the rest of the wine before moving to the bed. Matthew had pinned my wrists down against the mattress and told me not to move. I loved him being in control. So often I've slept with guys

121

who don't know what they're doing, their touch hesitant, but with Matthew . . .

'Good night?' Hugo asks.

'What?' I say, jolted from my thoughts. There is something so innocent and wholesome about Hugo as he sits at the table eating his buttered toast and runny honey, chubby cheeks cleanly shaven.

'I said, good night?'

'I'm so sorry, Hugo. It was Janey.'

'Janey. Right.'

'She was really upset.' He doesn't believe me. 'Will's been cheating on her. You got my message, didn't you?'

He nods. 'How is she?'

'Not great.'

We hear a door slam. 'Is someone here, Polly?'

'Uh-huh,' I say.

'Have you called Alex's girlfriend?' Clipped tones again.

He knows I haven't.

'I will, today.' I open the fridge, grab the milk. 'Are you in tonight? I could cook us something . . . I promise this time I won't go out.'

'Morning.' Matthew enters the kitchen naked. 'Oh shit,' he says when he sees my brother, but he makes no attempt to cover himself up.

'Matt, this is Hugo. Hugo's my brother.'

'Sorry, I didn't know we had company.' Matthew shakes Hugo's hand. 'Otherwise I'd have put some clothes on.'

'Oh don't worry, Hugo can't see your you-know-what.'

'Come here, Miss Stephens.' He grabs me, smacks me hard on the arse, both of us laughing.

'And even if I could, I'm sure there's not much to see,' Hugo says, shutting us both up, before leaving the kitchen.

Later that morning, after Matt has left, I think about Janey. I must call her. I know she was trying to put on a brave face last night, but she'll be hurting right now. She'll also want to know what happened with Matthew, but I'll play it down. The last thing she needs is me going on about a bloke. When he kissed me goodbye at the front door, he promised he'd call. All my instincts are telling me to stay away. Besides, it was a one-night stand, wasn't it? It was sex, that's all. There's no way he's the kind of guy who wants a serious relationship. Imagine taking him home to meet my mother! Just as I'm about to call Janey, my mobile vibrates. When I see the text I am unable to wipe the childish grin off my face.

See you tonight? Wear that short skirt again. Mx

15

2013

@GateauAuChocolat Happy Valentine's Day! Have a romantic lunch with us. It's Parmesan chicken breasts & my famous passion fruit roulade.

'Ta-dah! Happy Valentine's Day,' says Janey, arriving at my flat later that evening with flowers and a bottle of elderflower fizz.

'Sh.' I press a finger to my lips, gesturing to Louis's bedroom door. We tiptoe into the kitchen. 'Thanks so much for the flowers and this.' I open the bottle. 'You know, I'd never mind if you wanted a proper drink.'

'I know, but I don't want to.'

In the early days of my recovery I did find it hard when I was out with friends. I'd try to avoid bars and pubs at all costs, as I'd only have to look at their glass and wonder, 'Can't I have just one?' There's a saying in AA, if you hang around long enough in a barber's, you'll eventually get a haircut.

Now it's almost irrelevant what anyone else drinks, but I'm touched that Janey brings elderflower. Hugo's the same. He always brings round a bottle of Diet Coke and celebrates the fact that I'm doing him a favour since he'll have no hangover.

'So, how many Valentine's cards did you receive?' I ask Janey. 'Did you need your secretary to open them?'

Janey now runs her own film location business with a contact she made in the industry. Shortly after I gave birth to Louis, she was made redundant, so after months of looking for a job, she decided to set up her own business. 'How many cards did I receive?' she says out loud. 'Let me see. None. Diddly-squat. Gave the postman a day off. I remember the days at school when I used to get double figures. What's gone wrong?'

'Oh Janey, that's too bad. Better luck next year.'

'Watch it! Did you get any?'

'I did. I got two.'

Her mouth opens wide. 'How exciting! Who are they from?' Janey sits down on one of the stools in the corner of my kitchen while I check on the salmon. I'm baking it with crème fraiche and I've made a watercress salad. 'I don't know. One of them wasn't signed.'

'Even better! Any ideas? Where are they?' She hops off the stool in search of them.

I tell her one is on the mantelpiece, 'Along with all my party invites.'

Janey dashes into the sitting room, but returns slowly with the card. It's a giant heart with a couple of red crayon scribbles in the middle of it. Inside it reads, 'Mummy, my heart bursts with love for you'. Aunt Viv and I had shed a tear when I'd opened it at work.

'Ah, Louis is so sweet, but for a second . . . ? Where's the other one?'

I take the card out of my handbag. It's a picture of a champagne bottle and two glasses.

Janey opens it. It's blank inside, apart from the printed message in capital letters, 'EVERY MOMENT WITH YOU IS A CHAMPAGNE MOMENT.'

I tell myself to stop being so paranoid. It's not Matt's style; it's far too corny.

'Crikey.' Janey examines the card again. 'I wish people would just have the courage to sign it. Any ideas who it could be from?'

I shake my head. How would Matt even know where I live? 'It's probably a joke,' I suggest.

'I don't think so. If someone's bothered to get a card and stick it in the post, someone's *hot* for you.'

'Don't be ridiculous.'

'I'm not being ridiculous! Come on, Polly. We're attractive women in our *prime*. We're babes!'

Janey is conventionally pretty, with honey-blond hair,

petite features, pale-blue eyes and creamy marshmallow skin. She likes to wear tops that show off her generous cleavage. I'm the opposite in looks with my long dark hair and dark-brown eyes to match, large wide mouth and an enormous dimple in my right cheek that has always attracted attention.

'We don't have any warts, or chicken legs,' she continues, 'or unfortunate facial hair, or bad breath . . .'

'You do have a bit of a . . .' I press my top lip.

'Sod off. I do not have a moustache. Your beard needs trimming,' she adds.

I laugh.

'I mean, when you see some couples out and about,' Janey continues, 'I do wonder where we're going wrong. It used to be so much easier picking up men. Is there no one on the horizon, Polly? No one you can think of who could have sent this to you?' She shakes the card at me. 'You must be able to think of someone?'

'These are beautiful.' I arrange the pale-pink roses in a vase.

'Polly Stephens, you're avoiding the question!'

I think about Ben for a split second, but shake my head. 'How about you?'

'Well, there is this one guy.'

'Now you tell me.' I sit down on the stool next to her. 'Come on, don't keep me in suspense.'

'There's nothing to tell yet. He's called Paul. He's a

photographer. I met him last week at this stately home in Guildford. It was booked for a fashion shoot, some country clothes catalogue. Amazing place.' As she describes the sweeping staircase and the unusual domed reception room, I stop her mid-flow with, 'Back to Paul.'

'Oh yes. Anyway, we swapped numbers and he called. We're going out this Friday.'

'What's he like?'

'Bald.'

'Bald?'

She smiles. 'Yeah, but *sexy* bald. Think . . .' she clicks her fingers, 'Think Bruce Willis, no hang on, not quite right, think . . . Jason Statham. He's easily confident enough to carry it off and he was really funny, Polly. He's older than us. Think he's early forties. The models were falling over themselves to get his attention. He was cracking all these jokes to make them relax. Anyway, we'll see. I don't want to curse it, we haven't even been on a date yet. He might be an idiot when he's not behind the camera. He could be married for all I know. Or he might not pay. I think a guy *has* to pay on a first date, don't you? There's plenty of scope for it all to go wrong.'

'Yeah, but plenty of scope for it to go right too.'

Over supper Janey asks how her favourite godson is.

'You only have one,' I remind her. Very few of our friends

are married or have children yet. I was certainly in the minority having Louis aged twenty-eight.

'He's naughty,' I tell her. 'His name was in the red book again.'

'Why?'

'Well, his latest trick is taking his money out of his piggy bank to buy biscuits from the school canteen. It's hardly surprising he hasn't been eating his sandwiches.'

'I wonder where his naughtiness comes from?'

'Can't think.'

Janey and I reminisce about our schooldays. 'Do you remember our hairdressing camp in the corner of the lacrosse field? I think I paid you fifty pence for hacking my hair off. I'll have it back, thanks.' She holds out her hand and I slap it. 'This salmon is delicious by the way. You always were a good cook.'

I tell Janey about all the regulars today wanting a slice of the raspberry and passion fruit roulade. 'Ben came in . . .'

'Hang on, Ben . . . Is he the one looking after his niece? The one you've been spending time with?'

I tell Janey about him in more detail, mentioning how much I admire him for looking after Emily.

'Blimey. What an amazing guy.'

'He is.'

'Hang on a minute, why didn't we think of him before?

Ben sent you that card,' she says in triumph, refusing to let the mystery go. 'That's it! Do you fancy him?'

'No.'

'Why not?'

'I just don't.'

'Why?'

'I can't explain.'

'Have a go, 'cos it seems to me this guy could be perfect for you.'

'He's not interested in a relationship, Janey. All his energy is taken up with looking after Emily and he's lost his sister. He needs a friend right now, not a complication.'

'Maybe, but . . .'

'I don't need a complication either. Much better this way. I've never really had a bloke who's been a good friend,' I admit. 'I'm enjoying it.'

'Do you want to meet someone?'

'Think so.' I clear the plates. 'But what will be will be.'

'Oh don't give me that bollocks!'

'I believe in fate.'

'Polly, tell me if I'm way out of line,' she says quietly, 'but is this because of Matthew?'

'Is what because of him?'

'Not wanting to go on any dates?'

'I've been out with a few men since, you know,' I mutter.

'Mr Two Cubes was the last, wasn't he?'

'Yes, but . . .'

'You and I, we're not going to meet anyone unless we put ourselves out there, you know? Some lovely man isn't going to crash-land on our sofa.'

'I wish he would. In fact I wish you could order a bloke like you can a takeaway. "I'll have a George Clooney, please."'

Janey doesn't smile. 'I wouldn't blame you, I'd be scared too.' She pauses. 'But Matthew was a long time ago.'

'I know. I've moved on.'

'When I think what he did to you . . .'

'Don't, Janey. My fault too, for falling for him.'

'Yes, but . . .'

'Let's change the subject.'

'I'm sorry, it's just . . . well, I want you to be happy. Aren't you lonely, Polly?'

'No. I have you, Hugo, Ben, all my friends, Aunt Viv, Louis, I'm lucky.' I don't tell her that part of the reason I did go out with David was because I was lonely. I desperately wanted to be in a normal relationship after Matthew, prove to myself I could do it. 'I have all my AA friends. Some of the people who come to AA only have the clothes on their backs.' I look at Janey, who seems so sad all of a sudden. 'Are you lonely, sweetheart?'

She nods. 'I know I'm lucky in many ways too. I have my work, my health, I love my job, but sometimes it's still not enough. Like today . . . I know Valentine's Day is tacky, but it's like Christmas. It highlights being alone, having no one to hold you at the end of the day. I hate coming home to a dark empty flat. I'm being silly. Ignore me.'

'Janey, you won't be alone forever. You're beautiful and funny and you're about to go on a date with a hot bald photographer. He doesn't realise yet what a lucky man he is.'

We clutch hands. 'This time next year, Polly, you and I will be having a different conversation. Deal?'

'Deal, but for the time being . . .' I get up from the table and open the fridge, 'how about some of my special Valentine's cake?'

That night my dreams are muddled. One minute I'm on a yacht with Ben, we're laughing in the sunshine; then Hugo is angry with me, flushing a bottle of wine down the sink. I'm in Norfolk next, at school with Janey, cutting off her hair with a pair of jagged scissors. I'm in a school fight, defending my brother, telling a crowd of bullies to stop calling him names. Mum and Dad are disappointed in me. 'We warned you,' Mum is scolding, wagging her finger at me, 'you know what happened to Aunt Vivienne and Granddad Arthur.' Next I see Louis as a baby lying in the middle of a main road, vulnerable and alone, cars and lorries heading towards him. Matthew is watching. I scream, 'Pick him up!' but he's laughing at me. Next Louis's hand is about to touch a blazing-hot hob. I wake up in a sweat. I gulp down my water, recover my breath. I rush into Louis's room. I see him in bed, his breathing even. The relief is overwhelming. He looks perfect when he sleeps, so innocent. I'd kill anyone that hurt him.

Quietly I head into the kitchen. Why am I dreaming about him? I don't want him to take up any of my thoughts. I find myself walking over to the fireplace. I pick up the card, now displayed next to Louis's on the mantelpiece. Janey had insisted I show it off or give the card to her so that she didn't feel like such a loser in love. Without thinking I rip it in half. I head back into the kitchen and open the fridge, lift out the cake. Just one little slice; tomorrow I'll do an extra long run.

After finishing off the entire cake, I go back to bed feeling guilty I've eaten so much. I close my eyes, drift off to sleep, determined not to see Matthew's face again.

16

Tonight is Janey's birthday. She's hired a room in a hotel in Brook Green. It's crowded, the music loud, and I'm too far away from the bar, listening to one of Janey's friends telling me how she recently developed a curious dairy allergy. She's short and busty with long mousy-coloured straight hair and as she talks she blinks in a really off-putting way. 'It was most peculiar,' she says. 'It all started after I'd eaten some Boursin, you know that soft creamy cheese? I used to eat it all the time.'

'Uh-huh,' I say, glancing over to Matt at the bar.

'And you'll never guess what?' She blinks at me again, as if about to reveal the most exciting secret ever. 'That night I started to itch . . .' She scratches her arm.

Give me strength, I think, as she continues to reel off further disturbing symptoms that caused her serious alarm.

I look over to Matt again, still sitting at the bar, and this time he smiles at me, raising his glass. Bastard.

I catch his eye again. Matt and I have been seeing one another for four months and it's been four months of parties, flowers and silk underwear, nightclubs, bar crawls and skiving off work to stay in bed. He's been staying over most of the time; Hugo says only half jokingly, that he should pay rent. If we don't have a party to go to we stay in and create our own, ordering takeaway that I hardly touch and drinking until the early hours of the morning, music playing at full volume – causing the neighbours to complain. There's one guy in particular, ginger-haired Fred, we call him, a computer geek who runs some online company from home, who is always knocking on the door saying he's trying to work. Hugo isn't impressed either. 'Sadly I'm not deaf,' he'd said one morning, 'only blind.'

I know we should be more considerate, I do feel guilty the morning after when Hugo says we kept him up. I say sorry, like I always do, but the trouble is that the moment I'm with Matt, I lose myself in his company and forget the rest of the world. He's wild and outgoing, confident and charismatic. I look over to him again, talking to Janey now. I love the fact he left school when he was sixteen. He told me he didn't need qualifications to be a property developer, just a finger on the pulse and an eye for a good deal. 'I'm a risk-taker, Polly. Borrow from the bank and hold your nerve.' So far he has found most of his houses by getting in his car and driving about, targeting the right area and knocking on the door of some unassuming old granny and turning on his charm.

However, I'm aware it's not the healthiest of relationships in that apart from Janey, I've more or less stopped seeing my own friends and I haven't met any of his. If I ask Matt about his friends he shuts down. Mum keeps on asking when I'm coming home, that she and Dad have forgotten what I look like. Aunt Viv is living in Los Angeles with a film producer called Gareth. She went back to America after Granddad Arthur died. He had a heart attack when I was nineteen and died a couple of days later in hospital. His death crushed Aunt Viv more than Granny Sue. I knew from the way she talked about him that her father had been the only one really to support her after being released from prison. Aunt Viv and I email regularly; she wants to know all the gossip about Matt, always complaining when I give little away except to say I'm happy.

Matt doesn't have a relationship with his parents. He says they were too wrapped up in themselves to notice he was even alive. They travelled like gypsies when he was a child; he never settled long enough in one place to make friends. The most I discovered about his father was he's called Ron, Ron the Con, Matt had called him, but I could see talking about his dad hurt. Ron the Con was a fraudster and a gambler. Matt often found wads of cash under the sofa. 'I'd get a clip round the ear if I asked any questions,' he said. 'Or worse. Mum was scared of him.' When I'd asked if his father were violent, his silence answered my question.

His parents had met in a restaurant, his mother a waitress. His father was repeatedly unfaithful; he had the idea that he was the big guy. 'I give you the money and good sex; you cook and clean for me and turn a blind eye when I sleep with other women.'

When I asked him about his mother he said very little about her as well. 'She wasn't really a mum. We had no routine, no rules.' It was the first time I'd seen him emotional and I felt so protective, cradling him in my arms like a child.

Matt hasn't had much love in his life and I want to be the person that changes that. But if I'm honest, deep down I'm also relieved he's not close to his family. My last boyfriend, a doctor called George, came from a much more traditional background. His family lived in a grand house in Wiltshire with a swimming pool and a tennis court. He was blond, sexy and charming and I'd tease him by saying all his patients must be in love with him. When I look back there are two occasions when I truly disgraced myself. The first was at a Christmas drinks party with George's family, neighbours and friends. I remember champagne flowing freely and after one too many glasses George sending me up to bed like a child, telling his mother I was coming down with a bug.

The second occasion was in a Michelin-starred restaurant for George's father's sixtieth birthday. After the main course

I staggered to the bathroom, tripping over the pudding trolley on my way. As I plucked the cream and raspberries out of my hair George didn't see the funny side of it at all. Enough was enough. He couldn't go on making excuses. I'd had every fake bug and virus under the sun. 'You know what the real problem is? It's you, Polly. You've got a drinking problem,' he said the following morning.

I denied it, I mean, how stupid is that? I don't have a problem. He threatened that if I didn't stop drinking he'd leave me, so I left him instead.

I am brought back to reality when Janey's friend nudges me. 'And in the morning, if you can believe it, my face was out to here . . .' She stretches her hands out with exaggeration.

'Out to where?' Matt says, finally rescuing me, introducing himself. He wraps his arms around my waist and rests his chin on my shoulder.

She blushes as she touches her mouth, gazing at him doe-eyed. 'I've been boring Polly about my cheese allergy.'

'Not at all,' I say, gulping down my drink.

'Your cheese allergy,' Matt repeats, and I'm trying not to laugh when he pinches my stomach. 'Sounds fascinating, but can you excuse us for just two secs?' He pulls me away.

'You took your time,' I say when we're at a safe distance.

'I was enjoying your acting skills.'

'Oscar-winning, I thought,' I say as he pulls me towards

him and we kiss. But soon Janey is upon us, saying it's time to head downstairs for cocktails and dancing. We all head off, but I feel someone grabbing my arm, pulling me back. 'I'm sorry you got stuck with her,' Janey whispers. 'She's a family friend, just moved to London, I promised Mum I'd invite her.'

'Don't worry. Nothing I don't know about cheese allergies now.'

She smiles. 'Let's go out soon, just the two of us. I haven't seen you properly for ages.'

'I'd love that. How are you doing?'

Janey's been single for the past four months, giving herself time to get over Will. 'I'm good. How's it going with Matt? And you don't need to play it down. I can cope being around loved-up couples.'

'It's amazing,' I confess. 'I'm so happy, Janey.'

For the rest of the evening Matt and I keep an eye on one another all the time. I know I'm never out of his sight. 'I saw the way you were talking to him,' he whispers in my ear, standing close behind me after I've just been speaking to some random bloke. I lean back into him. 'And what way was that?'

'All flirty, getting him to buy you a drink.'

'Jealous, were you?' I say, turned on.

'Very.'

Later that night, back at the flat, Matt and I stumble into the sitting room to find Hugo and a friend watching a film, the lights dimmed. 'It looks cosy in here,' I say, wondering if this could be a girlfriend. Hugo introduces us to Rosie. She's slim with silky blonde hair.

I kick off my shoes before plopping down onto the old leather pouffe. It tips over and I can't stop laughing as I roll across the floor.

'Polly!' Hugo gasps. 'Get up! What are you doing?'

'I'm doing breaststroke!' I break into laughter. 'I'm swimming! Come on, let's do the butterfly!'

'Ignore her,' Matt says. 'She's bonkers. How did you two meet, Rosie?'

'In our choir,' she replies tentatively.

'Hallelujah!' Matt sings, making me scream with laughter and kick my legs even more, this time knocking a couple of glasses over. 'Kumbaya, my Lord,' I sing at the top of my voice. 'Kumbaya!'

'Polly, go to bed,' Hugo says.

I sit up, cross my legs on the floor. 'Sometimes, Hugo, you can be such an old *prude*.'

Lost for words, Rosie looks awkwardly from me to Hugo. Matthew lights up. Hugo squints when he smells the smoke, before gesturing to the television. 'Look, we were kind of in the middle of watching this thriller.'

Matt looks confused. 'Sorry mate, but what's the point? You can't see the bloody action!'

'You bastard,' Hugo says, staring at the screen.

'Matt!' I stagger to my feet and tug at his sleeve, the room spinning as if I'm on some boat and we've hit choppy waters. 'That was horrible!'

'I was only saying . . .'

'Say sorry,' I cut him off.

Rosie touches Hugo's knee. 'Don't let him get to you.'

Hugo walks Rosie to the front door, apologising profusely. 'I hope we can do this again?' he says.

Later on that night, when Matt is snoring, I hear the vague sound of footsteps in the hallway, but seconds later, pass out again.

The following morning Hugo storms into the kitchen, where I'm nursing a particularly bad hangover at the table. I make a promise to myself to stop drinking, especially on an empty stomach. 'You left the hob on.' Smoke is practically coming out of his nostrils.

'I don't remember using it,' I say blurry-eyed.

'You never remember anything. You and Matt were un-believably rude last night.'

Were we? It's one giant blank.

'This has got to stop, Polly.'

'I know,' I say, hearing the frustration in Hugo's voice. 'I'm sorry.'

'Saying sorry isn't enough! You can be unbelievably selfish—'

'Look,' I cut him off, 'I hadn't eaten anything all day yesterday and I've been on these antibiotic things—'

'What antibiotics?'

'I picked something up from one of the children at school.'

He doesn't say a word, but his silence speaks volumes.

'I didn't drink that much last night,' I continue. 'It's just that wine goes to my head if I haven't had any food.'

'Well, eat! And why are you drinking at all if you're on antibiotics?'

'Hugo, stop!' My head is pounding. 'It's like living with the cops. Why don't you tell me what the real problem is?'

'You can date who you like, Polly, but if you want my opinion he's a nasty piece of work and you should walk away.'

Over the next month I'm back at school after the Easter holidays and Matthew has identified a new project, a house in Wandsworth that is going to sealed bids. He's confident he'll come out on top, telling me the market is great and the banks are falling over themselves to lend him cash. He's borrowed a scary amount of money. 'It's well over six figures,' Matt had said, before cupping my face in his hands, 'but nothing for you to worry about, sweetheart.'

To earn more money, I have signed up with a catering company to do some waitressing in the evenings, after school. Mounting bills and rent, plus partying with Matt, have burned a hole in my pocket. All I have to do is stick on a black miniskirt and white top and serve drinks at parties and dances. It's easy money plus I get to take home the leftover bottles at the end of the evening.

Hugo barely sleeps in the flat. He stays over with Rosie, who is now his girlfriend. Part of me is relieved. Matt and I can walk around the flat naked if we want to. We can get up at noon at the weekends, stay in bed all day. Matt jokes saying that I'm free to scream when I have an orgasm now. No longer do I have to field questions from Hugo about Matt, like, if he's such a hotshot property man why doesn't he own his own place by now? Hugo doesn't get how it works. Of course Matt doesn't want to tie up capital buying his own place. No, it's a relief Hugo's not around. 'We don't need him, Polly. It's just you and me,' Matt says. The other half of me, however, is anxious that we're drifting apart. Hugo has been my anchor for many years; without him I feel adrift.

One Sunday morning I wake to find Matthew's side of the bed empty. I swing my legs over the edge of the bed, kicking over the bottle of vodka I'd bought late last night from the twenty-four-hour shop. I walk unsteadily into the kitchen and find him with Hugo. I'm surprised. I didn't even hear him come home last night. I glance at the clock. It's close to eleven.

'What's going on?' I ask, sensing the frosty atmosphere.

'Why don't you tell her what you've just accused me of, Hugo?' suggests Matt, crossing his arms.

Hugo pushes his plate to one side. 'I'm sorry if I made a mistake, Matthew. I've lost my appetite.' As he walks out of the room Matt pushes out a chair, causing Hugo to trip and lose his footing. I rush to Hugo's side.

'I'm OK, Polly,' Hugo says without flinching, placing the chair back under the table and leaving the room.

I stare at Matt, demanding an explanation. 'Why did you do that?'

'Why don't you ask him?' is all he can say.

'What's going on?' I ask Hugo, as he's about to leave.

'I had a couple of twenty-pound notes in my coat pocket.'

'You think Matt took them?' I place a hand over my mouth, feeling a wave of sickness overwhelm me.

'Who else? What do we really know about him?' he whispers.

'What do you mean?'

'He's so vague about his life. He swans around doing God knows what. He doesn't seem to have any roots.'

'He hasn't bought his own place yet because he's putting everything into this new project.'

'He makes me feel uncomfortable in my own home.'

'I know.' I reach out to touch Hugo's arm. 'That's my fault as well, but that doesn't make him a thief.'

'Come on, Polly. Money doesn't just disappear. I had forty quid in my coat pocket. I remember where I put things . . .'

'Hugo, stop . . .'

'You know how careful I have to be. I'm sure I saw him in

144

the sitting room earlier this morning and now the money's gone.' Hugo can see outlines of people and he has an innate sense of someone being close to him or in a room. He knows me by the sound of my footsteps and by my scent.

'But . . .'

'There's something about him,' Hugo continues, 'something I don't trust.'

'He didn't take your money,' I say.

'Polly?' For a moment I'm relieved he can't see the guilt written all across my face, but he can sense it, of course he can.

I clear my throat. There's a long pause.

'It was me, Hugo. I took your money. I'm so sorry.'

He doesn't shout, or scream. All he says is, 'I want my sister back.' Quietly he leaves, taking his disappointment with him. That makes me feel even worse, if that were possible.

I head to the kitchen and find Matthew drinking a black coffee as if nothing is going on. 'It's over,' I say, a tremble in my voice. 'You and me, we're done.'

He looks up from his mug, smiles. 'Oh come on, Polly. You know as well as I do that we're far from finished.'

17

2013

It's Friday and I'm at AA, sitting in between Harry and Aunt Viv. Aunt Viv normally goes to a Wednesday session; we decided not to go to meetings together, that we needed to be independent, but occasionally she joins my group. Denise is at the end of the row, knitting a multicoloured stripy blanket. Neve is sitting next to her.

'I started drinking when I was eight,' Ryan says, dressed in scruffy jeans and a cap. Part of me wonders if he's sharing today because there's a stunning new woman here, all legs and long blonde hair. She makes me feel fat.

'People often want to know why. I mean, eight! I was a child! I was bullied at school for being stupid. I'm dyslexic, still write my words backwards.' He smiles. 'Anyway, I figured if I can't be the brainiest kid on the block let's be the funniest. When I had my first drink, I stole some brandy from the kitchen. It made me feel like a rock star. Freddie

Mercury, eat your heart out. As the years rolled on no one realised I had a problem. I formed a band at school, played the guitar, became the cool kid. I loved an audience and thrived off the attention because I didn't get any at home.' He pauses. 'It's funny. When I was in rehab I snuck my guitar into the treatment room but I couldn't play a note, and the reason I couldn't play was 'cos I'd never gone on stage without having a drink first. The shame of playing sober, making a mistake, it kind of paralysed me. It's better to opt out than make a mistake, better not to enter the race. Then you can't lose, right? But I've got my act together, been clean now for four years and I work in the music industry, have a top dog called Kip and I'm happy. Just need to meet a nice girl now,' he says, grinning at the blonde woman. 'So, thanks guys, just wanted to share that.'

Harry nods vigorously as he offers me a toffee humbug before sticking his hand up in the air. The chair nods. 'Hi, I'm Harold and I'm an alcoholic.'

'Hi, Harold.'

'I was really moved by what you said, Ryan. I got my act together too, in the nick of time. I'm ashamed of my past. I lied practically my whole married life. What a weasel.' He slaps his thigh. 'Betsy wouldn't allow me to drink in the house, so I'd pretend I had meetings to go to, places to be, when all I was doing was heading off to the Dog and Parrot. Hah! The only reason I got clean was the doc said I had six months to live and Betsy threatened to leave me if I didn't do as he said. I go to the Heath now, find a quiet spot on Parliament Hill to think about my life and everything I have. I thank the Lord Betsy stuck by me. Sometimes I get down on my knees and pray to the angels for courage. Often I can't get up again. My knees aren't quite what they used to be.'

We all laugh affectionately. 'I might be over eighty, but my life is full of adventure now. I know my grandchildren. I'm dipping into my pension pot and taking Betsy on a cruise this summer. We're doing a Mediterranean Medley.'

Everyone claps and cheers. Harry winks at me. 'I'm a lucky chap. I've got my fellowship, people who know me and still love me, warts and all.'

Knitting needles stop clicking. 'Hi, I'm Denise and I'm an alcoholic.'

'Hi, Denise.'

They start again. 'I had a run-in with some biscuits.'

Over the years Denise has attended Overeaters Anonymous (OA) as well as AA.

'Millionaire's shortbread,' she continues in her deep husky voice. 'They were a present from my grandchildren. "Freshly baked, Granny," they said! Ate the whole lot in front of Corrie, about twelve of them there were. Felt sick as a parrot afterwards, cross with myself, you know. Why can't I be normal, have one or two after my main meal and then put them back in the biscuit tin.'

It makes me think of David, Mr Two Cubes.

'That's the thing about addiction. It's like having five

boiling saucepans but only four lids. When we slam down one lid another pot boils over, doesn't it? When I stopped drinking I took up coffee, drank so much I developed a frozen shoulder and had to see the doc. Poor old doc, he must have been sick of the sight of me. Either that or he thought I had the hots for him.'

Many of us smile and laugh.

Denise chuckles. 'I weighed myself this morning. Never mind, they were bloody good biscuits.'

We all laugh again.

I raise my hand.

'I'm Polly, I'm an alcoholic.'

'Hi, Polly.'

'I've had a bad day today. I was furious with Louis for making us late for school. I hate being told off by the head-mistress.'

A few laughs.

'I didn't sleep well last night. He's been asking a lot of questions about his dad, and it makes me feel guilty. I know I dwell too much on the past, but I can't help it sometimes. I hurt many people,' I clutch my mug of tea, 'especially the ones closest to me. I lied all the time.' Harry, sitting next to me, nods knowingly. 'It starts off with white lies, but they become bigger and bigger, to the point where you can't work out what is true or false anymore. Sometimes I look back and I don't recognise the old me, this selfish, spoilt brat.' I reach across and take one of Harry's handkerchiefs from him and wipe my eyes. 'I realise now addiction is all about instant gratification. It's a disease of the emotions. I'd felt wrong since I was a child, really since my brother went to boarding school. I missed him. I couldn't deal with my feelings of emptiness, of nothingness, so I numbed my feelings with drink. I was dishonest with myself too, fooling myself for years. What's even worse is I stole people's peace of mind. I once nicked forty quid off my brother, Hugo, so I could buy a couple of bottles of vodka and some fags. I've been clean for over four years now and never been closer to Hugo, but I want to be a better person, make up for all those years of selfishness.' I think about Ben, how close we have become. I want to support him and Emily. I think about Matthew and how naïve I was. I look at Aunt Viv, knowing she will relate to this. 'I am so grateful to have a second chance.'

At the end of the session we hold hands to say the serenity prayer. Harry's hand is small and frail in mine.

'God grant me the serenity to accept the things I cannot change, courage to change the things I can and the wisdom to know the difference.'

Neve and I catch up after the meeting. 'It was good you talked today,' she says. 'You OK?'

'I've been thinking about the past a lot recently.'

'Because of Louis?'

'He won't let it go. That's why I lost it this morning. On and on, like some broken record. "Where does my dad live?

Why can't I see him?"' I think about the Valentine's card and the few calls I've received on my mobile, where the person at the other end hangs up. 'Neve, I've been having these nightmares.'

'Go on.'

'I keep dreaming he's going to knock on my front door. It's daft, right? He'll never come back . . . will he?'

18

It's early June. I ended it with Matt, only to crawl back to him a week later, saying I'd made a mistake. 'I can't live without him,' I said to Hugo, trying to make him understand. 'I love him.'

Matthew has won the sealed bids for the house in Wandsworth and is consumed by architectural plans for extensions in every direction, up, down and sideways. 'It'll be double the size by the time I'm finished,' he claims. Most of the planning goes over my head. All I know is that he's borrowed a seriously scary amount of money, well into six figures, but he's convinced this project is going to be his biggest yet. 'It's all about leverage, Polly. No point me tying up my own capital.' In the meantime nothing much has changed in my life . . . except I've skipped two periods.

One Friday afternoon, back at the flat after school, I take a pregnancy test kit out of the bag. For weeks I've been telling myself I can't be pregnant, but the truth is I can't keep on blaming my morning sickness on drink, since I don't drink every night. I flop onto the sofa and turn the television on. Matt's not coming home tonight. He's catching up with Graham, his old flatmate.

Ninety-nine per cent accurate, I read on the back of the box, and not only that but this test will tell me how many weeks pregnant I am. I inhale deeply. Am I ready for a baby? It was earlier than I'd imagined but then again, I've always wanted children. I know I'd love him or her more than I can imagine. Perhaps it would force me to change? Stop living the way I do. But it makes me nervous too. I try to anticipate Matt's reaction if it's positive. He's not exactly the most paternal of people but it's different when it's your own, right?

I discard the box, heading into the kitchen to pour myself a glass of wine to relax. The second glass is for courage. The rest of the bottle is because . . . well, do I always need a reason?

'Polly, wake up. Wake up.'

Slowly I open my eyes and see a blurred face in front of me that eventually I recognise as Hugo. *The Sopranos* is playing in the background. I glance at the clock on the mantelpiece. It's 8.15. 'I must have fallen asleep.' I stretch out my arms, pretending to Hugo that I've had a really hectic day at school. 'What are you doing here, stranger?' I try to sound normal, but since the money incident, and my getting back with Matt despite Hugo's warnings, our friendship has been strained.

Hugo tells me Rosie is away this weekend. 'Besides, I hoped you'd be here. I brought round some pork chops and frozen chips.'

Pork chops and oven chips are Hugo's speciality. 'Sounds perfect.' I follow him into the kitchen.

'You're what?' he says so quietly I can barely hear him.

'Pregnant.'

'How?'

'Well, when two people have sex . . .'

'Stop it. I mean, when did you find out?' He pushes his plate aside.

'Tonight.'

'And it's his?'

'Of course it's Matt's!'

'What are you going to do?' Hugo unbuttons his shirt, as if trying to breathe.

'Keep it.'

'Right.'

I wait for him to say something positive, though I know full well what the problem is, or who the problem is. 'Hugo, please be happy. You're going to be an uncle.'

'It's a lot to take in.'

'You're not happy because of Matt.'

'Polly, I can't pretend.'

'But if you could get to know him like I do – he comes across all macho, but deep down he's not like that, not really. He's never had proper parents or the things we've had and there is another side to him . . .'

'I'm pleased for you, I am . . .'

'But?'

'I'm worried.' Hugo bites his lip. 'You're in denial, you have been for years.'

'Denial about what?'

'Drinking.'

'Hugo, I haven't had a drink for three days,' I say, which is true, up until this evening. 'I had one tonight,' I go on to lie, 'before you arrived, and one over supper. Lots of women drink while pregnant, it's . . .'

'I used to find empty bottles under your bed and in your wardrobe.'

'So you're monitoring me now?'

He steadies me by the shoulders. 'I'm worried. I'm really worried about you.'

'Nothing's wrong. I'm happy! I'm having a baby,' I say as I head to the sink. I need to lie down. 'I can't believe you want me to kill my baby.'

'I don't! That's not what I'm saying at all! I love you and would never make you do that!'

When I turn back to him I almost burst into tears. Gentle, kind Hugo. Part of me wants to hug him. I see us as children in our bright-yellow lifejackets, out on the lake, heading towards the sunken boat. I see his face when we dropped him off at school, a vulnerable boy clinging onto Fido, his toy dog. We were inseparable. We'd share a bedroom, hold hands when watching *Jaws* on television. I hate us arguing, but . . .

'Please be happy for me. I need you, Hugo . . .'

'Listen to me! I'm here for you. All I'm saying is if you're going to be a mum, you need help. You're a mess, Polly.'

'I'm not, I'm fine, I'm . . .'

'Be honest with yourself! I remember Aunt Viv saying alcoholism is an illness, it's like a scale . . .'

'What?'

'. . . and you need to arrest it, put the brakes on before it's too late.'

'I can't believe I'm hearing this. I enjoy a drink. I like having a social life. Now that I know I'm pregnant, I'll stop.'

He shakes his head. 'No, no you won't.'

'I love Matthew and I'm having his child, whether you like it or not.'

He gets up from the table without saying a word.

'Hugo!' I call after him. Seconds later he returns and hands me some brochures.

'Action on Addiction! Alcoholics Anonymous! AA!' I picture a group of losers sitting in a circle.

'Polly, you need to see someone,' he pleads, 'especially

now. I'll support you. I love you. If you could just see your GP . . .'

I throw the brochures at him.

'Polly, grow up!' he says, furious now.

I put on my coat.

'Where are you going?'

I turn to him as I reach the front door. 'Don't you dare come near me. I never want to see you again, do you understand?'

When I return to the flat a few hours later I glance at one of the leaflets left on the kitchen table. '*Addiction is the biggest preventable killer in the country. It destroys lives, breaks up families . . .*' I tear the paper into shreds, tears flowing down my cheeks.

Later that night I wake up drenched in sweat hearing Hugo's voice in my head. I hug my pillow, missing my brother already. 'You need help, Polly. Aunt Viv says alcoholism is like a scale, you need to arrest it, put the brakes on before it gets too late . . .'

19

@GateauAuChocolat It's another fishy Friday & it's Mary-Jane's fish chowder, Jean's fish pie and Polly's choc-peanut butter cake!

'Thank Crunchie it's Friday,' Louis and I had said to one another this morning, like we always do on a Friday. He's looking forward to the weekend; I'm looking forward to AA.

I slide the cake folder out from the bookshelf. Mary-Jane is stirring the fish chowder. Aunt Viv joins me in the kitchen to make herself a coffee. She looks sophisticated even in a pair of charcoal palazzo pants; her brown hair is tied back accentuating her cheekbones and nut-brown eyes. Aunt Viv practises yoga every morning; it's something she got into whilst living in Los Angeles. She swears by it, saying it helps her tap into a kind of calmness.

'Jean is driving me mad,' she says, glancing at the menu board. 'Fish soup *and* fish pie?'

'I heard that!' he shouts from upstairs.

'And fishcakes for pudding,' I joke. Mary-Jane shoots me one of her famous disapproving looks.

Aunt Viv and I try not to laugh. Aunt Viv says she's Mrs Danvers in Marigolds.

'How's Louis?' she asks as I melt butter in a pan.

'Good.' His questions about Matt have calmed down in the last few days. 'He's beginning to enjoy cooking too.' I tell her that when I'd taken him to the supermarket last weekend, telling him he could eat whatever he liked as a special treat for getting a gold star at school . . . 'He went for red bream because he liked the colour. We grilled it and made a tomato salad.'

'He's a lovely boy, Polly. And how's that handsome man? The uncle.'

I smile, knowing she's fishing for gossip. 'Fine.'

She raises an eyebrow. She doesn't trust the word fine. Fine means nothing. 'Is he a friend of Bill's?' she asks.

Bill Wilson, or Bill W., was the co-founder of Alcoholics Anonymous, so when we ask if someone is a friend of Bill's, it's code for asking if he's in our tribe. 'How do you know?'

'I sort of sensed it, Polly.'

'Well it was a good guess. Actually Aunt Viv, can I have some advice about Ben?'

'Sure.'

I remove the butter from the heat before leading her to the communal table; we sit in the corner. 'You know, more than anyone . . .' I take her hand, 'what it's like to lose someone.'

She nods.

'I've been reading up about bereavement and how language can confuse a child.' I tell her that Emily isn't sleeping because she's terrified that something might happen to her at night. Ben had told her that Grace had died in her sleep, so now Emily doesn't dare shut her eyes. 'How stupid can I be?' Ben had said to Jim and me one Monday morning at the school gates. 'Children take things so literally.' She's also convinced that her mum will come back for her birthday this summer; she can't understand that death is a permanent state.

'Tell me if this is stupid,' I continue, 'but I was wondering if they should have some kind of ritual for their old dog, Patch, to show he's never coming back?'

'Yes,' she replies, and immediately I feel relieved that she's not laughing at my suggestion.

'Maybe they should get another dog?'

'Maybe, but it's important Emily doesn't think life can be replaced, just like that. When did Patch die?'

'Over a year ago.'

'Does Ben like dogs?'

'I don't think he's ever thought about them either way.'

'You care for him, don't you?'

I nod. 'And Emily too.'

Jean joins us. 'I couldn't help eavesdropping.'

'Nosy bugger,' says Aunt Viv.

He ignores her. 'Have you heard of Bernard Crettaz?'

I shake my head.

'He set up the Mortal Café in Switzerland and France, a place where people come and drink tea, eat cake and talk about life, death, mourning, the loss of a spouse, a child . . .' He looks at Aunt Viv with deep love in his eyes. 'The café is the opposite of the British stiff upper lip.' He pulls a face that makes both Aunt Viv and me smile. 'In this country, we go to the funeral and then after a set amount of time we are supposed to move on. No more tears. As children we are told not to cry, we pull ourselves together, so it's not surprising that we find it hard to show emotion. I think a dog for Emily is a wonderful idea, it will remind her of those happy days with her mother. Ben needs to keep those memories alive.'

Three days later, Jim, Ben and I are having coffee after the Monday morning school run and moaning that given it is March, shouldn't it be a little warmer? I've prepped Jim to encourage the dog idea. I won't mention it immediately; maybe buy Ben a blueberry muffin first. Ben is letting off steam, something I've become used to. Emily will not brush her teeth in the mornings and he cannot seem to get through to her that it's unhygienic.

'What do you say to her?' I ask.

'That all her teeth will fall out if she doesn't do it.'

Jim and I glance at one another.

'Then she cries. You see?' He shrugs, registering our faces. 'I'm hopeless.'

'No, you're not,' both Jim and I say at the same time.

'I can't do this. I'm never going to be enough for her.'

'What Emily has gone through, is going through, is horrific, but she has *you* and you are making progress. I see it in Emily, I do. I'd love Louis to have a father, of course I would, but he'll be just fine, I'll make sure of that.'

'I know my position is completely different to yours, Ben, but I feel inadequate most of the time as well.' Ben and I turn to Jim, unsure how he can quite compete in this arena. 'Just hear me out, OK?'

We nod.

'I live with constant guilt because a mother's pair of shoes are a hard pair to fill. I only started looking after Maisy when she was four and all she used to say to me was, "When's it Mummy's turn to be at home again?" It's better now,' he admits. 'She realises this is how it is. Emily will also grow to understand that you are her father, the person she can trust. Children are resilient, much more so than adults sometimes, and they're good at adapting, don't underestimate that. There is one thing I am much better at,' Jim goes on, brewing a smile. 'Maisy loves me driving her to swimming classes or dancing.'

'Why?' Ben and I ask at the same time.

ONE STEP CLOSER TO YOU

'"Because when I drive with Dad," Jim says, imitating Maisy's voice, "there are so many buggers and wankers on the road!"'

We all laugh.

'You've got to laugh sometimes, haven't you?' Jim says. 'Otherwise you'd cry. Muffins?' I feel a soft kick under the table.

As Jim heads over to the counter to order a slice of banana bread and two blueberry muffins . . .

'What is it?' Ben asks me. 'You look constipated.'

'Thanks.'

'Spit it out.'

'OK, I've been thinking . . .'

'Always overrated.'

'I've been thinking about Emily and how she grabs hold of the leads of other people's dogs when we're out walking.'

'I know. Awkward, that.'

'She really misses Patch.'

'You think I should get a dog?'

'A dog! What a great idea,' says Jim, overdoing it as he hands us our sweet fixes.

'I think it could help Emily,' I suggest. 'It would give her something to care for. I know someone whose dog has just had puppies, she's . . .'

'I'll think about it,' Ben interrupts, before heading outside for a cigarette.

It's the Easter holidays and in front of me is a bright-eyed and bushy-tailed Scottie, who has the most enormous ears you have ever seen. 'Do my ears look big in this?' I joke to Ben.

We'd visited the puppy last Monday, and of course it was a done deal the moment Emily clapped eyes on her rolling around and playing in the pen. 'You can have her for free,' the owner had said, knowing Ben's background. He thanked her for her enormous generosity, holding the puppy in both hands and promising to take great care of her.

The ball of black fluff makes her way into Emily's bedroom, all of us following closely behind. Each time I visit Ben's flat I notice yet more small changes. Luckily for Emily, Ben has replaced the painting in her room that looked like a nosebleed with an old-fashioned fairy print they found together in a second-hand bookshop in Primrose Hill. Emily also has a new dressing table that shows off a collection of snow globes she found with her mother.

I also noticed a small framed picture of Grace in Ben's room, placed on his bedside table. She's sitting on a lawn, her hair held back in a patterned scarf. Ben tells me it was taken in her garden.

The puppy darts out of Emily's room, skids across the floor and is now back in the sitting room, where she decides it's a good time and place to do a piddle, missing the nappy mats Ben has strategically placed throughout the flat. He rushes over to the scene of the crime with his cloth and small bowl of soapy water. 'I've counted fourteen bloody wees,' Ben says when Louis, Emily and puppy are out of earshot, 'and three poos already this morning. She escaped her pen, the bugger.'

'Once she's trained, she'll be fine,' I say, before adding, 'but we've got to give her a name.'

'Patch!' Emily jumps up and down, before Ben and I try to explain that Patch can't be replaced. We have to think of something new.

We watch Emily rocking the puppy in her arms, a look of pure joy on her face. Ben stands close to me, his arm brushing against mine. 'Thank you, Polly.'

'What for?'

'This. She's a different girl.'

20

2007

I'm at the kitchen table, preparing myself to tell Matthew. It's great news, I reassure myself. A new life! When I have a baby I won't want to party all night or drink until dawn. I'll be so wrapped up in my baby that even if I were invited to the best gig in Hollywood I wouldn't want to go. I'm looking forward to having a break from teaching in the first six months. I'll miss the children, but already I can see myself slipping into a new routine. I'll bake again, like I used to. We'll have pancakes with maple syrup for breakfast, go for walks in the park, swings in the playground and feeding bread to the ducks. I'll meet the other mums and we'll go out for coffee mornings. Matthew will be a great father; he'll be the kind caring dad that he never had. His business will provide for us. Maybe we'll buy our own place with a garden and a paddling pool. I can learn to garden.

When I hear the key in the lock, I pray it's Hugo. I couldn't concentrate at school today; all I could think about was our argument last night. He sent me a message saying he was moving out. He'd pick his things up at the weekend.

'Polly?' he calls.

'In here,' I say, registering my disappointment.

Matt drops his overnight bag by the kitchen door. 'What are you doing sitting in the dark, Miss Stephens?' He switches on the light, walks towards me. He takes my face in his hands and kisses me as if he hasn't seen me for a year. I hold him close and breathe in his scent. I can't get enough of his touch. He pulls me to my feet and makes me sit on the kitchen table.

'Matt, I need to tell you . . .'

'Shh.' He unzips the back of my skirt, only one thing on his mind. His hands are running down the insides of my thighs; slowly he spreads my legs apart.

'We don't need one,' I murmur when he produces a condom from his pocket.

'What?'

'I'm having a baby,' I whisper, my heart beating hard and fast.

He stands back. 'But we were being careful, weren't we?'

'Not *all* the time, Matt . . .'

'How many weeks? You don't look any different.'

'Twelve.'

'Are you sure?'

'I can show you the blue line. I've done it three times.'

He remains silent.

'You're not happy, are you?'

He runs a hand through his hair. 'I don't know if I'm ready. Are you?'

'It'll be fine. I can look after it,' I assure him. 'Babies are like puppies to begin with; all they need is plenty of food and sleep. It'll be fun.' I try to kiss him, remind him where we were, but the moment has gone.

Later that evening, when we're in bed, I tell him about Hugo moving out, pretending he'd wanted to give us more space.

'Polly, he hates my guts, doesn't he?'

'He's not your number one fan.'

Matthew strokes my cheek. 'What with the baby and all, why don't I move in, permanently?'

Eight weeks later it's the morning of my twenty-week scan and Janey and I are in the crowded waiting room at Queen Charlotte's Hospital, flicking through magazines. Matt couldn't come today. He has an important meeting with his architect, going over construction plans for the Wandsworth house. 'See if Blondie can go with you,' he'd said.

'Oh look,' Janey says, stopping on a page. I lean across to see what she's reading. 'Am I an Alcoholic?' is written in bold. 'Has binge drinking become a way of life?' Below are questions and all you need to do is tick yes or no in the boxes besides them, add up the numbers of yeses and nos and the test will tell you the rest.

'This should be interesting.' She digs into her handbag for a pen.

"Are you more in a hurry to get your first drink of the day than you used to be?"

'Definitely,' Janey says, heading straight for the 'yes' box. 'I tell you, the first thing I do when I get back from work is open a bottle. I'm convinced I'm going to be made redundant. *"Do you feel uncomfortable if alcohol isn't available?"'*

She ticks the 'yes' box. 'I was at a wedding recently and all the people on our table, even the men, were talking about which bloody schools they were going to send their kids to and all the wine had run out. It was awful.

'*"Have you ever been unable to remember part of the previous evening? Has a family friend expressed concern about your drinking?"'*

'Stop it, Janey. We both know we drink like two old fish.'

'I could do with a nine-month detox. Have you had any cravings by the way?'

'Wine and fags.'

We both smile. She closes the magazine, chucks it onto the table. 'You definitely don't want to know the sex?'

'Matt doesn't want to find out.'

'How's it all going with him?'

I detect concern in her voice so overcompensate by saying, 'Great! He's really thrilled, can't wait!' I glance at the other couples in the room. It's not odd he didn't want to come, I reassure myself.

'How's your mum?' Janey continues.

'What do you mean?'

'Is she excited?'

I shrug. 'She calls Matt "that man".'

Janey narrows her eyes. 'To be fair, she hasn't met him.'

'Because I know it will be a disaster. Nothing I do is good enough for her. This . . .' I gesture to my bump, 'is another disappointment. I'm not married, no ring on my finger . . .'

'She's probably looking forward to being a grandmother though,' Janey says. 'You should take Matt up to Norfolk. Give your mum a chance to meet him.'

The nurse is telling me to relax as she performs the ultrasound but all I can think of is Mum meeting Matt. I'm also waiting for her to tell me something is wrong. I can tell from the way she's looking at the screen that my baby has two heads.

'Everything looks healthy.'

'Really? Are you sure?' I burst into tears. Janey squeezes my hand.

The nurse smiles at me sympathetically, as if she's used to hormonal mothers-to-be. Gently she points out to me on the screen where my baby's spine is, and those are the little fingers and toes. When I see its heart, my eyes fill with tears. There is a little person inside me, breathing. I need to cast aside any doubts. I can do this. I am going to be a great mother. I can't let him or her down.

21

'I was good at drinking,' says Alex, our chair. I like Alex because he says exactly what he thinks and after years of drinking he got his life back on track. He's in his mid forties and has always worked in the building trade but now runs his own company. His first marriage collapsed but since putting the pieces of his life back together he has married again, his angel, as he calls her, and they have one daughter aged three. 'By the age of thirty I was a pro,' he continues. 'If drinking were a job I'd have been a higher-rate taxpayer. I really liked the man I saw in the mirror, the guy who could still drink anyone under the table.' He lifts up his shirt collar for effect, making a few of us laugh. 'Check me out.' He clicks his fingers, winks at a woman in the first row. 'I could talk the talk and walk the walk. I was the geezer who was the first on the dance floor and the last to leave the party, and always ready to do a quick deal on the side. If I saw anyone on a Sunday washing their car at midday I thought they were flipping mental. The pubs are open! What I didn't understand was the progression of my drinking, right, how dangerous it was becoming. If I had a bad day at work, you know, like something crucial was being delivered on site and it was the wrong bloody thing and time was critical, I'd tell myself all would be fine, I'd feel calmer once I'd had a couple of pints down the local.' He takes in a deep breath. 'I got married at twenty-eight. Bad decision. I loved her, I hurt her, but looking back I was a mess, in no fit state to take on any responsibility or take on a mother-in-law. If she threatened to come over . . .'

There are lots of smiles in the room, Harry nudging me gently. Neve, sitting on my other side, gets that one.

'A right old dragon I have to add . . .'

Denise looks up from her knitting muttering, 'Cheeky sod.'

'I'd have a couple of pints before she visited and sneak off to the bathroom or bedroom when she was chatting to my wife. Mother-in-law always wanted to know when we were going to have kids. I couldn't do anything without a glass or bottle in my hand but I didn't see it then. All I knew was drink was becoming my friend, my parent – I needed it around me, to function. Ironically it was tearing me apart and it's only when I realised that moment, that rock bottom moment that we all have, that I could suddenly look in the mirror and see a very different person. Someone pretty pathetic, actually,' he says, his tone more sombre now. 'Someone lost, frightened and powerless over alcohol.'

I find myself nodding in recognition as he says, 'Someone who needed to change.'

22

2007

It's September and I'm just over six months pregnant when Mum calls, telling me she's driving to London in a fortnight to go to the theatre and will combine it with a visit to see me. There's no question about it; she wants to meet Matthew and if we won't go there, she'll come to us.

Slowly, I put down the telephone. 'Who was it?' demands Matthew, entering the kitchen. He looks rough; he hasn't shaved properly for days. He's been in a disgusting mood in the last few weeks because things aren't going his way. He bought the property in June and three months down the line, the elderly neighbours in Wandsworth are objecting to his plans. 'Fucking old fossils. It's called progress!' he'd ranted last night, pacing up and down the kitchen. When I told him everything would work out fine . . .

'You don't understand. There's no guarantee, Polly, that

175

planning permission will go through. By now it should have happened!'

He's not sleeping, doesn't like my body changing, I can't remember the last time we had sex, and he seems completely uninterested in our baby.

'It's not your mum again, is it?' Matt opens the fridge. 'Where's the sodding beer?'

'It's there. You're not looking properly.'

'Where?' he shouts, as if I'm deliberately hiding it from him.

'Bottom shelf.'

Finally he produces a can. Opens it. 'I'm not going to Norfolk to play happy families.'

I tell him he doesn't have to. She's coming here instead.

'Oh that's just great.'

Something seethes inside me. 'We're having a baby so you're going to *have* to man up and meet my parents . . .' I stop when I see that flash of anger in his eyes, something I've seen before when I demand anything of him.

'I don't have to do anything,' he says before hurling his can of beer towards the sink and kicking the kitchen chair over.

'Matt!' I gasp. 'What's got into you?'

'What's got into me?' He shakes me by the shoulders. His closeness makes me feel intimidated and when I try to move he won't let me go. His grip hurts.

'I don't have to do anything,' he says slowly, staring right into my eyes. 'Don't tell me to man up and don't ever tell me what I have to do or . . .'

'But Matt . . .'

He strikes me so hard across the face that I can barely breathe. 'When I say don't, Polly, I mean don't. Understand?'

Terrified, I nod, my cheek burning.

'Good.' He shoves me away, before leaving the room, slamming the door behind him.

The day my mother is due to have supper with Matt and me, I'm at school, dreading the evening ahead. It's going to be a disaster.

Just before class begins I head outside for some peace and quiet. I need space to think. Hugo isn't coming tonight. I miss him. We've patched things up, but only really papered over the cracks. My relationship with Matt is a little better since our argument a week ago. He has said sorry repeatedly for lashing out at me, swearing it was a one-off. He blamed his work and stress levels on the way he'd behaved. I picture him cupping my face in both hands. 'You know I love you. Of course I'll meet your mum. Just give me plenty of warning before the old witch arrives on her broomstick,' he'd said, hoping that would get a smile out of me. I noticed how I'd pulled away when he'd kissed me. Something has changed. I feel as if I am in deep water; I'm out of my depth, but I've come too far now to turn back.

Later that afternoon, after a lightning trip to the supermarket to buy the supper ingredients, along with a bunch
of lilies, I drag the Hoover out from the cupboard and give
it one hell of a workout after a long sabbatical. I polish the
furniture until there isn't a speck of dust. I make our bed
and scrub the kitchen surfaces until they are gleaming.
Once I start, I can't stop. As I clean the smoke-stained
mirror hanging over our fireplace I catch a reflection of
myself. My eyes are bloodshot, my skin blotchy in patches.
I look tired. I'm not eating my five a day. Things are going
to change. I'm going to take better care of myself and
when I have our baby and once Matt's job is back on track,
we'll be back on course. We were happy to begin with,
weren't we?

The table is laid, candles lit, lilies are in their vase, a homemade quiche is warming in the oven. I'm wearing a navy
wraparound dress that shows off my neat bump, and my
soft leather ballerina pump shoes. I've pinned my hair into
a tortoiseshell clip, applied some blusher and mascara and
put on some pearl studs. Matt calls, saying he's on his way.
He asks what my mother likes to drink; he'll pick up a bottle
on the way home. I tell him my mother doesn't drink.

'You sound in a good mood.' I ask hopefully.

'I'll tell you about it later. And, Polly, baby?'

'Yes?'

'I'm sorry I've been on lousy form.'

When I hang up, relieved, I fidget with the cutlery, straightening each knife and fork. I can't drink tonight, not in front of Mum. It's fine. I don't need a drink. When the buzzer rings I take a deep breath. This is going to work.

Mum enters the flat dressed in tailored beige trousers, a cream silk shirt and raspberry pink cashmere cardigan. She's staying the night with an old school friend in Notting Hill, close to the Portobello Market. We hug, Mum always the first to pull away, before she hands me a square slab of beeswax honey that she professes is delicious on toast and over natural yoghurt. 'The flat's looking lovely,' she says, as I lead her down the hallway, past the spic-and-span sitting room and back into the kitchen with a small wooden table laid for three, the vase of lilies in the middle. She tells me I'm looking well. The miracle of make-up, I think to myself.

'What a tidy bump,' she exclaims. 'I was much larger than you when I was pregnant with Hugo. People used to say to me, "Any moment now, dear!"'

I ask her how Dad is.

'Set in his ways. I did ask if he wanted to come, but you know what he's like now. Likes to hold the fort.'

Typical Dad, I think to myself irritably before offering her a drink. Elderflower? Lime? She goes for elderflower.

'I haven't seen you for months, darling. I'd forgotten what your face looks like.'

'Oh Mum, it's just been really busy, a lot going on at school.'

'You do look a little tired,' she admits now. 'You're not overdoing it, are you?'

'No no, I'm fine.' I glance at my watch. 'Matt should be home any second now.' I show her the ultrasound scan taken at twenty weeks, on the fridge door.

Mum sighs. 'I would have come down to be with you.'

'It's a long way, Mum.'

'I could have stayed the night,' she says as she looks more closely at the scan. 'I'm glad you didn't find out the sex.'

'Matt didn't want to.'

'Hugo hasn't told me much about Matthew or why he left the flat? It doesn't sound as if they hit it off?'

I hear that familiar criticism in her tone. 'Oh no, Mum, they get on fine.'

I turn away to check on the vegetables. 'But I don't think it's ever much fun being gooseberry.' I see us arguing in the kitchen, Hugo handing me the leaflets on addiction, me throwing them in his face. God, I miss him, I miss him, but . . . 'Anyway, he wanted to move in with his girlfriend.'

'Rosie's charming,' she says. 'They came to stay last weekend.'

Thankfully we hear a key in the lock and Matt sweeps into the kitchen with some flowers, striding straight over to my mother and kissing her on both cheeks. 'How lovely to meet you, Mrs Stephens,' he says, clutching her hand. 'I'm so sorry I'm late. The traffic was appalling.' Matt has clearly showered and shaved at the gym and is wearing a smart pair of trousers with a freshly ironed white shirt. I can smell his aftershave. He's scrubbed up almost as well as this flat. I always fancy him when he wears white shirts.

'I've heard so much about you,' he says to Mum. 'And I'm sorry we haven't been able to visit you in Norfolk.' What an act! I'll give him that. 'I don't know if Polly mentioned this to you, but I've been embroiled in planning disputes, which . . .' he turns to me, 'are all sorted! Permission finally came through today, Polly. All systems go!'

'Oh, what a relief!' I say before he sweeps me into his arms and kisses me.

'How's my gorgeous bambino or bambina?' He touches my bump. 'Isn't your daughter looking blooming marvellous, Mrs Stephens?'

I realise Mum has barely said a word since Matthew arrived and began his Oscar-winning performance. She's looking at him as if he's *nothing* like what she'd expected.

'Yes,' she says at last. 'Do call me Gina.'

Over supper Mum asks Matt how long he's been in property development. 'Not long, about five years. I started off small with my first flat, ex-council. From little acorns do big oak trees grow. It's all about buying the right house at the right price. It's not a game for the faint-hearted, but if you do your homework right, Mrs Stephens . . .'

Mum sniffs. 'Please call me Gina.'

'There are a lot of cowboys out there,' he continues as

I'm pushing my broccoli around the plate, 'but I've always been able to spot a good deal.'

'What did you do before all this?' Mum asks.

'Good question. I was an estate agent, for my sins. I learned a lot about the market, but I didn't like being a small fish in the big tank. I'm living the dream being my own boss now.'

How many more clichés can Mum take?

As Matt fills her in on how he's going to extend and modernise the Wandsworth house with a high-spec kitchen, underfloor heating and a basement conversion with a cinema room, Mum begins to look sceptical. 'I'm sorry, Matthew, I don't mean to interrupt,' she says, 'but my husband and I were watching the news about Northern Rock collapsing and we're a bit worried about the economy. Do you think this is a safe investment?'

'Oh it's fine, Mrs Stephens, that was an isolated incident.'

I excuse myself, saying I need the loo, before rushing into my bedroom, opening the wardrobe and lifting the lid off one of my old shoeboxes. I take a bottle out. I'll just have one sip, that's all I need. Lots of women drink the odd glass of wine when they're pregnant. Trust Mum to put a dampener on Matt's good news. I'm not sure she likes him. She really liked George, the doctor, who accused me of being an alcoholic. What a nerve! I swig down another mouthful before reluctantly putting the bottle back. I sneak into the bathroom, pull the chain and gurgle some mouthwash.

When I head back into the kitchen I ask if either of them would like seconds.

'It's delicious,' Mum replies, though declines, saying she's full. Matt tucks into a second helping of quiche, claiming he's famished.

'So, how are the baby arrangements?' she asks, before adding, 'Polly, don't bite your nails.'

I take my finger away from my mouth.

'I thought, Polly, while I was here, we could go shopping for a few bits and bobs, after you've finished work.'

'That's a great idea,' says Matt.

'I'd love to buy you something you really need. Maybe a cot or pram, Polly?'

'That's incredibly kind,' chips in Matt again.

I nod. 'We haven't bought a cot yet.' We haven't bought anything, but I can't tell Mum that.

'I was wondering,' she begins tentatively as I clear the plates, 'what you're planning for the future? Will you be buying a place of your own, Matthew?'

'Well, I reckon this Wandsworth project will take six to nine months, Mrs Stephens, so after the baby's born and I've sold the house, we'll take a view, won't we, honey?'

'Absolutely,' I say, not listening to a word, thinking only about my shoebox. I touch Matt's shoulder. 'Lots to think about. Very exciting.'

'It's important to make plans,' Mum advises. 'Once the

baby is born, it's exhausting so it would be nice to be settled, wouldn't it?'

'Agreed,' he says.

'And will you go back to teaching?' Mum asks me.

'Of course,' Matt says. 'I've got enough to cover us and then when I sell the place in Wandsworth . . . It's all under control, Mrs Stephens.'

'I want to be a full-time mother,' I say, touching my bump. 'At least to begin with, but I love my job, Mum.' I think affectionately of my class, of Lottie calling me Miss Polly. 'I'd really miss it if I gave up.'

Mum plays with the edge of her napkin. 'Your father and I were wondering about wedding plans, too? Do you think you might . . . ?'

'Oh, Mum!' I burst out.

'That's further down the line,' says Matt. 'Not so sure she can wear the white gown now.'

Mum looks stony-faced.

'Excuse me,' I say, slipping out of the room, blaming my weak bladder.

I sit on the edge of my bed and take another deep breath. I wish Mum would go. I knew she'd bring up wedding plans. Having a baby before marriage goes against everything she and my father stand for. Quietly I lift the lid off the shoebox.

'Polly?' Mum stands in the doorway, staring at the bottle in my hand.

I stand up, trapped. 'I was just . . . er . . .'

'You're drinking?'

'I've had a sip, that's all.' It's that nervous laugh again. 'It's not what it looks like.'

'Why are you hiding in here then?'

'I'm not.'

'Polly, what's going on?'

'Nothing.' I smile. 'Matthew's great, isn't he?'

'Polly, you're pregnant.'

'I've had a couple of sips,' I insist again.

'Hugo mentioned . . .'

'Oh, here we go again. You always believe what Hugo says.'

'He's worried. Be honest with me. Are you drinking a lot?'

'Can we not do this now? Matt will be wondering where we are.'

'He's not right for you.'

'Excuse me?'

'He's full of hot air.'

Angry, I say, 'I can't believe we're having this conversation.'

Mum grabs my arm, stops me from leaving the room. 'Polly, listen to me, you've got to listen.'

'Oh, what do you care, Mum! You've never really cared about me, so why the hell should I listen to you now?'

Mum stands back. 'That's not fair.'

'You can't waltz in here and pick my life apart.'

'But I don't trust this man . . .'

'Well, you're wrong.'

'You need help.'

'Help? What's Hugo been saying . . . ?'

'It's not too late to . . .'

'What's going on?' Matt says, glancing from my mother to me.

'Nothing,' I reply, dusting down my dress. 'Mum was just leaving, weren't you?'

23

It's the Easter holidays, spring is in the air and Louis, Emily, Ben and I are taking Nellie out for her first walk on Primrose Hill. Nellie is eleven weeks old now, vaccinated and ready to socialise.

'She's my dog!' says Emily, snatching the lead from Louis.

Ben pulls them apart. 'Now listen here, we'll go home if you two carry on like two old fishwives. Take it in turns.'

'You can hold her,' says Louis, letting go of the lead.

'You can have her.' Emily gives Louis the lead.

Ben turns to me in disbelief. 'I was expecting World War Three.'

'Well done,' I whisper. 'I wouldn't like to get on the wrong side of you.'

Nellie is sniffing every blade of grass and bounding up to every single dog. We pass weekend joggers, a dog walker with five Jack Russell terriers in a variety of fashion accessories scurrying in front of her. Nellie approaches a black-and-tan Rottweiler wearing a thick studded collar, off the lead. Ben and I glance at one another. 'Is he friendly?' I burst out, unable to keep my cool when I see the dog licking his or her lips.

'He's fine.' The owner shrugs. 'Rocky doesn't *normally* go for puppies.'

Nellie is rolling on to her back submissively as Rocky towers over her.

Emily must sense my fear as she jerks the lead to pull Nellie away and on we go. '*Normally* isn't good enough,' I mutter to Ben.

'We were told at puppy school not to judge on size, Polly,' he says.

I raise an eyebrow. 'Size is always important.'

He smiles. 'Is that right?'

Ben decides it's time to let Nellie off the lead. He rattles the treats. 'Remember our special call, Emily.'

'I don't want to let her go, Uncle Ben, not today.'

'Trust me.' Ben unclips the lead.

Unleashed, Nellie springs into action, racing up the hill, lots of dog walkers watching and admiring her and commenting on her large ears. 'Uncle Ben!' Emily says in distress as Nellie becomes a smaller and smaller black dot.

'Let her play!' Ben calls out, trying to sound calm, but when Nellie tears down another path, chasing the flight of a bird, Ben picks up pace and starts to sing 'Nellie the Elephant' as he rattles the fishy treats.

Emily is crying. Ben sprints like a madman but Nellie is hell bent on enjoying her freedom. Just as Ben's about to seize her collar she rockets off in another direction, towards a dog hopping along on three legs. It's like some awful cartoon and if it weren't Nellie, it would be funny.

'We must have looked as if we'd been let out of the loony bin for the day,' I say, later that afternoon when Louis and Emily are watching *Mary Poppins*. Nellie is fast asleep in her pen, conked out on her back with her paws suspended in the air, and Ben and I are still recovering.

'The gentle stroll didn't go quite the way I'd hoped,' admits Ben, sitting down at the kitchen island and moving his paperwork to one side. Since we've met he's taken on a couple of new clients, one a graphic designer, the other has just set up a kitchen company. I pull out a bar stool, and sit down next to him. He rests his elbows on the table, turns to me suggestively.

'What?' I say.

'I need to get laid. Badly.'

'Right. Where did that come from?'

'A very frustrated man.'

'Give Gabriella a call.' I hop off the stool, push my chest towards him, 'Benjamin,' I say in a strong Italian accent, pretending to be carrying a dish. 'I bring you my special spaghetti bolognese, just for you.'

Ben laughs as he digs into his back pocket, producing his wallet. He takes out a small scented card with a number on it.

'She gave you her number?' I'm shocked.

'I met this woman.'

'When? Who?' I notice I'm a tiny bit put out that he hasn't told me about her until now.

I discover he met this Naomi girl in the library when he was helping Emily choose a book. She's a single mum, has two boys aged eight and six. She divorced a year ago. 'I know I said I wasn't going to have a fling but . . .' He stares at the number.

'Ben, it's just sex. Call her.'

Ben sings James Brown's 'Sex Machine'.

'Call her,' I repeat watching him dance now. 'What have you got to lose? Besides, how can she resist your moves?'

He sits down. 'Maybe. How about you, Polly? Are you into anyone right now?

'Being a single mum is a great contraceptive, although clearly not for Naomi. Is she pretty?'

'Yeah. Very. When was your last relationship?'

'Over a year ago.' I tell Ben briefly about David the lawyer. 'He loved the theatre, the opera, ballet.' I picture us walking hand in hand around museums. 'He treated me to all the good things in life.'

'So what was the problem?'

'There wasn't enough snap, crackle and pop.'

I can tell Ben is amused by me. 'You can't make yourself fall in love with someone,' I continue. 'There has to be passion, at least to begin with. He was lovely, but I think I went out with him because he felt safe,' I say quietly. 'He was the opposite to Matthew. Does that make sense?'

Ben nods.

'How about you?' I ask.

'I fell in love in my early twenties. Juliette. She was half French. Beautiful. She had long dark hair like yours and she was a bright, 'seize the moment' kind of girl. She worked for a Swiss airline, ran the office, thrived on stress. We lived together while I worked in the City and it was amazing for the first few years, we were a good match, but . . . she didn't like the man I was becoming,' he admits. 'The truth is the City sucks. There's a lack of culture, there's greed, sharp elbows, people earning a lot of money but with no imagination about how to spend it. She became bored with me. I became bored with me.'

'If you could have anything you wanted, Ben, what would it be?'

'Emily to be happy.'

'That's lovely, but what do you want for you?'

'Live on a tropical island with a nice normal woman. You?'

'Wow, the same, please.'

'Ah, you're a lesbian.'

I nudge him playfully.

'There's really no one on the scene?' he asks again.

'It's complicated with Louis. I don't want him to meet someone, get attached and then we break up.' I glance at my little boy on the sofa, begin to sing 'Meet me in St Louis, Louis.' It was my favourite song when I was little. Dad used to sing it to Hugo and me on long car journeys or we'd sing it as we rowed towards the sunken boat. I stop, aware of Ben's gaze.

'I like this,' he says with a smile. 'Us hanging out and singing songs. It's funny. I haven't had a girl "friend",' he uses his fingers to make speech-marks, 'before. I've never had someone like you in my life, Polly, someone I can talk to.'

'Me neither.'

'I love spending time with you.'

'Me too.'

'Great. So maybe we can be friends with benefits?'

Ben laughs when I hit him. But then for a split second I do imagine us together. Of course it's crossed my mind, just as it's crossed Janey's, Aunt Viv's and Hugo's. Do I fancy him? Maybe I do, just a little, but am I confusing it with enjoying his attention? I'd never forgive myself if it all went wrong and I lost this friendship, which has become one of the most important things in both Louis's and my life.

'Worth a try,' he shrugs. 'Guess I'll have to make do with a mint tea.' As he switches on the kettle he says more seriously, 'You hardly ever talk about Matthew. What was he like?'

'He was . . .' I chew my lip, 'messed up. He had problems.

What hurts me most is Louis is the one who suffers.'

'What was he like when you first met him?' His tone is surprisingly gentle.

'Exciting. Different. I thought I was in love with him. Things began to fall apart when I fell pregnant. I made the classic mistake of thinking a child would change him. I regret so much.'

'Don't regret, Polly, just learn. It's what my shrink says.'

'Mine too. What a pair we are.'

We remain quiet for a minute. 'Whatever this Matthew guy did to you, you have Louis and he's a great boy and I . . .' He hands me my cup of tea. 'Well, I wouldn't have met you both.'

Ben is right. Matthew gave me nothing and everything.

24

15 September 2008

It's six o'clock on Monday morning when Louis wakes me up. Foggy-headed, I heave myself out of bed, leaving Matthew snoring, and tiptoe out of the room.

My little boy is almost nine months old. I haven't returned to work. I'm not ready. Besides, when I looked into childcare costs it made little financial sense to rush back to my job. I settle him down in the sitting room with a bottle of formula and sing our song quietly, 'Meet me in St Louis, Louis'. I gave up breastfeeding after a few weeks. I tried, but Louis cried so much, and then I became frantic with worry that either I didn't have enough for him or that my milk wasn't good enough. Was the alcohol in my blood affecting him? I had to stop; it was causing too much stress for both of us. I'm much happier now feeding him from a bottle. That way I'm in control and know how much milk he's taking. I'm a good mother, I tell myself. There's no need to feel guilty;

lots of mothers don't breastfeed. I love him, deeply. That's what counts.

His birth is a blur.

I don't remember getting to the hospital, but I do recall the relief of seeing Hugo. Aunt Viv had flown back from LA to visit the family a month before for Christmas, and had forced the two of us to meet. 'What do I have to do? Knock your heads together! I *lost* my brother, Polly. You have a chance to make things right with Hugo.'

As Louis gulps down the bottled milk, I remember the pain, the agony of pushing and nothing happening. I hated Matthew with a passion. He had done this to my body and the miserable sod couldn't even be bothered to show up! He's more interested in doing up houses than me. When I'd called Matt to say the baby was on its way, his phone went to voicemail. He was in Brighton, visiting some rundown warehouse that was up for sale. Immediately I'd called Hugo. He was the only person I wanted to see.

Hours later and still no baby, I was wheeled down to theatre, papers flung in my face. I couldn't focus on the small type; it was some three to four sides of single lines, way too much information for someone half-drunk and about to give birth. Hugo told me to sign it; it's a consent form. I didn't really care if I died; just get me out of this pain. I'd managed to laugh at chubby Hugo alongside me, dressed in his scrubs and plastic blue shoes. 'I could give George Clooney a run for his money,' he was saying, feeling for my hand. He knew I'd been drinking, I could tell, but he didn't say a word. I'd murmured to one of the nurses that I'd been out for an early Christmas drink, that's all.

Nine months after the birth, Hugo is renting a flat off Baker Street, close to the BBC and is still dating Rosie. 'We love Uncle Hugo, don't we?' I say to Louis, rocking him in my arms. In his free time he's been writing a blog about being blind. He's decided he wants to raise awareness. 'Not every blind person needs a white stick or a guide dog. I want people to understand what it means.' It made me think back to Matt saying, 'You can't even see the action!' Why didn't I break up from him there and then?

Janey is still working at her film location company and is single again. She and I have become even closer than before. I could not have done without her support. Often she comes round in the evenings, where inevitably we stay up too late drinking and putting the world to rights. 'Why did we open another bottle?' she groans the following morning. 'I don't know how you do it, Polly. At least I only have myself to look after.'

Aunt Viv has left her American film-making boyfriend. She has moved back to London for good. The news came as a shock to me. She'd seemed, on email, so happy in LA, but now she claims the relationship had run its course. She was tired of being an extension of his life and besides none of Gareth's films were being made. 'I miss tea and scones. I even miss the rain and snow in spring. My travelling days are over. I want to settle down close to my family, to you and Hugo. I want to get to know Louis.'

She rents a tiny flat close to Primrose Hill. She's met a Frenchman called Jean.

My mother visits occasionally. She's enjoying spending time with Louis, but our relationship is strained. She tolerates Matthew, just as Hugo does, but every now and then she can't help herself. 'I've never seen *that man* wash up or change a nappy,' she says. 'What does *that man* do all day? When is he going to sell this wretched house in Wandsworth so the two of you can buy your own place? I'm worried he's going to end up saddled with debt. You are going to buy somewhere soon, aren't you, Polly? Or at least rent somewhere with more space,' she says, gesturing to the washing drying on plastic racks in the cramped sitting room.

The Wandsworth project is finally on the market. It has taken a lot longer than predicted to finish. Six to nine months stretched to almost a year. During that time Mum and Dad were ringing regularly, banging on about the credit crunch. When I tentatively questioned him about why it was taking so long he became aggressive. He told me they'd discovered dry rot under the bath. It had spread like a virus and this setback had cost him a fortune. When I mentioned Mum's concerns he dismissed her as a boring old nag and became defensive about the economy. Even though it's on the market now, I'm nervous about how much cash he has haemorrhaged into this one property when we need the money ourselves, but he's convinced he'll get the money back with interest. 'There are plenty of rich people out there with cash to splash: this place will be snapped up.'

Matt interrupts my thoughts when he enters the room. 'You look pretty awful,' is the first thing he says to me, turning on the television.

'You wouldn't look so great if you had to get up three times in the night.'

Matt opens the fridge, takes out the milk and drinks it straight out of the bottle. He spits it into the sink. 'Bloody hell, Polly, it's off.'

'Well, I asked you to get some more on your way home last night.'

'I've got a full-on day today, I'm trying to get this house sold for us and . . .'

'We're live from Canary Wharf on a dramatic day for the financial markets,' says the news reporter.

'You say full-on, but what are you *actually* doing, Matt? It's up for sale, there's nothing . . .'

'Quiet,' he snaps.

'The financial news overnight was grim,' the reporter continues. 'Lehman Brothers, the fourth-largest US investment bank, has filed for bankruptcy.'

'My day is pretty full-on too,' I continue. 'Having a baby to look after isn't exactly a picnic.'

'Shut up, Polly!'

' . . . Merrill Lynch has agreed to be taken over by Bank of America . . .'

'I mean, you could at least come home to bath Louis. You don't have to go to the gym every night . . .'

'POLLY!' Matt is closer to the television now, waving his arm aggressively in my direction.

'. . . Insurer AIG is trying to raise funds to save itself from collapse . . . the effect on the markets has been predictable: stocks have tumbled in value, and banking shares have been hardest hit.'

'Oh,' I say, finally shutting up and looking at Matt. He's staring at the screen, the colour draining from his face.

'The big question is,' the reporter asks, 'what went wrong and, crucially, who might be next?'

I jiggle Louis in my arms. 'Matt, what does this mean?'

'This is unbelievable,' he mutters.

'We can still sell the house, can't we?' I ask, fear lodging in my stomach. Louis wrestles in my arms. 'It won't affect your deal, will it?'

Matt turns the television off. 'Of course it will! If we're about to enter a recession people are going to be cautious, aren't they! I've borrowed up to my eyeballs and if I can't get even close to the asking price I'm screwed, Polly!'

Louis starts to cry.

'I swear,' he says, walking past us, 'I don't want to see you or hear that baby cry until I have my fucking coffee.' He storms out of the kitchen. I shudder when I hear the door slam. I have no idea if he's coming back. I stare at the head-line band at the bottom of the television screen. 'BREAKING NEWS,' it flashes. 'Lehman Brothers has crashed.'

Three weeks later, and I'm drying Louis after a bath. I'm so relieved to get to 6 p.m. because it's bath-time and bed. After a quick dunk, I dress Louis in his pyjamas and read him a story, rushing to get to the end, before retreating as fast as I can into the kitchen to pour myself a glass of wine. Our landlord called today. Matt promised he'd paid this month's rent, but he hasn't. He wants to be paid by the end of the week. Mum keeps on calling too, sounding increas-ingly desperate as she asks what the news is on the house. I stare blankly ahead. Janey is coming over later. What am I going to cook her? I open the fridge and stare at the empty shelves. I could give her . . . I pick up the jar . . . Louis's pureed parsnip. Takeaway it is.

Janey arrives an hour later, with a bottle of wine. 'I've had a shit day,' she says on my doorstep. 'What's happened?' I ask, inviting her inside.

She gestures that her head's been cut off. 'Given the axe. Made redundant.'

'Oh, Janey. Oh, I'm so sorry. Let's open this.' I shake the bottle at her. 'Quick.'

She follows me into the kitchen, the sink filled with pots and pans. She notices me chucking the empty bottle that

I'd polished off earlier, into the black binliner. Sensing she's shocked by the mess, I say, 'Sorry, hectic day.'

'Here, let me help.'

'No! Honestly it's not normally like this,' I lie, pushing her away from the sink. 'Anyway, tell me about your job.'

'My ex-job you mean. We were all warned. Every single one of us was holding on to our chairs. It was like the gallows, Polly. In some ways it's a relief, but what am I going to do? Oh, God,' she groans, taking the wine gratefully.

'You'll find another job. Something better will turn up.'

She shrugs. 'How's your day been? I hope better than mine.'

I want to scream, 'The same as the day before! Louis and I went to the park. We fed the ducks. I called a few friends to see if they were around for lunch, but everyone was busy so I came home, opened a bottle of wine and fell asleep in front of the television. 'OK,' is what I end up saying, not able to own up to the loneliness. 'We went to the park.'

'Any news on you know what?'

'Nothing.'

'Oh shit.'

'It's a disaster,' I tell Janey. 'I don't have much left in my savings now. I don't know how we're going to pay the bills and the rent.'

'Could you go back to work? I thought that was always the plan?' she says tentatively.

'Have you seen how much childcare costs?'

'Yes, but . . .'

'I'll get a new job,' I say, 'when he goes to nursery.'

'What about Matthew? Where is he?'

'Who knows? He won't answer my calls; he's not inter-ested in Louis.'

It's a relief I can talk to Janey about Matt. I can't be honest with anyone else, but with my best friend I don't need to wear a mask all the time.

'That's not good enough. What happens if you can't sell the bloody house?'

I refill our glasses. 'I don't want to think about it.' I pick up the takeaway menus. 'What do you fancy? Thai or Indian?'

'Oh come on, stay,' I plead with Janey after supper, opening another bottle of wine. 'It's only 10.30.' I plonk myself back down on the sofa and refill our glasses.

'I'm shattered, need an early night.' She gets up. I push her back down.

'Just one more! Come on, you can't go yet.'

'I don't want any more. And you need to stop too,' she says, raising her voice. 'I've lost my job, Polly, and you're . . . well you're in a mess. This . . .' she picks up the bottle of wine, shakes it at me, 'isn't always the answer.'

'Yes it is. It solves everything,' I slur.

'I'm tired. I don't want a hangover tomorrow. I need to work out what I'm going to do next and how I'm going to pay my bills, and so do you.'

'It'll be fine,' I say.

'You don't get it, do you? You don't listen. Nothing is fine,' she says. 'You and Matt can't carry on like this. He's *useless*, Polly, and you're not coping and . . . look at this place. It's a tip.'

The words are whirring around me.

'I love going out, I love partying,' she says, 'you know that, but sometimes we have to take some responsibility for ourselves . . .' She gets up, gathers her coat. 'You're drinking way too much.' She stares at me, waiting for a response.

'It's all I've got.'

We hear Louis cry.

'No, it's not,' she snaps back.

Slowly I stir myself off the sofa and stagger across the room. 'Go then, I'll see to him. Enjoy your early night.'

Janey grabs me by the arm. 'Polly, where are you?' She shakes me. 'Where's the old Polly? I know how hard things are but you're seriously worrying me.'

She follows me into Louis's bedroom. Clumsily I lift my son out of his cot and rock him from side to side. 'Is Matt treating you OK? If things are really bad you need to talk to him. Is this why you're drinking so much?'

I shrug. 'I wanted one more, no big deal. If you need to go, just go.'

'Fine.' Janey kisses Louis goodbye. When I hear the front door shut I begin to cry, holding Louis close.

*

I hear noise. Half-asleep I feel for the light switch and see Matt, crashed out beside me, fully dressed. 'Where have you been?'

'Out,' he murmurs.

'Clearly. Where?'

'Just out.'

'That's not an answer.'

'Well it's all you're getting.'

'I've been trying to call you all day.'

Matt rolls on to his other side, his back facing me. 'Not now, Polly.'

'Yes, now. I'm worried.'

He stands up, walks out of the room. Next I hear the bathroom tap water running.

I stand at the door, watching him splash his face with water.

'Go back to bed,' he says.

'Is there any news on the house?'

'You know there isn't.' He grips the edge of the sink, his head bowed.

'I don't know. I don't know anything because you don't talk to me. If we're in trouble . . .'

'Don't push me, Polly.'

'I have to know! We have a son! Why can't you sell that house? What's going on?' Why, why, why?

He turns to me.

'OK, if you want to know, I missed a couple of payments

. . . I can't pay the mortgage and the bank's decided to call in the debt. Happy now?'

'Well, that's really going to help,' he says when he finds me in the kitchen draining the last of the wine.

I feel sick with worry. All I want is to pull the duvet over my head; escape this life. 'We'll be homeless, you'll be made bankrupt . . .' I say. 'It's all one big giant mess. I should have listened to my friends, to Hugo, to Mum . . .'

'Oh shut up, Polly!' He grabs the bottle from me. 'Who the fuck are you to criticise? Call yourself a mother? You're nothing but a drunk.'

But I'm not listening. I'm far away. 'We'll be homeless . . .'

'Shut up!'

'. . . out on the street.'

I feel the force of his hand against my cheek.

The sting of his slap.

'Oh, Polly, I'm sorry, I'm sorry,' he says, pulling me into his arms. 'I love you,' he's saying repeatedly, words I'd longed to hear when we first met, but now, never have I felt so desolate and alone.

25

Jim, Ben, Nellie and I have dropped the children off at school on Monday morning and are sitting at our usual corner table in Chamomile. Jim is tired this morning. He tells us he had a weekend from hell. It started on Friday night when he had to go to a corporate event with his wife.

'What does she do again?' Ben asks.

'She's a lawyer.'

'So what was so awful about Friday?' I ask.

'These events are like endurance tests.' Jim stirs his tea. 'These men see me as the boring old stay-at-home dad.'

'I'm sure they don't,' I say, imagining that's what many of them do think.

'They do. I can almost hear them thinking, 'God, what do we talk to this freak about?''

'Look at me,' chips in Ben. 'If half the guys I used to work with could see me walking Nellie and drinking tea that smells of' – he lifts his mug and gives it a sniff – 'compost, they'd laugh, but I don't care.'

Jim nods. 'I know I shouldn't care, I should rise above it, but it's hard not to feel irritated when they come up to me and say, "I wouldn't know where to begin changing a nappy," or this one guy clamps me on the back and says, "Where's your apron, Jimmy boy?"'

'If I had it, I'd strangle you with it,' I suggest, making Ben laugh.

'I go "ha ha ha" when all I want to say is, "You know what, buddy, I could do your job standing on my head, but could you do mine?"'

Jim goes on to tell us that Theo, his youngest, was sick the entire weekend. The first time was at the fish counter at Sainsbury's; the second at the cashier's checkout. He managed to get Theo and Maisy home, but Theo threw up in the car. After a day of staying indoors, they all developed cabin fever and Maisy wanted to kill her brother with her toy rolling pin.

'Poor you, not fun,' I say. 'Where was Camilla?'

'Office. She doesn't normally work weekends, but she had this deadline.'

'Would you like to swap back?' Ben asks.

'No. All I'd like is a little recognition here and there. I know it's the same for mums, so why should men be hero-worshipped for doing the same job, but . . . anyway, enough whingeing,' he says as my mobile rings.

I dig into my handbag. Again it's a number I don't recognise.

'Hello?' Pause. 'Hello?'

'What?' Ben and Jim ask when I hang up.

'I've been getting these calls. It's probably nothing,' I say, trying to disguise my concern. I put the phone down on the table. 'What were you saying, Jim?'

'What kind of calls?' Ben asks.

'They hang up. It's only been a couple of times . . .'

'Oh listen, I get *loads* of crank calls,' Jim says. 'I've had deep breathing, a whistle blowing, deathly silences, you name it, I've had it. Too many bored people out there.'

'Have you tried calling the number back, Polly?' Ben suggests.

'Nothing happens. It keeps on ringing. It's probably nothing, like Jim says, a hoax or wrong number.'

'Sure.' Ben nods with me.

'Gather you're going to Hugo's concert tonight, Ben?' Jim says, moving on.

When my mobile rings again, both Jim and Ben stop talking abruptly and stare at it. I don't normally feel so relieved when I see my mother's name on the screen.

Hugo's concert is in St Peter's Church, a tangerine-coloured building in Notting Hill. '*I want to meet this so-called friend you're spending so much time with*,' Hugo had said.

When Ben waits outside the front entrance he almost doesn't recognise me because I'm wearing a dress and heels. It's a simple red dress with long sleeves and lace buttons.

'You look good,' he says, taking off his shades. 'I like your . . .' He looks at me quizzically again, as if unsure what it is I've done to myself. 'Your hair,' he decides. 'I like it down.'

'Thanks. You look good too.' I gesture to his pale-pink shirt and dark jacket.

He grins, giving me his arm.

'You know, Ben, you're really very handsome when you smile.'

Inside the church, there's a buzz of activity. We head towards the front, squeezing ourselves into a pew next to an elderly couple.

'How long does this last?' Ben scans the Mozart Requiem programme.

'Oh, at least three hours, with no interval and prayers at the end.'

He turns to me, about to protest, but then sees me smiling. 'You are so easy to tease, Benjamin,' I say, looking over to the group of singers at the side of the church, dressed in black tie and trying to line up into some kind of order, ready to take their position on the stage. Hugo tells me their leader in charge of the seating plan is always in a state of meltdown minutes before a concert, and how they pull it together is anyone's guess.

There's a buzz of anticipation as members of the orchestra settle down in front of their music stands and begin to tune their instruments. The choir begins to file onto the stage with their music folders. 'There's Hugo,' I say, pointing to the tallest member, towering over his colleagues like an enormous palm tree, his bow tie skew-whiff. 'And that's his ex, Rosie,' I say, nodding towards a blonde woman near the front. They split up amicably when Louis was about two. 'I didn't want to marry her,' was Hugo's simple explanation. 'I had to be honest.'

Hugo is a bass, so he takes a seat on the back row next to a small balding man with spectacles. The choir is like a bus, or AA for that matter, filled with a motley crew of passengers of all shapes and sizes.

'I couldn't stand up there,' I say.

'Why not?'

'Well I can't sing for starters. At school they used to tell me to mouth the words during assembly. I sound like a strangled cat. I can shatter glass with my vocal cords.'

'You can't be that bad.'

'Trust me.'

'Would you get up on stage for a million quid and sing a solo?'

I hesitate. 'No. Seriously, I cannot sing and the audience would pay a million quid *not* to hear me. Hugo got all the singing talent in our family.'

'Unfair.'

'And all the height.'

'Double unfair. But you obviously got the beauty and the brains.'

I smile, aware he's still looking at me. He turns when the plump conductor walks to the rostrum to a round of polite applause. There's a hush. The concert begins.

Midway through the Requiem I forget where I am. As I watch Hugo, a feeling of pride swells inside me. When I was drinking I was never present for anything, not even the birth of my own son. Tonight, I'd have made some excuse as to why I couldn't be here just so I could be in the pub. I'm so relieved things have changed, that I have changed. When one of the professional soloists is singing I am in awe of her voice and beauty. She is willowy and blonde and wearing a pale-turquoise silk dress. She moves her body with the music. How can it be that when she opens her mouth this amazing pure sound comes out? Where does this gift come from? I picture Louis and me singing along to his *Annie* CD at home. When I sing 'Tomorrow', Louis laughs and puts his hands over his ears in protest.

During the Lacrimosa I glance sideways at Ben. He's sitting quietly, completely absorbed. Towards the end there are tears in his eyes. When the choir takes a bow the audience claps and cheers, Ben and me included.

As Ben and I wait for Hugo to get changed we remain seated. 'I didn't think I'd enjoy that,' Ben says emotionally. 'In fact I was dreading it.' Soon we are the only two left in the church. 'Ben, are you OK?'

He begins to cry, apologising and telling me to ignore him.

'Ben?' I touch his shoulder. 'What is it?'

'I was thinking about Grace. She used to tell me I was a Philistine, you see I've never appreciated classical music. She'd listen to Mozart while she cooked, or a bit of the other guy, Bach, I think. Tonight made me think of her . . . I miss her, Polly,' he says, his voice trembling.

I rub his back.

'All I was thinking was how she won't see Emily again. She won't see her daughter grow up. We didn't have much of a childhood. A rich but empty one. It would have been better to live in a caravan with next to nothing but with parents that were around rather than live the way we did. We only had each other and now she's gone. The kindest and most gentle woman who never resented the world or felt bruised by the hits she was given. All she wanted was to be a good mother and even that was taken away from her. Emily should have a mum, not me.' He curls his hand into a fist, 'I miss her and I'm scared because she was all the family I had. There's so much you don't know about me, Polly, so much bad stuff.'

'Come here,' I say, pulling him towards me. He clutches my arm, falls into my embrace. I hold him while he sobs, stroking his back like a child. I cry with him. 'You're a good man, Ben, don't ever think you're not, and Grace would be so proud of you, I know she would.' When his breathing subsides he looks up at me. 'Don't tell Hugo I cried. I feel such an idiot. Perhaps you should have taken Jim,' he suggests, making both of us smile. 'A safer bet.'

'Perhaps. But who wants a safe bet?'

Ben, Hugo and I find a table in a crowded Italian restaurant on Westbourne Grove, close to St Peter's Church.

After Ben and I heap praise on Hugo's choir, me adding that the bass soloist was hot and I want his number, I read out the menu for Hugo. 'Four seasons,' he says when I come to the first pizza on the list. 'That'll do.'

A slim waitress in a black apron takes our order. 'Any wine?' she asks, her pen poised.

'No,' we all say at the same time.

Briskly she clears away our wine glasses.

As we wait for our food, Ben asks Hugo about his radio show.

'I'm glad you asked, you might have some ideas. Next week we're talking about all the things we'd do if money and time were no object.'

'Oh, that's a good one,' I say. 'I'd take myself off to Ballymaloe in Ireland.'

I tell them it's this amazing cookery school in the middle of nowhere. 'I'd love to grow my own food, go out in a boat and catch crayfish.'

'I can't think of anything worse,' says Hugo.

'Me neither,' claims Ben. 'I've only had to learn to cook

because of Emily, and when I say cook, it's more like pressing a button on the microwave.'

'What would you two do then?'

'Cricket,' says Ben without even thinking. 'Doesn't matter what I'm doing, I will stop and watch a match wherever I am, whoever I'm with.'

'Even if you were in bed with Kelly Brook?' Hugo asks, mischief in his eyes.

'I'd still stop. Well, maybe not.' He laughs. 'Played it at school, fell in love with the game. Granny and I would watch the Test matches in the summer holidays with orange juice and a plate of choccie bics. She'd send me newspaper cuttings, too, of our favourite players. I used to play a lot down in Hampshire, with a few of my sister's friends. We formed a club. Travelled all round the place in the summer playing matches.'

Hugo tells us he'd live in the mountains and ski all day long.

'I don't mean to be rude,' says Ben, grabbing a bread roll from the basket, 'but how can you ski without knocking someone over or flying off the edge of the cliff to your death? Isn't it terrifying?'

'Actually, Hugo won two silver medals in a World Championships,' I say proudly.

'How very British of you to come second,' quips Ben. 'Who came first?'

'Some Swiss wanker,' Hugo says, making us all laugh.

'Well, first the worst, second the best,' says Ben. 'I'm impressed. You must have started young.'

'At school. I was picked for the British Ski Club. It was all about getting people like me up into the mountains to give us confidence. My racing career began when I was about fourteen. I had a guide in front but apart from that I just went for it. I'm a speed freak,' Hugo admits. 'Got the scars to prove it.' He points to the faded scar above his left eyebrow. 'For me skiing is the substitute for not being able to get behind a wheel. I love cars, so it's ironic that I can't drive. Now that would be an accident waiting to happen, but on a mountain the reflective light is great, I can see much more than I can sitting opposite you.'

'I'm tall, dark and devastatingly handsome, that's all you need to know.'

They laugh, a natural chemistry between them. 'Anyway, skiing is one of the only ways I can throw caution to the wind. I have my guide yelling left and right as we turn, and I go hell for leather.'

'I've seen him,' I chip in. 'He's like a high-speed train.'

'Some people imagine "the blind" sit at home and read Braille, live in the dark and hobble around on a white stick.'

'Guilty,' says Ben, raising his hand. 'Not about the hobbling, but I wouldn't have put skiing with blind people.'

'Don't worry. But what you said earlier, about it being terrifying? I was petrified before the start of the downhill race

215

and I was pretty scared when I fell down a crevasse while training on a glacier in Italy. It's about trust and freedom. Skiing conquered a lot of my fears. Both of you know all about that.'

Aunt Viv slips on her coat.

'Thanks so much for babysitting,' Ben says. Aunt Viv babysat Louis, Emily and Nellie at my flat tonight.

'Any time,' she replies, kissing us both goodnight. 'So glad you two had fun.'

After Aunt Viv has gone, I show Ben the photograph of Hugo skiing, all six foot four of him, donning his skin-tight yellow plastic suit and crash hat to race the downhill in Colorado.

'How does he get home?'

'By reference,' I say. 'He knows the bus routes, that's fine, and he knows there are six trees along his road and his door is just before reaching tree number five. When we were children we'd count the stairs together and after a while he knew the house off by heart. It's kind of the same in London. He knows little pockets. It's instinct more than anything. Often he'll catch cabs in the winter, but he hates that, says it's like throwing money down the gutter, but sometimes life is too short to get freezing cold and lost.'

'He's pretty special, your brother,' Ben says.

I place the photograph back on the mantelpiece. 'Yes. Yes, he is.'

After a mug of mint tea, we tiptoe into Louis's bedroom. I watch Ben carefully lift Emily out of bed. She was sleeping on our pull-out mattress. She wraps her slim arms around his neck. They look more together now; a puzzle that's beginning to fit.

'Is Ben Emily's dad now?' asks Louis when I kiss him goodnight.

'I thought you were asleep.' I sit down at the edge of his bed. 'Yes,' I add, 'he is.'

'Do you want to kiss Ben?'

'He's a friend, sweetheart.' I am aware I hesitated.

'Then he could live here, and he could be my dad too.'

'Oh, Louis.' I brush his cheek. 'Ben is a friend, just like Emily is your friend. He won't be moving in with us.'

'Emily wants you to be her mummy, that's what she said.'

For a second I'm flattered. 'I can't be Emily's mum, but I can be her friend,' I reassure him. 'Now, are you going to go to sleep?'

'Emily says her mum died in her sleep. You won't die in your sleep, will you, Mum?'

I lift the duvet, telling him to budge up. 'I'm not going anywhere,' I promise him.

26

I'm sitting outside my counsellor's office, waiting to be called in. Stephanie apologised, saying she was running late. I flick through a magazine of celebrities with toned bodies on the beach, only months after giving birth. I toss it back on to the coffee table. It's the summer holidays and for the next six weeks I'll need to juggle work with Louis. In a way, it'll be a relief to stop the grinding routine, no longer having to clock-watch to get to school on time.

As I continue to wait for Stephanie, I think about the past few months leading up to the end of the summer term. I have spent virtually every weekend with Ben. Neither one of us wish to go anywhere near a pub or bar at a weekend, and we'd prefer to give parties a wide berth unless they're for close friends or family, so we've naturally begun to do things together with the children. Recently we visited Grace's grave in Hampshire. We laid down flowers, Louis keeping aside a pink rose to give to Emily in case she was sad. We have seen the dinosaurs in the Natural History Museum and one

Sunday we went to the National Portrait Gallery and the children dressed up in costumes and learned all about the famous people in the paintings. Louis and Emily were fascinated to hear about Henry VIII chopping off his wives' heads.

We take Nellie out for long walks on the heath. We love our Sunday picnics on Parliament Hill, watching all the other dogs playing as we eat our homemade sausage rolls and cupcakes. In the evenings Aunt Viv often babysits for us, shooing us off, saying we need adult time. 'Have a meal,' she insists, 'or go dancing. Stay out as late as you want.'

Ben and I usually take it in turns to choose a movie and head to the cinema on Belsize Park Road with the comfy leather seats. We laugh, saying how sad it is to be eating popcorn on a Saturday night, but at the same time it's a relief not to be in some seedy nightclub.

We go on shopping trips. Ben and I bought Emily and Louis chef's hats and aprons and I've been teaching them how to bake in Ben's kitchen. Much more space in his flat and, besides, Ben has all these mod-con gadgets that need to be used before they turn to rust. We listen to Emily's favourite group, One Direction, as we make shortbread, chocolate cookies and orange and lemon cupcakes with fancy icing – it all gets a bit messy, but Ben's beginning not to care. When we're all dancing around the kitchen table to 'Live While We're Young', sometimes I catch that look in Ben's eyes that says, 'A year ago I could not have imagined myself doing this.' Like me, I sense he's a lot happier. I feel a connection to Ben because there's always been something missing in his life. It's not as simple as a wife or family or money. It's something you can't describe. I felt spiritually bankrupt for years; I didn't care about anything, and I see that in Ben too. I see him as one of my tribe, and I'm beginning to think he sees me in the same way.

We've talked about our friendship, both of us admitting again that this is a first for us. Sometimes I sense he might want more, but in the next breath he's saying he doesn't want a relationship. Surely what we have is too precious to risk. Janey keeps on saying how unusual it is to spend so much time with a single man and for there to be no hint of romance. But that's why it works, I tell her. If I want sex I'll look for it elsewhere.

'Polly,' Stephanie says, standing at the door, dressed in a cream blouse and linen trousers. 'Come in.'

'How are you feeling today?'

'Good.'

'Can you expand?'

'Happy.'

That throws her. 'Right. Good.' She adjusts her glasses.

'This morning, when I woke up,' I continue, 'I felt a beam of sunlight through my bedroom window, before Louis jumped on to the bed and said, "Mum, do cows have normal feet?" He's always coming up with the most random questions.' I smile. 'Half of them I don't know the answers to. Anyway, we cuddled in bed and I felt so lucky to be alive. I've been clean for four and a half years. I'm proud of myself. I don't feel so empty anymore.'

Stephanie remains poised. 'Why do you think that is, Polly?'

'I don't know, a sense of well-being I guess. I'm still single, don't have a high-flying job but I have a job I really enjoy. I don't even miss sex that much. I've become quite the nun.'

Stephanie wants to smile.

'I overdosed on sex in my twenties.'

'What do you think was missing from your life before, that you're getting now?'

'I'm enjoying my friendship with Ben,' I admit. 'It's given me a lot of confidence, being with someone who under-stands the "addict" thing.' I keep on thinking until at last it dawns on me why I am happier. 'The thing missing from my life for so many years has been intimacy. I enjoy laughing with Ben about the funny things that have happened during my day, tucking Louis up in bed, taking Nellie for a walk. It's nothing earth-shattering, it's just doing all the normal things normal people do.' I sip my water. 'Ben's asked me on a camping trip.'

I think back to how he'd come into the café to ask if I'd consider going with him. 'It's for Emily,' he pointed out when he clocked my hesitancy and making it even harder for me to say no, he went on to tell me that Grace had made a promise that they'd go to this festival in the summer holidays. 'Do you like camping?' I'd asked. 'Can you put a tent up?'

'Of course not, but how hard can it be banging a few pegs into the ground.' He went on to show me a picture of a fairytale castle set in acres of land. 'It's my treat, Polly, for you and Louis, as a thank-you.'

'That is *such* a big deal,' Janey had exclaimed. 'You'll be sharing a tent!'

I look back at Stephanie. 'I don't think my past can hurt me anymore. I've looked over my shoulder for too long. I feel as if I have so much to look forward to now, even a camping trip in the rain.'

27

2008

It's been two months since the announcement that Lehman Brothers crashed.

Someone knocks on the door. It'll be Matt. When we argue he always storms out only to have to come back to get his car keys. I open the door, stare blankly at our thirty-something ginger-haired neighbour from downstairs who acts like some social worker.

'Er, I was just wondering,' he says, dressed in sloppy trousers and a U2 T-shirt, scratching his head. 'I heard a lot of shouting again?' He looks over my shoulder, into the hallway.

'Everything's fine,' I reassure him with a smile. The telephone rings. 'But thanks anyway. Better get that.' I shut the door and head to the sitting room. It's Mum. She's kindly agreed to pay for us to live here for now, until we know what's happening to the house. 'I'm doing it for Louis more than anyone else,' she'd said, when I'd promised to pay her back. She couldn't help adding that Matt had been reckless. There had been warning signs, but he'd refused to listen to them, gambling with his money and with our future. Now what's going to happen? Will the bank repossess the house?

'Everything's fine, Mum.'

'Did you see your GP?'

'*You're depressed, extremely common I might add*,' he had assured me, when I told him I wasn't sleeping. '*Being a first-time mother is exhausting.*' I didn't argue with him when he wrote out a prescription for antidepressants.

'Nothing's wrong, Mum, just the normal tiredness.' I make a knocking sound against the coffee table. 'Someone's at the door . . .'

'Hang on! Polly! Call me later . . .'

I hang up abruptly, thinking of the day ahead, the loneliness of sitting here in the flat, staring at these four walls or pushing Louis round the park like a zombie, worrying if Matt is going to come home tonight and what mood he'll be in. I glance at my watch, wondering how long I can let Louis sleep. I think about calling Janey, but then decide against it. Since our argument we've patched things up. She said sorry, I said sorry, but we've barely seen one another since she's been busy job-hunting. She's been approached by someone in the film location industry, to see if she's interested in joining forces to set up their own company.

I haven't told her the full story behind what's going on

between Matt and me, but I know Janey doesn't like him. When there's no food in the fridge and I point out that there's nothing stopping him from a trip to the shops, he hits me, saying I waste our cash on vodka. Then he says sorry, he always says sorry, pleading with me that he didn't mean it and saying it won't happen again. I know it will. Deep down I think Matt hates me as much as I hate myself. Pretty much whatever I do or say now provokes him, and Louis isn't his son; he's some screaming child who wakes him up in the middle of the night. Matt never wants to hold him. During heated rows he blames me for having a baby. 'I never wanted this life,' he says. 'You did. You trapped me.'

I know Matt's in deep trouble. As he keeps on telling me, he's up to his eyeballs in debt and if I make any more demands on him he's going to crack.

I force myself off the sofa when I hear Louis crying. It's like drilling in my ears. I understand why women say they could kick and scream at their children. I love my son, I do, but I wish he'd stop crying, just for five minutes. I lift him out of his cot. 'Stop crying, baby boy,' I say, rocking him in my arms. 'Please stop crying. STOP CRYING.'

Later that morning Louis and I are in Cathnor Park, around the corner from our flat. I can't even remember dressing Louis in his dungarees and hat, or getting here. I push Louis on the baby swing. What day is it? Maybe I should call Hugo?

I need to tell someone about Matt. He and Aunt Viv both understand we're not happy, but along with Janey, I don't have the courage to tell them what really goes on behind closed doors. They suspect, but neither could imagine it was this bad. It's my fault. I'm so ashamed that I'm in this position. Each time I have a fresh bruise I swear I'll leave him, but end up talking myself out of it, especially when he tells me he didn't mean to, and that I have to support him. Even if I could leave, where would I go? Surely it will get better when Matt sells the house. The truth is, I don't want to be alone. There's comfort in being with someone, even someone like Matthew.

Irritably I lift Louis out of the swing. He protests, kicking his arms and legs, he begins to cry again, snot running down his nose. I shove him back in his pram and look for some tissues. He needs changing too. I swear I could leave him here, leave him and run. I unscrew the vodka bottle I stuffed into my bag, but there's barely any left. I walk away from the pram. One step, two steps . . . Go, that internal voice is saying to me. Escape. Leave Matt and this life behind. Grab your passport and take off, Polly. Go anywhere but stay here and face the mess you're in. I take another step and another step away from my son. Then I hear him cry out. I can't breathe. I turn back and run. What is wrong with me? I'm a monster. I look at his trusting eyes. I don't deserve you. I don't deserve to be alive. I pick him up and cradle him in my arms. 'I'm so sorry, so sorry,' I say, smothering him in kisses. I am a bad person, bad friend, bad daughter, bad sister, bad girlfriend and a bad mother. Bad everything. I'm thankful Louis is too young to see the real me.

We have to get home quickly. I walk past a bin and chuck the empty vodka bottle into it, but stop abruptly when I see a bottle of beer. I glance around; there are a few mums playing on the swings and climbing frame with their children. I rummage in the bin to grab the can and also take out a plastic cup, stained with lipstick around the rim. I pour the dregs of the beer into the cup. There's a good fingers'-worth. It's accompanied by a couple of cigarette butts. I fish the butts out and drink every last drop.

Someone is shaking my shoulder. 'Sweetheart,' he says, in a voice I don't recognise, 'you have a visitor.'

Aunt Viv is in the sitting room. Matt stands next to her, acting like the concerned husband.

'You only have to sit down for one second.' I exaggerate a yawn. 'Such a busy day, Aunt Viv.'

'Glass of wine, Vivienne?' Matt heads into the kitchen.

'You know I haven't touched a drink for over twenty years,' she says coolly.

'You must be pretty strong to be able to give it up. Wish I had that willpower.'

'I'm not strong,' she says, her eyes fixed on mine. 'It's only because of my weakness that I can't drink anymore. One is too much and a thousand isn't enough.'

'Well, I'm full of admiration,' Matthew says, before excusing himself, shutting the sitting room door behind him.

When he's out of the kitchen Aunt Viv grabs my trembling hand.

'What's wrong? How much are you drinking?'

I feign ignorance. 'What do you mean?'

'You can tell me, you know I'm the last person to judge.' Aunt Viv searches my face, my eyes for clues. She glances at the door. 'I don't want to see you get hurt. Nor does Hugo.' She picks up my glass, sniffs it. I grab the vodka from her. Half of it spills onto the table. 'Aunt Viv! What are you ...?

'Shut up, Polly!' She shakes me by the shoulders. 'And tell me the truth. The truth. Do you understand? How much are you drinking?'

I edge away from her. 'I don't know. A lot, but ...'

'How much?'

'I don't know!'

'Is Matthew ...?' She looks at the door again. 'Is he hurting you?'

'No! I mean, things aren't great, the house hasn't sold and the bank is on his case so he's very worried ...'

'I don't care about him. I care about you. What's this?' She touches my face. 'Don't tell me you banged your head against a door *again*. Let me help you.'

Every part of me wants to tell her.

'You can trust me,' she says. 'Drink isn't the answer. Look what it did to our family.'

I place my hand over hers, look into her eyes, and for a moment I recognise myself.

I release my hand when we hear the loo flushing, a door unlocking, footsteps heading towards us.

'Leave him,' she urges.

'What were you talking about when I came in?' asks Matt, the moment Aunt Viv leaves.

'Nothing. I'm going to bed.' I walk past him; he takes my arm roughly. 'What were you talking about?'

'Let go.'

'Not until you tell me.'

'It was nothing.'

'You're lying.'

I try to manoeuvre myself out of his way. 'You were talking about me, weren't you?'

'Not everything's about you, Matt.'

He follows me into our bedroom, paces up and down. 'She doesn't like me. Hugo's been poisoning her, I bet. That's why she was here, checking up on you.'

'Don't be so paranoid.' I sit down on the edge of the bed and kick off my shoes.

He walks over to my side of the bed. 'It's difficult not to be when you *lie* to me.'

'Matthew, if you hit me again I swear . . .' I reach for the telephone on my side of the bed, 'I'll call the police.'

He grabs the telephone from me; hurls it against the

wall like an animal. Terrified now, I edge away from him, muttering I'm going to sleep next door, in Louis's room.

'I'm sorry, Polly, I'm sorry. This isn't me! I'm under so much pressure,' he says, pressing his head into his hands. He looks at me desperately, before trying to kiss me; I push him away. He's about to raise his hand to me when we hear a knock on the door.

I get up, but he shoves me aside, before heading out of the bedroom and shutting the door behind him.

'I left my gloves,' I overhear Aunt Viv saying.

'Here they are,' he says. 'What beautiful gloves.'

I lean against the door.

'Is Polly . . . ?'

'She's having a bath. I think she's rather tired from being on her feet all day.'

My hand rests against the door handle. I know this is my moment. All I have to do is open it. I could get out of the house before it burns. Take Louis with me. I could escape with only a few scars.

'Right.' There's a long pause.

'Is there anything else, Vivienne?'

'No. Thank you.'

'My pleasure.'

I hear the click of the door and await my fate, realising I have made my choice.

28

It's Friday afternoon and Ben is driving us to the camping festival in the New Forest. Nellie is being looked after by one of Ben's friends who lives in Cambridge. He's staying in Ben's flat and enjoying a weekend in London.

'Can we listen to something else?' I suggest, turning off the soundtrack to *Mary Poppins*. Next Louis and Emily are singing along to Little Mix, 'Wings'. Ben and I join in, and the sad thing is we know most of the words. 'I mean, who doesn't love Little Mix,' Ben says. 'But it's our turn next.'

I look out of the window, wondering if Ben has had any doubts about the weekend. Up until last week I was looking forward to it, but now we're actually on our way . . .

'Camping?' Janey had repeated, still open-mouthed after telling me that this was *such* a big deal. 'And you don't fancy each other *at all*?'

'I can see why women find him attractive.'

'But not you?' She was like a terrier with a bone.

No one gets that we want to protect our friendship. Both of us have had chequered pasts and this is the one thing we don't want to jeopardise; sex would make it complicated. Janey has met Ben a few times. She and her now not-so-new boyfriend, Paul the bald photographer, met up with us one weekend for a pizza. 'We're like a couple, but without the sex,' I'd explained to them both when Ben was outside smoking. 'It works well. I suggest you two try it.'

'No chance,' Paul had replied.

In the last few days uncertainty turned into major anxiety. I noticed that creeping feeling inside, grabbing hold of me. It was a feeling I wanted to numb with drink. Immediately I called my sponsor, Neve. She said my nerves were understandable, that it was good to acknowledge them and that I can't go wrong if I'm always honest with Ben and myself. 'Don't drink, don't worry, take one day at a time and have fun.'

'In one hundred yards, take the next left,' instructs Ben's satnav.

We turn left, down an even narrower winding road and hit traffic. Surprised, I turn the map upside down. 'Hang on,' I mutter, 'we're still at least three miles away.'

In front of us is a Volvo Estate with lots of luggage on the roof rack and a colourful sticker on the back windscreen that says, 'New Forest Festival Rocks!' Ben and I glance at one another, realising that in front of us are all the other merry campers.

Excitement builds. At last we can see the castle, tents and marquees. Ben parks the car in a field. The family parked in the four-by-four next to us, get out in their waterproofs, wellies and matching rain hats. Ben and I watch the father unclip from the roof rack a contraption that unfolds and turns into a trolley. With the help of his wife, they assemble their luggage on to this light trolley and off they zoom, in high spirits.

'Can we go?' Louis asks when Ben heads off to find a trolley.

I'm rummaging around in the boot trying to find the children's raincoats. We have so much kit. Keep calm, I tell myself. This is a new experience. Let's unload and then off we go! Finally Ben and I push the trolley across the field at tortoise pace, me ordering the children not to leave our side.

When we approach the check-in area, a second queue snakes its way in front of us. After half an hour we present our tickets and a guard begins to open our cases. What's he looking for? Booze? Drugs? I lean towards him. 'We're both clean,' I say quietly, winking at him. 'I mean *squeaky* clean, sir.'

Unimpressed, the guard tells me to stand back as he rifles through my underwear and make-up bag while seeming to take great pride in mentioning that we won't be in need of any suncream.

Ahead of us are acres of land laid out in different zones. There's a glamping area that I walk past, trying not to covet the luxury. Next there are the pre-erected tents squished together like sardines. Finally, there's a zone for the likes of us.

Ben is reading out the instructions. The first tip is to practise putting up the tent in the garden. 'Never mind,' I say, as it begins to rain.

Ben continues, 'Lay the flysheet . . .'

'Flat sheet?' I glance at the family closest to us, Mr Speedy Gonzalez putting up his tent at lightning speed.

'The flysheet, Polly.'

'What's that?'

'The tent!'

I laugh. 'Right. The tent. I knew that. Well, lay it out then.'

Louis and Emily giggle. 'Now what do we do?' I watch this flimsy piece of material on the ground flapping furiously around in the wind and am unable to imagine how it's going to remain upright for longer than two seconds.

Slowly Ben assembles the poles together. I nudge Louis. 'Go ask Speedy Gonzalez if he can do ours.'

'I heard that.' Ben hands me a pole. 'Thread it through this sleeve. We're doing this ourselves even if it kills us.'

Ben and I do a high five. My socks are drenched, but we've put up a tent!

'Bagsy this one,' says Louis, charging into one of the pods. Emily takes the other, leaving only one compartment left.

'Ben?' I prod him.

'Let's blow up the mattresses,' he says, an awkwardness

lingering in the air as we continue to stare at the three pods.

By the time we've unpacked and blown up mattresses it's late Friday afternoon and we're sitting in our family tent, the rain lashing against it.

'I need the loo,' Louis says.

'Where are the loos?' I ask Ben.

'Good question.' He hops up.

'It's filthy out there,' I say.

'Mum, I need to do a poo.'

Ben whacks on his hood and says he won't be a sec.

'Right,' he says when he returns ten minutes later, looking like a drowned rat. 'The loos are pit loos.'

I stare at him. 'I'm sorry?'

'They're holes with a loo seat.'

'There aren't bathrooms?'

'Polly, we're *camping*.'

Camping. Right. But where is the fun in this?

Ben composes himself. 'Once you've done your you know what . . .'

'Poo!' says Louis and Emily, both of them laughing madly.

'You have to lay it with compost,' Ben explains.

Toughen up, Polly. This is a treat. The great outdoors! 'Fine, but you did bring some loo paper, didn't you?'

'I thought you did?'

'Uh-oh,' says Louis.

*

235

After we have bought some loo paper from the family in the next-door tent and Louis has done his business, Ben suggests we head out. It's some two miles to the main arena and we find ourselves amongst stampedes of families wrapped up in a million waterproof layers, hats and boots, trudging in the same direction, like little refugees.

Pop music is blasting and everywhere I look, people are drinking. Someone holds a can of Pimm's, another drinks beer. We come across a puppet theatre, art and craft tents, science and travel marquees, a kids' disco. Louis and Emily want to go into the dressing-up tent. Ben and I watch Emily transform herself into Cinderella and Louis emerges as Robin Hood. Next we're in the face-painting tent. Watching them having so much fun makes me happy.

'I'm beginning to love her,' Ben says, clapping when Emily shows off her butterfly cheeks. 'She grows more and more like Grace, every day.'

Later that night, after heading off to the communal food tent to buy ourselves some burgers and sausages in baps for supper, we head back to our base. It was decided that Louis and Emily share a pod to give the grown-ups their space. Louis thanks me for the day as I tuck him up in bed.

When the children are finally asleep, Ben and I sit down together in my compartment. It's only eight o'clock. We can't go to sleep yet.

'I'm sorry, Polly.'

'What for?'

'I didn't realise there were only three sections.'

'Don't worry. The children are fine sharing.'

'I wasn't trying to have my wicked way.'

'Ah, shame.' Ben smiles back at me. I hug my knees to my chest. 'I could do with a drink right now, couldn't you?'

'It's funny. I don't really miss it. The moment I went into rehab the desire went.'

'Tell me more, about rehab.' I now cross my legs, making myself more comfortable.

'I shared a room with a guy called Ed. He snored. He was addicted to prescription drugs, sweated a lot. He needed much more medical attention than I did. Nice bloke. I often wonder what's happened to him.'

'What was South Africa like? I've never been.'

'Beautiful. It was a world away from London. I remember feeling so relieved to be there, Polly. It wasn't like some prison, we weren't strip-searched when we arrived.'

'Not like this camp.'

He grins. 'I saw a psychotherapist three times a week. We had lectures on lifestyle and diet. We had craft mornings. I remember painting a picture of a tree and turtle for Grace. My sister loved turtles. There were tea and biscuits at four.' He stares ahead. 'I liked the structure. You see, as a child I'd never had a routine, but I didn't think our family life was any different to how other people lived, didn't think it was odd hearing my stepfather shouting across the table at my mum or throwing food at me. During the holidays he'd stick a wodge of twenty-pound notes in my pocket and tell me to sling my hook. Maybe that's every child's dream, but . . .'

'No,' I say gently, 'it's not.'

'I learned a lot about myself in rehab. I felt a fraud in many ways.'

Ben tells me about the people he met. 'There was this one woman, a model with an enhanced chest, who loved to strut around in ripped jeans and a bubblegum-pink bikini. Turns out she was raped by her grandfather when she was eleven, repeatedly, and couldn't tell anyone because her parents were drunks. Then there was this lovely mother whose son had died of cancer. He'd been brainwashed by some kind of cult not to take medicine and that the power of prayer would heal. He died. There were heroin addicts, a different beast altogether, and I was surprised by how many eating disorders there were too. Then there was me. What did I have to complain about?'

'Your father dying when you were little and being scared of your stepdad,' I volunteer.

'The thing is, Polly, I wasn't angry when I was a child. Anger is reactive to something and I knew no different,' he stresses again. 'The anger came out when I was older. It flooded out in rehab,' he admits. 'Grace felt it, but in a different way. She was determined not to let our childhood ruin her life. She used to say it was a miracle that we were so close, that we should hold on to that. One of the things I learned in our lectures is we live our lives by our intentions,' he continues. 'When drink and drugs get in the way, you lose enthusiasm for what you want to do, it drains your ambition. That was definitely true for me. I had everything on a plate: a swanky flat, the flash car, beautiful women, a well-paid job, but I was stuck in this rut. I wasn't treating life with any respect.' He stops. 'Sorry, Polly, I'm talking too much, I must be boring you.'

'No,' I say sincerely, 'carry on.'

'Giving up drink was the simple part. I know people have this idea that you're left in a room shivering and sweating, but it wasn't like that for me. I was apprehensive leaving rehab because I had to change my lifestyle and find a new job. I spent a lot of time living with Grace . . .'

'That was when she was pregnant with Emily, right?'

'Exactly. I lived with her for about six months, helped her through her break-up and pregnancy, we worked on her business. I enjoyed it. It helped being busy, but I'm not saying it was easy. The hardest part was leaving Grace. In a way we'd become security blankets for one another. I felt foolish. Here was a thirty-something man terrified of the future. I still see my shrink once a week, I can't do it all alone . . .'

'I wish you'd come to AA.'

'I go to the odd one, but you and me, Polly, we're not the same. I know it saves lives, but for me I just need to keep on telling myself to stay away from the drink because it goes hand in hand with that destructive empty lifestyle I was leading.'

'In this life we need three things,' I reflect, 'something to do, someone to love and something to look forward to.'

'What are you looking forward to?'

'Watching Louis grow older, get his first girlfriend . . .'

'What about love? Someone to love?'

'I have Louis.'

'Yes, but you can't marry him.'

'Would you like to meet someone, Ben?'

'Definitely.' He turns to me. 'You?'

I nod.

Just as Ben is about to say something, my mobile rings. I hunt for it in my handbag, don't reach it in time.

'It was Janey,' I tell him. 'I'll ring her back tomorrow.'

'By the way, have you had any more of those strange calls?'

I shake my head. Thankfully I haven't, not since the day of Hugo's concert, but I still can't quite shake off this feeling . . . 'Ben, can I ask you something?'

'Go on.'

'No, forget it.'

'Forget what?'

'You didn't. No, of course you wouldn't have.'

'Polly, what are you on about?'

I compose myself. 'You didn't send me, as a joke,' I add, 'a Valentine's card this year?'

'No. I'm terribly sorry, but I didn't.'

I laugh nervously. 'I'm so stupid, of course you didn't. Ignore me.'

'It was probably Jim. I think he still does have a little crush on you.'

'No, he doesn't. I'm such an idiot,' I say, wishing I'd never opened my big mouth. 'Forget I mentioned it.'

'I can send you a card next year if you like?' Ben nudges me. 'As long as you send me one back. Deal?'

'Deal.'

There's a long silence until I say, 'Well I'm pretty tired,' wondering when we're going to get into our pyjamas.

It's only nine o'clock.

'One of these days, Polly, we should go out dancing, remember we're still young.'

'Why wait?' I grab his hand and lead him out of the tent. 'What are you doing?' He's smiling at me.

'Dancing,' I say, 'with you.'

'Polly?' Ben rubs my shoulder. 'Are you all right?'

I sit up, disorientated. Where am I? I see his face. 'Ben?' He tells me that I was shouting in my sleep.

I recover my breath, slowly remembering I'm in a tent. 'Bad dream.'

'Here.' He hands me a glass of water.

I confide that often I dream about Matthew. 'He's gone, but he's never far away.'

'Do you want me to stay with you for a while?'

I find myself nodding.

Ben grabs his sleeping bag from his next-door pod before settling down beside me. 'Do you want to talk about it?' he whispers.

Lying in the darkness, I take Ben and myself back to that cold December morning when finally I had the courage to leave him. How can I forget the date? December 8th. It was my birthday.

29

2008

I wake up. Matt's side of the bed is empty.

He doesn't sleep. He knows he can't pay the mortgage; the house hasn't sold, so it looks as if this can only go one way. Repossession. I know he's tormented by worry, but my resentment towards him is building up. He does nothing to support me but, most importantly, he's no father to Louis. I get out of bed and head into the kitchen, sticking my mobile into my dressing gown pocket, hoping Louis won't wake up just yet.

As I pour myself a vodka I hear a key in the lock. Matt enters the kitchen, his face unshaven, his clothes reeking of perfume and London nightlife. He throws his jacket on to the sofa. 'That kid,' he says when Louis cries.

'That kid is our son.' I walk out of the room, returning with Louis in my arms, only to find Matt emptying the contents of the fridge onto the floor. 'We don't have a fucking thing to eat in this house.'

'It's my birthday,' I tell him.

'Whoopee.'

'You bastard.'

'What did you just say?' He kicks the stool over. Picks up the vodka bottle, hurls it against the wall, glass shattering. I edge away from him, jiggling Louis up and down in my arms, but he's coming closer. He grabs Louis but I manage to wrest him back. 'Don't you dare hurt him,' I say.

'I might go bankrupt and all you can think about is your birthday?' He laughs in my face. 'That's why I stay out all night. I can't stand the sight of you. What's wrong? Want another drink?'

'You bastard.'

He hits me so hard I taste blood on my lip.

I move away, so angry now that I can't cry. 'It's all right, Louis, it's all right my darling,' I say, rocking him in my arms.

'I'm sorry, Polly, I'm sorry. I didn't mean to, I didn't . . .'

There's a knock on the door. 'Leave it!' Matt calls after me.

Never before have I been so relieved to see Fred, our ginger-haired neighbour, asking if everything is all right.

I shake my head vigorously. 'No.' I take out my mobile and scroll down my contact list. 'Wait here.'

Matt comes to the door. 'There's been a misunderstanding. Everything's fine,' he says to Fred as Aunt Viv's phone goes to voicemail. 'Let's all calm down,' he suggests, attempting to take my mobile, but I snatch it back.

'If you touch Louis or me ever again, I swear I'll call the police. Fred knows what's been going on, don't you, Fred?' He nods, avoiding eye contact with Matt.

'Aunt Viv,' I say, my voice trembling when the phone beeps. 'I'm leaving him. I need your help.'

30

'So, what's the big news?' I ask Janey when we meet for lunch in a brasserie on Chiswick High Road. She called me on Sunday night, just when Ben and I had returned from our camping weekend, to ask if I could meet her today, on my day off. 'It's important,' she'd said. 'I want to tell you face to face.' Louis is with Ben and Emily. Ben said he'd take them to the zoo.

'So come on, what is it?'

Janey looks hesitant.

'You're joining a circus?' I suggest.

She shakes her head.

'You've won the Lottery?'

'We'd be whooping it up in the Ritz if that were the case.'

'You're not moving out of London, are you?'

'No.'

'Just tell me. You're pregnant?'

'Warmer.'

'You're engaged?'

Her smile says it all.

I think I must scream because the people at the next table are staring at us.

I grab her left hand, but her finger is bare.

'It needed altering,' she says, before telling me she went for a sapphire. 'So you're pleased, Polly?'

'I couldn't be happier for you.'

The waitress clocks the mood, telling us that champagne is on the house. 'You have one, it's fine,' I insist. 'For all the calories in fizz I can have chips instead.'

Janey laughs. 'Well in that case.'

Over chicken Caesar salads and a bowl of chips to share, I ask Janey how Paul proposed.

'Petrol station. We were buying the Sunday papers. Who says romance isn't dead?'

'Oh Janey, this is unbelievable. It's happened so quickly.'

She tells me they're marrying in September. Paul has been married before so they don't want the church and the white dress. 'We don't want fuss and frills. We want to save up to buy a house.'

They have booked the registry office on Marylebone High Street and are organising a party for friends in the evening.

'It still feels like a dream,' she sighs.

I remind her of our evening on Valentine's Day, only five months ago, Janey despairing that she'd received no cards, no chocolates or flowers, nothing. 'Shows how things can turn around so quickly,' I say.

Janey looks at me with affection. 'I want the same for you.'

'Then we could have a double wedding and go on honeymoon together.'

'Oh Polly, you always joke, but I'm worried deep down that you'll never trust anyone again. You put on this brave front, but . . .'

'I'm happy, I really am,' I cut in, before telling her about my recent camping weekend. Janey bursts out laughing when I describe Ben and me putting up the tent. I describe our satnav disaster on the way home too, TomTom telling us to go straight on, so we happily drove deeper into this tiny lane until we realised we were stuck and couldn't go forwards or backwards. Louis laughed hysterically, as he always does. Emily was terrified. With much revving of engines we did manage to get ourselves out of trouble. 'Honestly, Janey, the whole weekend was such a drama, but it was fun.'

'And the sleeping arrangements?' That's what Janey *really* wants to know.

'I hate to disappoint you.'

'No hanky-panky under your sleeping bag?'

'No, but . . .'

'You sit up talking half the night, you have so much in common . . . you bare your souls to one another . . . I know I go on about this, but . . . you don't fancy him *at all*?'

'We're much better off as friends.'

'Honesty is important, right?'

I nod, dreading what's coming next. Honesty can be inconvenient at times.

'Well, I'm really pleased Ben has become such a good friend . . .'

'But?'

'You're seeing so much of him, you don't think it's stopping . . .'

'Me from meeting someone else? I'm not fussed, Janey. I don't want to go on dates with strangers off the internet and . . .' I stop dead when I see a man sitting down at the table by the window, his back facing us. He has dark-blond hair and there's something about the slant of his shoulders.

Janey turns round and then back to me. 'Is that who I think it is?' she whispers. As if imagining being spied on, he looks over his shoulder towards us. When I see his face relief overwhelms me, but there's also a tiny part of me that's disappointed, the questions that keep me awake at night remaining unanswered: Where did he go? Does he ever intend to see his son again? Has he been trying to call me? Is he dead or alive? Is he hurting anyone else? Should I have reported him? Would the police have taken me seriously? My priority was Louis and getting clean, but the guilt still haunts me.

Over a shared passion-fruit cheesecake Janey and I talk about dress shopping and the invitation list.

'And if you want to bring Ben, as a friend,' she's quick to add. 'Out of interest, does he want to meet anyone?'

'Definitely.'

'Interesting. This mate of mine, Diane . . .'

'The pretty one with the long hair? Works in publishing?'

'Exactly. I saw her the other day. She's bored of being single. All she wants is to meet a nice straightforward guy . . .'

'I wouldn't exactly call Ben straightforward.'

'. . . Well, anyway, she asked if I knew anyone . . .'

'I'll talk to him if you want?'

'Would you? You're sure you're definitely not keen?'

I roll my eyes. 'I'm sure,' I say, though each time I say it I become less convinced.

On the bus on my way home I ring Ben. 'How was the zoo?'

'Great. We saw some bears and monkeys. Where are you?'

'On my way, I'll be home in twenty. Janey's engaged.'

'They don't waste time.'

'Ben . . .'

'Um?'

'I think I might have a date for you.'

'A date? You mean a girl date as opposite to a sticky thing with a stone in it.'

'She's one of Janey's friends. Diane.'

'Diane,' he repeats to give himself time. 'What's she like?'

'Pretty.'

'That's a good start.'

'She's pretty *and* she has big wotsits,' I say, causing the man next to me to stir in his seat. 'Ben? Are you there?'

'I'll think about them – I mean, it.'

31

@GateauAuChocolat More sunshine! It's lentil, fennel & rocket salad & save the best 'til last . . . choc meringue roulade . . .

Mary-Jane is off sick today so Jean is working in the shop, Aunt Viv is wearing the Marigolds instead and I'm rushing around serving everyone. It's not so crowded since it's a beautiful summer's day and many locals are on holiday during August. 'Lucky sods,' Aunt Viv says at the sink. All morning she has been grilling me about the camping weekend. 'Speak of the devil,' she says as Ben comes in with his entourage of Louis, Emily, Nellie, two scooters and a football.

Jean makes himself a coffee, before deciding that today he doesn't like dogs, especially not when the customers are eating. 'Oh, don't be such a stick-in-the-mud,' Aunt Viv tells him, poking her tongue out and making Louis and Emily giggle.

Jean shrugs before heading back upstairs to finish preparing his workshop on baking bread.

'He can be so French at times,' Aunt Viv apologises to Ben and then to Nellie.

'Don't worry, we're not staying.' Ben turns to me. 'I was just checking we're still on for tonight?'

Aunt Viv pretends not to listen, busying herself clearing one of the tables.

'Look, if you've forgotten we can cancel,' Ben says.

'No!' she bursts out. 'I mean, why would you want to do that?' she mutters, before saying sorry again and serving a new customer.

'Where you taking our lovely Polly?' one of the customers asks.

'Honestly, it's like working in a goldfish bowl,' I say, causing a few laughs across the tables.

'Uncle Ben is going out with Diane,' says Emily, the laughter stopping abruptly.

I smile. 'And I'm the hired babysitter.' Ben and I make arrangements for the evening before I hug Louis goodbye. 'Be a good soldier for your mum.'

Aunt Viv carries on washing up but I sense she's longing to say something about Ben and his date. Finally . . . 'Who's this Diane then?'

'I am the commander!' claims Louis, shaking his toy submarine in the air victoriously, before submerging it in the water and watching it whir around, making underwater battle noises. Emily wriggles out of the way when he fires a torpedo into the make-believe enemy gunship. 'Attack!' Water splatters over the edge of the bath.

'Gently,' I say. 'You've got company.'

Ben joins us with Nellie pattering closely behind. She jumps up against the side of the bath to see what's going on, tail wagging.

I turn to him. He's cleanly shaved and dressed in jeans and a pale-blue shirt that brings out the colour of his eyes. His face is tanned from taking Nellie and the children out for walks. 'You look handsome,' I say. 'Doesn't he, Louis and Emily?'

Louis is too busy with his torpedoes and Emily is cleaning the other submarine with a flannel.

Ben has left. Supper is cooking in the oven. Louis and Emily are in bed. I'm on the sofa, Nellie curled up beside me, when Hugo calls.

'Oh,' says Hugo, when I tell him the reason I'm baby-sitting Emily. 'Who's Diane? Two fingers up to her.'

We laugh, before I explain myself yet again, although I get the sense that no one wants to listen. All Janey, Hugo, Aunt Viv and even Mum want for me is the happy-ever-after ending. I can hear Mum saying to her tennis friends, 'If only she could meet a nice young man and settle down.'

'You don't feel at all jealous?' Hugo asks.

'It was my idea.'

'What happens if he falls head over heels? Then you won't have him to hang out with.'

'That won't happen,' I say without thinking. 'I mean, even if he does, we'd still do things with the children.'

'Right. Well, I still hope there's no snap, crackle and pop.'

'How are you?' I ask, changing the subject, sensing he's in a good mood.

'You'll never believe it, Polly, but I went on a date last night and . . . well for once there was plenty of snap, crackle and pop.'

Later on in the evening, after taking Nellie out for a quick pee, I flick through the television channels and glance at my watch. It's quarter to ten. I think about Hugo's call. There is he, putting himself out here and what am I doing? I'm babysitting. Maybe Janey has a point. If I spend all my time with Ben, how am I going to meet anyone else? Hugo met a Spanish artist on his radio show, Maria. 'She has this lovely gentle voice and laughs at all my jokes,' Hugo had said. I grab my ancient laptop from the coffee table and google the single-parent dating website that Janey mentioned months ago. Up pops a colourful picture of a family of four; a mum and dad with pearly-white teeth and two smiley kids. It reminds me of a Boots holiday snapshot. *'Being a single parent doesn't mean you have to sit in night after night with nothing but a cottage pie for one as company. Join our matchmaking site for free and see how finding love when you're a parent no longer need be a pipe dream.'*

Tentatively I click the register box.

I read: I am a man . . . woman. I click 'woman'.

Looking for a man . . . woman. I click 'man'.

The age range goes from nineteen to ninety-nine.

Crikey. For a moment I am tempted to scroll down to ninety-nine, just to see who comes up. I decide I'm looking for a man aged thirty-five to fifty.

I wonder what Ben and Diane are chatting about. Will they have a first-date kiss? I haven't had many of those. Normally I went the whole hog, but that was the drink talking. It's different now. I don't think Ben has had many serious relationships other than the one he had in his twenties. I imagine Ben walking her home or to the bus stop. It's quite awkward getting to the lunge moment when you're stone-cold sober, much easier after a drink. I feel ashamed of all those times I've woken up with strangers, little recollection of how it all started. Strangely enough, I didn't want to be with anyone else when I was with Matt. Our relationship was too intense; I was addicted to him, he was more than enough for me, well at least to begin with.

It's simple going to bed with someone when you're drunk. It's not so easy saying you have feelings for someone when you're sober.

'Polly?' he whispers.

I wake up with a start, Ben kneeling down, his face so close to mine. Disorientated, I turn on the light by my side and look at my watch. It's nearly eleven o'clock. 'I didn't hear you come in. How did it go?' I ask, trying to gauge his mood.

'Good.' He picks Nellie up; she covers his face in wet kisses, treating him like a long lost friend. 'How's my little girl?'

'Expand. What did you talk about?'

'Oh, this and that.'

'Did you think she's pretty?'

He nods. 'How was Emily?'

'What was she like? Come on, I want *detail*.'

'She was nice.'

'Nice?' Frustrated I ask if he wants a cup of tea. 'I'm not sensing you were bowled over, Ben.'

'She was a little loud,' he admits, joining me in the kitchen, 'especially after she'd had a couple of drinks. Janey must have filled her in about Emily because she seemed to know all about that.'

'That's good, isn't it? At least you didn't have to explain.'

'She also knew I didn't drink.' He smiles dryly. 'When the waiter approached us with a bottle she kept on placing a hand over my glass. She meant well, but I did find it a bit irritating.'

'Will you see her again?'

'Not sure. Anyway, while she was in the bathroom I was looking up some places in Cornwall. I really like the sound of Fowey. It's near the coast and we could take a boat to . . .'

'You were doing that on a date?'

'She was taking an inordinately long time in the bath-room. I want to show you one place, you'll love it.' He grabs my laptop, glances at the screen. 'What's this?'

I blush. 'Oh, that!' Flustered I try to retrieve it.

He doesn't let go. 'You don't trust these sites, do you?'

'Ben, it's for single parents,' I say, as if that makes it all right. 'It's no big deal. You could join,' I tease.

'I'm not happy about you meeting some sleazebag online. I mean, look at this idiot.' He reads his profile. 'There's no way he's into long country walks. I doubt he even has a child!'

I look at a picture of a plump unhealthy-looking man, his hair greasy and styled with a mini-quiff. 'You haven't registered, have you?' he asks.

'I might, we'll see. You and me, Ben, we're young, as you pointed out last weekend. You're a warm-blooded male,' I remind him, 'and I wouldn't mind a bit of excitement.'

He snaps the laptop lid shut. 'Fine, but don't date Mr Quiff.'

'If you had to describe online the kind of person you'd like to meet, what would you say?' I ask him. This was one of the questions.

'Easy. If I want to be with somebody more than watching a Test match at Lords, I'm in love.' He laughs gently. 'Be careful if you do this, Polly. You don't know the kind of people you might meet.'

'For two people who've lived quite a rocky past, we're surprisingly risk-averse.'

'Perhaps that's because we care more about our lives now.'

After Ben has left I think about what he said. *'Perhaps that's because we care more about our lives now.'* The only thing I used to care about was the next drink. When I left Matt and walked into the AA meeting the following day with Aunt Viv, I wanted to be anywhere else but in that church with a bunch of losers. I wanted a drink, that's all. My life had boiled down to nothing more than that.

32

The day after I've walked out on Matt, Aunt Viv leads me into a small church in Primrose Hill, filled with chairs lined up in rows. Dread cramps my stomach. I feel angry that she made me come here when I could be with Louis. I fidget, scratch my arm, run a hand through my hair again and again. I reach into my handbag, pull out a piece of chewing gum. Louis is with Uncle Hugo. 'I'll manage,' he'd said to me. 'How hard can it be changing a nappy? Can do it with my eyes shut.'

I bite my lip, wanting to turn and run.

I told Aunt Viv and Hugo repeatedly that my drinking was under control, and now that Matthew and I had split up, everything would change. '*He* was the problem. I'll stop now,' I'd promised. But instead, Aunt Viv has arranged an assessment tomorrow with a psychologist who specialises in addiction. 'I met her through AA and I know you'll like

260

her.' And not only that, here she is, leading me into this room with a bunch of losers. When I see the Twelve Steps written on a large board at the front, the word 'God' keeps on flashing in front of me.

'This isn't for me.' I tug at her arm, like a child wanting to leave a grown-up party. 'Please, Aunt Viv.'

Slowly she walks on as if she can't hear me.

There are a couple of guys near the back wearing headphones, one rocking back and forth in his chair. The other man's arms are covered in tattoos. There's a woman, heavily made up with bright-yellow hair and green eyeshadow. She looks as if she's married to a packet of cigarettes. I notice another woman wearing a pearl necklace over her polo-neck and carrying a Cath Kidston bag. She looks as if she's on her way to the Chelsea Flower Show. Aunt Viv stops at a table laid out with mugs and biscuits and asks an old man wearing a tweed jacket for two cups of tea. 'Sugar?' He smiles sympathetically at me. 'Or are you sweet enough, pet?'

I pay no attention, deciding to keep my head down from now on. I don't fit in here. I am not one of these people.

'Can I remind you, it's no smoking?' says a man sitting behind the front desk. 'So if you need a cigarette, please go outside, but can you keep the doors shut at all times? Right. I think that about covers the house rules. I'd like to warmly welcome all our regular members and also any newcomers.

Is there anyone new here today who would like to introduce themselves?'

Blood rushes to my ears. My heart thuds against my chest. I keep my head down, but can sense Aunt Viv willing me to raise my hand.

'Don't worry, it's not to put you in the limelight,' the man continues, 'but simply to welcome you.'

There's another long agonising silence. I can hear someone unwrapping what sounds like a sweet wrapper. Finally a man says, 'Hi, I'm Ryan. This is my first meeting.'

'It's really good to have you here with us, Ryan.' A further silence follows, and I continue to stare at my feet, noticing how old and grubby most people's shoes are, except for Aunt Viv's heels. 'Right, well I'd like to introduce you to our chair today. Lots of you will know her. Neve, over to you.'

'It's lovely to be talking to my home group,' Neve begins, people still entering the church hall. 'I had a rather funny journey here. You lot will appreciate this story. So I'm in a bit of a hurry after work, going too fast, and a police car stops me. I step out of my car, cop pretends to be examining my tyres and then he asks me when was the last time I'd had a drink. I reply, rather smugly, "Twenty-ninth September 2005, 5 p.m., Phoenix Airport, Arizona."'

A few people laugh and mutter to themselves.

'I came to my first meeting seven years ago,' she continues. 'I had lost my home, my marriage, my friends and I was facing the possibility of losing my children too.'

The room turns silent.

'I started drinking when I was eleven. I don't know why; it's a question I often ask myself since I had everything you could ask for. All I can say is I felt this hole in my heart, like I didn't belong in my school, to my family, to anything around me. Growing up, I'd hang out with my older step-brother and his friends. They wanted to form their own band. At the time I thought they were cool. Looking back now they were pretty seedy, letting a schoolgirl drink and smoke pot with them. I loved the feeling drink gave me, the buzz. I was a hyperactive child, in a bad way, and needed the pot to stop me doing crazy things. I didn't think much of school, it was a waste of time when all I wanted to do was smoke weed and carry a guitar on my back.'

I shift in my seat, hearing myself saying the exact same thing to Hugo.

'I carried on drinking throughout my teens and twen-ties. It was fun at first. Let's face it drinking *is* fun. I loved dancing on tables, flirting with the guys, grabbing the microphone off the father of the bride and belting out Whitney Houston.'

A few people laugh.

'But it becomes fun with consequences. The stories get darker. I began to let people down; I'd put myself in danger of blacking out, waking up and not knowing where the hell I was, or cycling home from the pub in my flip-flops, pissed and without a helmet. I went from one bum job to another, never lasting long because I couldn't stand any responsibility. One time I slept with my best friend's boy-friend, something I regret to this day because I lost the most important friendship in my life. Before you know it, the fun stops and all you're left with is consequences.'

Slowly I lift my head when she stops talking, hoping she'll carry on.

'I married in my late twenties, thinking that would put a stop to my drinking, but I can't have been that confident since I was determined to have the wedding at noon so I couldn't get plastered first.' She laughs sadly. 'I fell pregnant shortly afterwards and was certain that this, *surely*, would be the end of my drinking and wild days. Automatically I'd stop, right? I wasn't career-minded in any way. I wanted to be a mum. I wanted to be a good wife. Despite my rebel-lious streak, deep down I'm a fairly traditional girl at heart, brought up by conservative parents.'

I glance at Aunt Viv. Is this some kind of set-up? Is she going to tell me her husband hit her next and she escaped and lived with her aunt and she has a partially-sighted brother? But she's sitting peacefully beside me, her eyes closed.

'I couldn't give up, even when I had my first child. I had affairs. One moment I was committing adultery; the next I was in Homebase choosing paint for the nursery. I mean, that's surely insanity, isn't it? Some affairs were with abusive men. I thought I deserved it. In a way it made me feel better. I was sinking deeper and deeper into a black hole. When I had child number two, my parents begged me to see a doctor, but I was still in denial. My husband wanted a divorce and threatened he'd file for custody. In the end my father booked me into rehab.' She coughs awkwardly. 'I know I was fortunate to have parents desperate to help, but still . . . I wanted to die,' she says with emotion. 'I was broken physically, mentally, spiritually. I was riddled with guilt and shame. How could someone like me, who was given the best start in life, screw it up so badly?'

I begin to cry, feeling pain from years ago, lodged in my chest.

'I began to understand that alcoholism isn't a choice. Who would choose this life? It's an illness. I was sick, not some monster. In rehab I got down on my hands and knees and prayed for a second chance. The moment I realised I needed help was the moment when I could start doing something about it. Those weeks in rehab taught me that I'd lost enough; I wasn't going to lose my children. They were only little. I loved them. I returned home and came straight to AA. I tried to work it out with my husband, but it was too late, our marriage was over, but he was willing for the sake of the children to stay on good terms. My parents looked after my kids, or I arranged babysitting. I did ninety-ninety. Ninety AA meetings in ninety days. If I could take drugs and drink every day I could definitely do an hour's meeting each day too. I owed it to my children, to myself. People with cancer need chemo. AA was my medicine. During my first meeting I was scared. I was crying, snot streaming down my nose.'

The old man who was serving tea hands me a handkerchief with the initial 'H' in the corner. Until now I hadn't even noticed him sitting next to me.

'I got myself a sponsor. She took me through all the steps, made me confront the things I'd done, the hurt and damage I'd caused others. The truth is, once I said "I'm an addict", giving up drink wasn't as hard as I'd expected, but I was still a broken person inside. It wasn't easy, but each day, with support, I grew a little bit stronger. And then, one morning I woke up and noticed a ray of sunshine coming through my bedroom window. It had been a long time since I'd seen the sun, even bothered to look outside. Then my children jumped onto the bed and we laughed about something stupid, before they asked me if we could make pancakes for breakfast. I felt hungry for the first time in years. The black was lifting; the clouds were parting. There was no grand event, no major turning-point, I just had this feeling deep inside that everything was going to be all right.'

Finally I look up at Neve, wiping away a tear. I blow my nose again. Aunt Viv clutches my hand.

'I'm now in a new relationship with someone I met in AA.'

There are a few smiles and nods, as if this happens a lot. 'And a lot of you will know I trained to become a yoga teacher. I like to work with people who have been through illness or trauma.'

I want to be like her. I want to swap this chair for hers.

'I never thought I *deserved* to be happy again. For anyone here struggling, for any newcomers, please believe you're in the right place. Don't waste time. Get a sponsor . . .'

'Will you be mine?'

There's a long pause. Chairs scrape, people mutter. A few people turn round and face me. Why are they are staring at me? Why's everyone talking? It's only then that I realise the words came out of my mouth.

'Of course,' she says warmly, locating where I am sitting. 'Come and chat to me at the end of the meeting.'

After Neve's talk, the room opens up to members who want to share. There's a pilot who confesses he's been drunk many times before flying innocent passengers to their holiday destinations, none of them realising how lucky they are to step off the plane alive.

There's an actress who says Hollywood turned her mad. 'You have to be a certain person, fit in with the in crowd, be as thin as a stick insect. I feel like I've been wearing a mask all my life. When I ended up in some car park giving a random stranger a blow job during the Cannes Festival . . .' She shakes her head with shame. 'I don't know who I am anymore.'

I discover the woman with bright-yellow hair and tight curls is called Denise and Denise had a difficult childhood. 'My mum had what you call baby blues, but in those days you were assumed mad and stuck in some loony bin. My dad blamed me. I was living on the streets by the age of fifteen. I'd find bottles in dustbins and drink the dregs. I'd sleep with dealers in exchange for alcohol. Made me feel like shit, until one day I walked into AA, got myself clean.'

The man in the tweed jacket who offered me his handkerchief is called Harry. He tells the room it's his birthday and that he's been sober for twenty-three years. There's clapping and out comes a chocolate cake lit with candles.

At the end of the meeting everyone stands and holds hands. Harry offers me his and to my surprise I take it. Aunt Viv takes my other hand, and together we say the serenity prayer.

33

It's the afternoon of Janey's wedding, and I'm waiting for Ben to pick me up and drive us to the registry office.

I look out of the window. The house feels quiet now that Louis is back at school. I think about the night before the autumn term began, how we went through all the things we were grateful for, Louis tucked up in bed.

'Uncle Ben, Nellie and Emily. I've had the best summer, ever, Mum.'

Words that make my heart sing. 'What was the best part of it?'

'All of it! We did such *interesting* things. I liked the surfing on my little board.'

Ben, Emily, Louis, Nellie and I went on holiday to Polzeath a couple of weeks ago. We hired a self-catering cottage two minutes' walk from the sea. I was in charge of the sun-cream and picnics. Ben taught Louis and Emily to surf on their child-friendly boards. Ben loves the sea. As a child he went on many holidays abroad. 'Even if I hated my stepdad,

Grace and I did love the sandy beaches, jumping off our boat and snorkelling.' He described to the children the colourful underwater world with its jellyfish and octopuses.

I was content to be watching them all from a distance, reading books on my Kindle, looking after Nellie and waving when they were up on their boards. Each time I venture into the water I hear the theme tune to *Jaws*, but Ben did persevere with me, and by the end of the week I could surf too, nothing ambitious, just on the boogie board. I found myself laughing out loud, it was so exhilarating coming in with the waves.

'I liked the cricket with Big Ben too,' Louis continued, making me realise with relief that he hadn't asked questions about his father for some time.

'I love you, Mum,' he said when I turned off the light and left the room.

That evening I felt proud of us.

I glance at my watch. It's close to four. Aunt Viv will have picked Louis and Emily up from school and taken them back to the café, and then she's taking them on to my flat. A dogsitter is looking after Nellie. 'She's like my second child,' Ben said.

The wedding is at five o'clock and then we're heading to a Greek restaurant for supper and dancing. I jump when I hear my mobile ring. That's probably Ben saying he's running late. I dig it out of my handbag and glance at the screen. Tentatively I pick up, only to hear a recorded voice saying I've won some money. I jump again when the buzzer rings.

Ben watches as I approach his car. I give him a twirl in my rose-pink dress that used to belong to Aunt Viv. 'I can't get away with it anymore, but you can,' she'd said. My long dark hair is in a chignon, making me feel like a film star.

'Ben?'

'You're beautiful,' he says.

'What's the best wedding you've been to?' I ask in the car, on our way to Marylebone.

He taps the wheel. 'I went to an Indian-themed one, boiling hot day. The marquee was decorated with elephants, not real ones, now that *would* have been interesting. Great band, curry and cold beer. It was back in the good old days.'

'Worst one?'

'Oh, there are many. Well, not exactly bad ones, but awkward. I went to one in Greece and during the speeches the best man spoke for a little too long about the groom, if you know what I mean. You could have cut the atmosphere with a knife.'

'Are they still married?'

'To my amazement, yes.'

'I remember one where you had to buy your own drinks.'

'Shocking.'

'Wouldn't be so bad now.'

'You can't expect guests to buy drinks, that's mean. Reminds me of a wedding I went to where we all had to clear up the morning after. I remember us scurrying around with black binbags.'

I laugh. 'I've been to a few and made a total fool of myself. I'm looking forward to this one because I know I'll behave.'

Ben glances at me. 'Behave? Where's the fun in that?'

The blue room smells of fresh flowers and is decorated with cream and lilac panelled walls. Upholstered chairs are lined up formally and Ben and I take a seat. Paul is at the front, dressed in a suit, looking relaxed as he greets guests. Janey's mother is sitting close to him, wearing a lilac skirt and matching jacket. I go over to say hello and she asks warmly after my parents. When I return to my seat, I mutter to Ben that I used to go round to Janey's house after school. I've never confessed to stealing a half bottle of wine and on another occasion, two cans of cider from their kitchen. 'I stuck one up each jumper sleeve,' I whisper naughtily.

Registry offices miss out on the theatre of a wedding, but there's still a strong sense of anticipation as we wait for Janey to arrive. There's a hushed silence when we hear footsteps from the corridor outside, Paul composing himself. She enters the room on the arm of her father, in a turquoise dress that floats down to her knees, her fair hair tied up in a fresh pale-pink rose that matches the rose in

Paul's buttonhole. When they say their vows, their happiness is contagious. I want to stand up and clap.

After the service, guests pile into taxis and head to a restaurant in Chalk Farm. I know this place well; it's owned by a Greek family and is one of Janey and my favourite haunts. When we arrive there is cheering from all the waiters and diners as we're ushered upstairs into the private room, a large open space with its own bar. The tables are laid out in a U-shape and covered in white linen cloths, flowers and candles. A couple of waiters serve flutes of champagne and elderflower cordial. There's a buzz of chat until Paul clinks his glass with a spoon, telling everyone that supper is served.

Janey approaches, squeezing my hand, before we both say how beautiful the other looks. 'Now, Polly, I've put you next to Nat. He's the only single guy here,' she says. 'He used to live with Paul at college. Lovely bloke but apparently snores *a lot*.'

Ben laughs.

'And Ben, you're over there.' She points to the seat at the far end of the room 'Next to Tatiana, recently divorced. A dentist.'

'Ha ha,' I say back to him, 'a dentist. Open wide.'

Everyone sits down at the table, a feast of colour. There are lots of small white oval plates filled with different dips, meats, fish and vegetables; my mouth waters at the sight of prawns marinated in olive oil, lemon and garlic. The single man next to me, Nat, has dark hair that he styles with a substantial amount of gel, rather like the man on the dating website. He picks up the bottle of wine, aims it towards my glass.

'Thanks, but I don't drink,' I say before he can get any further.

He looks at me oddly, as if I'm mad; it's the way I used to look at people who didn't drink. 'So, how do you know Janey?'

'We're old school friends.' I watch Ben take his seat next to the dentist.

He nods. 'Paul definitely got lucky.'

'So, what do you do?' It's a question I hate, but out it comes, like some nervous disease.

As Nat tells me he's an animator, my mind drifts to what Janey keeps on saying about us, especially after Ben's date. 'Diane really liked him, couldn't understand why he didn't call her again, but I think I know why.' Why aren't we together? It seems everyone thinks we should be a couple except for us.

As Nat tells me he's shot some television commercials and animation films and lived in California, I find myself looking over to Ben again. It wouldn't be true to say that I haven't thought about it at all. When Ben said I was beautiful earlier this afternoon my heart did melt. But it's Ben. I keep on fast-forwarding, only to imagine it coming to some horrible sticky end where we lose our friendship, our weekends together, Louis misses him and asks why he never sees

Uncle Ben anymore; it's awkward at the school gates, both of us keeping our heads down, Jim caught in the middle. What Ben and I have is perfect so why go and ruin it with some romantic notion that we're destined to be together? Look at how all my other relationships have turned out! I glance at Janey. She couldn't believe we were in Cornwall for a week and, 'not *once* did he try and make a move?'

I have no idea if Ben is attracted to me in that way. I've noticed a definite closeness, a few jokes about shagging, and he's determined to put me off this single-parent dating website, but he hasn't actually asked me out on a date. I'd be lying if I said I hadn't thought about our camping trip, replaying the two of us dancing, his hand on my back, both of us laughing and feeling so free. I can tell him anything, and equally he can talk to me about anything too, and neither one of us feels judged. But surely, by now, something would have happened if Ben and I were into one another? As Janey had said, we spent a whole week together and if Ben did feel something for me, then that would have been the time to show it.

Nat distracts my thoughts, asking if I came to the wedding with anyone.

'Ben,' I say, gesturing to him. I tell Nat we went on a beach holiday recently to Cornwall, with our children.

'How long have you been seeing him?' Nat asks, faint disappointment in his tone, or am I imagining it?

'Oh, we're not together.'

'Right,' he says, perking up, but looking mildly confused.

I turn to him. 'Do you think men and woman can be just friends?'

'No way, not if the bloke finds the woman really attractive, like *When Harry Met Sally*.'

'So it's possible if he thinks she's unattractive?'

'Yeah.' He looks at me. 'But you're not ugly.'

'Thanks, I think. So you don't have a *single* friend that's a woman?'

He has to ponder on this. 'One. Beth, but she's a bit funny looking.'

'Funny looking?'

'She's got these . . .' He places his hands behind his ears, wiggles them, 'sticky-out ears. To be honest, I mainly hang out with the lads. My industry is pretty male-dominated. I couldn't go on holiday with an attractive woman and lie next to her on the beach, see her in a bikini and rub suncream on her back and not, you know, want to do it.'

Ben didn't blink twice at me in my spotty bikini, and he slapped the suncream on my back as if it were Polyfilla.

'Nicely put,' says the man sitting on my other side. He's Paul's brother. 'Sorry, couldn't help eavesdropping. I was really close to this girl, Annie, right, and we'd been friends through college until we blew it one night getting drunker than usual and ended up in bed.'

'Ah yes, alcohol always has a way of becoming involved,' agrees Nat, asking me again if I'm sure I don't want a drink.

'Did you regret it?' I ask.

'Bitterly. We lost that trust, that sense of ease. We wasted something really special for nothing but a stupid drunken roll in the sack.'

You see. Paul's brother gets it. It's too bad if others don't.

'I have lots of friends who are men,' says a blonde-haired woman in her forties placed opposite me. 'I get different things from both. I love my girly friends, but I also like a male perspective.'

'Rubbish,' dismisses the man sitting next to her. 'Sorry, but there's no such thing as friendship between men and women, there's always an imbalance somewhere.'

Soon comments are flying across our end of the table, the debate heating up.

'Men can't be just friends. We need more. We're only human.'

'Of course they can.'

'What if that male friend has a partner though, or a wife?' says Paul's brother.

'Good point. If Ben were dating, I'd have to take a step back. We wouldn't be able to play chess at midnight,' I say, thinking of our evenings in Cornwall.

'You play chess at midnight?' asks Nat. 'That *is* weird. Why not strip poker?'

I laugh.

'I bet you if Ben started dating,' says Nat, 'you'd turn into a green-eyed monster.'

'Keep your voice down,' I mutter. 'No. I'd be happy for him.'

'Well then,' concludes Nat, 'if Ben isn't into you, you can take comfort knowing he thinks you're a bit funny looking.'

Paul comes down to our end of the table and asks if we're all happy, before refilling wine glasses.

'We're talking about men and women and if they can be just friends,' says Nat.

Paul nods. 'They can be.'

'See.' I nudge Nat.

'As long as the man's gay,' Paul winks, 'or the woman's funny looking.'

At the end of the speeches, Janey stands up. I can see she's flushed from champagne and wine. 'I know it's not normal for the wife to say anything . . .'

Everyone in the room cheers.

'But I've never done things normally. I *love* this man.' She turns to Paul, 'And I'm so excited to be your wife.' We all stand up and raise our glasses to Janey and Paul.

Soon the tables are cleared and music is playing.

'Mercifully short speeches,' Ben mutters as we watch a couple of Paul's friends dancing, including Tatiana and Nat. 'What was Nat like?'

'Nice.'

'What were you talking about?'

'Oh, this and that. How about you and the dentist?'

'Nothing I don't know about root canal treatment now.'

'Ouch.'

We watch Nat and Paul's brother, both of them competing for the world's worst dancer. They remind me of Hugo on the dance floor. 'When you're drunk you dance as if nobody is watching,' says Ben, 'and when you're sober, you should still dance as if nobody is watching. Shall we?' He offers me his arm.

Ben and I dance. We dance for the rest of the evening, me thinking how I shall remember every single moment of this wedding when I wake up tomorrow morning, and how lovely it is to be in the arms of a man who can dance.

At the end of the evening, on our way to the car, Ben and I notice Nat and Tatiana stumbling across the road hailing a cab. The taxi pulls over and they hop onto the back seat together. 'That turned out well,' I say.

'I'm guessing I was meant to be going home with the dentist, so that turned out well for me too.'

Inside the car, Ben turns on the engine. 'Are we ever going to meet anyone, Ben, if we spend all this time together?' I try not to sound serious, but deep down I know now Janey has a point.

'I like spending time with you,' he says, driving us back home. 'I don't want to be with anyone else.'

I look out of the window. 'I hope the children behaved for Aunt Viv.'

'You don't get it, do you?'

'Get what?'

He's gripping the steering wheel now as he stares ahead. 'I have . . . oh, God, I don't know how to say this . . . I've wanted to say it for some time.'

'Don't,' I say, panic growing inside me.

'I have feelings for you.' He turns to me.

'But Ben . . .'

'I have to tell you how I feel.' He pulls over at the side of the road, switches the engine off.

'What are you doing?' I keep on playing the fast-forward button. I want things to stay the same.

'I've never felt this way . . .'

'But we're friends, good friends.'

'No! It's more than that. I've fallen in love with you, Polly.'

'But . . .' I stop, lost as to what to say.

'You can't tell me that the thought hasn't crossed your mind once?'

'Yes, yes it has.' I turn back to Ben. 'But . . .'

'There you go again. I hate the word but.' He looks at me beseechingly. 'We know each other so well, there's no pretence, no secrets, and . . .' His hand touches my cheek. 'When you're in the room no one else stands a chance.' He smiles at me, deep affection in his eyes. 'What's stopping us?'

I edge away from him. It feels wrong.

'I've wanted to tell you for some time,' he continues, 'but I . . .'

'Please! Stop! I'm sorry if I've led you on, if I've given you the wrong impression, the last thing I want to do is hurt you, but . . .'

'No more 'buts', Polly,' he cuts me off. 'I'm sorry.' He turns on the engine, stares ahead. 'I thought maybe you felt the same. Clearly I was wrong.'

I feel pain swell in my stomach as we drive home in silence.

When I wake up the following morning I wish I wasn't so clear headed. The memory of the night before rushes back to haunt me. I want to pull the duvet over my head and stay in bed all day. I can't face seeing Ben and Emily at school.

Aunt Viv knew something was up last night. The moment we walked through the door she said, 'You two look as if you've been to a funeral, not a wedding.' Her smile vanished when neither of us said a word. Ben simply thanked her and said he'd wake up Emily and then be on his way.

I toss and turn, kick my legs against the mattress. How could I have been so stupid? How do I feel about Ben? I feel so guilty about the way I spoke to him. Louis jumps onto my bed, asking if he can play dressing-up games before school.

'Not today.'

'Can penguins fly, Mum?'

I bite my lip. 'No. They swim. They fly underwater.'

'Why can't they fly in the air like other birds?'

I want to scream. Instead I say, 'I don't know, sweetheart. Now go and get dressed and we'll make some breakfast.'

Food is the last thing on my mind. I couldn't eat a thing.

As we're about to head out the door, Louis decides to tell me he needs to take something into school beginning with the letter 'P'.

'Why tell me now? We've had all morning!'

His chin wobbles. He begins to cry as I storm around the house trying to find something, anything will do. I grab a colouring-in pencil before demanding we go right this minute otherwise we'll be late.

As we walk down Primrose Hill Louis is still crying. As I attempt to calm him down and say sorry, all I can think about is facing Ben and the panic grows inside me again.

At the school gates I bump into Jim.

'Polly? Are you all right?'

'Fine, but I'm in a real rush.' I kiss Louis goodbye before heading to work as fast as I can. That voice inside my head persists. 'Drink,' it tempts me. 'Go on, have a drink. You can have one now, can't you? You've grown up, Polly. You haven't touched a drop for years! Good on you! See, you can be responsible. You have a job and a home. You pay your rent and bills. You love your son. Surely you can have just one? Don't you deserve one little drink? It would help take the edge off, give you courage to face Ben.'

I open my bag, hunt for my mobile. I call her.

'Slow down,' Neve says. 'Remember H.A.L.T. Hungry angry lonely tired. You're probably feeling all these things right now?'

'I'm not hungry. I feel sick. I'm so *angry* with myself. I don't know how I feel about Ben. I'm confused . . .' I see my friendship with Ben, so precious, crumbling into tiny pieces.

'Polly, stop. Take a deep breath.'

'I'm sorry, Neve,' I mutter.

'Listen, you've called me instead of having a drink, that's good.'

'But I could die for one. I haven't felt this way in a long time, it's terrifying.'

'A craving should only last for about half an hour,' she reassures me. 'Drink loads of water. Eat something sweet when you get to work. Pray to your Higher Power for strength. This seems like the worst imaginable thing right now, but the answer doesn't lie in drink. Can you get to a meeting today?'

'Can I come and see you after I pick Louis up?'

'Sure. Remember, Polly, the important thing to do when we think it might be a good idea to have a drink is to play the tape forward. So we have a drink . . . Then what? We have another? Almost definitely. You know as well as I do, it can never be "just one". Then we might decide to go to a bar and pick up some random man,' she says, making me think of how Matthew and I began. 'Look at where that one drink will take you. Is it a place you want to go?'

34

2008

The following morning, after my first AA meeting, I am sitting at Neve's kitchen table, drinking my third cup of coffee that day, Joey, her black cat, stretched out on the island.

Nervously I read the Twelve Steps.

1. We admitted we were powerless over alcohol – that our lives had become unmanageable.
2. Came to believe that a Power greater than ourselves could restore us to sanity.
3. Made a decision to turn our will and our lives over to the care of God . . .

I stop abruptly. 'Neve, I'm not religious. I'm not even sure I believe in God.'

She sits down beside me as if expecting this. 'Polly, I can't stress enough that AA makes no religious demands on you.

AA was founded by Christians but it's open to everyone. Our home group that you came to yesterday will be made up of Christians, others agnostic, a Buddhist, Harry prays to the angels. Everyone is different. AA merely advocates appealing to a Higher Power, a belief in a power greater than oneself. It's not about going to church every Sunday. AA is not some cult either. You can leave whenever you like. If you look at Step Three, there are three important words. Can you see them?'

I read the Step out loud. 'To the care of God as we understand Him.' All I can see is the word 'God'.

Neve helps me out. 'As *we understand Him*. We only recover from our addiction when we admit our powerlessness and the need for "the God of our understanding" to help free us.'

'What's your God?'

'At school I used to picture God in the sky sitting on a puff of clouds, dressed in shrouds, but now God is a shaft of sunlight that you see through the trees, or it's seeing my two children eat their vegetables.' She smiles. 'When I hit my rock bottom and finally admitted I needed help, I began to hear this strong and loving voice that over time helped the madness, the insanity going on in my head. I had a problem with food as well as drink and drugs,' she confides. '"If you eat cereal out of a mug instead of a bowl it doesn't count," said this gremlin in my head, or "Throw the food in the dustbin, Neve, you don't need it." Then I'd wake up with that bloody voice telling me to eat it, so I'd rush out in the middle of the night and fish the food out of the bin. Something has to give! This madness is unsustainable. Praying helped me get moments of sanity and gradually I began to hear a much calmer voice guiding me through this wilderness. People might laugh . . .'

'I'm not.'

'A voice told me to talk to my father, say sorry before it was too late. I visited him in hospital and he died only hours later. Cynics will think it was just a coincidence, he was ill anyway, but I believe it's something deeper than that. Some people think only they know best, they want to quit their own way. Well, that's fine, but the thing you need to ask yourself is, "Can I stay sober alone?" We all need help sometimes, Polly.'

35

@GateauAuChocolat Autumnal flavours today . . . Butternut squash soup, aubergine, feta & thyme tart & Polly's banana cake!

I haven't seen Ben for two days and I've missed him. I need to sort out this mess. I can't keep on running away. I don't want to go back to the old Polly.

The shop is quiet. Mary-Jane is washing up in her Marigolds. Aunt Viv is eating her soup. 'What's wrong, Polly? Sit down.' She indicates to the chair next to her.

I decide it's time to tell her exactly what's going on. She listens. I can tell Mary-Jane's ears are pricked too.

'Don't keep on avoiding him, Polly,' Aunt Viv says.

I nod. 'I feel so bad. There he was, confessing he loved me, and I threw it back in his face.'

'Darling, are you sure you don't feel the same way?'

I feel far from sure. My head is spinning, nothing is clear to me anymore.

'After he told you, why did you want to have a drink?' she asks gently.

'I was scared, panicked, unprepared for it. I don't like not feeling in control, I don't trust myself when I feel that way.'

'I understand. Even now, after all these years, I find change or anything out of the ordinary makes me have that moment too. Listen, tell me if I'm wrong, but maybe you're scared of being vulnerable again? It's easier to cruise along and not put yourself out there. You're nervous of entering a relationship where it might actually *mean* something.'

'I've had a few relationships since Matt.'

'Yes, but both with men who weren't going to break your heart, and if you're honest with yourself, I think that's exactly why you picked them. Ben has broken down your defences.'

I'm quiet.

'What else did he say to you that night?'

Tears fill my eyes thinking how much I must have hurt him. '"When you're in the room no one else stands a chance."'

Mary-Jane takes her hands out of the sink and heads towards me with grim determination. 'You have this very nice man saying he loves you and here you are . . . all sad, as if it's the end of the world, boo hoo! Happiness doesn't come along often, so when it does . . .' she thrusts her Marigolds towards us, warm soapy water spraying on to my face, 'you grab it, you stupid girl.'

'Mary-Jane is right,' says Aunt Viv. 'I've made more than

my fair share of mistakes, but when I met Jean, as annoying and French as he can be . . .'

'I heard that,' he calls from upstairs.

'I took a chance on this place and on him, and boy am I glad I did.'

'Thanks. I heard that too.'

I stand up. 'You're right.'

'So go!' Mary-Jane shoos me away like an annoying fly. 'I can finish up here.'

Just as I'm about to call up to Jean to ask if it's all right to leave, 'Go, Polly!' he says. '*Bonne chance!*'

I put on my jacket and run towards the door, but before I leave I turn to Aunt Viv and Mary-Jane. 'Thank you,' I say, 'I needed to hear that.'

Outside, I dial Ben's number. The moment he comes on to the line I know something is wrong. 'It's Emily,' he says. 'She's hurt her arm.'

Ben tells me he can't talk; he's about to pick her up from school and take her straight to hospital.

'Do you want me to come with you?'

He hesitates.

'I'll jump in a cab and be at the school gates in five,' I say, giving him no choice, before I call Aunt Viv, asking if she can pick Louis up later and look after him until I get home. There's been an emergency with Emily.

*

289

Ben, Emily and I walk through the doors of A & E. Emily has one of Ben's woolly jumpers wrapped round her shoulders. She's crying, punctuated little sobs. When we're seen by a duty doctor, he looks carefully at her arm and I do my best not to turn away when I see a big swollen lump where there shouldn't be. Ben informs the doctor that she'd fallen hard onto the stone steps leading to the classroom, her hand outstretched, and she must have hit the ground at an odd angle. 'I'd seen a dead bird,' Emily mutters tearfully, 'and it made me scared when someone said my mum was dead too, like the bird.'

The doctor promises her everything will be fine, before informing us that Emily will need to have an X-ray. My mobile rings. Flustered I dig into my handbag, apologising. Without looking at the screen I switch it off. 'I suspect she's broken her arm above the elbow.' The doctor turns to Emily with a warm smile, 'But don't worry, you'll be as right as rain in no time.'

'Do you want me to stay?' I ask Ben, when Emily is led into the X-ray room.

It's early evening when Ben and I are on the children's ward, waiting for Emily to be taken down to theatre. Ben had to sign a consent form, the doctor warning him that as with any operation there are risks. She will need her arm pinned and will be put under a general anaesthetic; the operation should take an hour or so. Ben is perched on the edge of her bed. I'm sitting beside her, on a deeply uncomfortable bright-blue plastic leather armchair with a high back. Emily looks pale in her white hospital gown. 'I want my mummy,' she says, her face crumbling.

Ben moves closer, puts his arms around her. 'I'm so sorry, Emily, but I'm here. Uncle Ben is here. And Polly is here too, and everything is going to be fine.'

'I want Mummy,' she repeats, Ben helplessly trying to comfort her.

When Emily is wheeled off to theatre, he turns to me, anguish in his eyes. 'She's so little,' he says. 'If anything happens to her . . .'

'It won't,' I promise.

For the next hour, while Emily is in theatre, Ben and I take a walk around the hospital. I suggest we find something to eat, buying us both a tired-looking chicken salad sandwich that neither of us wants from the canteen. When I turn my mobile back on, only to make sure Aunt Viv hasn't called, I see I have five missed calls, all from a number I don't recognise. 'If you need to call someone,' Ben murmurs. I tuck the phone firmly back into my bag. 'No, it's fine.' I try to keep the conversation going, unsuccessfully. It's as if the clocks have stopped for Ben. Time is suspended. He's not with me; he's lying next to Emily. I sense he's thinking of Grace too, how her death was so unexpected, that anything can happen when you least expect it. 'I know it's only a broken arm,' he mutters when we're returning to the ward, 'but . . .' He pauses. 'I can't lose Emily. I know I'll never be enough for her, she wants her mum, but she means the world to me. She's the only part of Grace left. Does that make sense? What if something goes wrong?' He glances at his watch for what feels like the millionth time. I realise that whatever I say isn't going to calm him, so I put my arms around him instead.

When the nurse tells us that Emily is in recovery and that the operation went well, the relief on Ben's face is over-whelming. 'When can I see her?' he asks, strength returning in his voice.

'Now,' the nurse replies with an encouraging smile, 'but she will need to stay in hospital overnight to be monitored, it's standard procedure.'

I call Aunt Viv to give her an update. 'Stay as long as he needs you,' she says.

Emily is woozy when she wakes up, her arm in a cast. I stand back, making sure Ben is the first person she sees. Disorientated, she looks around, as if searching for some-thing lost. 'Mummy,' she says.

Ben grips her hand, kisses her cheek. 'It's Uncle Ben. Mummy's not here,' he says softly, 'but that doesn't mean she's not thinking of us. She's watching over you and me, especially you, and she loves you. I love you too. What a brave girl you are.'

292

'Daddy,' she says. Ben glances at me for a split second, before turning back to her. I am almost in tears.

'Daddy,' she repeats, trying to hug him with her good arm.

Tears are in his eyes as they hug, Ben trying not to touch her cast. 'Don't scare me like that again, you're so precious.' Ben gestures for me to come forward. I kiss Emily on the cheek and hold her hand, realising how much I need to talk to Ben. In front of me are two people I care about deeply. They have become my family.

Back on the children's ward it's quiet, the lights dimmed and visiting hours over. Emily is settled in bed, having her blood pressure and temperature taken. She's exhausted, drifting in and out of sleep.

'Don't hang around,' Ben says to me. 'You must be tired.'

'What are you going to do?'

'Stay here. They said I could sleep on the chair.' He gestures to the uncomfortable bright-blue plastic thing next to the bed.

I gather my jacket and handbag, still desperately wishing I could say something to Ben about the other night, but . . .

'I'll walk you to the lift,' he says.

The hospital corridor is eerily quiet, the lifts at the far end of the building. 'She called you Daddy,' I say.

I can see pride in his eyes. 'All I want is for her to feel loved. I know what it's like not having a father, and then losing her mum so suddenly. She hasn't had the easiest of starts,' he says, putting it lightly.

'Grace would be so proud of you both, you know.'

'Thank you. And thank you for being here.'

I inhale deeply, my pace slowing down as I pluck up the courage to say, 'I know now probably isn't the best time to talk . . .'

'Let's not.'

'I'm so sorry, Ben, about . . .'

'You don't need to explain.'

'Yes. Yes I do. What you said that night, it came as a shock.'

He raises an eyebrow. 'A rude shock.'

We both smile for the first time that evening. 'What you said, it must have taken courage, but . . .' We both stop walking, the lifts getting too close.

'No more buts, Polly.'

'But I need to say this.' We continue to walk on slowly. 'I do care about you.'

He stares ahead. 'But you want to be just friends. I understand.'

'I don't know. All I do know is my life wouldn't be half as happy if you weren't in it. I feel . . .' I shrug, trying to understand my feelings for him. 'The thing is, I haven't wanted to look at you in that way.' I think back to our first evening together, when I taught him how to plait Emily's hair. 'There was so much going on with you looking after Emily and grieving for Grace, I didn't think . . .'

'Nor did I. I didn't plan to feel this way, you can't plan falling in love or making it fit into your diary.'

I nod. 'I haven't had such a close friendship in years, well, ever,' I admit. 'What we have is special and I want to keep it safe.'

We reach the lifts and Ben gently turns me towards him. 'I have an idea.'

'Go on.'

'Why don't we go out on a few dates without the children? Give us a chance, Polly. I'll keep my hands off, they'll stay firmly in my pockets, but maybe you'll see me in a different way, maybe you might grow to love me.'

'I don't think it'll be hard.'

'Thank you for being with me tonight,' he says again.

'I wouldn't have wanted to be anywhere else.'

He touches my cheek, the palm of his hand warm against my skin. 'I'd better go. See how Emily is.'

'Be careful of that blue chair,' I warn him, since I'd been playing with it while Ben had been talking to the anaesthetist. 'It snaps back into the upright position when you're least expecting it. If I were you, I'd sleep on the empty bed next door.'

'Thanks for the tip.'

I'm about to enter the lift when I turn back to him. 'When did you know, Ben?'

His face softens. 'Camping. When we danced in the mud.'

He leans forward, kissing me gently on the lips. I don't pull away. 'Now go,' he says. I inch backwards into the lift, smiling at him as I press the down button. Ben stands there, waiting, as the doors shut.

As I head up the stairs to my flat, a wave of excitement overtakes exhaustion. I feel hope in my stride. I want to give us a chance. I think of Janey and how much has happened during her honeymoon. I can't wait to talk to her when she gets back. My mind returns to Ben again. I imagine him sitting on the ugly blue chair, trying to get some sleep. Emily has been unlucky in so many ways, my heart breaks for her, but she's also won the lottery with him.

I turn the key in the lock and enter the hallway, taking my jacket off. Louis's bedroom door is slightly ajar, the lights off. Quietly I poke my head round the door and see my boy all curled up, in the shape of a kidney bean, looking so peaceful. Aunt Viv approaches and ushers me into the kitchen. I plonk my handbag on to the barstool. 'I didn't think I'd be this late,' I say. 'I'm so sorry if I've kept you up.'

'Don't worry. Polly . . .'

I put the kettle on. 'Emily's fine. The op went well.'

'Good.'

I reach for the tin of herbal teas. 'Want one?'

'No. I'm all right.'

'Ben's sleeping at the hospital. Oh, Aunt Viv, it was so emotional, she called him Dad for the first time.' I turn round to face her. 'And then after all the drama we managed to talk. We were walking to the lifts . . .' I stop, noticing Aunt Viv looks pale and distracted. 'Are you OK?'

'I'm not sure,' she says, before sitting down on the other barstool. 'Sit down, Polly.'

Nervous, I obey her.

'He called.'

'Who called?'

'Matthew. Somehow he tracked you down.'

'Matthew,' I repeat, suddenly remembering my mobile ringing earlier in hospital. Those strange missed calls. The times I didn't recognise the number. The silence on the other end. I pace the room. 'Did you speak to him?'

She shakes her head. 'He left a message on your machine. I almost deleted it.'

I walk over to the answer machine in the corner of the kitchen and press 'Play'.

'Polly, it's me.'

I shiver at the familiarity of his voice.

'I know it's been a long time, but don't hang up, give me a chance to explain. I've been trying to pluck up the courage to talk to you for a long time, but each time I called you, I lost my nerve. I mean why would you want anything to do with me ever again? But we need to talk. There are things I need to say, sorry most importantly, and that I've changed.

Can we meet?' He clears his throat. 'I want to see my son. I want to get to know Louis.'

'Men like him never change,' Aunt Viv says, unable to keep the loathing out of her voice.

I sit down again, trying to get my head round it. Why now? Why wait nearly four years?

'What are you going to do?' Aunt Viv is saying. 'If I were you I'd call him, say you don't want to meet, say . . .' Soon Aunt Viv is background noise. I'm seeing us in the flat the day I walked out. I'm seeing the other side of me, the me that did nothing but drink, the me that loved Louis but was a useless mum who put her son in danger. I have changed. Is it possible Matt has too?

'We were given a second chance,' I mutter, still deep in thought.

'That's different.'

'Is it? Why?'

'It just is. Polly, don't forget what he did to you, and Louis.'

'I won't, but . . .'

'And what about Ben?'

'But what about Louis?' I raise my voice for the first time. 'When he's older, and he asks more questions about his dad, which he will, he's already asking them now, how can I lie to him?'

'You tell him the truth.'

'How can I tell him that his father did try to get in

touch but I wouldn't see him, I wouldn't give him a second chance? *He's* the one that loses out. It's not about me or you, it's about my son.'

'All I care about is you, Polly. That man has no rights. He gave those up the day he hit you,' she says, a tremble in her voice. 'How can you even *think* of seeing him?'

I press my head into my hands. 'I'm not making any decision right now.'

'You can't let him back into your life,' she stresses again. 'You've come so far and now you have a real chance of happiness with Ben.'

'It's not that simple! You're saying I just ignore him and he goes away and Louis never sees his dad again. Aunt Viv, you don't have children . . .' The moment I say it I want to take it back. She looks as if I've plunged a thorn in her weak side. 'I'm so sorry, I didn't mean, oh, Aunt Viv, I'm so sorry.' I reach out to her. 'But it's not black and white. Aren't we being hypocritical? We ask for forgiveness, look at the people we hurt, but the moment someone hurts us, we turn our backs on them.'

'Sometimes we need to protect ourselves. I've never seen you this happy. I couldn't bear it if that man comes back and ruins everything.'

'I won't let him. I'm stronger. I'm not the same Polly.'

That night I sit in my bedroom rocking chair, questions filling my head until I can no longer think straight. One minute I'm with Ben. I feel his lips on mine, can see his face at the lift doors, but then his face becomes Matthew's. I fantasise about him holding Louis's hand in the park. I know there's a void in his life; as much as we love one another there is a vital piece of the jigsaw missing. What if he really has turned himself around? I think of those times when he must have called me and then hung up. How did he get my number? Has he been doing it to scare me? Or did he really lose his nerve? Is it possible he feels remorse? I pick up my mobile, call my counsellor, Stephanie, praying she'll answer. She says she's always on the end of the line in case of an emergency. When she picks up, she sounds sleepy.

'Polly?'

'I'm so sorry if I woke you, I didn't know who else to turn to, who can be objective,' I say, knowing Neve would be in Aunt Viv's camp. Stephanie tells me to slow down and tell her what it is worrying me.

'Doesn't he deserve a hearing, at least?' I ask, waiting for her to say something, anything.

'Listen to your gut,' she says finally. 'What is it telling you to do?'

'Sometimes I just wish you'd give me the bloody answer.'

'I don't have the answers, Polly.'

36

2008

Aunt Viv drops me off outside a flat on Cambridge Gardens, Ladbroke Grove. She's borrowed Jean's battered old car. I turn to look at Louis, sitting on the backseat, none the wiser that his mum's messed up and off to see a shrink.

I feel like a schoolchild as Aunt Viv tells me she'll pick me up in an hour and a half. As I head towards the front door I sense her gaze, making sure I don't change my mind and run off. When Stephanie Green opens the door, I hear the sound of the engine, a car driving away.

Stephanie Green is small, with pale skin and chestnut brown hair, strands tucked neatly behind both ears. She wears simple clothes and flat shoes, barely any make-up or jewellery. She leads me up a flight of stairs and gestures to a sofa covered with a checked throw and a coffee table stacked with a few glossy magazines, along with a bottle of Evian water and a couple of glasses. 'Make yourself comfortable, I won't be long.'

Alone, I fidget with the strap of my handbag, wondering what she's going to ask me. My mind drifts to Matt. Would I be here if we were still together? Was I wrong to walk out on him when he's about to face bankruptcy? Should I have understood why he lashed out at me? He was under huge pressure and I certainly didn't help. I was a handicap. I'm sure he didn't mean to hurt me. It was the worry and stress and . . . I curl my hand into a fist, trying to stamp out that persistent voice in my head as Stephanie calls me into her room.

'Tell me about yourself, Polly,' Stephanie asks, sitting comfortably in her black chair.

A big fat blank comes to mind. 'I'm fine.'

She nods.

'I have a son, Louis. I used to be a teacher.'

She asks me about my childhood.

Again nothing much comes to mind. 'It was fine. My parents are still together.'

'Do you have siblings?'

'Hugo.'

'What's your relationship like with him?

'We're close.'

'How are you feeling right this moment?'

I hunch my shoulders. 'Fine.'

'Can you be more specific?'

'I'm good.'

'Your aunt was keen I see you. Can you think why she might be concerned about you?'

Silence.

'I understand this is hard, Polly.' She gives me time.

I look out of the window. 'I've been drinking a lot. I'm not now.'

'How much were you drinking?'

I was expecting this question. I halve it and don't include the vodka. 'About a bottle of wine a night, sometimes less.'

'And what did that do for you?' Her expression remains neutral.

'Er, it helped me cope with stuff.' I look down to my lap, can't stop fidgeting with my hands. 'Made me feel less lonely, I guess.'

'What's that loneliness about?'

'I've messed up my life.'

'What makes you feel that way?'

'Where do I start?' I blurt out. 'Mum said I was always a rebel, I didn't . . .'

'Let's put your mother's voice to one side for now. Can you tell me how *you* think and feel?'

I can't talk about *feelings*! My head is busy, working over-time, but I don't know how to articulate a single sentence in this room. After another long silence Stephanie tells me not to worry. We go back to my childhood. 'Tell me anything,' she says. 'The first thing that comes into your head.'

I end up telling her about rowing on the lake and visiting the sunken boat. I talk about Hugo, mentioning he's partially sighted and went to a special school for the blind.

At the end of the assessment, Stephanie closes her notebook and takes off her glasses. 'Polly, I have two rules when I see clients. The first is I won't see someone who carries on drinking or using while they're seeing me. The second is that it's your choice to be sitting here, not your aunt's or your mother's, or Hugo's. I have a gap in my diary. How does that sit with you?'

'Good.' I try to give more. 'I'd like that.'

She nods. 'Now, I need your GP to refer you to a psychiatrist. I know someone I think you'd like. Don't worry, Polly,' she says, registering my anxiety. 'But it is important that you have a medical assessment. Don't stop drinking until you've seen him, OK? It can be dangerous cutting drink out immediately. You'll need to be weaned off and he might prescribe some medication to help. I'll liaise with your psychiatrist and we'll devise a care programme. How does that work for you?'

'Good,' I mutter.

'There's one last thing I advise. Go to as many AA meetings as you can and get yourself a sponsor, preferably female.'

'I already have one.'

When Stephanie smiles she appears more human. 'That's the best possible start.'

37

@GateauAuChocolat Lots going on here! A pasta class on Weds so book a spot. And today is serious comfort food – braised beef macaroni & cakes galore . . .

It's the morning after Emily's operation.

The chocolate peanut butter cake is made and a coffee sponge is baking in the oven. The smell is comforting after a sleepless night spent haunted by Matthew's voice on my machine. '*I have changed, Polly. I want to get to know my son.*'

As a trickle of customers come in and I begin on the meringues, Aunt Viv stares at me like a hawk from behind the shop front desk; she's been watching my every move since I arrived. As I whisk the egg whites in a porcelain bowl, I think about Louis and how blissfully ignorant he was this morning. I have to confront Matthew at some stage, I reason, watching the egg mixture thicken. Vaguely I've made a plan in my head that I see him first before I involve Louis, and then I can make a decision.

My mobile rings. The knot in my stomach twists again. When I see Ben's name lighting the screen I turn the whisk up to full speed instead of turning it off. 'Bugger!' I screech, egg mixture splattering everywhere before finally I switch it off. I consider screening since I haven't had a moment to think about what happened between us last night.

'Emily's been discharged,' he says when I pick up. 'She's back at home, watching television and eating a chocolate bar, basically being spoilt rotten.'

'Oh good,' I say. 'Send her my love.'

'Polly, about last night. You being there, it meant a lot.'

'I'm glad I could be with you.' How can so much have changed in the last twenty-four hours?

'So,' he continues, 'I was wondering about our date. I thought maybe I could take you out for some Thai food, we could try that new place . . .'

I catch Aunt Viv staring at me again. 'Ben, I can't talk right now. It's a bit busy in here.' Distracted, I wipe some egg mixture off my cheek.

'Sure, sorry, but are you free this weekend?'

I pace the kitchen, dodging out of Mary-Jane's way. 'Can we talk later?'

'Is everything all right?'

'It's fine.'

'Are you sure? Have you changed your mind?'

'Ben, I can't do this now.'

'You can't chat now, or you can't do us?'

I hesitate, feeling cornered in by everyone and so tired I want to scream. Quickly I head outside for privacy, avoiding eye contact with Aunt Viv.

'Matthew called.'

There's a lengthy pause. 'I see.'

'I need a bit of time, that's all I'm saying. I can't think about us right now, but that doesn't mean . . .'

'I understand,' he cuts in, his good mood buried. 'Are you going to meet him?'

Listen to your gut, I hear Stephanie saying.

'It's not just about me. If it were, it would be simple. I have to let him see his son.'

Until I meet Matthew, I can't rest. Despite everything I owe it to Louis to see if his father has changed.

38

2009

As I wait to see Stephanie, I flick through *Hello!* magazine, thinking how much has happened over the last three and a half months since I first met her back in December. I have been to ninety meetings in ninety days – 'doing a 90/90' as they call it in AA – Neve reinforcing again that if I can drink heavily for years I can make time to go to an hour's meeting each day for three months.

I am enjoying AA, if that is the right word. Slowly I'm getting to know Harry in his oversized tweed jacket and Denise who chews nicotine gum manically, her hair turning a more buttery yellow by the week. I have a crush on Ryan. He's a music producer in his mid-twenties. 'What I like about it in here is there are no docs, no men in white coats,' he'd said during our last meeting. 'No shrinks. We're all equals who have one thing in common, to stay sober.'

I have confided to Neve that at times I feel like a fraud,

especially when listening to how the man next door to me was brought up in poverty and became a drug dealer by the age of fifteen, and the woman on my other side was haunted by a violent childhood. 'You can't compare,' Neve said. 'We all need the same help.'

A turning-point for me was towards the end of the first month, when finally I raised an arm and said, 'Hi, I'm Polly and I'm an alcoholic.' My heart was pounding and I felt sick with nerves sharing my story, but saying it out loud changed something inside me. It was as if, at long last, I was opening a locked gate. When I told them I hadn't touched alcohol for twenty-four days I could feel the waves of support in the room.

I like working the steps with my sponsor, Neve. She's funny and compassionate, but she's also tough. We've found a lot of common ground, especially in our relationships. She had an affair with an abusive man, but kept on going back for more at the cost of her marriage. 'I couldn't be intimate with *anyone*, not even my husband. In my messed-up head this guy was perfect for me, I thought he was what I deserved for being such a screw-up. You were brave, Polly, you escaped from Matthew. Some stay in abusive relationships for years and don't know how to leave.'

Matthew hasn't been in touch. What did I expect? I threatened that if he ever came near me again I'd report him to the police. I had witnesses in Aunt Viv, Hugo and my ginger-haired neighbour. Sometimes I miss what we used to be. I find myself wondering if he thinks about me too. Is he relieved that he no longer has any responsibility? Were we ever happy? Deep down I know he never wanted a child. Was it just about the sex? What is he doing now? When Matt was in control, he was attentive, funny, loved to spoil me with gifts. The moment things spiralled out of control . . . Questions crowd my head. What if, what if, what if . . . ?

I've been through Steps One to Five with Neve. Step One was the most powerful for me, writing down a list of all the times that I had put myself, or others, in danger because of my drinking. One thing that strongly came through was the guilt I felt, and still feel, for drinking when I was pregnant.

Along with AA and Neve, I have been seeing Stephanie twice a week and my psychiatrist once a month. None of this would have been possible without Mum and Dad. They have been able to pay for it since my father has a family health care plan that covers my treatment. 'It's a relief it's being used,' Mum had said, in her twisted kind of way of showing support. 'We've paid into it long enough.'

'It's no wonder I can't show emotion,' I told Stephanie during my last session. 'Mum is so tight-lipped. She didn't do hugs with me, only with Hugo. I wasn't allowed to cry, I had to be the grown-up sister. When Hugo went to boarding school I had to pull my socks up and get on with it.' I told Stephanie that my father has never really played much of a role in my life. He's always been Mum's puppet. I have also told her about Aunt Viv being kept a secret and the time when this mysterious figure had turned up on our doorstep, such a contrast to my own mother in her navy skirt and silk blouse.

I flick over another page. Aunt Viv has been my fairy god-mother, letting Louis and me live in her rented shoebox, as she calls it. She laughs, saying aged fifty-four she still has no roots, no home, she's never had a mortgage – will she ever grow up? I pray she'll be staying put for a while yet. She's very much made her flat her home, with her pictures of her travels and the things she's brought back from abroad, like her Moroccan lantern and kilims.

When I suggested to Aunt Viv that perhaps I was invading her privacy (something Mum had strongly hinted at) she shook me by the shoulders. 'Getting you to meetings and to your appointments with Stephanie is all that counts right now.'

In return I made her promise to let me at least cook, and this is when she suggested I work temporarily in Jean's café. 'I remember how much you used to enjoy cooking,' she'd said. Aunt Viv had it all worked out. I could take Louis to the shop, or she could look after him on her days off, or we could employ a childminder temporarily and arrange for him to go to nursery. A job will give me independence and restore my confidence.

I chew my thumbnail. My interview is tomorrow morning.

'Polly,' Stephanie says, holding the door open.

*

'How are you feeling today?'

'Fine.'

'Can you be more specific?'

I knew she was going to ask me that. Fine will never do. Fine means 'fucking incapable of normal emotion'. 'I'm OK,' I say, knowing that will be rejected too.

'Are you sure?'

'Yes, I'm sure.'

'You sound . . . '

'I'm fine!'

She waits.

'All right, I'm a bit nervous.'

'Tell me why.'

'I have this interview tomorrow, for a job.' I explain where it is, before adding, 'It's not a big deal really, don't know why I'm so worked up.'

Stephanie nods, not giving anything away. 'So what are the physical sensations you're feeling?'

I rub my palms together. 'I'm a little sweaty,' I whisper, as if someone can hear me. 'And I've got this tightness in my chest, as if something's stuck in here.' I tap my heart. 'Like some nasty chunk of meat that I haven't swallowed properly and each time I breathe it feels odd . . . Oh, I can't describe it.'

'You've described it well. These are feelings of anxiety. They are an entirely appropriate response to you having an interview tomorrow.'

'It's not like it's some hot City job though, is it? It's only working in a café.'

'You're putting yourself down. It's a step forward and any kind of change is unsettling. In this life we often have a dangerous sense of entitlement, that things should come easy. Life isn't easy. There are times when we're supposed to feel anxious, scared or uncertain. Job interviews are one of those times.'

'*I'm sure Jean will give you the job*,' Mum had said on the telephone last night, again trying to be reassuring, but not understanding how hurtful she can be.

I'm biting my lip, trying to hold my anger in.

'It's all right to be nervous,' Stephanie reassures me. 'You're meeting life on life's terms.'

'When I got my teaching job, do you know what my mother said to me?'

She shakes her head.

'She said, "Well done, but I doubt many other people applied."'

Stephanie doesn't react in the way I'd hoped. I want her to slam the desk and say, 'What a thing to say!'

Instead she asks me, calmly, 'Are you scared of being angry?'

'No,' I say, rage building up inside me.

'Your anger is a battery to change, Polly. Let it drive you, not hold you back.'

I want to scream, but I can't.

'Anger isn't always negative. Don't be scared of it.'

'I'm not scared,' I lie.

'Let's have a look at your mother again.'

'Nothing I've ever done is good enough! Nothing!'

I think of that evening when I'd overheard Mum and Dad talking about Hugo, the day we'd driven him to school for the first time. Dad was furious that Mum was having a go at him for drinking. '"It's hard not to love Hugo more,"' I say out loud, recalling her words vividly, like a stab in the heart.

I look at Stephanie. 'I was sitting on the stairs. I should have been in bed. They were talking in the kitchen. She said, "It's hard not to love Hugo more,"' I repeat, not even aware I'd been carrying this conversation around with me for over twenty years. 'She doesn't love me the way she loves Hugo. She never has and never will. I was always a disappointment. And here I am. No job, no prospects, I'm nothing but a waste of space.'

I stop; hesitate.

'No one's here,' she says, as if she can read my mind.

I scream, and then I scream again, before I begin to sob.

'You know, Mum wanted me to go back to Norfolk.' I wipe my eyes at the end of the session, wishing I didn't have these feelings poisoning me inside. 'She hates me staying with Aunt Viv, but it's nothing to do with me, it's her being jealous, nose out of joint, you know. She tolerates Aunt Viv but, after all this time she still hasn't forgiven her. She hates us being close. Aunt Viv has paid for what she did. Even Granny Sue hasn't forgiven her. I thought parents loved you unconditionally, no matter what.'

'You wouldn't go back home?'

'No way.'

'Why?'

'Because that's where all my problems started,' I say, without even understanding I'd felt that way. I pull another tissue out of its box. 'Can you help me?'

'You've started doing that yourself.'

'When will it go away, all this pain?'

'You can't force it. You need to give yourself time and we've only just begun. We need to work from the inside out, Polly. You've held on to a lot of things from your childhood and it's time to let them go. You're doing really well today.'

'Mum called Matthew, "that man". She was right about him, but of course I didn't want to listen. I thought I was in love. You know that feeling of being intoxicated with someone?' I close my eyes, smile. 'It can be better than sex. For the first few weeks I had that rosy glow, that sweet sense of anticipation. I want that again, but with the right man. I want to feel alive. I feel dead inside, bankrupt.' I open my eyes. 'Without drink there's nowhere to park my feelings.'

'You have to acknowledge them instead. It's painful, but to change we must suffer. You can be happy. There's nothing stopping you from meeting someone and falling in love again. You can have all those feelings, but I have some advice that I often give my clients. Steer clear of relationships in the first year of recovery. You need to fix your relationship with yourself.'

'That's what scares me.'

'What is that?'

'Finding out who I am.'

39

It's Saturday morning. Janey returns from her honeymoon today. Finally, I have made the decision to meet Matthew.

Jim opens the door to his flat and Louis barges on through, heading towards Maisy who is sporting her bed-hair look and wearing a blue cord dress with woolly tights. She grabs Louis by the arm saying, 'I want to show you something.'

'Thanks so much for having him, Jim. I should be back in a couple of hours.'

'Remind me where you're off to?'

'Seeing a friend,' I say, already slipping back into my old ways, but sometimes you have to tell the odd white lie. 'She's going through a tricky time and it's hard to talk with . . .'

'Sure. Can't chat when the little people are around. By the way, I thought Ben was a bit odd the other day.'

'Odd?'

'Yeah, down. Has something happened that I don't know about?'

'It's complicated.'

'I knew it!' He breaks into a smile. 'I thought you two . . .'

'Complicated,' I repeat, heading down the steps.

I set off towards Chalk Farm tube. I didn't want to meet Matt close to home. I'd imagined bumping into Aunt Viv or someone from AA or even worse, Ben and Emily, so I suggested a café in Notting Hill. As I zap my oyster card I try to ignore my nerves. Hugo took down the name of the café, saying he'd be free all morning in case I needed him. He'd even wanted to come with me. 'You owe him nothing,' he'd said. 'Nothing.'

The train pulls into the platform and I step into the carriage. It's crowded for a weekend morning. As the train doors close I think about the person who has surprised me most: my mother. 'Oh,' she'd said, 'where's he been all this time?' and 'Why now?'

'Well I suppose if nothing else, it's worth trying to get some money out of him. It's about time that man shouldered some responsibility. Is Hugo going with you?'

Deep down I know Mum cares, but she's removed from the situation in a way that Aunt Viv and Hugo aren't. Aunt Viv saw the crash. She nursed me in her home, washed the dried blood off my lips and chauffeured a quivering wreck to her first counselling session. I urged Aunt Viv and Hugo not to tell my parents the whole truth about Louis's father. The version we gave, in return for me cooperating and going to AA, was that Matt became impossible to live with when he couldn't sell the house or pay the mortgage; I couldn't take it. We split up. My priority was to get better. He vanished off the face of the earth.

As I approach the coffee shop it begins to drizzle and my stomach is clenched with anxiety. I glance at my watch: 10.30. I'm fifteen minutes early. My mobile rings, making me almost jump out of my skin. Janey's name lights up the screen. Relieved, I take the call, wondering how I am going to tell her the events of the past week. 'How was your honeymoon?'

Janey and Paul went to Puglia in southern Italy. 'Think turquoise sea, shaded courtyards planted with lemon and orange trees, meals al fresco,' she sighs as drizzle turns to serious rain. 'I'll bore you senseless with Paul's pics. Where are you?'

'Notting Hill.'

'What are you up to?'

'Meeting someone,' I say, my heart in my mouth.

'Who?'

I shelter myself in the doorway of St Peter's Church, where Hugo sang in his choir. I tell Janey the whole story, from the moment Ben revealed his feelings towards me after their wedding, to Emily's broken arm, to our kiss and then finally to Matthew calling.

'Fuck me,' Janey gasps. 'I should never leave the country.'

'I have to see him, don't I?'

Janey is ominously quiet until she says, 'Do you really think people can change?'

'I did.'

'Yeah, but that's different. You were always a good person, Polly.'

When I enter the café I scan the room, but there's no sign of Matt. I rush into the ladies to dry off and find myself standing in front of the mirror, brushing my hair and applying lipstick. I take off my jacket. I'm wearing a slim-fitting navy tunic top with jeans and suede boots, my long dark hair falling down my shoulders. I scoop it into a pony-tail. Dissatisfied, I let it go and grab a tissue, wiping away the lipstick. What am I doing?

The first thing is I see is his dark-blond hair, cut short again. He's clean-shaven and wearing a pale-blue shirt. When he sets eyes on me, he stops playing with the menu and gets up from the table. My pulse is racing. He looks like the old Matthew, the Matthew I was so attracted to in the bar. When he holds out his hand, as if greeting a client, it occurs to me that he might be as nervous as I am.

'Thanks for agreeing to see me. Can I order you a coffee? Tea? Something stronger?'

His mouth curls into a slight smile, that quickly vanishes

ALICE PETERSON

when I say, 'I don't drink anymore. I gave up a long time ago.'

Matt pulls out a chair, beckons me to sit down. His politeness makes me feel uneasy. 'I'll have a green tea,' I say, after looking at the drinks menu.

After Matt has ordered an espresso and green tea, he asks me if I'm cold. 'We could sit at a table further away from the door?' he suggests, when a couple walk in, bringing a blast of cold fresh air with them.

'I'm fine,' I say, placing my mobile on the table. 'Matthew, why did you get in touch?'

'I want to get to know my son, that's all.'

'Why now?'

'That's a fair question, and the only thing I can say is I've grown up. I have different priorities now. I want to be a part of his life and make up for lost time. When I think of what I put you through, it's, well, terrible.' He raises a hand to stop me from speaking. 'Let me explain, please. It's the least I can do.'

I nod.

'I was in a mess with the house, bogged down in debt and fear, but that's no excuse,' he concedes, just as I'm about to pre-empt him. 'You have every right to hate me. I bet Hugo and Aunt Viv are hiding round the corner with cricket bats,' he attempts as a joke to break the ice, but I remain cool. 'How is Louis?' Matthew asks, warmth in his voice.

'He's well.'

'Does he ask about me?'

'Of course he does. Most of his friends have dads and he's getting to that age when, well, it's hard knowing what to say.'

'What do you say?'

'That you had problems.'

'That's a kind way of putting it,' he says, looking ashamed. As our drinks arrive, my mobile vibrates.

'Please. Take it.' He empties a sachet of sugar into his coffee.

I shake my head. 'So what has happened since . . . since . . .'

'Since I . . . hurt you,' he says quietly. 'After you'd gone I got help, Polly. I wasn't fit for anything, least of all to be a dad. When I think of the way I treated you, it makes me feel sick.' He drinks his espresso in one go, orders another, unable to meet my eye. 'But a man can change. Once I declared myself bankrupt I wiped the slate clean, went to see a counsellor to sort my shit out. I went on this anger-management course, I was sceptical at first, as you can imagine, but when I met others like me I realised I wasn't alone.' He leans closer towards me. 'I didn't set out to hurt you, or Louis. I lost it . . . up here.' He taps his head. 'I wasn't sleeping, I was drinking too much, we both were, and I couldn't handle the shame of failing. I'd put my life into that house . . .'

'But you weren't the only one who lost out when the market crashed.'

'I know, I know, but I didn't have the tools to deal with it,' he says. 'All sense of perspective went out the window.

I took it out on you and I'm sorry. I still see a shrink. She told me I was ready to see you again. I couldn't risk doing anything until I was certain I was fit to be a father, to be in your life again. I can't step in and out and cause any more damage.' My mobile vibrates again. 'I'm guessing all your friends and family . . .'

'They're protective.'

He shrugs his shoulders. 'I don't have that problem. I'm lucky, or not so lucky, maybe.' There's that vulnerability in his eyes; it's what attracted me to him in the first place. Despite his outward confidence I saw another side to Matt that no one else saw.

'What's he like, our little boy?' he asks. 'Have you got a picture?'

I pick up my mobile and find a picture of him, grinning like a clown, chocolate cake smudged on his lips. It was taken at Maisy's birthday party. I hand it over to Matthew. He smiles. 'He's cute. Lovely big brown eyes like yours,' he says. 'He's got your thick hair too. He's beautiful, Polly.'

I find myself softening. 'He's the best.'

'When can I see him?'

'I don't know.' *He has no rights, Polly. Walk away.*

'I promise you can trust me.'

'I don't know,' I repeat. 'I need time.'

As I head back towards Notting Hill Gate, trying to make

ONE STEP CLOSER TO YOU

sense of the morning, my phone keeps on ringing. First, it's Aunt Viv, then it's Hugo, followed closely by . . .

'How did it go?' Janey asks. 'Are you going to see him again?'

That night I tuck Louis up in bed. 'We're very grateful for Jim and Maisy, aren't we,' I say, 'and for all the fun you had with them today. We're lucky to have so many lovely friends and family.' I think about Matthew again and try to imagine being in his shoes, having no Aunt Viv, no Hugo, no Janey. Whatever he did to me, I didn't help matters by drinking, and he's never had any family to support him.

'Big Ben and Emily too, Mum.'

'Yes, of course sweetheart.' I feel guilty. I've barely had time to think about him through all this. I don't want to shut him out. I stroke Louis's hair. How do I tell him his father is back and wants to see him?

'Meet us tomorrow,' I'd said to Matthew on the telephone earlier this evening, 'at the top of Primrose Hill, where the William Blake etching is.'

Aunt Viv is struggling to support my decision. I tried to reassure her, but it was in vain.

'What about Ben?' she tried again. 'Don't throw a chance of real happiness away.'

'I'm not taking him back. This is about Louis.'

As I make my way into the kitchen I remember Aunt Viv

and me, almost four and a half years ago, sitting in here, having lunch, Aunt Viv telling me the games she'd played with Louis while I'd been to an appointment with Stephanie. She'd created a safe haven for Louis and me.

I understand why she is the most protective of all. When I left Matt I was a broken vase. Aunt Viv picked up the shattered glass and slowly pieced me back together again.

40

2009

'I'm back,' I call, turning the key to the flat.

Aunt Viv approaches me, Louis by her side dressed in denim dungarees.

'Wow!' I clap my hands as I watch him tottering towards me, before he topples over. Aunt Viv helps him up and he takes a few more steps before I scoop him into my arms. 'You are such a clever monkey.'

Aunt Viv tells me they've been playing with pots and pans and wooden spoons.

'Pots,' Louis repeats.

'We've been emptying wastepaper bins too.'

'Sorry,' I mouth when I see her sitting room now looks like a hurricane has visited.

She laughs. 'We've danced around the flat as well, haven't we, Louis? And we've made you a card.'

With Louis in my arms, I follow Aunt Viv into the sitting

room and she shows me a piece of paper with red and yellow pencil crayon scribbles. 'You have been a busy bee, haven't you, with your great-aunt?'

'Don't call me that,' Aunt Viv says looking away. 'It makes me feel *so* old.'

While I put Louis down for a nap, Aunt Viv makes us something to eat. 'So, how did it go?' she asks, trying to sound casual when I know she is longing to talk about my session with Stephanie.

'Aunt Viv, when did you start drinking?' I ask. I have so many questions, questions neither Hugo or I had the courage to ask when we were younger.

'I was ten. I stole some wine from the kitchen after overhearing someone in the village shop saying my father was having an affair. I was confused and certain Mum would find out. It didn't occur to me at the time that the drink was numbing my fear; all I knew was it was like swallowing cough medicine.'

'Mum never told me Granddad Arthur had an affair.'

'He had a few, Polly. Granny Sue turned a blind eye many times.'

'I worshipped him when I was little.'

'Of course you did! So did I. Addicts are often good with children because they've never grown up themselves. Dad was fun, charming, lovable and forgiving too. He was a good man, until the drink got the better of him.'

'You and Mum, you're so different.'

'Gina went the opposite way because she saw how drink damaged our family. She frets and worries because she's always had to play the big sister role. I was the emotionally immature one.'

'Our family had so many secrets. Mum should have told us about you.'

'She had her reasons. We always think we're doing the right thing to protect our children.'

'How did you pull through?' I ask, unsure if I would have had the strength of spirit to carry on if I'd lost my son, my brother, sister, my entire family and ended up behind bars.

'I did want to end my life,' she confides. 'I understand why people hang themselves in their cells. All my waking hours were spent feeling tormented, wishing I could rewind, grieving . . .' She pauses, as if this conversation is causing her too much pain. 'Drugs and alcohol were rife in prison; they were the only things left. People self-harmed. To begin with I thought, "What the hell?" I took heroin inside. "Have a go on this, it'll make your bird fly,"' she says. 'Your bird was your sentence.'

'What changed?'

'My father. Your Granddad Arthur visited me regularly. He was the only one. He forgave me and promised the others would too, in time. Mum never has. She's tried to but . . . I'd had so many lives before the car crash. You need to see

329

ALICE PETERSON

it from their side too, I'd used them all up, and more. Even prison wasn't punishment enough.'

Aunt Viv tells me that Granddad Arthur sent her money when she was released; enough to help her fly to LA and get help.

'So you had treatment in America?'

She nods. 'I booked myself into a rehab clinic. I met this incredible man there, Tate. We became close. I lived with him for a time. He made me laugh. When we were encouraged to find true spirituality through God or a Higher Power he said, "Why God? Can't we find it through George Harrison?"' Aunt Viv smiles. 'He loved the Beatles. We'd dance to them all night long.'

I ask her about the Higher Power stuff.

'I believe God puts people in front of you when you need them. Tate was a gift. Often you'll find people come into your life for a reason. Sometimes they'll stay, sometimes they're only meant to be around for a short time to help you find your way. I believe I'm meant to be here now.' She touches my cheek with the palm of her hand. 'With you.'

When I wake Louis, I breathe in the smell of sleep and warm blankets and milky skin. Holding him in my arms makes me realise how much I want to stay clean and live a fulfilled life. I owe it to Aunt Viv, to Hugo and, most importantly, my boy. He deserves a mother who will be there for him. I also owe it to myself. I've made some bad choices in my life. 'I won't ever let you down again,' I promise him, touching his cheek.

Aunt Viv stands in the doorway, watching.

'Here,' I say, holding him out towards her.

She cradles him in her arms.

'It must hurt, every day,' I say, thinking of her loss.

'It does, but I've done my time grieving. I have to live for today now. There's a beautiful reading,' she says, rocking Louis in her arms.

'Is it the one in your bedroom?' I ask. 'In the frame?'

She nods. 'I'm not sure who it's by, but I know it off by heart.

'There are only two days in every week,

That we should not worry about.

One is Yesterday

With its mistakes and cares,

Its faults and blunders, its aches and pains.

Yesterday has passed, forever beyond our control.

All the money in the world cannot bring back yesterday.

The other day we shouldn't worry about is Tomorrow.

Tomorrow is beyond our control.

Tomorrow's sun will rise either in splendour

Or behind a mask of clouds – but it will rise.

Until it does, we have no stake in tomorrow, for it is yet unborn.

This leaves only one day . . .'

'*Today*,' we both say together. Aunt Viv smiles at me, before she goes on,

'*Any person can fight the battles of just one day.*
It is only when we add the burdens of yesterday and tomorrow
That we break down.
The experience of today doesn't drive people mad –
It is the remorse of bitterness for something
Which happened yesterday,
And the dread of what tomorrow may bring.'

41

It's Saturday morning and Louis and I are making pancakes for breakfast. Louis is wearing his little chef's hat and apron, reminding me of being in Ben's flat with Emily. It's been a week since I saw Matthew, and I have agreed to meet him with Louis, for the first time, tomorrow morning. I keep on telling myself, one day at a time. Don't worry about yesterday or if he'll turn up next weekend or stick to his promise next month.

I watch Louis eating his pancake, sugar coating the corners of his mouth. 'Louis, I have something to tell you, sweetheart.'

'Can I have another one, Mum?'

'In a minute. Louis, your father has been in touch with me.'

The room turns silent, as if someone has pressed a pause button over us.

I put on a smile. 'He wants to meet you.'

Louis thinks about this. 'Today? Now?'

'Tomorrow. I thought we could go for a walk on Primrose Hill together. What do you say?'

'I could show him my stomp rocket.' He slides off his stool and rushes into his bedroom, the thought of another pancake forgotten.

I see Matt from a distance, standing by the William Blake etching. He looks stylish in boots and jeans and he's holding a large rectangular-shaped box wrapped in paper and tied in the middle with a thick blue ribbon. I clutch Louis's hand with all my strength as I say, 'There he is, Louis.'

'The man with the present?' Louis releases his hand and tears towards him.

I watch Matt bend down to take his son's hand in his. 'I like your coat, buddy,' he says.

Earlier this morning I'd helped Louis dress in his best cords and navy-checked shirt and his army-print jacket. I'd brushed his hair, made sure his teeth were sparkling clean. Again, I found myself applying make-up. Why am I trying to impress him?

I can see Louis is more interested in the present than his father.

'Oh right, yes, this is for you,' Matt says, as I approach them. Matt mouths, 'Thank you,' as Louis unties the ribbon and greedily rips open the stripy wrapping paper. A few children stop to watch, reluctantly pulled away by their mother or father.

'It's a stunt scooter,' says Matthew, helping Louis open the box. 'Apparently it's the coolest two-wheeled stunt scooter around!'

'Wow!' Louis jumps up and down in excitement at this flashy silver thing on wheels. 'Can I have a go now?'

I stand back, irritated. Those scooters are expensive. It's over the top, so obviously a present to show off and make Louis like him.

'Let's not play with it now,' I say. 'You wanted to show Matthew, er . . .' I can't bring myself to say 'your dad', 'your stomp rocket.'

'But, Mum! I want a go on this.'

'Mate, you have to assemble it,' Matt says. 'Listen to your mum.'

'And we haven't brought your helmet,' I add.

'We'll play on it next time. I can give you some stunt lessons. Deal?' He holds up his hand to do a high five.

'Deal,' Louis agrees, hitting his hand and giggling. 'Do you want to play stomp rocket with me?'

'I sure do.' I hand the rocket over, telling Louis we need to find a more secluded part of the park. Louis and Matt go on ahead, me trailing behind with the scooter and bits of wrapping paper.

'I play stomp rocket with Emily and Uncle Ben,' he says, eagerly assembling the firing pipe and launch pad on to the ground.

'Uncle Ben? Who's he now?'

'Mum's friend. You have to see whose rocket goes the highest. I always win.'

'Do you now? Well, we'll see about that,' Matt says, glancing my way, hoping I'll join in, but all I can think is: have I opened some terrible can of worms? This doesn't feel real. How can he waltz back into our lives as if nothing has happened?

Louis attaches the foam rocket over the pipe, angling it towards the sky. 'You see this.' He gestures to the plastic launch pad, filled with air. 'You stamp on it, as hard as you can. I'll show you!' Louis raises his foot, stamps on the pad and the rocket is released, whooshing into the sky. Matt applauds, before Louis scurries to retrieve it.

'Nice one, mate! Can I have a try?'

Eagerly Louis hands the rocket to Matt.

Matt positions the rocket in the tube. He pumps up his fists, flexes the muscles in his arms, beefs up his legs, making Louis giggle, before he stamps on the pad, the rocket flying high into the air. I watch as they both run to pick it up, Louis saying, 'My turn next!'

Dog walkers and passers-by watch them; some smile at me. From a stranger's point of view we look like a normal family, enjoying a day out in the park, but I feel anything but normal inside. Is this an act? What if he meets up with Louis a few times, and then gets bored? The novelty could easily wear off. The damage it would cause Louis couldn't be undone. At the same time, there's a little voice also saying that this could be good. Give Matthew a chance. Ben and Hugo are fantastic, as is Jim, but they're not 'Dad'.

I watch them laughing as they race towards the rocket again. As I'm trying to mould this morning into something positive, I still can't get away from that feeling that I've let my son, my baby cub, into the lion's den.

And the one person I want to talk to about all this is Ben.

42

Ben and I sit at the kitchen table with a cup of tea. The table is covered with spreadsheets and paperwork. Emily is curled up on the sofa with Nellie, watching a Disney film, her arm in a cast now covered in bright stickers. 'What's up?' Ben had asked in an offhand way when I'd called him earlier today, after seeing Matthew.

After arranging to see Ben in the afternoon, I told Louis I needed to do some boring Sunday afternoon errands and that maybe if he was good, Uncle Hugo would come round and play a game with him. I didn't want Louis coming over, telling Ben and Emily all about seeing his daddy. He wouldn't understand that it's not the best thing to say right now.

I ask Ben how he is and what he's been up to, but he cuts through all my small talk with, 'So, have you met up with him?'

I nod. 'It was OK,' I downplay it. 'Louis had a good time.'

'*I've had the best day! When can I see you again?*' Louis had asked his father.

Ben gets up, opens a cupboard, offers me some biscuits. I cradle the mug in my hands.

'Well, that's good, isn't it?' He won't look at me.

'Maybe.'

'How did you find him?' Ben's voice is strained. He's pacing the kitchen, making me feel uneasy.

'Strange. It was like he was a different person.' I tell Ben how he'd turned up with an expensive scooter. It didn't make me feel comfortable, but of course Louis was over the moon.

'Will you see him again?' Ben asks.

'*Well, buddy, how about next weekend?*' Matthew had suggested to Louis, '*as long as your mummy is cool about it. We could go to the zoo, maybe have a pizza together.*'

I'd expected Matthew to be awkward, unsure how to interact with a six-year old, even if it was his own estranged son, but instead he was stepping into the role effortlessly, as if he'd never left.

'Maybe next weekend.'

'Ginger biscuits?' Ben now asks, shaking the packet at me.

I wish he'd sit down. 'No, thanks.' I pause. 'I'm caught between a rock and hard place, aren't I? If I do see Matt again, if I allow him back into our lives, I run the risk of him letting us down, but if I don't I'm the baddie in Louis's eyes, I'm the one stopping him from having a father. What would you do?'

Ben shrugs. 'You have to do what feels right, in your gut.'

'You sound like my shrink,' I say, aching for him to smile.

'Do you trust him?'

'I don't know.' I press my head into my hands.

'Well, only you can make the decision.'

I can't help registering the bite in his tone.

'I'm sorry, Ben. Here I am going on and on. I just needed to talk to you. I've missed you and Emily. How are you?'

'We're fine.'

I can't bear the coldness between us. I reach for his hand ,but he withdraws it. There's distance in his eyes.

He turns away from me. 'I can't do this, Polly.'

'Do what?' But I know what he means.

'This. Pretend it's normal between us, friends having a cup of tea and all that crap. I want what's best for you and Louis, of course I do, but Matthew coming back has changed everything.'

'It doesn't have to,' I say quietly.

'I can't be objective! I'm the last person you should be talking to! I don't like the man. I hate what he did to you. He's a bastard,' he says, forgetting Emily is watching television in the next room. 'I've done some bad things in my life, you know that, but no man has any right to hit a woman. In my book he's the lowest of low.'

'Yes, but he's . . .'

'Louis's father? Some dad!' He begins to pace the room again. 'He hasn't been in touch for years! I wish he'd never contacted you. I don't ever want to meet him and you know why.' He walks over to me now, holds my face in both hands and looks into my eyes, and for a moment I think he's going to kiss me, and part of me wants him so badly . . . but as soon as he's touched me, he lets go and walks away. 'I can't be your friend anymore. I can't be good old Uncle Ben, your confidant, the guy who picks you up when you're down. Don't you see?' He turns back to me. 'I'm in love with you and it's killing me listening about whether you do or don't meet up with the father of your son again when all I can think about is how we were *this* close to getting together and . . .'

'Daddy?' Emily comes into the kitchen and looks at us, wondering what's wrong, before asking me if I want to see her special box that she keeps by her bedside table. Inside are pictures of her mummy and Patch.

'Polly and I are in the middle of something, sweetheart. Go back and watch the film. I'll be with you in a minute. Here.' Ben burrows in a drawer and produces a dog chew. 'Give Nellie a treat.'

Emily looks from me to Ben, before sloping off back to the sofa, Nellie padding closely behind.

'Ben, this isn't about you, all I'm asking for is more time, while I work out . . .' I look at him, unsure what I want to work out.

'You don't know what you want, that's the problem, but I do, and I can't sit around hearing about you and Matthew getting closer.'

'Oh my God! You think I'm going to get back with him?'

'Who knows? Is he seeing anyone?'

'I don't know! Even if he weren't . . .'

'He comes back, all Mr Charming. You fell for it before.'

'That doesn't mean . . . Ben, I don't want to get back with him. It's never been about that! You can't be jealous, there's nothing to be jealous of. This is about Louis. Louis. That's what no one understands! If Emily's father suddenly turned up, swearing he wanted to be a part of her life, would you slam the door on him? How would you live with yourself?'

Ben sits down again. 'I wouldn't let him anywhere near her. You don't pick and choose when you want to be a father.'

'Daddy?' Emily says again, clearly troubled now by us arguing.

'I shouldn't have come. I'm sorry.' He watches as I pull my jacket on.

'You're scared of moving on, Polly.'

I stop dead. 'That's not true.'

'Isn't it?' His voice softens for a moment. 'I know what I want.'

'I don't want Matthew. You know how much you mean to me.'

He nods, as if he almost believes me.

'I understand that his coming back is a huge deal and that he wants to be a part of your son's life. I get that it's scary, but that doesn't mean *your* life has to stop. You can't let your entire life revolve around Louis.'

Janey has said this too.

'This is the perfect excuse to put the brakes on us,' Ben goes on. 'You're terrified of being happy again, of taking risks.'

Determined not to agree with his theory, I say, 'Seeing Matt again is taking a risk for my son, but I don't want it to be at the cost of seeing you. It feels like you're giving me some kind of ultimatum, that if I can't make up my mind about us right now, when all this other stuff is going on in my head, that's it.'

'If you're in trouble, if that man dares to hurt you, I'll be there, but I can't meet you and Jim anymore on our Mondays, you and I can't go on camping holidays or head to the park every weekend. She's getting too attached to you too,' he whispers, gesturing to Emily. 'It's not fair to let her imagine that the four of us might become one happy family. I can't do that to her. I won't.'

'So it's over. We can't be friends.'

There's sadness in his eyes. 'We can't go back to the way things were. Too much has changed.'

43

2009

I'm on the tube heading to Oxford Circus, to see Hugo during his lunch-break. He's still working for the BBC, in Portland Place.

'Make an appointment, make it formal,' Neve had advised when we talked through Step 9, which is to 'Make direct amends to people wherever possible, except when to do so would injure them or others'.

So far I have apologised to Janey for not being there when she was made redundant. I have made amends with my father for being a terrible daughter. His reaction overwhelmed me. Never before had he shown much emotion. He'd hugged me, saying, 'You haven't let us down. We have. We love you and want you to get better. Please talk to Mum,' he added, 'she's been so worried.'

Yet I can't bring myself to say sorry to her, not yet. As for Louis, clearly I can't make an appointment with him but what I can do is make a living amend and be as good a mother as I can be.

As I watch a crowd of people entering the carriage at Warren Street, my mind drifts to Matthew again, something of a habit. I sometimes wonder what I'd do if I saw him amongst the crowd. Would I hide? It's been nine months since I left him.

What else has happened? Aunt Viv has moved in with Jean and I have taken over her small flat. 'You don't need to go,' she'd pointed out. 'You and Louis are comfortable here, you're close to work and I can pop round and babysit whenever you want.'

I miss the sound of her footsteps in the flat and the way she'd open the blinds and curtains to welcome a new day. I miss seeing her meditating on the sitting room floor and the smell of freshly brewed coffee first thing in the morning. I used to laugh hearing her sing in the shower, her voice almost as bad as mine. But at the same time I know it's good to be independent. Carefully I worked out that I could afford the rent. I don't have much left over, but then again I am saving thanks to family helping with childcare, a luxury many single mothers don't have.

I see Stephanie once a week now and am beginning to find it easier opening up. Sometimes I'd go so far as to say I enjoy our sessions. I fit AA around my work. I have become good friends with Harry, Neve and Ryan. How naïve to think they were all scavenging bins and sleeping rough.

Give Harry a globe and he'd tell you all the places he and Betsy have travelled to since being clean. Ryan left school when he was sixteen to pursue a career in music. He has just produced an album for a singer called Kitty Adams, who made her name on a talent show.

Jean gave me the job. Perhaps, as Mum had implied, it wasn't exactly stiff competition since I was Aunt Viv's niece, a bit of a charity case basically, but at the same time I have thrown myself into the role with a passion and even begun taking cookbooks to bed. Jean tells me people love to read about food almost as much as eating it. 'Many take a cookbook to bed,' he had said to me with a shrug when he was making both of us a coffee the other day. 'It can be better than a lover.'

'And at least a cookbook will never let you down,' Aunt Viv had added before he threw a tea towel at her.

Aunt Viv, Mum, Hugo and I have devised a rota for Louis. Mum travels down by train once a week, staying one night and two full days to look after her grandson. Aunt Viv looks after him two days a week. Hugo, who doesn't work on Fridays, takes Louis out for the day. Our routine is a little shambolic at times, but it seems to work and Louis is happy. I could look after him full-time, but Aunt Viv was right. Working again is not only helping me pay the rent but also restoring my self-esteem. I leave at four and have the rest of the day and evening with Louis, and I value every minute, especially bath and story time. No longer do I hurry through the pages just so I can get to the vodka bottle.

I approach the front desk, saying I've come to meet my brother, Hugo Stephens.

The guy behind the reception gives me a visitor badge and guides me towards the lifts.

I sit down in the waiting area listening to the end of Hugo's programme. His career is thriving. He now has his own weekly show on a Wednesday morning, alongside producing the daily lunchtime slot on Radio 2.

'When I was younger, I was too proud to ask for help getting around,' he says live on air. 'I didn't want to draw attention to myself. I went to a special school for the blind until I was eighteen. I was fortunate to go there, it gave me many opportunities, but it also sheltered me from the real world. Can you imagine going from this cocoon to the busy streets of London, me trying to blend in and get myself around! Often I'd torment myself by taking hours instead of asking the way. Men are bad at asking for directions at the best of times.' I can hear humour in his voice. 'Anyway guys, that about wraps it up. Remember to keep on sending those messages. I always love to hear from you.'

As Hugo and I make our way down Portland Place, I hear Neve's voice in my head. 'Don't make it into a drama.

You're just there to say "sorry". Don't expect anything in return.'

We push open the doors to a crowded café, people working on laptops, others on their mobiles.

Hugo grabs a table in the corner as I order one soya latte and a filter coffee. 'So what's this all about?' he asks, as I join him with our drinks.

'I'm sorry.'

'What for?'

'For hurting you.'

Hugo squints. 'For hurting me?'

'For telling lies, embarrassing you in front of your friends . . .'

'Polly,' he stops me. 'It's all in the past. Dead and buried.'

'And then when Matthew came along,' I continue, determined to say my piece, 'I was so stupid, Hugo. I drove you out of our flat . . .' I inhale deeply. 'I threw your support back in your face.'

He puts his coffee down. 'You weren't yourself,' he says with kindness. 'That's why I was scared. I was watching my sister disappear and there was nothing I could do about it.'

'Hugo, you're a much better person than I'll *ever* be.'

'That's not true.'

'You showed no resentment, took all my crap and still helped me when I needed you. You have had to deal with stuff through no choice of your own; you don't let anything stop you from doing exactly what you want. You never seem scared or . . .'

'Oh I'm scared all right. Been scared since the day I was dropped off at school.'

'You were only seven.'

'I used to cry myself to sleep, wondering how I was going to last until Friday.'

'I was lonely without you.'

He nods. 'I have an apology to make too. I stole all of Mum's love.'

'No, you didn't,' I say, a lump in my throat.

'Polly, I did. Parents shouldn't have favourites.'

'It's not your fault though.'

'Perhaps, but I know Mum is different with me.' He runs a hand through his hair. 'She's more protective, makes more allowances for me. She still treats me like that five-year-old boy, making sure I'm eating properly and insisting I bring my washing and ironing home. And I let her.'

'Mothers and their sons,' I say, a reservoir of tears filling inside me. 'It doesn't help future wives, you know.'

Hugo laughs. 'Rosie says that too.' He takes my hand. 'You didn't need to say sorry, but I'm touched you did.'

'I wish I'd listened to you. You were the only one brave enough to warn me about Matt.'

'He might be Louis's father, but . . . oh boy, it's rare I dislike someone, truly hate their guts,' he says, his voice churned with emotion. 'I used to panic that he might try and worm his way back into your life. I was worried you might drink again.'

'It won't happen,' I assure him.

'If I saw that man again I couldn't be sure what I'd do. Promise me,' he urges, 'promise me that if he ever comes back you'll have nothing more to do with him.'

'I promise.'

44

'I'm not taking any risks,' I whisper down the phone to Hugo as I tell him Louis and I are on our way to meet Matthew at the Odeon in Camden town. It's too cold and wintery to be outside today, so Louis asked if we could watch a movie instead.

'No, it's too soon,' I say when Hugo asks if he can meet him too. 'I know what I'm doing. Trust me.'

After our call, I shove the mobile back into my bag, understanding Hugo's concern, but at the same time, over the past two months Matthew hasn't once let us down. He has turned up on time to meet Louis and play stomp rocket in the park, or give him lessons on his stunt scooter. He always looks well-dressed and clean-shaven, his blue eyes bright with enthusiasm when he sees his son. I'm not immune to the glances he receives from women, especially when he's with Louis. One afternoon he brought a Union Jack kite to Hampstead Heath and taught Louis to fly it, both of them wrapped up in coats and woolly scarves, looking every inch father and son, as I watched from the sidelines.

Louis is ecstatic about being reunited with his father. At night, when we go through our list of all the things we are grateful for Matthew is always mentioned first now. I have to remind him about Emily, Ben, Aunt Viv and Uncle Hugo, but it's in vain. When he plays games with his friends I hear him say, 'My daddy will shoot you down!' Or 'My daddy will save you!' when it used to be, 'Big Ben will rescue us!'

On Monday mornings he tells everyone at the school gates about his dad. 'He bought me a kite. It went whoosh in the sky,' he said to Emily last week, Ben standing closely behind.

I felt awkward when Jim asked Ben if he wanted to join us for a coffee. Ben wouldn't look at me, making his excuses as he headed off for a run without as much as a glance over his shoulder.

I've talked to Jim about Ben. 'Give him time,' he'd said. 'When he understands this isn't about getting back with Matthew, he'll come round.'

Janey has said the same. 'Take it very slowly with Matt,' she warned me.

I am taking it slowly. However, despite myself I am warming to Matt. I'm seeing a new side to him, a paternal side that was lacking before. He is contributing financially too, paying a regular monthly sum into my account to cover school clothes, food and a percentage of my rent. He works for an estate agent's in Fulham. It's not the most exciting job, he concedes, but it's regular pay and no stress. I like this more modest Matthew. It suits him. 'I can't be a director, can't run my own ship anymore, but it doesn't mean I can't work my way up the ladder,' he said. 'Main thing is, Polly, I sleep at night.'

When Hugo and Aunt Viv ask questions I sense they are longing to hear he's back to his old tricks and ways. They want to pat me on the back and say I was brave for trying, but leopards never change their spots.

As Louis and I push through the weekend crowds, I see Matthew waiting outside the cinema. He waves, before Louis rushes towards him, throwing his arms around Matthew's legs. 'Hi, Matthew!'

Matt kneels down, ruffles Louis's hair. 'Call me Dad,' he says.

Louis sits between us, plunging his hands into a tub of popcorn. As the room darkens I find myself glancing at Matthew. When he catches my eye I turn away. As the film plays I close my eyes. During the first few months of our relationship my head felt giddy with longing for Matthew. At school I'd have butterflies in my stomach, anticipating being with him in the evening. The sex was amazing. Sometimes rough, sometimes surprisingly tender. When he'd won the bid for the Wandsworth house he'd called saying we were going out to celebrate that night. He took me to a fancy lobster restaurant and over drinks produced a box, lined with tissue, containing a black lace bra with matching knickers.

I remember that night, returning from the restaurant and dressing up for Matt while he watched from the bed as I faced him in my silk dressing gown, before slowly untying the belt and letting it fall to the floor. I can still feel that magnetic attraction, the way his eyes had found mine in the bar the first time we met.

After the film, Matthew suggests a mug of hot chocolate in a nearby café. While Louis is choosing a cake, pointing to every single thing with whipped cream behind the counter, I decide to ask Matthew if he's in a relationship.

'I haven't been with anyone since, well, since us.' He grins, that cockiness beginning to emerge. 'I know that's hard to believe. I haven't been celibate all that time, but I needed to get my head together, go to therapy.'

'Who did you see?'

'Sorry?'

'You said you went on that anger-management course? Saw a counsellor? You still see someone, don't you?'

He looks at me quizzically. 'Hugo been checking up on me?'

'No.' I remain composed. 'I'm interested, that's all.'

'Sam Colefox,' he says, making me feel foolish for asking. 'He encouraged me to do the course and to remain single until . . . ' He plays with the drinks menu, taps it against the table. 'After hurting you, I didn't trust myself. You know it was the last thing I ever wanted, to hurt you.' He looks over to Louis, still choosing something to eat. 'You were the only one who really understood me, Polly.' His hand inches towards mine. 'I want to get to know you again. It's been great seeing Louis, but I can't deny that seeing you again has brought back memories. Not all of it was bad, was it? We've both changed, got our acts together.' His hand is now on top of mine, his touch warm. 'Imagine . . .'

'Don't.' I pull my hand from underneath his. 'It's too soon.'

He raises an eyebrow. 'Does that mean that in time . . . ?'

'I don't know what it means,' I say, as thankfully Louis interrupts, returning to the table to say he wants a chocolate eclair.

45

A week later

'How are you feeling today?' Stephanie asks me.

'Confused. Uncertain about everything, really.' I agreed to see Matthew tonight, at my flat. 'All I want to do is *talk*,' he'd said when I looked hesitant, Hugo and Aunt Viv's warning voices in my ear. 'Christmas is coming up,' he went on, 'and I was hoping we could see one another. I'd like to be with Louis, enjoy my first Christmas with him.'

'What's "everything"?' Stephanie likes to pick on words; make me explain what I mean by them.

'Matthew, mainly.' I dig into my handbag to find the piece of paper with the name of Matthew's counsellor. 'Do you know Sam Colefox?'

'Polly. What's this about?'

Briefly I explain that Hugo wants to make sure Matthew really did attend counselling and anger-management courses.

'Do you understand why Hugo might be concerned?'

'Basically, he doesn't trust a word Matt says. I'm grateful to him, he's being protective. Anyway, I've googled this counsellor, but quite a few names crop up and I just wanted to make sure . . .'

'I know him,' she says. 'He practises in Fulham. He specialises in abuse, addiction, compulsive and obsessive behaviour and anger management.'

Relieved, I nod. 'Yes, but anyone can pluck a name out of a hat, Polly,' Hugo had said. 'I could tell you I'd seen this Sam Colefox person. Doesn't mean I have.'

'Polly, you seem anxious.'

'I am. I don't know what to do.' I confide about our recent cinema trip and coffee. Matthew taking my hand, telling me he wanted to make a go of it again.

'What's your heart telling you?'

'I don't know.'

'How about this? What's stopping you?'

'Where do I start? Fear. Reactions from others, Louis being hurt if this doesn't work, if he walks out on us or . . .' I take a deep breath. 'He hurts me again. Louis was a baby when that happened. He's growing up so fast. The damage would be terrible and . . . no, that's it.'

'That's all?'

I nod, unconvincingly. 'Ben,' I admit at last. 'Ben stops me.'

'In an ideal world, what would you like to happen?'

I'm torn. 'A part of me misses Ben and what we could be, but then again I've felt close to Matthew recently, slowly I've begun to enjoy seeing him, and he makes Louis so happy. What would you do?' I throw the question at her, knowing she can't or won't answer it. 'Sorry, I know you can't tell me what to do.'

Stephanie takes off her glasses and leans towards me. 'Polly, I see a lot of clients who relapse when they go back to a bad relationship – sometimes the only reason they go back is because it's easier to return to someone familiar, even if that person was abusive or destructive, and do you want to know why?' She closes her notebook. 'Because they don't believe they are worthy of anything better,' she says with passion. 'Someone who loves them is too overwhelming.' She looks at me directly. 'Polly, you do the same thing; you get the same result. Do something differently and you've got a chance at something new and better. The best thing for you, what could *help* you more than anything else is being with the right person. Over the last few years you have worked out that there were consequences to your mistakes and that you had to make sure you walked down a different path . . .' Stephanie stops. She tucks a strand of hair behind her ear as she gathers her composure. 'I can't tell you what to do.'

But we both know she just has.

As I approach the school gates I see Ben, hands deep in his coat pockets. Tentatively, I walk over to him and say hello, asking how he is.

'Good.'

'How's the work going?'

'Busy.'

'How's Emily? Would she like to come over and play one afternoon?'

'Maybe.'

Is this what our friendship has been reduced to? 'Ben, please,' I say, trying to reach out to him. 'Can we talk?'

He looks withdrawn, his eyes tired. 'It's good to see you,' he says finally.

'You too.'

'Polly, I'm sorry . . .'

'No, I'm sorry.' I remember the hurt and anger in his eyes when I'd said we couldn't be more than friends. *This is the perfect excuse to put the brakes on us.*

'This stinks,' he declares at last, making both of us smile.

'It really does.'

'I'm bored of not seeing you.'

'Me too. Insanely bored.'

'Can I come over? Tonight? Emily keeps on asking why we don't see you any more, and I, well, I miss you.'

'I can't, not tonight, but how about . . .'

'Are you seeing him?'

A crowd of children begin to emerge from the school building. 'He's coming over for supper but . . .'

'Are you back together?'

'No. He wants to talk about Louis, that's all.'

ALICE PETERSON

My mobile rings. Matthew's name appears on the screen. I catch Ben's eye. He's seen the name too.

'Take it,' he says as Emily rushes towards him, her satchel swinging off her shoulder, Louis following closely behind.

Emily says hello to me, my mobile still ringing. I reject the call, saying it can wait. 'Daddy is coming over tonight,' Louis mentions to Ben and Emily. 'I'm going to show him my pilot costume. I want him to sleep over.'

Ben looks at me, as if finally he understands there's no hope.

'See you around,' he says, managing a smile before taking Emily firmly by the hand.

46

After Louis has had his tea, he and Matthew charge around the house playing goodies and baddies. 'I'm coming to get you!' Louis shouts, before Matthew collapses on the sitting room floor, Louis handcuffing him and saying, 'You've been very naughty. I'm taking you off to prison now.' Louis jumps up. 'Again!' he says, his energy never failing to amaze me. 'This time I'm the baddie. Count to ten!'

'No, Louis, it's bedtime,' I say. 'Get into your pyjamas and then I'll come in and read to you.' I notice how formal my voice sounds.

'I'll read to him. Would you like that, buddy?' Matt asks, taking off the toy handcuffs.

Louis nods. 'I'll show you my bedroom again,' he says, taking Matt by the hand. 'Do you want to see my new rocket pyjamas, Daddy?'

'Don't forget to clean your teeth,' I call.

Fifteen minutes later, as I stand in the doorway of Louis's bedroom, listening to Matthew reading *Plop, the Owl Who*

Was Afraid of the Dark, I can't fight the feeling that it's all too good to be true. It still feels strange hearing Louis call him 'Daddy'. It took Emily months to call Uncle Ben Daddy. Ben never expected nor asked her to. He earned it. I picture them at hospital, the way Emily had opened her arms, invited him in at long last.

After the story is over, I kiss Louis goodnight. 'Mum, is Daddy sleeping here?'

Matt glances at me, raises an eyebrow.

'No, darling.'

'Not tonight, but maybe sometime soon.' Matt ruffles his hair. 'Would you like that, buddy?'

Louis nods before I grab Matthew by the arm and pull him out of the room. 'Don't encourage him,' I say when we're in the kitchen. 'You'll give him the wrong idea.'

'Don't tell me it hasn't crossed your mind.'

Already I feel backed into a corner, his stare predatory. 'It hasn't,' I say, moving away from him. 'You're here for Louis.'

Matt smiles in the old familiar way. 'Sure. Right. Louis.' He looks around the room. 'Nice place, this.'

I busy myself, opening the fridge, getting things out, checking on the chicken, chopping the vegetables, telling Matt to sit down. Instead he wanders around, picking things up, asking where they came from. 'What's this?' He's looking at the precious ceramic box Aunt Viv gave me with the AA serenity prayer engraved inside. He reads it out, a faint mocking tone in his voice, or am I imagining it?

He reads Louis's cards scattered around the flat, picks up my photographs, handles books and the candlesticks Hugo gave me for my birthday. 'Who's Louis with?' He's now holding a framed photograph of Ben, Emily, Louis and Nellie. I'd taken the shot on one of our dog walks.

'Emily. She's in his class.'

'Yeah, but who's he?'

I carry on chopping. 'Ben.'

I glance at the sofa, remembering all those times Ben and I have watched films together here, eaten takeaway, argued, laughed, played games with the children. I see Emily and Louis colouring in at the coffee table. I see Ben sprawled out on the floor helping me put together a bookshelf for Louis's room, both of us laughing at how impractical I am. We felt like a family, but I took it for granted at the time. Being with Ben, that's how it *should* feel.

'Ben? Louis mentions him too. Is he a boyfriend or something?'

'No.' I carry on chopping. Chop, chop . . .

'Really?'

CHOP. I see blood. I drop the knife and run my cut finger under the tap. This isn't going to work. I've let him back into my life too soon. 'He's a friend.' I resent having to justify him.

'You all right?' He comes over, takes a look at my hand. 'Something I said, Polly?'

'I'm fine.' Flustered I find a plaster in one of the kitchen drawers, aware of him watching my every move.

He leaves the room, muttering he'll be back in a sec. When he's gone I lean against the sink, take a deep breath. I pour myself a glass of water. Drink it in one go. What was I thinking? When I see Louis and Matt playing in the park I don't feel this way. I feel safer because I'm watching from a distance, on neutral ground. Being alone with him brings back bad memories. I don't want him here, putting fingerprints all over the past few years that have brought me here, to a good place. The oven timer rings, making me jump.

'Something smells good,' he says when he returns.

'It's only roast chicken.' I slide the roasting tin back into the oven. When I turn to him he's holding a bottle of wine. 'Thought we could celebrate.'

I blink. 'Sorry?'

'Seeing one another again.' He opens the kitchen drawer, takes out the corkscrew.

'I can't drink that, but you can.' I watch him opening my cupboard to find the glasses; he produces two. 'Surely you can have one?' He pours us both a glass.

'I don't drink. You know that.'

'Oh come on, Polly. One can't do any harm.' He holds the glass out to me.

Fury burning inside now, I chuck the wine down the sink. 'You don't get it, do you?'

'Sorry. I thought . . .'

'No you didn't. That's the problem.'

My mobile rings. Hugo's name lights up the screen. I reject the call. He'll be worried that Matthew is here when I promised we'd only meet in the park or in cafés. The only people who know about tonight are Stephanie and Aunt Viv. I'll talk to Hugo tomorrow. It rings again. It's Mum. Matt eyes my mobile.

I switch the damn thing off, saying it's time to eat.

Over supper I try to keep the conversation all about Louis and possible Christmas plans.

'He's a great kid,' Matt says. 'You've done him proud. It can't have been easy being a single mum, having no man around to help.'

'I've had support. Anyway, I was thinking you could see him for an early Christmas day here, before I take him to my parents.'

Matt picks up his glass of wine. I notice he's wearing a white shirt, similar to the one he wore the very first night we met. I remember us dancing; the look in his eyes when he said he wanted to take me home, his hands sliding down my back. I shift in my seat.

As if he can read my mind, 'Do you remember the night we met, Polly? You were with your friend . . .'

'Janey.'

'I couldn't take my eyes off you.'

It was all sex, booze and hedonism.

Life is different now.

'There was something wild about you, dangerous . . . '

'Would you like some more peas?'

He shakes his head; his eyes still not leaving mine.

'Carrots?'

'I know we had a rough time, but there were some good times too, weren't there?'

'Some. Now, what were you thinking about Louis?' I ask, trying to keep my voice in control. 'We need to sort out some dates and times.'

He leans towards me. I back away. 'You do believe I've changed, don't you?'

'We're here to talk about our son.'

He rolls his eyes. 'I'm not just here to talk about Louis, you know that.'

I put my knife and fork down, steel myself. 'We had our chance. It didn't work.'

He frowns. 'So? Doesn't mean it can't ever work.'

'I invited you here for Louis, no other reason.'

'But think what we could be. A family.'

'I've moved on.'

'Is there someone else I should know about?'

I feel threatened by his tone. 'No.'

'Don't lie to me.' I see that anger flare in his eyes.

'OK, Matt, there is someone.' I picture his face earlier this afternoon, the way he'd walked away with Emily, his steps defeated. What a fool I am.

'Who is he?'

'That's not really any of your business.'

'Anyone who's hanging around my son *is* my business. It's that Ben guy, isn't it, in the photo?'

Fighting to remain calm, I continue, 'Matt, you came back for Louis. I'm prepared to let you see him . . .'

'Prepared? That's mighty big of you. Come on! I buy Louis shit-hot presents, I turn up on time, I'm trying really hard here, and you've turned into some ice maiden. I want to know more about this Ben guy.'

'Keep your voice down. You'll wake Louis.'

'I don't fucking care about Louis!'

I stare at him, open-mouthed. 'This was a mistake.' I clear the plates. 'I think it's time you left.'

'I didn't mean it like that, Polly, it came out wrong. Oh come on, you must have realised I didn't come back just for Louis.'

Angry, I chuck the plates into the sink. 'I've moved on, Matt.'

'With this Ben guy,' he sneers.

'No. I've just moved on with my life. I've changed and . . .' I stop when Louis enters the room with Fido, Hugo's old toy dog under his arm. Before taking him back to bed, I slide my mobile, left on the kitchen counter, into my pocket.

When Louis is tucked up, lights out, I rush to the bathroom and lock the door, turn on the mobile, a sixth sense now that Hugo's earlier call was important. 'Come on,' I say as it's firing up, eventually stabbing in my password. I have five missed calls and two voicemails.

'It's me,' Hugo says. 'I know you're with him, Aunt Viv told me. I'm coming over. He's told you a pack of lies.'

'Polly?' I hear Matt calling.

'Won't be long,' I call back, before listening to one more message. 'Polly, it's Hugo. I've found out stuff about Matthew that you need to know about. Call me. It's urgent.' My finger trembles as I press the call-back button.

Matt is knocking on the door now. I flush the loo and turn on the tap as I hear Hugo's mobile go to voicemail. I hide my mobile in my pocket and unlock the door. He's standing over me. 'I want you to go,' I say quietly, gesturing to Louis's bedroom door. 'We can talk about supervised access . . .'

'Supervised access!' He grabs me by the shoulders, shakes me. 'What's that supposed to mean? I haven't done anything wrong!'

I try to get away from him, but his grip tightens, his face right up to mine. 'I can't see my own son without you policing me?'

The buzzer rings.

'Leave it,' he shouts.

'Matt, please,' I plead. 'Let me go. Think about Louis. Is this how you want it to be?'

The buzzer rings again. I'm about to call out, but he plants a hand over my mouth. 'I said, leave it.'

Hugo, don't go away. I'm here. I'm here. I hear footsteps coming up the stairs, voices outside. I hear a key in the lock. Aunt Viv and Hugo burst through the door.

'Let her go!' Aunt Viv demands, trying to come between us.

Surprised, Matthew stands back.

'Are you all right?' Hugo asks. I nod, rubbing my shoulder, and catching my breath, before he turns to Matthew. 'Are you going to tell Polly, or shall I?'

He shrugs. 'Don't know what you mean.'

'I think you do,' says Aunt Viv, standing firmly by my side.

'Polly, he's been feeding you lies,' Hugo states. 'He didn't finish the anger-management course. He quit therapy after only a couple of weeks . . . he isn't seeing anyone, no counsellor, nothing.'

'How do you know, Miss fucking Marple? You don't know what I've done . . .'

'That's where you're wrong. I had you followed, dug up all kinds of dirt.'

'You bastard.'

'He has a family, a kid, a little girl.' Hugo remains calm. 'Do you want to tell Polly more, or shall I?'

'Matt?' A coldness creeps into my veins.

'Don't believe him,' Matt says to me. 'I swear . . .'

'He left because he was dumped,' Hugo interrupts. 'Up to his old tricks, weren't you? Your girlfriend threw you out, so you came back to try your luck with Polly. You're nothing but a bully, Matthew.'

'I don't believe this,' I say, looking at Matt with disgust and feeling so ashamed and angry with myself that I fell for it again. 'Get out. Go.' I push him away.

He laughs. 'You and your support group, your entourage. Blind brother and . . .' He looks at Aunt Viv. 'Some decrepit do-gooding old aunt.'

'I think you heard her. Get out.' Aunt Viv opens the front door for him. 'Before we throw you out.'

'You can't tell me what to do.' Matt stares at Aunt Viv. She stares right back.

He turns to me. 'Polly, please, just hear me out.'

'What? Hear more lies? I want you to go.'

'You heard her. Leave,' Aunt Viv says, keeping the door open.

He stays put. 'You think you're all high and mighty now, don't you, Polly? Whiter than white, looking down your nose at me . . .'

'Leave!' Aunt Viv forces him through the door.

He turns on her. 'Get your hands off me! Who the hell do you think you are?'

There's a silence. 'I'm her mother,' she says finally.

Hugo and I stare at her.

I'm too numb to speak.

'I'm her mother,' Aunt Viv repeats. 'Polly, you're my daughter.'

47

'And then what happened?' asks Stephanie, two days after Aunt Viv told me she was my mother. 'After Matthew slammed the door and left.'

'I asked her for an explanation.'

'I can see you're upset. Are you ready to go on?'

I nod. 'Aunt Viv explained that the day she'd had the crash I was on the backseat, next to my baby brother, Sam. Sam was two; I was five months old. My brother was killed outright. Aunt Viv's brother was taken to hospital but he died the following day. The car had rolled over. It was miraculous that both Aunt Viv and I survived with barely any scratches. She was driving Sam to nursery, hammered, but she always hid it well, us addicts do. The rest you can imagine. My mother . . .' I press my head into my hands. 'My aunt never forgave Aunt Viv, she told her she wasn't fit to be a mother so she adopted me. Aunt Viv went to prison and here I am, telling the tale.'

'Polly, your anger is understandable.'

'I've been living a lie all my life. My biological dad was an addict too, some rich playboy. Money had done him no favours. He left Aunt Viv the moment she was pregnant. What chance did I have? Two parents, both as bad as each other. At least it makes sense,' I concede, as if it's finally sinking in.

'What do you mean by that?'

Trying to compose myself I say, 'All my life I felt like I didn't belong, that I wasn't part of the family. *It's hard not to love Hugo more.* Of course she said that. He was her son. Mum took me on to punish Aunt Viv; she didn't really want me.'

'Has your mother told you that?'

I shake my head. 'My aunt, you mean?'

'Your aunt, who raised you.'

'I haven't spoken to her. I can't. Not yet. I am the product of Aunt Viv. Mum, well my *aunt* . . . what a messed up family we are,' I say with a weak smile.

'I'm following,' Stephanie reassures me.

'I think she resented me. Each time she looked at me she was reminded of losing the brother she loved and all the damage Aunt Viv had done to our family.'

'Would you like to talk more about Matthew?' Stephanie suggests, after she's given me time to cry and to try to make some sense of the traumatic events of the past forty-eight hours.

'Done.'

'Done?'

'Over. What a fool I was to trust him again. So naïve. What an idiot.'

'You wanted Louis to have a father.'

'He has a father, in Hugo.' Tears come to my eyes. 'Hugo isn't my brother. I think that's what's thrown me the most, he's my cousin, but I don't care about titles or labels.' I think about Ben, what he'd said about his stepfather. '*Forget the title, it's the man that's important.*' 'He *is* my brother and he's the closest thing Louis has to a dad.'

Stephanie nods. 'How is Louis?'

'Upset. He doesn't understand. "Where's Daddy gone?" "Why isn't he coming to see me again?" "I won't!" is his favourite phrase right now. Digging his heels in whenever I ask him to do anything. Hugo and I told him too much, maybe, I don't know if it was right, but I said Matthew hurt me. Hugo talked to him too, explained that sometimes his dad wasn't kind and we *all* had to stop seeing him, that this wasn't a punishment, that it was best for all of us.' I pause. 'Unbelievable how so much can change in a couple of days. The last time I saw you, the night Matthew was coming over, I was confused. In my head I wanted it to be happy families. I wanted so much to believe he'd made a fresh start, for Louis, maybe for me, I don't know. I knew it was wrong when he offered me a drink. I nearly did, later, after everyone had gone. I went into the kitchen and the first thing I saw was that bottle of wine on the table. It was half-full. For the rest of the night I couldn't sleep, just rocked in my chair, working out what I was going to say to Louis, going over everything, how my whole life had become this sham overnight. I kept on thinking about that bottle of wine, sitting there. I couldn't concentrate. I went into the kitchen, picked it up, I needed something to take away the pain. I felt betrayed. The *one* person I have trusted more than anyone in my life, the person I felt safe with, and she'd lied to me for years. All those times I'd talked to Aunt Viv about my mother and confided about not fitting in, not feeling a part of the family, and she still couldn't tell me the truth. All this AA talk about honesty and amends and doing the right thing . . .'

Stephanie is quiet, letting me carry on.

'I carried the bottle back to my bedroom. I was *this* close. I was exhausted, it was almost as if I were sleepwalking, couldn't think straight . . . I was about to . . .' I stop, as if recalling that moment.

'What stopped you?'

'I heard a voice. It was your voice at first, but then another voice took over. My own.'

'What was your voice saying?'

'Don't throw your life away again. Throw away that wine. So I did. Went into the bathroom and watched it disappear down the plughole.'

'Polly, I'm proud of you. That showed guts.'

'I wouldn't have been able to do it without you.'

'Yes, yes you would. You chose not to drink, not me.'

'I wouldn't have been able to do it a year ago. I know now, whatever life throws at me, I have an inner strength, I have belief in myself, something I've never had before. There was no way I was going to have a drink, not after all the hard work to get sober. Besides, I have unfinished business.'

'Unfinished business?'

'One thing came through loud and clear that night as I chucked the wine away.'

She waits.

'I love Ben.'

Stephanie is trying hard not to smile.

'I think I've always felt this way about him, but I was too scared to admit it. Like you said, easier to go back to your old ways. But I love him. I love him, I *love* him.'

'Well, I know I shouldn't really give advice.' She pauses. 'But maybe you should tell him that.'

48

Shortly after my counselling session, I find myself running across Primrose Hill, rehearsing what I'm going to say to Ben at the school gates. I can't just blurt out 'I LOVE YOU!' in front of everyone. Maybe I should suggest he comes over with Emily tonight, and when they're playing I can explain. It's hard to talk about Matt with Louis around. My pace slows down. What if it's too late? What if I had my chance and Ben no longer feels the same way? After all, I let him down; I allowed Matt to get in the way of us. What if he believes I could hurt him again? He has every right to say he's not interested anymore. My pace quickens again. He won't feel that way. I know how much we mean to one another. I will make this work. He loves me and I love him; that's all that counts.

Outside the school gates I see the usual mob of mums and Jim. Out of breath, I swig down some water, try to compose myself. Jim looks at me curiously. 'What's going on?'

Adrenalin pumping, briefly I tell Jim about Matt, simply

saying it didn't work out and that I'll tell him in more detail soon, in private.

'I'm sorry.' But he looks relieved.

I shake my head. 'Don't be. In a way it helped. I've been looking over my shoulder too long.' I keep on scanning the crowd.

'He's coming,' Jim says.

I turn round and see Ben and Nellie walking towards us.

I face Jim again, my pulse still racing. 'I've been so stupid.'

'No you haven't. As you said, it was complicated,' Jim says kindly. 'But I've wanted to bang your heads together for ages.'

Ben is getting closer and closer. He's wearing his chunky navy jumper with jeans. Tentatively I wave at him, my stomach a tangle of nerves. 'Good luck.' Discreetly Jim slips away.

When Ben is standing next to me the first thing I do is bend down to stroke Nellie. 'How are you?' I ask, finally looking him in the eye.

'Good. You?'

'Great. Yes, very good. How are you?'

'You've just asked me that.'

'I'm sorry.' I pull him away from the crowd. 'Ben, we need to talk.'

'Right.'

'It's about Matthew.' There's so much to tell him, I'm unsure where to start.

He stands there, waiting. 'He hasn't changed, Ben. He's been lying to me all this time. I don't want anything more to do with him.' Children begin to emerge in the playground, walking towards the gates.

'I'm sorry,' Ben says with sincerity. 'Louis must be upset.'

'He is, he's, well he doesn't understand, but . . . Are you around tonight?'

'No,' he says, distance returning to his voice.

'Tomorrow? Or the weekend? Maybe we could . . .'

'I'm not sure, Polly.' He waves at Emily.

'Ben, I'm so sorry, about everything.' I want to tell him about Aunt Viv and Hugo, about my mother being my aunt, my dad not being my father at all, but most of all . . . 'I love you.'

'You love me?'

'So much.' I reach out to touch his hand, but he edges away. 'I've been so stupid, not seeing that the one person in front of me . . .'

'Polly, stop!' he says, raising his voice and causing a few mothers to turn to us and stare. 'It doesn't work out with Matthew, so you come running back to me?'

'I promise you it's not like that.'

'I'm not going to be the second prize because the other option didn't work out.'

'Ben, please, you mean *everything* to me.'

'Hi, Daddy,' says Emily, bending down to stroke Nellie,

who's jumping up and down against her legs, her tail wagging. Ben and I continue to look at one another.

'Polly, I'm sorry about Matthew, but . . .'

'Can't we talk tonight? I can come over.'

'Daddy has a date,' says Emily, adding that Louis has been naughty today. 'He had to write his name in the red book.'

Ben takes Emily's satchel in exchange for Nellie's lead.

'I'll see you around,' he says, briefly touching my shoulder before walking away.

49

'According to my son, allegedly I'm an alcoholic.'

Neve nudges me. We've heard that one many times before.

'*Daddy has a date.*' Who with? He can't just switch off his feelings for me. Feelings don't go away overnight.

'I feel so angry with my mother,' says another voice. 'I understand why some people murder, kill one another, I really do. Don't worry, you're all safe in here.'

Neve laughs, nudging me again.

'*I'm not going to be second prize because the other option didn't work out.*'

'I was drunk taking out someone's bowel,' says someone else, telling us he's a surgeon.

'I hope he never operates on me,' murmurs Harry, sitting on my other side.

'*Daddy has a date.*' Why hasn't Ben returned my calls?

'Why do we care so much what other people think?' says another. 'For years I wouldn't admit I was an addict, wouldn't dare walk inside here in case the neighbours saw me. I wore a wig and shades during my first meeting and immediately spied my Pilates teacher. Turns out AA is like going to a drinks party, but without the drink.'

'Polly? Are you OK?' Neve whispers.

I wake up, telling myself to put Ben out of my mind, so what if he has a date . . . ? I'm going to try to talk to him again; I won't give up . . . I stop when I hear crying coming from the end of our row. I see a young woman with tousled blonde hair, wearing an old baggy jumper, black smudged around her eyes. I haven't seen her before. She looks as if she's in her late twenties. When I glance at her again, she's wiping her nose on her sleeve. 'Harry,' I whisper, gesturing to his handkerchief tucked into his pocket.

Harry passes the handkerchief to me, I pass it to Neve, Denise stops knitting to pass it to the person sitting next to her, who finally gives it to the woman. She looks up to see where it came from. When I smile at her, she looks down at the floor again.

After the meeting Harry, Neve and I help clear up the tea and biscuits.

'You seem quiet today,' Harry says to me, tottering towards the sink with a couple of dirty mugs. 'Is this about your Aunt Viv, I mean, your mother?'

I nod. 'I have a few things on my mind.'

'It's Ben, isn't it?' guesses Neve, leading me away from the sink before asking what has happened between us. She wants detail. 'Your life is like a soap opera. You're giving me a run for my money now,' she says.

Neve listens as I tell her everything. 'His date won't come to anything,' she predicts, as if the date is nothing more than a pesky insect getting in the way. 'Listen, he's hurt. I can understand him thinking he's second best. It does look as if you went for one apple and discovered it was rotten, so picked another.'

'I didn't.'

'Yeah, but that's what he thinks. Try and talk to him again,' Neve advises. 'Explain. Make him listen.'

'No, no!' Harry pipes up, clearly having listened to every word too. 'Not the way to go!' He approaches us, waving his tea towel.

We stare at him.

'Actions speak louder than words, my dear. When I had to win Betsy back it was no good saying sorry a million times, I had to show her I meant business.'

'So what did you do?' Neve asks impatiently.

'I'm coming to that,' Harry snaps. 'What I did was think to myself, "what does Betsy love doing more than anything else in the world?" The answer?' He leans towards us. 'Dancing.'

'Dancing,' Neve and I repeat.

'When we first met all she talked about were her dancing pins. She has beautiful legs too,' he says, veering off the point. 'Anyway, I've got two left feet me, but in secret I took myself off to lessons, while she thought I was down the boozer.' He raises an imaginary bottle to his mouth, pretends to drink, 'But I was dancing the night away in the local community centre, learning the waltz . . .' Harry grabs me by the hands and we dance around the table and chairs, 'and the foxtrot! So what you need to do, young Polly, is do something special just for him.'

I stop. 'Like what?'

'Use your imagination. Do something he knows will have required strength or effort. No good just baking him a cake, you do that all the time.'

I'm beginning to think Harry might be right. 'So Betsy loved your dancing?'

'Oh yes. For her birthday I asked her to put her best dress on, she thought we were going to some fancy fish restaurant.' He cackles as he claps his hands. 'I took her to the London Ballroom Dance Club! We danced all night. It paid off all right, in more ways than one.' He winks at us.

'Thanks, Harry, but we don't need all the details,' says Neve, while I'm still lost in thought, trying to work out what I can do for Ben. It's got to be something to make him realise I really do love him.

50

Two weeks later

Aunt Viv and I meet in Chamomile, Christmas music playing in the background. Christmas has been the last thing on both our minds.

Aunt Viv looks tired, dark rings under her eyes and her hair pinned away from a pale face. 'I wanted to tell you, Polly, of course I did, but I'd made a promise.'

I stir my coffee. 'Were you *never* going to tell me?'

'I know it's hard to understand, but I made peace with my decision years ago. Whatever you think of my sister, she gave you a home, she provided for you in a way I never would have been able to. I couldn't come back and destroy that. What a way to repay her! We made a deal and I had to honour it. It broke my heart, it wasn't easy, but . . .'

I can't listen . . . 'How about being honest? You lied to me!'

'If I'd told you, it could have done unthinkable damage.

I made a promise to be as good an aunt as possible, treat you like my own, love you like my own. I was determined to be a part of your life; no one was going to stop me from doing that. I never stopped thinking about my little girl,' she says tearfully. 'I came back from America to be close to you. I watched with terror when you were with Matthew. I admire the way you've brought up Louis and had the courage to turn your life around. I have loved every single minute of being close to you, especially these past few years. And Louis . . . well, of course I loved babysitting him. He's my grandson.'

'I wish you'd told me,' I say again, fighting not to cry, and then thinking what the hell, just cry. 'I can't call you Mum.'

'I don't expect you to.'

I look up at her. 'Maybe one day.'

She takes my hand. 'That's good enough for me.'

We sit quietly for a while, until Aunt Viv says, 'There are many things I'm not proud of Polly, but I'm so proud of you.'

I look up, tears in my eyes. 'You won't be very proud of me when you hear me sing.'

'Sorry?'

I end up telling her about my plan, based on Harry's advice. 'It's the Christmas school fundraiser tonight, 'Stars in Their Eyes'. I'm singing a song for Ben.'

'But you can't sing.'

'I get that from you.'

We laugh for the first time and it feels good. 'I always

used to wonder how Hugo could have such an angelic voice.'
I look at Aunt Viv, not wishing to fight or argue with her
anymore. 'Will you come? I need all the support I can get.'
Janey is coming with Paul; Hugo and his Spanish girlfriend,
Maria, along with Jim and his wife, will be on our table.
Thankfully I know Ben is coming because Gabriella told me
he's helping behind the bar.

Aunt Viv appears surprised and touched. 'Of course I'll
come. I'll bring earplugs.'

51

Jim and I are at Louis's school, rehearsing my song. Jim turns the music off.

'I told you I couldn't sing,' I say, breaking into a helpless smile.

Jim coughs. 'You're a little out of tune.'

I stare at him, knowing he's using artistic licence.

'OK, let's say there's plenty of room for improvement. One more time,' he insists as I'm about to jump off the stage.

Reluctantly I get back into my starting position, clutching the microphone.

'This time don't stand so stiffly, Polly. Walk around more, strut your stuff.' Jim glides across the floor, clicking his fingers, begins to sing my song effortlessly. 'It'll be easier when you're in your red-hot dress, you'll feel . . .'

'Terrified.'

'I was going to say a million dollars. Think sexy. Think sultry.' Jim pouts, making me forget my nerves for a second.

'Remember you're singing this for Ben. You want to show him how much he means to you, right?'

'Right.'

'So make every single word count. Think about the lyrics and what they mean to you. Old Frankie boy had a way of singing out a beautiful woman in the audience and making her feel like he was singing the song only for her. That's what you've got to do.' Jim presses play. 'Just think of Ben and forget about the rest of us.'

The school assembly room is adorned with Christmas decorations and filled with small round tables covered with red-checked cloths and candles. People are heading to the kitchen bar to buy crisps and cheap warm wine.

'What number are you on the list?' Aunt Viv asks, detecting my nerves. 'Good to go fairly early on and get it over with.'

'I'm last.'

'Oh,' everyone says.

'Exactly.' I look over to the next table. Gabriella is with her husband and friends, everyone merrily drinking wine and filling in their quiz sheet. She's performing 'It's Raining Men', by the Weather Girls with Violet, head of the PTA. I watch her pick up the bottle and pour another glass.

It's hard enough singing in front of a crowd, let alone singing stone-cold sober.

*

ONE STEP CLOSER TO YOU

'Welcome to the second 'Stars in Their Eyes', back by popular demand,' says our host, dressed in black tie, holding
a clipboard. 'My name is Mike, and I know you'll be truly
bowled over by some of tonight's performers, some of the
finest acts you'll ever see . . .'

Everyone laughs.

'. . . and some of the most amazing outfits you'll ever set
eyes on too. So without further ado, let's meet our first act.'

Janey squeezes my hand. 'He's not here yet,' I whisper,
thinking there's no way I'm doing this if he doesn't show
up.

'He'll come,' Janey assures me.

'Have faith,' says Aunt Viv, crossing her fingers.

Hugo nods. I watch him and Maria together, so comfortable, his arm around her shoulder. I ache to see Ben. Where
is he?

Jim is on next. 'So, Jim, can you give us a clue who you are?'

'Sure. This song was used in a Quentin Tarantino film,
Reservoir Dogs.'

'And your UK sell-out tour going well?'

Everyone laughs.

'Very.'

'Well, Jim, tell us who you are. We're on the edge of our
seats here.'

'Well, tonight, Mike, I'm going to be Stealers Wheel
singing 'Stuck in The Middle with You'.'

389

'Of course you are! Go and get changed.'

Jim's wife covers her eyes when five minutes later he returns on stage dressed in brown trousers, stripy shirt, droopy moustache, wig and shades, playing a guitar.

I forget about my ordeal as Hugo and I stand up and wolf-whistle. Jim can sing. He kept that a secret.

I head to the bar. Still no sign of him. 'Have you seen Ben?' I ask one of the school mums.

She nods. 'Apparently Emily's been unwell or something.'

My heart sinks.

'He left a message. He might come later, if he thinks he can leave her with the babysitter.'

I report the gloomy news.

'Oh, bloody children,' Janey exclaims.

'I can't believe this,' I mutter.

Hugo leaves the table, asking where the loos are.

Gabriella and Violet are on next, both of them modelling low-cut silk dresses that show off their ample cleavages. Gabriella belts out 'It's Raining Men' like a diva. Panic seizes my stomach. I'm rubbish and everyone else is good. They have talent. Gabriella has a beautiful voice. This isn't just some school fundraiser; I'm watching mums and dads who have dreamed of the stage since childhood and this is as close as they are going to get to fame. As for me . . . all I'm going to do is make a fool of myself. Aunt Viv stops me from fidgeting and looking towards the bar. 'He'll be here,' she says, touching my arm. 'But even if he doesn't come tonight, there will be another way to show him.'

After a show-stopping version of Shirley Bassey's 'Hey Big Spender', our headmistress comes on singing a Susan Boyle number. 'Damn it,' I mutter to Janey. 'She's amazing too.'

'Apparently she's always wanted to be an opera singer,' mentions Jim.

I've given up hope of Ben arriving.

Janey grips my hand. 'It doesn't matter about Ben. Just go up there and show us what you're made of.'

'Everyone on this table will be clapping,' reassures Maria.

'Exactly!' continues Janey. 'Who cares if you can sing or not? You give it attitude! Own that stage.'

I nod, yet feel positively sick with nerves and disappointment as the host announces, 'Well, we've saved the best till last, folks! Come on up, Polly Stephens.'

Hugo encourages me to go, but I can't feel my legs. I'm going to faint.

'Polly,' our host greets me when finally I join him on the stage. 'I've been really looking forward to your act. Give us a clue who you're going to be.'

'Er, she was an American singer and actress, big in the 1920s and 30s.' I look towards the back of the hall, still waiting for Ben miraculously to show up.

'And tell us about the song you've picked,' continues the host.

I can see Aunt Viv and Janey willing me to continue.

Come on, Polly, you can do this. 'Harry Connick Jr. sang it in my favourite film, *When Harry Met . . .*' I stop dead.

I want to jump off this stage and into his arms.

'Go on,' Ben mouths at me, leaning against the wall at the back of the hall.

'*When Harry Met Sally.*'

'Well it's great you're singing this for all the children at Eastwood's.'

'I'm not doing it for the school,' I say without thinking. 'Sorry, but if it were for the school, I'd have rather donated a tenner.'

A few more laughs.

'I'm singing it for someone,' I say, looking directly at him now. 'Someone who's here tonight.'

'Well, on that saucy note, I think it's time to tell us who you're going to be.'

'Tonight, everyone, I'm . . . I'm . . .' I catch Ben's eye. 'Ruth Etting.'

'She's Ruth Etting!' the host repeats with way too much enthusiasm.

I return to the stage in a full-length red-sequin dress with matching lipstick, dangerously high-heeled shoes, my dark hair falling down my shoulders. The audience cheer and wolf-whistle. 'I can do this,' I mutter to myself, my heart thumping.

The orchestral music starts to play the introduction to 'It Had to Be You', everyone in the audience clapping already. I take a deep breath. He's here. He is here, Polly. This is my chance. Don't be nervous.

'It had to be you,' I sing, my voice surprisingly bold.

As the song picks up momentum, I glide across the floor and gesture to Ben, just before my heel gets caught in the hem of my dress. I disentangle myself and on I go, reminding myself I am a glamour puss. Some of the audience turn to see who I'm looking at. 'Go for it, Polly!' I hear Jim shout, as my entire table gets up to clap and encourage me on.

I sing every single word for him, from the bottom of my heart. When the song comes to the end, I must be dreaming. I'm getting a standing ovation.

Backstage, I rush to get dressed, laughing with tears of relief that it's over and that he came. At least I didn't go through that ordeal in vain. I can't have been that bad? A standing ovation! Maybe I *can* sing? I hop around on one foot trying to find my other shoe. Come on, where are you? I look under the rail of clothes. I've got to see him, before he goes . . .

'Here it is,' a voice says.

I turn, my heart skipping a beat when I see Ben standing in front of me, holding my shoe.

'How's Emily?' is the only thing I can think of saying to him, not taking the shoe.

'She picked up some bug.' He doesn't take his eyes off mine.

'I'm sorry. Poor Emily. But you came, saw me make an idiot of myself.'

'When Hugo called to tell me his sister was singing a special song for me in a stunning red dress . . . well that kind of offer doesn't come along more than once in a lifetime. Well, I hope not anyway, for the sake of my ears.'

I take the shoe and slip it on, building myself up to say, 'How was your date?'

'Good.'

I look away.

Gently he turns me back towards him. 'It's my turn for a "but" now.'

'But?'

'But she wasn't you.'

I take his hand. 'I'm so sorry, Ben . . . and if I could rewind time . . .'

'What time would you go back to?'

'The time when you told me you loved me.'

'What would you do differently?'

'Everything. You were right. I was scared. Terrified that if things didn't work . . . but I shouldn't have trusted Matthew so easily, or let him get in the way of us.'

'You're forgiving.' He shrugs. 'We've had second chances. Everyone deserves that, and I understand that he's Louis's father. Hugo told me about what happened that night Matthew came over,' he says, moving closer towards me, our fingers now interlocking. 'That he uncovered a lot of untruths about him. He's quite something, your brother.'

I nod, tearful. 'So are you. It was always you, Ben. I was just so stupid. You were never second best.'

He wipes a tear away from my eye with his thumb and our faces are only inches apart before he puts his arms around me. I do the same, clinging on, knowing I will never let him go again.

'I was wondering,' he says, when finally we pull apart.

'You were wondering . . .'

He pulls me towards him again; our foreheads touch, his mouth so close to mine. 'What do you fancy doing on our first date?'

'This,' I say, as we kiss.

52

Six months later

It's a glorious summer's day and Ben is driving Emily, Louis, Nellie and me to watch him play cricket at Stoneleigh Abbey in Warwickshire. A few months ago Ben contacted his old village cricket club, based in Crawley, close to where Grace had lived. He was missing the matches, the league tables, seeing his team players, a mixed bunch from a professor of neuroscience to the maintenance man. 'That's what makes it fun,' he'd told me. 'Everyone is different.'

Ben tells me Stoneleigh Abbey is stunning, one of the best venues in the country, and that the Abbey and grounds are often hired for weddings.

'Are you going to get married, Daddy?' asks Emily, ears pricking up at the idea of dressing up. 'Can I be your brides-maid?'

'Sweetheart, we're not getting married,' I say.

'Not yet.' Ben glances my way, touching my knee.

'Why don't you ask me – see what I say?'
'Maybe I will.'

As we drive on, I think about the past six months. Despite my life being turned upside down, I have never felt this safe and happy, nor so in love.

Ben and I moved in together a month ago, a big step for both of us, but we were ready. He asked me one Sunday morning in bed. 'Polly, I've been thinking,' he said, wrapping his arms around my waist, our naked bodies warm under the covers. 'We should make this *our* home.' He turned me towards him, took my hand as if about to propose, kissing each finger in turn. 'Will you live with me?'

We spoke to Louis and Emily separately. Emily was easy to persuade, loving the idea of Louis and I sleeping over for good. Louis was quiet at first. He no longer asks questions about his father, but I have reassured him that any time he wants to talk to me, he can. I won't let Louis grow up in a house filled with secrets. 'Does that mean Big Ben will be my dad now?' he asked after thinking about it for a long time.

I nodded. 'But you don't have to call him Dad, you can call him whatever you like. We want to be together, a family. I think we could be so happy, but your happiness is the most important thing to me, Louis.'

'Ben won't leave us, will he?' he said, clutching on to Fido the dog.

I shook my head. 'No. We love each other very much.'

Ben then came into the room. 'I'm sorry, couldn't help overhearing.' He knelt down in front of Louis. 'I'm not going anywhere. I'm afraid you're stuck with me.'

I felt sad saying goodbye to my old shoebox. It was the home where I became close to my mother and it symbolised a fresh start in every way, but moving in with Ben is the next adventure. I've begun to put my past behind me; what matters now is my future, with Louis, Emily and Ben.

Mum, well not my mother, really my Aunt Gina, and I have slowly begun to heal wounds. When we first met, after Christmas, she explained that she'd thought she was doing what was best, but even she could see that this explanation was too rehearsed, it wasn't going to be enough for either of us. When I pushed her, stressing it was important for Hugo to know the truth too, she agreed that part of it might have been to punish her sister. I do understand the damage caused by Aunt Viv not only killing her baby son but also her younger brother. I understand how angry Aunt Gina must have been that addiction was tearing the family apart, first with her father, my Granddad Arthur, then Vivienne and of course, later on, me. When was it going to stop? She had given her sister so many chances, Aunt Viv swearing she'd change, promising she'd quit, all of which had been thrown back in her face. 'Vivienne wanted me to adopt you. She agreed. She knew she wasn't capable of looking after you. We promised one another it would remain a secret, but I'm so sorry we hurt you, Polly. That I hurt you.'

It is the deceit I have found most difficult to deal with. I have sat in my rocking chair, going over and over it again. I don't understand why, at some stage, they couldn't have told me? I also now understand why my father took a back seat, why Aunt Gina was always the disciplinarian. I wonder if he ever really wanted to adopt me? We're close, but we never had a father-daughter bond. He was simply there, a gentle presence, working hard to support his family and Aunt Gina's decision. It seems Aunt Viv's addiction impacted on everyone's lives.

The one thing that has remained constant is my deep friendship and love for Hugo. Like me, Hugo has been angry, confused and wanted answers, but nothing has changed between us. Louis, Hugo and I went out for a meal last weekend, just the three of us. He seemed different. He's in love with Maria, I can tell. I'm so happy for him. Hugo deserves only the best.

During the past six months I have also found strength through my friends at AA, especially Neve. I am now a sponsor to the young woman who came to her first meeting in tears. Her name is Iona, and she had been raised by foster-parents all her life, shunted from one place to the other with no sense of belonging. We're working through the steps and I am enjoying being on the other side, giving something back.

Harry and his wife Betsy are joining their children and grandchildren for a summer holiday in Barcelona. 'Going to whoop it up, Polly, live every day like it's my last. Life is too short.'

Of course Harry was also delighted that his ploy to show Ben how much I loved him worked. Ben's support and love has helped me so much. We all make mistakes. What counts is how we move on. I don't want to be bitter for the rest of my life. I want to live it. I've wasted enough time. All that is important is that we can find a way to forgive. I am not blameless. I *was* a pretty bad daughter, but Aunt Gina also recognises now that many of my actions were the actions of someone who was deeply insecure. Someone who felt unloved.

Since we've been together, Ben has been able to build up his business, taking on new clients, and in the past few months I've been thinking about going back to teaching, only this time I'd like to teach older children. When I was packing my things up in the flat I came across an old canvas box-file filled with random photographs. There were some taken in Paris, others of Janey and me at school, Hugo and me in our bright yellow life jackets rowing on the lake towards the sunken boat, pictures of Louis as a baby, and right at the bottom, an official-looking document. Curious, I dug it out to see it was a reference from my old school. I felt a surge of guilt, remembering how irresponsible I'd been at times, and that if I knew now that one of the teachers at Louis and Emily's school was anything like me . . .

'*Polly is a delightful member of staff, who brings to her les-*

sons warmth, humour, charm and above all, she makes children understand learning is all about having fun. She will be a hard act to follow.'

I reread it, wondering why it hadn't meant that much to me the first time. When I showed it to Ben he asked me why I seemed so surprised. When I told him I wanted to teach again, that it was time to think about leaving Mary-Jane in the kitchen in her Marigolds, he told me that I could do whatever I set my mind to.

Ben and I fill one another with confidence. It's as if we are the missing pieces in each other's jigsaw, and now that we've found one another, joy has crept into our lives.

Stoneleigh Abbey is as beautiful as Ben described: a large country mansion set in acres of parkland, overlooking the River Avon. Lots of friends and family have come to watch the match, picnics adorning rugs. I help the children to egg sandwiches and sausage rolls from the coolbox, telling them not to feed Nellie. There's something so lovely and British about watching cricket, not that I've done it before, mind you, but I'm not complaining about the view: handsome men in whites on a fresh green lawn. I try to find Ben amongst the crowd. 'There he is!' I point him out to the children. He's talking to one of his teammates, his pullover and cap showing off his club's crest. Ben's team are fielding first. I sit back and relax, enjoying the sun beating against my face, not paying too much attention. After lunch, Louis takes Nellie for a quick walkabout, promising he won't go far. We laugh when we see Louis telling Nellie off for eating someone's sandwich.

Emily grows taller by the day and eats pretty well now, I think to myself when she asks, 'Mum, can I have another custard tart?' She enjoys ballet and dance. She also loves to cook, telling me that when she grows up she wants to own a restaurant. Louis wants to make a lot of money in America and drive fast cars. Sometimes I see Matthew in him, but all I can tell myself is that Matthew didn't have the best start in life. His father was some dodgy criminal who clipped him round the ear when he spoke out of turn. He probably did more damage than I'll ever know. His mother was absent. I think about him, from time to time, but no longer look over my shoulder or have nightmares. I know I won't see him again. That chapter in my life is finally over.

It's the second half of the game. I have stopped plaiting Emily's hair and reading my magazine. This is impossibly tense. Stoneleigh Abbey scored one hundred and sixty-five all out and Ben's team have scored one hundred and sixty for nine. All they need is six runs from two balls to win, a daunting task, and Ben is batting. I feel charged with nerves.

'He has to hit the ball really hard, over the boundary,' I tell Emily and Louis.

'Go, Daddy!' she says when we see him positioning himself in front of the wicket, dressed in his pads, gloves, thigh pads and helmet – the whole works. The bowler is polishing the ball against his trousers.

He runs towards Ben, bowls . . . Ben hits the ball, down to deep mid-on, only making him two runs. I shriek with disappointment, it's not enough. He's got to make a boundary from the last ball.

I'm unable to watch. It's too much. I shield my face. Emily and Louis are on their feet, cheering him on, as are all the other supporting families.

'Go, Daddy!' Emily jumps up and down, clapping her hands.

'Go, Daddy!' Louis says.

I look over to him, a tear in my eye. It's the first time Louis has called Ben Daddy.

I tell myself that if Ben hits it across the boundary I will ask him to marry me, tonight.

The bowler bounds towards him, releases the ball . . . Ben makes contact. The ball strikes against the bat, a clean crisp sound. The ball soars into the air. Emily, Louis and I watch as it flies across the field and into the stand.

He's done it.

THE END

Acknowledgements

Firstly, lots of thanks go to Jane Wood and Katie Gordon at Quercus for their wonderful editing. To my agent Charlotte Robertson, thank you so much for your amazing support.

This book was helped enormously by a number of people talking to me about addiction. Mark Hjaltun – thank you for our many fun lunches together and for being so open about your experiences, both light and dark. To Johnny S for sharing his stories; to Virginia Graham, a psychotherapist and counsellor with a wealth of experience in this field. A huge thank-you to you all.

There are other parts of the book that many friends have helped me with. Masses of thanks to Sam Boyero for telling me about her life as a single mum and her touchingly warm relationship with her son.

To Mark Chamberlen, for giving me an insight into being born partially sighted. I think you are funny, inspiring and quite incredible.

I'd also like to thank my friends, SJ, Ju, Debbie and Ed F-S for helping me in very different but important ways. To Diana Beaumont for her invaluable input, as always.

To *Books For Cooks*, in Notting Hill, my favourite haunt for a bowl of soup and slice of cake.

To my parents, for always being there for me. To my sister, Helen. You are the best.

Finally, Catty Thomas. Thank you for your patience, wisdom, courage and humour. You helped me to get right under the skin of my leading character, Polly. Through you I have learned so much about addiction, especially the vital importance of AA. This novel could not have been written without you.